REV IT UP

BLACK KNIGHTS INC.

JULIE ANN
WALKER

sourcebooks
casablanca

Published by Sourcebooks Casablanca, an imprint of Sourcebooks, Inc.
P.O. Box 4410, Naperville, Illinois 60567-4410
(630) 961-3900
Fax: (630) 961-2168
www.sourcebooks.com

Printed and bound in the United States of America.
LSC 10 9 8 7

To my mother. I owe all of this to you.
You supported me and encouraged me through
all my endeavors, and instilled in me a love for the
written word that has shaped and enriched my life.
Oftentimes, there wasn't enough money for those
designer jeans I thought I couldn't live without, but
there was always enough extra for book clubs and
book fairs. Thanks for keeping my priorities straight.

Not the glittering weapon fights the fight, but rather the hero's heart.

—Proverb

Prologue

High in the mountains of the Hindu Kush
October...

"THIS IS SERIOUSLY MESSED UP, GUYS," PREACHER whispered as he kept the business end of his M4 aimed at the Taliban leader sitting cross-legged on the dry, shale-strewn ground. Al-Masri's mouth was covered with duct tape, but even so, it was hard to miss the bitter twist of his bearded cheeks or the undisguised hatred glowing in his black eyes.

Messed up. Jacob Sommers, aka Jake "The Snake," couldn't help but agree with that incredibly concise, if somewhat tame, assessment. Personally, he would've qualified their current situation as *fucked up*. Fucked up from the ground up, to be more precise, but that was the difference between him and Preacher. He cursed like the sailor he was, and Preacher was actually known to bust out with the occasional *golly gee*.

Of course, what you called it didn't really matter, because it all boiled down to their entire mission having been plagued by disaster from the get-go. Starting with their one and only satellite radio getting bashed to smithereens on the side of the mountain when its strap broke during their fast-rope insertion into enemy territory. Continuing after they'd snatched al-Masri from his bed in one of the tiny houses crammed in the valley below, only to be spotted by one of his men who'd chosen the unholy hour of oh-three-hundred to go take a piss. And ending with the Taliban leader's army boiling from the village to fan out across the valley, effectively cutting off Jake and his team's planned route of escape and causing them to miss their evac out of this godforsaken hellhole. As a result, they'd been forced to take cover in a tiny outcropping of trees clinging precariously to the side of one hellaciously sheer barren-ass mountain.

And to add a shiny turd on top of this crap sundae, the sun was coming up, slipping over the mountains to their east and spilling its disastrous light all around them.

"So whatchu boys wanna do now?" Rock asked in his slow Cajun drawl. Jake glanced at him briefly before turning his attention to the CO's scarred face.

"Kill 'im," Boss said, spitting on the ground like a visual exclamation point. "If we don't, we probably won't make it outta here. And if we try to take him with us, this douchebag will give away our position the first chance he gets. Intel says his army consists of between 80 and 120 fighters, which means at best that's twenty-to-one and, at worst, thirty-to-one. We're good, gentlemen, the absolute best, but those aren't odds I'm comfortable entertaining."

The four of them, Navy SEALs from Bravo Platoon, had been tasked with snatching Hamza al-Masri—the local Taliban leader personally responsible for the barracks bomb resulting in the deaths of over two hundred good Marines—and bringing him back to face some old-fashioned American justice. But that outcome was looking less and less likely as the hours and list of what-the-hells mounted.

"Those aren't our orders," Jake murmured, pissed beyond measure at the entire assbag of a situation. "We were told to bring him in still breathing."

"Yeah?" Boss scoffed, his face full of derision. "And just who gave those orders, do you suppose? Some pencil-pushing prick in DC who wouldn't know his ass from a hole in the ground when it comes to how quickly things can go from sugar to shit out here on the battle-field, that's who. But what we're talking about here is serious, guys, something that could get us reprimanded at best, busted down in rank, or worse. I won't make the call. We all have to agree."

Jake knew Boss was right. He knew killing al-Masri was their best chance at surviving. And Lord knew, *he* certainly wanted the guy dead, had wanted his head on a spike ever since that bombing. But that was a big part of Jake's growing problem, now wasn't it?

"No one would need to know," Preacher mused. "We could kill him, bury the body, get the heck out of Dodge, and say we never saw him." But even as he said the words, it was obvious from the look of disgust that passed over his camo-painted face that the idea didn't sit real well with him.

It didn't sit real well with *any* of them.

Among patriotism and loyalty and honor, one of the characteristics most SEALs prided themselves on was honesty. Lies tended to stick in their craws.

"No. If we do this thing, we're doing it out in the open," Boss said, his jaw sawing back and forth. "We get back to base and say, 'This is what we did because it was our only viable option.' And anyone who knows anything will understand that's God's honest truth. I'm not falsifying reports. I refuse to do that."

"Maybe we kill him, report it, and nothing comes of it," Preacher proposed. "They're going to give him life in Gitmo or string him up by his neck anyway, so what's the point? I think the brass will have our backs on this one."

Say what?

Jake resisted the urge to glance overhead—just in case pigs were singing R. Kelly's "I Believe I Can Fly" while zooming past.

He liked Preacher, he honestly did—despite the fact that six weeks ago the guy had up and married the only woman Jake ever loved. Of course, given that whole pride and honesty thing, he had to admit Preacher's marriage to Michelle was mostly *his* fault. He *had* been the one to push the two of them together…

And was it really any surprise they'd hit it off?

Um, that'd be a big, resounding negative. Considering Michelle Knight was the finest, sweetest woman on the planet and Steven "Preacher" Carter was the nicest, absolute *nicest* guy Jake had ever met, it should've been a foregone conclusion they would be a perfect match.

And, yes, he realized that most people would consider labeling a guy who was philosophically discussing slicing open a man's jugular as *nice* was more than a bit bizarre, but besides being nice, Preacher was also one hell of a soldier.

He knew the score here.

Then again, if he really believed they could come out of this shit-storm of a situation totally unscathed, he should be voted mayor of La-La Land.

"Gimme a break, brohah," Jake growled, reverting back to the surfer lingo he'd grown up with, as he tended to do in stressful situations. "You *know* better than to trust the brass to have our backs. The good ol' U-S of A wants al-Masri as a prize, a warning to all the other fanatics on the planet that there's no place you can hide where we won't find you and bring you to justice. We'll be skewered if we kill him. No," he shook his head, "we have to take him back in one piece."

Although, if he was honest with himself, it wasn't the thought of being demoted or ripped a new one by the rapier tongue of the general that prompted his dissent. No, no. He didn't care about rank or any of that other bullcrap. It was the fact that his heart beat with a terrible, hungry rhythm at the thought of slipping his knife from its sheath and ending al-Masri's existence right there and then that scared the breath right out of his lungs. Because he wasn't supposed to have any particular feeling one way or another about his missions. He was supposed to remain cool and levelheaded. *Detached.* But lately that was becoming nearly impossible. Ever since the bombing, ever since the horror of sorting through all those bodies had planted a seed in him that'd steadily grown into a poison-fanged monster, he'd been struggling against a mind-numbing fury that obliterated all thoughts save those of vengeance.

And, yo, wasn't that just dead-eye wrong? Wasn't it the exact same type of mentality terrorists employed to justify bombing buildings and embassies and marketplaces? Of course it was. But even though his rational mind might yell *Dude, what the hell are you thinking?*, the monster inside him seemed to be growing louder by the day. And it screamed one line over and over: *Kill them all. Avenge your brothers…*

He was ashamed to admit he'd nearly let the reins slip

on that monster once. The thought of doing so again terrified him. Like right now? He was piss-his-pants scared that if he unleashed his need for revenge and killed al-Masri outside of his orders, there'd be nothing to stop him from doing it again. And then again and again and again...

"Ya really think it's possible we can get ourselves outta here before al-Masri's guys surround us, *mon ami*?" Rock asked.

"Check it," Jake said as he wrestled back the bloodthirsty beast growling inside him and the accompanying fear it evoked. Taking out the topographical maps and surveillance photos of the area, he motioned for his teammates to follow him a short distance away, out of earshot and eyesight of the Taliban leader, before spreading them on the ground. "If we go up the mountain and reach the plateau," he pointed at the map with a dirty finger, "our cell phones should be able to receive a signal. We can call back to base and request an airlift out. Let's say it takes us fifteen minutes to make the climb, two minutes to make the call, eight minutes prep time for the helo, and thirty minutes flight time for the bird to reach us. That's fifty-five minutes total. It'll take al-Masri's army at least forty-five to fifty minutes to climb up the mountain from the valley. That's cutting it close. But we'll have the high ground and can hold our position for those remaining few minutes."

It wasn't cockiness that assured him four guys could hold off 120. It was training, superior shooting accuracy, premium weaponry, and better positioning.

"All right then," Preacher said, nodding once, "you've convinced me."

"Rock," Jake asked, turning toward the Cajun, "what do you think, bro?"

Rock eyed him for the space of a few interminable heartbeats, and Jake knew his teammate was accurately reading the situation. Rock was there the day Jake had nearly done the unthinkable, and the ragin' Cajun had to know it was the flat-out, ball-shriveling fear of what he was on the brink of becoming that was driving Jake to make this decision right now.

"*Oui, mon frere*," Rock finally nodded, sliding him a look of...*Please, God, don't let that be pity.* "Let's try it."

Jake blew out an unsteady breath, and for the first time in his recent memory, nary a swear word left Boss's lips even though the big man must have thought they were making a colossal mistake. Instead, Boss took the vote in stride and simply walked back to al-Masri, pointing at him and motioning for him to stand.

The Taliban leader shook his head, his nostrils flaring. In answer, Boss grabbed the guy under the arm and yanked him up like a ragdoll, giving him a little shake before setting him on his feet and propelling him forward with a hard shove.

"Move out," Boss ordered.

In less than two seconds, they were all slogging it up the side of the mountain. The loose shale and rocky rubble gave way beneath their desert-tan boots, and for every two steps forward, it seemed they slid one step back. It didn't help matters that al-Masri fought them every inch of the way, slowing their progress until it seemed they'd never reach their destination. By the time they'd covered half the distance to the plateau,

sweat streaked their camouflage face paint and damp-
ened their clothes.

Jake was dying of thirst, his tongue sticking to the
roof of his mouth. And just as he made a grab for the
hydration tube on his CamelBak, the biggest, ball-
twisting sight he'd ever seen manifested before his
gritty eyes...

Taliban fighters swarmed the plateau like ants on an
anthill. All armed with AK-47s. All with only one thing
in mind: *Kill the Americans*.

Holy shit!

Somehow they'd managed to climb up the backside
of the mountain even though Jake's maps had shown
nothing but a sheer cliff face...

Well, obviously his maps had been wrong. Go figure.
Because that's *exactly* the kind of day he was having.

"Get him in front of us!" Boss roared as they shuffled
in behind al-Masri, using him as a human shield, knowing the Taliban leader's men wouldn't risk opening fire
on their esteemed commander. But as they began to inch
back down the mountain, al-Masri stuck out his foot,
tripping Rock who was directly behind him.

Jake and Boss made a grab for their teammate as
Preacher scrambled to secure the Taliban leader, but
they were too late. Somehow al-Masri managed to
snag Rock's KA-BAR from the sheath around Rock's
waist and, in the blink of an eye, he'd driven all seven
inches straight into Rock's shoulder. A heartbeat later,
he ripped out the blade and aimed it straight for Rock's
carotid artery.

What happened next was like something beyond reality.
This is the man who's responsible...

It was a fleeting thought, but it was enough. Because no sooner did he have it than Jake lost his grip on the thing inside him. Rage poured through his system, hot and violent.

This man, this evil *man has killed and injured enough of my comrades. It stops. Now!*

Then it was if he'd been catapulted from his own body. With an odd sort of detachment, he seemed to watch himself. Watch as he raised his weapon, aiming it at al-Masri's turbaned head. Watch as he pulled the trigger.

Blood sprayed from the Taliban leader's skull in a terrible arc of crimson gore, and Jake was suddenly slammed back into his body just in time to feel a delicious sense of justice right before he realized what his impulsiveness…what his *bloodlust* may have cost all of them.

Oh, shit! What have I done?

"Fall back!" Boss roared as the first volley of rounds sprayed around them, biting into the shale, kicking up razor-sharp flecks of rock that turned one projectile into fifteen.

Fall back. Yo, Jake didn't need to be told twice. And *fall* was the operative word.

He tried turning and getting his feet under him so he could at least *attempt* to snake his way down the mountainside, but if he thought going up was difficult, going down was impossible.

At least, it was impossible to manage with any sort of control…

He slipped and slid, his thick-soled boots skidding on the loose shale as he occasionally turned to fire behind him.

SEALs were trained to make their rounds count, so while al-Masri's men wildly sprayed the side of the mountain, Jake and the guys only fired when they had a target they could hit. By the time they'd slipped back into the relative safety of the little copse of trees, he could see the bodies of at least seven Taliban fighters littering the steep slope.

It wasn't enough. Not nearly enough. Especially since more of al-Masri's men rushed over the brim of the plateau. The intel they'd received on the number of fighters the Taliban leader commanded was clearly off.

Way off.

He'd bet his left nut there were at least two hundred hard-faced militants closing in on their position.

"This is bad!" Preacher yelled from behind a small tree trunk as he continued to acquire targets and fire. He was trying to protect their left flank while Jake covered their right. Boss quickly dispatched anyone stupid enough to come at them head-on, and Rock picked off anything that managed to slip by all three of them.

"We've got to get off this mother-sucking mountain!" Boss yelled, his suppressed M4 quietly spitting rounds uphill as more Taliban fighters breathed their last.

The acrid smell of cordite perfumed the air around them as hot rounds bit into the trees behind which they took cover. Jake's particularly weak, little sapling wasn't going to last much longer under the barrage.

"If we can make it to the valley, take over one of those houses, we can hold our position until help arrives!" he yelled, slamming in another clip.

They had the ammo; they had the weapons. The plan just might work.

Of course, making it down to the valley was going to be the tricky part and, yeah, he couldn't deny the fact that it would've been a whole helluva lot easier for them if they'd still had al-Masri to use as a shield and bargaining chip.

What the hell *have I done?* Again, the question blasted into his head, and waves of guilt and recrimination washed through him, compounded by the adrenaline coursing through his veins.

"Fall back!" Boss shouted and, once again, *fall* was exactly what they did.

The mountainside below the outcropping of trees was even steeper—if that was possible—and controlling their descent proved hopeless. Soon, all four of them were rolling and tumbling like clothes in a dryer. Sharp rocks and debris grabbed onto straps and gear, snatching it away, and all the time bullets rained down from above.

They landed in a giant heap of screaming muscles and tangled limbs at the foot of the mountain beside the tiny village houses. Boss and Rock both made for one helluva hard landing spot, but Jake figured Preacher, who'd ended up on top of the pile, would say something similar about him.

The four of them managed to untangle themselves only to fire and retreat, fire and retreat, leapfrogging each other as they raced toward the village.

Thankfully, they weren't met with any resistance from the village's inhabitants. It seemed all the guys with guns were on the side of the mountain.

Well, mahalo *to the Big Kahuna in the sky for small miracles.*

As Jake, Preacher, and Rock laid down covering fire,

Boss planted one of his big boots against the door of a little mud-brick house and, two seconds later, they all stumbled inside.

It was blessedly empty.

Again, Jake took the right, Preacher the left, and Boss held steady smack dab in the middle while Rock covered their six. They kept plugging away at the approaching army, acquiring targets and squeezing their triggers. During a small lull in the action, Jake felt for his cell phone and came up empty-handed. *Damn!* He must've lost it somewhere on the long tumble down the mountain along with two extra clips, his M203 grenade launcher, and his pack.

"I lost my phone!" he yelled, and watched from the corner of his eye as Boss, Rock, and Preacher started patting pockets, searching for their phones, their one and only chance of making it out of this god-awful situation alive.

Both Boss and Rock came up with a big handful of *nada*. Thankfully, Preacher hit the jackpot.

He held up the device triumphantly, but Jake could tell by the look on his face, they were too close to the side of the mountain to get reception.

"Cover me!" Preacher yelled.

Before any of them could stop him, Preacher raced through the front door and down the packed dirt street. Bullets slammed into the road all around him, kicking up great puffs of dirt as he serpentined his way toward the open poppy field at the south end of the village where his chances of acquiring a cell signal would be the best.

It was the bravest thing Jake had ever seen, but he didn't have time to watch the heart-wrenching spectacle because he had to keep shooting, keep disposing of as many of the men operating those AKs as he could so Preacher could make the Hail Mary call back to base.

He didn't know how much time passed. It seemed like days but was, in reality, probably only about fifteen minutes.

Then, the most delightfully welcome sound he'd ever heard came thundering down the valley. A couple of U.S. Air Force boys in stealth fighters began dropping twelve-hundred-pound bombs on the side of the mountain beyond the village in a beautiful, tightly packed barrage of fire and death.

The blasts were beyond belief, the concussive effects loud enough to render everyone deaf for long moments afterward.

In their little house, the three SEALs warily eyed the roof as one entire mud wall cracked and splintered like shatterproof glass. The ground beneath them heaved in a series of rolling waves but, thankfully, the roof held. And when the bombardment finally ceased, they peeked from the door and windows.

The main body of al-Masri's men was obliterated. Nothing left but gaping, charred holes where previously whole groups of men had been firing. Only a few Taliban fighters, dazed and wounded, stumbled upright to try and continue the battle.

Jake took aim and started picking off the survivors. They needed to finish this and find Preacher.

The guy had been gone too long. Outside. Exposed.

When no more fighters popped up to aim rusted-out AK-47s in their direction, they abandoned their cover and hoofed it down the dusty road toward the poppy field. They pushed into the middle of the field just in time to see one of al-Masri's men jump up and take aim at Preacher's unprotected back.

"Preacher!" Boss and Rock yelled at the same time Jake shouted, "Steven!" They raised their M4s, but not before the gunman squeezed off two rounds.

Preacher spun as the scorching lead slammed into his body, and Jake freight-trained it toward the Taliban fighter, screaming like a berserker as he plied his trigger again and again.

The man jerked as round after round tore through his flesh, but even after he'd fallen to the ground, Jake didn't let up. He continued to riddle the body with bullets.

His monster was free for the second time today…

When he got close enough to see the man's face, he squeezed the trigger one more time, putting a round right between those evil, sightless eyes as he spit on the corpse and cursed the bastard to hell.

Of course, the person he should be cursing was himself.

If only he hadn't been such a chicken shit, so scared of the thing he was becoming that he couldn't make the tactically sound decision—which would've been to kill al-Masri on the side of that mountain—they could've made it to the plateau *before* al-Masri's army, and from their superior position, they might've held off the fighters until an extract team arrived.

And, as if of that wasn't bad enough, then when they'd actually *needed* al-Masri, he'd gone and lost control and killed the guy. Now, because Jake had screwed up on every level possible today, Preacher was lying in an expanding pool of dark blood.

He ran to where Boss and Rock knelt beside Preacher

and choked when he saw the gaping hole through Preacher's chest and its twin through his lower abdomen. Amazingly, Preacher was still conscious, still clutching his M4 in one hand and his open cell phone in the other—the same phone that'd called in the airstrike that had saved their lives.

Jake fell to his knees, helping Boss and Rock apply pressure to those gruesome wounds as blood pumped hot and heavy between his shaking fingers.

"Hang on, man," he whispered, glancing up as Boss stood and whipped off his shirt. They'd lost their field medical gear in the headlong plummet down the mountainside and had no bandages or QuikClot. Their clothes were the only things they had to try and staunch the life-taking river of fluid pouring from Preacher's body.

"Helo on…the…" Preacher choked and coughed, foaming blood oozing from both corners of his mouth, "…way," he finally finished.

"Yeah man, yeah," Jake murmured, not trying to fight the tears streaming down his cheeks as he ripped the shirt Boss handed him in two, pressing each half into Preacher's wet, ragged wounds. "You did one helluva job," he said around a heart that was sitting and throbbing in the back of his parched throat. "Gave those Air Force boys perfect coordinates. They obliterated al-Masri's guys."

"Good," Preacher choked, and Jake had to resist the urge to throw his head back and shriek his grief into the hot Afghan air.

No way was help arriving in enough time to save Preacher's life.

"I'm going to go look for our medical gear," Boss said.

"I'll go with ya," Rock murmured, blood oozing from the deep gash in his shoulder to slide down his arm and drip from his fingers into the dark soil of the open poppy field. "Fours eyes are better than two."

Jake nodded and numbly watched his teammates race back toward the side of the mountain.

"S-Snake?" Preacher coughed wetly, and Jake knew that sound. Most folks referred to it as the death rattle.

"Yeah, bro?"

"Sh-Shell," more coughing, more awful rattling. "She's..." Preacher's eyes flew open, and the coughing turned to choking.

Jake could do nothing. Nothing to help his teammate, his fellow soldier, his *friend* as the Grim Reaper hovered overhead. He felt that bastard's presence like a cold, wet blanket, and knew if the sonofabitch were corporeal, he'd blast him full of holes before sending him back to the stinking black abyss from which he'd sprung.

"She's..." from somewhere Preacher found the strength to finish, "pregnant."

Pregnant? Dear God...

"C-congratulations, bro." He choked on his tears, hoping Preacher didn't know the extent of his feelings for Michelle, or about that night in the bathroom of the Clover Bar and Grill when he'd *almost* let things get out of hand with her. The same night he'd shoved her into Preacher's arms.

Of course, at the time, he'd never dreamed she'd go and do the *smart* thing and actually fall for the guy...

With one last mighty heave, Preacher tried his best to fight Death.

But in the end, Death was too strong.

And Jake could do nothing but sit, crying and cradling the lifeless body of one of the finest men he'd ever known.

He refused to let go of Preacher even after Boss and Rock returned, empty-handed, from the mountain and sank down beside him, tears streaking their faces. He refused to let go when the Night Stalkers arrived and loaded them all into their Chinook. He refused to let go until it was time to clean and prepare Preacher's body for transport back to the states.

And all the while he was thinking, *This is my fault. This is all my fault…*

Chapter One

Chicago, four years later…

"JUST LEAVE THEM ON THE PORCH," MICHELLE instructed, peeking through the peephole at the flower delivery man as she wiped her flour-covered hands on her apron.

Something wasn't right.

For one thing, the delivery man held up the blue roses so she couldn't see his face. For another, she wasn't expecting any roses.

Of course, maybe she was just being paranoid, but that's what she got for being the kid sister of a covert government defense contractor. She had the tendency to see villains lurking around every corner.

"But I'm s'posed to get a signature, ma'am," the guy said, his deep voice muffled by the flowers.

Nope. Her brother had told her on numerous occasions—drilled it into her head was more like it—to follow her instincts. Always.

"Sorry," she called. "I'm not expecting any flowers. You'll just have to take them back."

The guy seemed to hesitate. Then he shrugged his shoulders behind the giant bouquet before turning and dropping the roses on the top step. He quickly crossed the street and, shoving his hands into his jeans pockets, strolled down the block and around the corner where he'd no doubt parked his delivery van. She still didn't get a good look at his face, but stitched across the back of his baseball cap in white lettering was the logo for Silly Lilly Flower Shop.

Crap. She was obviously jumping at shadows.

Opening the door, she retrieved the bouquet and fished through them for a card.

Nothing.

Huh...

Shaking her head in confusion, she walked into the kitchen and took down a vase from above the refrigerator. She filled it with water, then arranged the brilliant blue roses and placed them in the middle of her kitchen table before skirting around the counter to resume her task of rolling out dough for homemade pasta.

She was still frowning at the flowers when her brother slammed in through the back door, wincing when his cast accidently banged against the jamb.

"Something wrong with the front door?" she asked as he ambled toward the refrigerator.

"Thought I'd try something new," he replied as he took out a gallon of milk and twisted off the cap, tilting his head back to drink straight from the carton.

"Lovely," she muttered, shaking her head as she threaded a piece of dough into her pasta machine.

There was no use scolding him. She'd tried that, and it'd never made any difference except to exacerbate her own frustration.

"Snake's back," Frank blurted, wiping the back of his hand over his mouth before replacing the milk and strolling over to lean a hip against the counter.

Great big, fat, cricket-chirping, tumble-weed blowing silence.

That's what followed his announcement for all of about thirty seconds, until she could swallow down her stupid heart. She'd been dreading the day she'd hear those words, though a part of her always knew it would eventually come.

"Oh, yeah?" she finally managed to ask, glad to discover her voice wasn't shaking like her knees. "What does he want?"

"He says he'd like to see you," Frank admitted nonchalantly, popping a ball of dough into his mouth before she could swat his hand away.

Her belly did a good impression of an Olympic gymnast at this second declaration, but she chose to ignore the sensation.

"You shouldn't eat that!" she admonished, evading his last statement because, truthfully? She couldn't go there. Not yet. "Okay, fine. Go ahead and eat it, you big dummy. But if you get salmonella, don't come crying to me."

"I won't," he assured her with a wink. "I'll go crying to Becky. She makes one helluva nurse." He patted the blue spica cast that held his newly reconstructed shoulder immobile, grinning like a loon. She knew that particular head-in-the-clouds smile was because Becky Reichert, the hotshot motorcycle designer who provided the cover for Frank and all the guys over at Black Knights Inc., had agreed to become his wife.

It'd be a marriage made in motorcycle designer/secret-agent heaven, no doubt.

Here comes the bride. All dressed in...studded black leather?

Shaking her head, she tried to envision that particular wedding ceremony and failed miserably.

"Uncle Frank! Uncle Frank!" Franklin raced into the kitchen from the living room, clutching the blue construction paper upon which he'd glued colorful, crazily shaped tissuc-papcr fish. Hcr heart warmed at the sight of her rough-and-tumble son with his mop of unruly, sable-colored hair and his stormy gray eyes. "Look what I made with Miss Lisa today!"

Frank scooped the boy up in his good arm, regarding the sticky, slightly limp piece of art like it was the *Mona Lisa*.

"Well, would you look at that," he mused, his deep voice infused with the appropriate amount of awe to bolster a three-year-old's ego. "Looks like you've got a burgeoning artist on your hands here, Shell."

Franklin pressed a tissue-paper fish more firmly onto the construction paper with one stubby finger. The tangy aroma of Elmer's glue wafted from the soggy work of art.

"In fact," her brother continued, "this little man might just be the next Picasso."

Franklin's lips puckered. "No way! I'm not gonna be no pistachio! I'm gonna build motorcycles with you, Uncle Frank," he declared hotly before squirming to be let down.

Her brother deposited him on the floor, and Franklin trotted toward the living room, the conversation apparently having reached its conclusion in his brain until her brother said, "Well, you can do anything you want to do, kiddo. The sky's the limit."

Franklin turned back, blinking twice as if truly grasping the magnitude of this last statement. Then he swung around and raced away, singing "On Top of Spaghetti" at the top of his lungs as the lights in his sneakers blinked happily.

"You and Franklin should come back with me tonight," Frank declared.

Her stomach did another quick flip at the thought of actually coming face-to-face with Jake Sommers.

She should've been ready to see him again. She *should* have been.

She wasn't...

"We're trying to take Becky's mind off what happened yesterday evening. She's still a little shaky," he continued, and Michelle pushed aside her aversion to the thought of seeing Jake just enough to think a *little shaky*? Becky Reichert had *shot* and *killed* a villainous, bloodthirsty man not more than twenty-four hours ago, and she was only a *little shaky*? "Rock says he's gonna grill up some steaks and brats. And it's such a beautiful evening for a barbeque."

There he went again with that loony grin. It was almost eerie. Like attack of the pod-people eerie.

Come on," he cajoled when her face filled with mutiny. "With Snake back and Rock finally home, it'll be like old times."

"You mean the kind of old times that made you hide me away from your coworkers at Black Knights Inc. for the past three and a half years?"

After everything that'd happened in Coronado, after the horror of it, her brother had thought it better to keep her separate from *that* part of his life, the government operator part of it. He'd thought he was protecting her by keeping her a secret from his employees at Black

Knights Inc., protecting her from more fear and heart-break. And maybe he was right. But she'd become sick and tired of being a peripheral figure in his world. So she'd shown up at the hospital after his shoulder surgery and introduced herself to all the Knights who'd been waiting for him to come out of recovery.

Oopsie. My cover's blown!

Aw, shucks…

"Well, the jig is up anyway, thanks to you," he scowled and feigned punching her in the shoulder. "So you might as well come out to the shop and see what I've been up to."

"I've got to finish rolling out this dough," she hedged, getting desperate. When Frank got that particular look in his eye—yep, there it was—there was no nay-saying him. Of course, that wasn't going to stop her from giving it her best effort. "Plus, I've got an early appointment in the morning."

"Well that's perfect. You two can pack some bags and spend the night."

"A-are you insane?" she sputtered. *It just gets worse and worse.* "First of all, you know I don't like to mess with Franklin's schedule. And secondly, do you really want a three-year-old running around your—" she peered into the living room to make sure her little pitcher wasn't listening in with his big ears, "—super-secret spy shop?"

"I wouldn't let him go up to the command center." Her brother's expression very succinctly conveyed *gimme some credit*. "You guys could sleep out in the old foreman's house. Dan doesn't use it anymore."

The thought of seeing everything her brother had

built for himself was tempting, but not nearly as tempting as avoiding Jake. "I really can't. I've got some work
to finish tonight. Franklin needs a bath. There's a load
of laundry to fold and—"

"Michelle Knight, are you making excuses?"

She glared at him. "I'm Michelle *Carter*, remember?
And I don't understand why you'd want us to come
spend the night. It's preposterous."

"Like I said, Snake wants to see you. This way, it'll
give you guys plenty of time to catch up."

"Why would I want to catch up with him?" *After the
way he abandoned us.* She didn't need to say that last
part. It was there in her tone. Directly after Steven's
funeral—God, Steven's funeral. She still got sick to her
stomach every time she thought of it—Jake had transferred to Alpha Platoon and signed on for a two-year
mission that'd taken him to parts unknown. And when
he'd finally returned to CONUS—continental U.S.—
when she'd swallowed her pride, disregarded her better
judgment, and sent him a letter begging him to come
back to them, telling him they were his family and they
loved him and needed him, what had he done?

He'd completely ignored her, that's what. Acting
as if she was nothing, as if her brother, his *best friend*,
was nothing.

"Shell?" Frank reached forward and placed a hand on
her shoulder. She hoped he couldn't feel the trembling
there. "What happened between you two? Did he treat
you like he treated all those other—"

"No," she was quick to interrupt him. Because even
though four years ago she'd been determined to be the
last notch on Jake's bedpost—and they'd been close, oh

so close that night at the Clover—she couldn't let her brother go on thinking his best friend had pulled one of his typical Austin Powers moves on her.

Shall we shag now? Or shall we shag later?

Much to her surprise and dismay, Jake's sense of loyalty and friendship, and whatever other noble notion you could possibly think of, had overcome his libido that night.

"Jake wasn't like that with me," she admitted, having lost count of the number of times she'd asked herself how things might've been different had they actually *finished* what they'd started in that bathroom.

"Good." He nodded decisively, his frown turning into that weird pod-person grin again. "So there's no reason why you can't come out to the shop and help me welcome him back."

No reason? *Oh, sweet Lord…*

Of course, maybe it was better this way. They say, whoever *they* are, that in order to conquer one's fears, one first had to face them.

Swallowing, rolling in her lips, she called for Franklin to grab his jacket and tried not to pass out cold on her kitchen tiles as she wrapped up the remaining ball of dough and went to the sink to wash her hands.

The darn things were shaking like gravel on a dirt road during an earthquake.

Black Knights Inc. Headquarters
Goose Island, Chicago

"So, *mon ami*," Rock murmured in his slow Cajun drawl

as the breeze wafted the meaty smell of steaks cooking on the grill and mixed it with the waxy scent of the burning tiki lamps and the slightly fishy aroma of the nearby Chicago River, "ya said you're here for Shell?"

Uh…yep. That was the first thing Jake blurted upon his arrival the evening before. *I'm here for Shell*.

Geez. Just call him Captain Obvious.

"That's what I said," he grumbled uncomfortably, adjusting himself in the brightly painted Adirondack chair.

Rock grinned, his teeth flashing white against his dark goatee as he sat forward in gleeful anticipation. "Tell me, what size must a guy's balls be in order to walk up to his former commandin' officer and declare his intent to plant his flag, so to speak, in the man's baby sister? Texas-sized, maybe? Alaska-sized?"

"Cut it out," Jake growled, avoiding Rock's gaze as he took a sip of locally brewed ale and let his eye wander around the enclosed courtyard located behind the motorcycle shop that was the front for Black Knights Inc.

Black Knights Inc…

They'd really done it.

All those years the three of them, him and Rock and Boss, had talked and planned and dreamed of building their own clandestine government defense firm, and they'd really gone and done it.

Without him…

He didn't know whether to burst with pride for his former Bravo Platoon teammates or break down and cry because he'd missed it all. What he *did* know was he'd made himself sick on the ride from the west coast to Chicago, wondering what his reception might be.

But he shouldn't have worried. Men who fought wars

together had a connection, a soul-deep connection that time and distance and familial affiliation couldn't touch.

Rock and Boss welcomed him back with open arms. And for the first time in a very long time, glancing at the familiar, sardonic expression on Rock's face, he felt like he was home.

If home included the pins and needles he was sitting on as he waited for Shell's arrival, that is...

Because no matter how hard he'd tried—and you better believe there'd been times he'd given it his all—he'd never stopped loving her.

He hadn't stopped loving her that night in the Clover when, scared out of his mind, after barely stopping himself from nailing her up against the wall of the men's bathroom, he shoved her in Preacher's arms and saw the hurt and disbelief fill her eyes. He hadn't stopped loving her that rainy day when she caught him at the base's front gates to tell him she'd fallen for Preacher. He hadn't stopped loving her that afternoon two weeks later when Preacher pulled him aside on the way to mess to softly inform him, *Shell and I are getting married*. He hadn't stopped loving her that day in the mountains of Afghanistan when he learned she was having another man's baby. And he hadn't stopped loving her in the long, too long years between then and now. If anything, his love for her had grown, become an overwhelming thing.

And any minute she was going to come through that door. Any minute.

He snatched a glance at the door in question. Did the knob turn?

No. Just his eyes playing tricks on him and, *good grief*, he was *so* totally losing it.

"And Shell?" the Cajun broke into his spinning thoughts. "How d'ya think she's gonna feel about havin' you back around?"

That was the question of the hour, wasn't it?

He shrugged and stared past Rock's right ear, the air inside his lungs getting sucked out like he'd stepped into a vacuum.

"Dunno, brohah," he wheezed, trying and failing to drag in a much-needed mouthful of oxygen. "But I think I'm about to find out."

Why does he still *have to look so darned good?*

That was Michelle's first thought as she stepped into the courtyard and set eyes on Jake. He was lounging in a bright red Adirondack chair, sprawled there as if he hadn't a care in the world. And the audacity of that pose considering… well…*everything* that'd happened, burrowed under her skin like a chigger.

Since this was her first time inside the big gates of Black Knights Inc., she should have been scoping out the place. She should have been overcome with curiosity, checking to see exactly what her brother had been building for himself over the last three and a half years.

And she was…*Sort of.*

With a teeny-tiny portion of her brain, she registered the mammoth, three-story factory building with its aged brick and leaded glass windows. Through the most fleeting of observations, she took in the various outbuildings surrounding the tidy brick courtyard covered by a red-and-white striped canopy. With the most miniscule portion of gray matter, she noticed the unlit fire pit, the mammoth stainless steel grill, the basketball hoop standing next to the furthest outbuilding, and the odd assortment of brightly painted lawn furniture.

But she was able to catalog all of this by using only about 0.1 percent of her brain, because from the moment she set foot inside the courtyard, her eyes were glued to Jake's ridiculously handsome face and that body of his that could've been the model for an anatomy class, and the other 99.9 percent of her mind was wholly occupied with one and only one thought…

Why, why, oh why *does the lowdown, no-good cad* still *have to look so frickin' good?*

Couldn't the universe have taken pity on her, for once, and let wonderboy get fat or go bald? Couldn't it have allowed him to develop a rather tragic case of full-body psoriasis or fall victim to a series of odd facial tics?

No?

Damn you, universe!

Of course, if he *had* acquired some strange affliction, bleeding heart that she was, it would've probably only softened her toward him.

And she couldn't afford that.

Oh, no. She definitely could *not* afford that.

Taking a deep breath, reminding herself of the way he'd treated her four years ago, the way he'd treated all of them, she marched forward on knees threatening to give way with every step.

What she wanted to do was crawl into the nearest hole and hide until he went away again—and he *would* go away again; that's what he did. But since that wasn't an option, she mustered all the composure she could and blurted the first carefree-sounding thing she could think of.

"I see the years haven't had any sort of positive effect on your fashion sense, Jake." Her voice didn't come out sounding as shaky as her gelatinous insides felt, thank God. She'd never be able to make another JELL-O mold again without thinking of this moment right here, right now, and the way her stomach was quivering inside her. "You're still wearing those god-awful Hawaiian shirts like you're auditioning to be the next Magnum PI."

Although, with his shaggy mop of sun-bleached hair, Coppertone tan, and five o'clock shadow which, at the moment, looked more like the twelve o'clock version, he more closely resembled Josh Holloway.

Crap.

And *yes*, she'd watched each and every episode of *Lost* simply because of the resemblance between the two men...

Crap, crap, crap.

"Magnum PI! Ha!" Rock hooted with laughter, slapping his knee. "Good one, Shell."

"Mmm," Jake rubbed his chin, his beautiful, emerald green eyes sparkling with warm humor as he glanced down at the shirt she'd just insulted. The hideous thing was coupled with ratty jeans and a pair of dingy, leather flip-flops. A California surfer until the day he died.

And, man, he made it look good. Heaven help her...

"I don't know if I've ever heard two words more oxy-moronic than fashion and sense," he murmured, grinning. *Oh geez. There are those dimples.* "And dude" he added, glancing pointedly at Rock's faded Green Day

T-shirt, holey jeans, and scuffed alligator cowboy boots, "you're not one to talk."

"Okay," Rock admitted, still chuckling, "so a couple of Giorgio Armanis we ain't."

"On that we can agree," Jake said, clinking his beer bottle against Rock's. And just like that, they seemed to fall into their old rhythm, the give-and-take. As if nothing had ever happened. As if he'd never crushed her soul and abandoned them all.

It was all so familiar and heartbreaking, her throat closed up like she'd swallowed the industrial-strength cleaner she liked to use on Franklin's potty-training toilet. And then she couldn't breathe at all when Jake winked at her in that flirtatious way he had before tilting his head back and sucking down a mouthful of suds.

She took the opportunity of his distraction to do two things. One, she tried to steady her thundering heart and drag in a much-needed lungful of air before she passed out. And two, she let her hungry gaze travel over his face.

There were webs of fine lines at the corners of his eyes that hadn't been there four years ago, and a little crescent-shaped scar near his left temple. And even given all that, he still looked like he belonged on a billboard selling expensive shaving cream or designer cologne.

It wasn't fair! Particularly when he dropped his chin, letting his bright eyes leisurely wander down her frame.

Her cheeks heated under his rather…*thorough* scrutiny as if she'd shoved her head in a four-hundred-degree oven.

And *now* she could breathe. She gulped in a mouthful of air like a drowning victim.

Ugh, stop looking at me! she wanted to shout like a petulant five-year-old. Because, despite the fact that she sported the fuller breasts, wider hips, and slight roundness to her lower belly that no amount of crunches or yoga seemed to remedy—the physical badges of motherhood—he was still watching her the same way he'd always watched her. With affection and humor and sweet, burning *desire* in his eyes.

It made her remember things she thought she'd forgotten. It made her question her decision—

No. She'd given him chance after chance, and all he'd ever done was let her down. He was a rake and a wanderer, just like her dear ol' dad, and instead of being mad about all of that, instead of slamming into him with vitriol like he deserved, like any *intelligent* woman would do, the only emotion she could seem to conjure up was sadness.

An intense and overwhelming sadness…

"You look more beautiful than ever, Shell," he murmured appreciatively. "The years have been good to you."

And how did he *do* that? How did he make her want to believe him?

"How long has it been since you've been to the optometrist?" she quipped, pushing back the urge to cry as she stopped beside Rock, bending to give the Cajun's cheek a sisterly peck before accepting the chair Frank pulled out from around the unlit fire pit.

Okay, Shell, you're doing good. Just keep up the mild banter so nobody guesses you're slowly dying on the inside.

"My eyes are just fine," he declared, the eyes in

question flashing to her jean-clad legs when she sat and crossed them.

At least that was one body part that'd bounced back after her pregnancy. She was proud to admit, she still had a rockin' good set of stems. Although, it wasn't like he could *see* her rockin' good set of stems, given they were covered in a tattered pair of jeans.

Okay, and *why* hadn't she thought to change into something a little more fabulous than an old Texas A&M sweatshirt and this threadbare pair of Levi's?

Oh yeah. Because she'd been scared out of her mind while walking out the front door of her town house, and all she'd been able to think about was getting this little reunion over and done with *double-time*, as her brother would say.

"They" said confronting one's fears was the only way to conquer them? Well, in her opinion, *"they"* were all a bunch of idiots.

"Hey!" he declared, frowning when she leaned back in the chair. "The ragin' Cajun gets the love, but I don't? I haven't seen you in nearly four years, woman. You better come here and put one on me." He tapped a finger against his cheek.

And there he went again, regarding her with such genuine pleasure she almost began to wonder if she'd imagined the way he treated her. Then, a brief image of her waiting for him in the rain outside the base stabbed into her brain like a pickax and the harsh words he'd spoken rang in her ear like a death knell.

Stay strong, Shell. Don't let him see how much this hurts.

"Rock gets the love," she grumbled, fighting the

tears clogging her throat. That particular memory always evoked the same reaction in her, "because although I don't know where he's been recently, I'm pretty positive it was woefully short on friendly faces. *You*, on the other hand…" She gratefully accepted the cool glass of chardonnay Frank handed her. She sure as heckfire wasn't going to say no to a little liquid courage right now. "…have probably spent the last couple of years with Alpha Platoon working your way through all the base bunnies you'd failed to sample during your stint with Bravo Platoon. And I'm sure they were *extremely* friendly."

Instead of coming back with a snappy rebuttal as per usual, Jake's jaw hardened to living stone, his eyes flashing in the low light of the covered courtyard.

Well, at least that took care of those dastardly dimples…

"Some things change, Shell," he said quietly.

Her heart somersaulted at the solemnity, and something else she couldn't quite put her finger on, in the tone of his voice.

"Yeah," she stared at the scuffed toes of her sneakers, trying to ignore the nearly overwhelming desire to believe him. She was such a softhearted fool. "And then again, some things never do."

A strained silence settled over the courtyard then, broken only by the sound of Rock's boots clacking against the pavers when he pushed up from his chair to stroll over to the giant stainless steel grill. He lifted the lid in order to transfer a load of sizzling steaks onto a big platter, and Michelle absently watched him cover the plate with tinfoil before he plopped half a dozen fat bratwursts onto the grill.

All the while, she could feel Jake's piercing gaze on her flushed face.

Yes, some things never change.

His effect on her body temperature being one of them...

"Woo-ee!" Rock exclaimed, adjusting his sweat-stained John Deere ball cap as he turned away from the grill and let his eyes ping back and forth between the two of them. "Y'all are making me nervous as a long-tailed cat in a room full of rockin' chairs. Why don't you kids just kiss and make up? Let bygones be bygones and all that?"

Let bygones be bygones?

As if it was that easy...

She glanced at Jake. Whatever odd tone she'd heard in his voice and whatever strange expression she'd glimpsed in his face vanished when he winked and once again tapped his cheek with a finger. "Yeah, Shell. Let's let bygones be bygones. Get your fine fanny over here and lay those famous lips of yours on me."

She knew she had no choice but to set her glass of chardonnay on the ground and push up from her chair.

With men like her brother and Jake, men trained to catch and analyze the smallest blip of human emotion, making a big deal out of one little peck on the cheek was tantamount to waving a pair of semaphore flags and yelling at the top of her lungs that she wasn't unmoved by Jake's sudden return.

She couldn't give him the satisfaction.

So, surreptitiously taking a deep breath, she gathered her courage and walked over to him. Hiding the trembling of her hands by lacing them behind her back, she bent at the waist, careful to keep any part of *her* body from touching any part of *his* body, and placed a perfunctory peck on his warm, rough cheek.

Something hard and painful unfurled in her chest as she sucked in the intangible mix of salty sea, warm sand, fresh laundry, and coconut suntan lotion.

Jake always smelled like a day at the beach.

"There, now," Rock drawled, grinning. "One big happy family."

Chapter Two

JAKE CLOSED HIS EYES AT THE FEEL OF SHELL'S LUSH, warm lips, and sucked in the sweet scent of vanilla that always surrounded her in a soft cloud.

He remembered the first time he'd ever seen her, the day she'd gotten a job transfer from Texas to southern California, making her San Diego's newest and brightest pharmaceuticals representative. He'd just pushed through the door of the Clover Bar and Grill when she launched herself into Boss's arms and then proceeded to break into a happy dance that'd had her dangerously curvy hips doing a shimmy-shake that immediately affected him below the belt.

He'd instantly realized three things...

One: She was, in a word, stunning. Or in surfer lingo: a babelini, a California dime, a perfect ten. That is, if most guys thought a perfect ten came in a size ten—which he most certainly did. Not only did she have one of those heart-shaped faces and an Angelina Jolie mouth complete with a little beauty mark, but she also possessed Amazonian princess height and a set of curves with enough kinetic oomph to give a big wave surfer heart palpitations.

Two: She smelled like vanilla, which had worked to remind him that his own aroma left a lot to be desired. After a thirty-six-hour training exercise where he'd been forced to belly through a swamp, he remembered thinking Eau de Old Gym Socks and Unwashed Armpits pretty much summed it up.

And three, the most important thing: She was his commanding officer's kid sister. Which landed her directly in the column marked "hands off."

Of course, he'd instantly forgotten number three when she finally noticed him, turning those eyes of hers that were gray and turbulent—like the Atlantic after a storm—in his direction. He'd very astutely thought *homina, homina, homina.*

And then when she'd smiled at him? Word, it straight-up stopped his heart.

And that'd been the end of it. Right then and there, in the doorway of the Clover Bar and Grill, he'd fallen ass-over-teakettle in L-O-V-E.

Opening his eyes now, his stupid, lovesick heart thundered in his chest. He watched hungrily as she retook her seat and delicately lifted the wine to her killer lips. What he wouldn't give to be that wine, sliding into that sweet-tasting mouth, over that soft, agile tongue...

Whoa.

Dock the love boat, Sommers.

He couldn't let his mind wander down *that* prickly little path unless he wanted to pop an immediate chubby.

Which he *so* didn't want to do.

Because then it'd be all over before he really got a chance to start. She'd take one look at his growing bulge and roll her eyes in that way she had, instantly dismissing him as the same skirt-chasing hound dog he'd been when she'd known him years ago. And that was the dead last thing he wanted.

Not if he hoped to win her. And he was determined

to win her despite the fact that every time she looked at him, her expression filled with a wary kind of sadness.

Of course, *not* having those kinds of thoughts was proving nearly futile considering it'd been over two years since he'd been inside a woman, and she had to go and get more beautiful on him.

At thirty-four, Shell was fast approaching perfection. She was just hitting that sweet spot in a woman's life when her body lost the last rough angles of youth and developed a certain soft magnificence a guy could really revel in.

He opened his mouth to ask her how she'd been, to tell her how much he'd missed her. But he was stopped when the shop's back door flew open, and a short blur of denim overalls and blinking sneakers came streaking into the courtyard.

"Uncle Frank! Uncle Frank!" the blur skidded to a stop beside Boss, attaching himself to the big man's leg like a barnacle to a battleship. He held a cherry lollipop in one hand and, from the red splotches around his lips and on his chubby little cheeks, it was obvious he needed to work on his aim. "That purty lady showed me the motorcycles, and I gotta sit on one. Not yours. But the red one with the fire. I like the fire. She told me she painted it. Can I have a red motorcycle with fire when I grow up?" He didn't wait for Boss to answer before he pressed on, "But then I wanted to go upstairs and, and, and," he stuttered in his excitement, "she wouldn't let me. She said it was only for grownups. Why is it only for grownups, Uncle Frank?"

"Frank" came out sounding like "Fwank."

Boss opened his mouth, but again he didn't manage

to get a word in edgewise before the boy was steaming ahead. "I don't care anyway, 'cause I got a sucker instead." He brandished the sloppy piece of candy frighteningly close to Boss's eye as the big man bent to scoop the little curtain-climber up in his good arm.

So this is Franklin.

Jake had wondered if perhaps he might suffer a few pangs of jealously when he first saw the boy, but thankfully, he didn't. Perhaps it was because it seemed somehow appropriate there should be a reminder of Preacher and Shell's union other than his near nuclear jealousy when he thought about the two of them together. Or perhaps it was because no matter how hard he looked, he couldn't see one ounce of Preacher in Franklin's little face.

The rug rat was 100 percent Shell or, more accurately, 100 percent Knight, because he happened to look exactly like Boss...if Boss wasn't covered in half a dozen scars, that is.

"Well, there isn't a single doubt as to who this little guy is, is there?" He pushed up from his chair and strolled over to Boss and the sticky little boy in his arms.

"Who're *you*?" Franklin asked, steel-gray gaze sliding suspiciously over Jake's shirt before dropping to his feet. "It's too cold to wear flip-flops now," he announced gravely. "Mama says so."

"Yo, little dude." Jake held out one hand and was surprised when Franklin tucked his head under Boss's chin, suddenly going all shy. The kid had been Mr. Life-of-the-Party two seconds ago. He tried a different tack. "My name's Jake. And your mama's right. It *is* too cold for flip-flops, but I can't help it," he shrugged and made a face. "My toes like to breathe."

The boy tentatively reached out to shake his hand with red, sticky fingers before surreptitiously glancing at his mother. He leaned toward Jake, grinning and whispering conspiratorially, "My toes like to breathe, too."

Jake laughed and turned to tell Shell she was suffocating her son's toes when the stricken look on her face had him frowning. "Shell? Is something wrong?"

———⁓———

Is something wrong?

Yes, something's wrong! *Everything's* wrong!

She shouldn't still have to catch her breath whenever Jake moved with that silky, sliding, big-cat grace of his. She shouldn't still get light-headed just by being next to him. *He* shouldn't be able to cruise back into their lives without so much as a by your leave, making her want to forget the awful things he'd done, the awful things he'd said. Making her want to second-guess her decisions about…well…*everything*.

And the sight of him with Franklin…

Dear Lord…

She opened her mouth without having the first clue what she planned to say—because she sure as heckfire couldn't tell him any of *that*. But she was saved, *thank you, baby Jesus*, from having to say anything at all when Becky Reichert, Vanessa Cordero, and a dark-haired woman she didn't recognize pushed through the back door.

"Sorry about the lollipop," Becky said as Shell lifted a hand to her temple. Sure enough, ten minutes in Jake's company, and she was on the fast track to Migraine-ville.

Why had she let Frank talk her into this again?

Because you're a pushover when it comes to your brother, that's why. And you were under the mistaken impression that this might actually be good for you.

She'd very much like to find whoever "they" were and kick them straight in the groin.

Raking in a deep breath, she tried to shake away the tension in her shoulders and neck as she turned toward her brother's fiancée.

Becky held a platter stacked high with baked potatoes and a bowl of salad just about big enough to bathe in. Vanessa and the dark-haired woman were each loaded down with French bread, plates of bratwurst condiments, and what looked to be pecan pies.

It appeared they intended to feed an army.

"It was the only thing I could think to use to distract him from going upstairs," Becky explained as Michelle set her chardonnay aside and jumped from her chair to help with the food.

"No worries," she was quick to assure her future sister-in-law, who didn't look the *least* bit shaky to her, by the way. In fact, she'd go so far as to say Becky Reichert looked incredibly calm. No wonder Frank had fallen head over heels. The woman obviously had nerves of steel—a characteristic her balls-to-the-wall covert operative brother no doubt found completely irresistible. "It's not like it'll ruin his dinner or anything. He takes after his Uncle Frank in the appetite department."

A brief look of abject horror flashed across Becky's pretty face as she turned to survey the cornucopia of food now straining the supports of the weathered picnic table. "Oh, great," she grumbled. "We probably didn't make enough."

"We'll manage." Michelle laughed, glad for the distraction Becky provided so she could take a few moments to gather herself.

But that proved to be easier said than done.

Because the whole situation, what'd happened between her and Jake, what'd happened to Steven after they'd just started to build their life together, what was *still* happening to Franklin every day, growing up without a father, was so unbelievably unfair that sometimes she had the urge to rip her hair out by its roots and scream at the top of her lungs.

And it was that last one that bothered her most. Because she remembered what it was like as a child to watch her friends crawl all over some dependable-looking guy—a guy who tickled and laughed and taught them to ride their bikes—and feel a dark, aching hole in her heart, knowing that'd never be her.

She'd tried so hard to ensure Franklin didn't experience that same throbbing void, but Fate, that unbelievably unfair witch, had stepped in and robbed her and her son of the future they deserved.

And she couldn't help but lay a good portion of the blame for how everything had turned out at Jake's big feet...

"I, uh, I used to call you Chesty McGivesItUp," Becky said in a quiet undertone.

Okay, and *that* managed to rip Michelle way from her unsettling thoughts. "Huh?"

"When I thought you were Frank's lov—"

"Gross," she held up a hand. "I don't even want you to finish that sentence."

Her brother had laughingly informed her that, before

she'd gone and blown her cover, the Knights had suffered under the impression that all his furtive trips up to Lincoln Park to visit her had, instead, been bootycalls to a secret lover—which was as hysterical as it was ludicrous. Especially considering that most times Frank had been re-grouting her tub or changing one of Franklin's dirty diapers. A far, *far* cry from satin sheets and soft whispers...

"Yeah, I know, right?" Becky made a face. "But, I, uh, figured I better tell you in case any of the guys bring it up."

She laughed; she couldn't help it. "Chesty McGivesItUp, huh?" Becky winced and nodded. "I think I like that. Boss Knight. Snake Sommers. Rock Babineaux. And Chesty McGivesItUp Carter. Has a certain ring to it, doesn't it? I always wanted a cool handle. Thanks."

"You're nuts," Becky declared with a snort, then glanced over at Frank, her dark eyes instantly softening. "It must run in the family."

"Oh, it does," Michelle assured her.

She opened her mouth to tell Becky how happy she was that her brother had finally met his match, when he suddenly looped his good arm around her waist and called over his shoulder, "Snake, get over here. I wanna introduce you and Shell to Becky's best friend, Eve." He flicked a finger toward the slim, dark-haired woman who was busy setting the table. She turned at the sound of her name. "Eve, this is my beautiful and talented sister, Michelle Carter. And that sticky little creature over there terrorizing Peanut..." Michelle glanced over to see her son petting the biggest, ugliest cat ever born. The thing appeared to be part American Shorthair and part It's-Anybody's-Guess. It was ten pounds overweight—at least—covered in scars, and apparently a victim of some sort of skin affliction if its patchy fur was anything to go by. "…is her son, Franklin. And this," he jerked his chin toward Jake, "is Jake Sommers."

"Good to meet you," Eve said, timidly shaking Michelle's hand before turning her attention toward Jake. "Mr. Sommers, it's a pleasure."

Michelle rolled her eyes when Jake flashed those lady-killer dimples of his at poor, ill-equipped Eve. "Call me Jake or Snake," he said, widening his dimple-inducing grin. "You say Mr. Sommers, and I start feeling my age."

And another one bites the dust.

Wonderboy just couldn't help himself, could he? Just like her father, if you put him in front of a beautiful woman, he naturally started oozing charm like a cedar oozes sap.

Not wanting to inadvertently get caught up in his sticky trap, she turned and wandered over to Franklin and the tormented tomcat he was now petting in the *wrong* direction. On the way, she studiously closed her ears to whatever charming bologna Jake might think to sling Eve's way.

She figured she'd heard it all before anyway…

Vanessa Cordero watched as Snake shook Eve's hand, amazed once again to be in the company of one of the most legendary SEALs ever to graduate BUD/S. The guy was known for not only being an absolute animal out in the field, but also for his unparalleled success with the ladies. When he flashed Eve those deep dimples of his, Vanessa could certainly understand why so many California girls had fallen victim to his charm.

Of course, when she caught the hot, longing look he shot toward *Michelle*, she figured his days as the SEALs' resident lothario were long gone.

So that's the way the wind blows…

She'd wondered what his whole *I'm here for Shell* thing meant last night. Now she knew. And it was strange thing indeed to witness the exact moment when a man's heart skipped a beat. Stranger still that Michelle seemed to be completely clueless.

"Hey, *cheri*, why doncha load up a plate for Toran at the front gate, and I'll mosey on out and take it to him." Rock's smooth voice dragged her away from her fanciful observations.

But she discovered, much to her embarrassment after she turned to him expectantly, he wasn't speaking to her.

Of *course* he wasn't.

Like he would ever refer to *her* by the sweet French pet name, or sling that leanly muscled arm around *her* shoulders.

As far as she could figure, Rock was barely aware she was alive. Which just made it that much more ridiculous when she turned into a Disney character anytime he came within ten feet of her. All big eyes and fluttering lashes and an overwhelming desire to break into song.

Good God, the absolute absurdity of the whole thing would've been funny if it wasn't so blasted embarrassing…

And for the life of her, she couldn't understand what it was about the guy.

It wasn't like he was all that handsome. Not in the movie star way Ozzie or Ghost or Snake was handsome.

But it wasn't like he *wasn't* handsome either.

He was just…there. The kind of man you'd pass on the street without noticing. Seemingly wholly constructed of perfectly average features. That is until you really *looked* at him. Because when you stopped to really *look* at him, you realized his brown hair wasn't really brown, but a deep, dark auburn. And his hazel eyes weren't merely hazel; they were warm whiskey-brown shot through with amazing striations of glinting gold and new-grass green. His nose wasn't average and uninteresting; it was actually quite perfect. And his mouth…well, anybody who took the time to get past that goatee *had* to recognize that mouth for the thing of beauty that it was.

And when you added all that up with a sexy Cajun drawl and a body that was long, lean, and honed to physical perfection by hard living and harder training, not to mention the overall effect of a plethora of tattoos and long-legged swagger on the female libido, it was easy to see why some women would find themselves quite enamored with the guy.

But *she* was not just some woman.

She was Vanessa Cordero, communications specialist superstar. She'd spent her entire adult life working with hard-bodied operators and never had she reacted to them the way she reacted to Rock.

The situation was not only highly unimaginable, but also highly unfortunate as it threatened to muck-up her new job with BKI, the most elite, most clandestine defense firm in the whole world.

"Hey." Becky came up beside her, shoving a tall

glass of iced tea and a plate with a giant slice of pecan pie into her hands. "Would you do me a huge solid and help Rock take this out to Toran at the front gate?"

"Uh," she glanced over at the heaping plate of food Rock carefully balanced in front of him. "Sure."

"Thanks." Becky sauntered away, completely oblivious to the butterflies she'd awakened in Vanessa's belly. The ones that took to frantically beating against her rib cage as Rock strolled in her direction while digging in the front pocket of his Levi's for his cell phone.

"Before we go out, I need to call the guys on the perimeter and make sure there aren't any unfriendlies skulkin' about the place," he told her absently, his deep, sexy voice making her shiver.

Or maybe it was just the cool evening breeze causing her skin to erupt in goose bumps. She certainly hoped it was the breeze because, *crud*, she wasn't that far gone, was she?

When he gave her a strange look, she realized she hadn't responded to his last statement and was, instead, gaping at him in slack-jawed fascination, mere seconds away from breaking into song.

Ack! Someone just shoot me now!

Of course, since some wiseguy out of Las Vegas had put a price on the head of each and every Black Knight, she knew getting shot was an actual possibility. Which was why most of the Knights were stationed in the buildings around the perimeter of the BKI's compound, keeping a close eye on their operation.

"Oh, uh, good idea," she murmured and screwed her eyes closed when she realized how impossibly lame that sounded.

Rock didn't seem to notice—*thank goodness*—because he was already pushing some numbers on his phone and listening to it ring on the other end.

Pull yourself together, Cordero. He's just another operator like all the other operators you've worked with your entire life.

Unfortunately, that wasn't true. She couldn't put her finger on it, but he was somehow…*different*…

To distract herself as Rock exchanged a few terse words with whichever Knight he'd called, she turned back to the group gathering around the table.

Michelle was in the process of taking a seat when she glanced at her son's sticky hands and quickly changed her mind.

"No way you're coming to the table with those hands, mister," she said.

Little Franklin groaned like having to go inside to wash was tantamount to Chinese torture, and it was impossible to miss the smoldering look in Snake's eyes as he followed Michelle's progress into the shop.

Boss obviously didn't miss it, because he punched Snake in the shoulder and grumbled, "Stop staring at my kid sister like she's five-foot-ten-inches of grade-A giggidy."

"Ow!" Snake howled, making a face as he rubbed his abused shoulder. Then he grinned, lifting his hands in a shrug.

"You're ruining my dinner," Boss rumbled.

"Like that's even possible," Becky snorted, and Vanessa could only shake her head. She was still having a bit of trouble consolidating the image of the world's most dangerous men with those of the guys she'd come to know at BKI, the ones who threw impromptu barbeques and razzed one another without mercy. Sometimes, the place felt less like a top-secret spy shop and more like a rowdy fraternity.

"Perimeter's clear. We're good to go," Rock drawled, reminding her that for next couple of minutes she'd be completely alone with him.

Oh dear. The butterflies in her stomach started crawling up into her throat.

"Hey, Rock!" Becky called before they could make it through the shop's back door.

"Yeah, *chère*?"

"While you're out there, would you do a sweep of Snake's bike to make sure it's free of bugs or any other nasty devices?" The Knights never allowed unsecured vehicles onto their premises. In their line of work, it paid to be vigilant. "I'm dying to get a closer look at that paint job. The snakeskin on the tank looks almost three-dimensional."

"That would be thanks to this amazing tattoo artist out of LA," Snake said as he dug in his front pocket and tossed Rock a set of keys.

Even balancing the mammoth plate of steak, salad, and potatoes, Rock caught the keys easily.

"You finally restored that ol' Honda?" Boss asked, and the conversation dissolved into flywheels, pistons, and cylinders, of which Vanessa knew absolutely nothing.

Amazingly, however, since joining the Knights, her interest in the subject matter had skyrocketed, because, *seriously*, what she wouldn't give to have her very own custom-designed Black Knights motorcycle.

She'd never really considered herself the type of

woman to go in for the whole MC lifestyle. But the first time she'd seen all the Knights mount up and head for the open road, she knew she wanted a piece of that action.

"Lead the way," Rock's drawl interrupted her thoughts, and she turned toward the shop's back door.

She'd only gone a few feet when she glanced over her shoulder. Something about having him behind her gave her the definite sensation of being...*stalked*. Of course, that particular feeling made a lot of sense when she caught him staring at her butt the way a hungry lion stares at a wounded impala.

Okay, so maybe he *was* aware she was alive.

Gulp. She wasn't sure if that knowledge made her giddy as a school girl or simply scared the crap out of her. But from somewhere deep inside her, some place she never knew existed, a little horned—or maybe horny was the best way to describe her—demon sprung up and said, "You see something you like, cowboy?"

Rock's eyes shot to her face, one dark eyebrow rose nearly to his hairline. "I certainly do, *ma belle*," he grumbled. "But I've learned most things I like tend to get me in trouble."

"Trouble can be fun," she heard herself retort and almost choked.

Who was this woman saying these salacious things? Certainly not her.

It's official folks. I've been possessed by a demon. A motorcycle-riding, sexy-talking succubus apparently.

"*Oui*." He slowly licked his lips, catching the bottom one between his square teeth before adding, "Trouble *can* be fun. Are you lookin' for some fun, *chère*?"

Oh gosh, and whatever demon had momentarily

possessed her suddenly vanished without a trace, leaving her flustered and tongue-tied and completely incapable of thought. The best she could manage was an audible gulp followed by the tentative lifting of one shaking shoulder.

Rock's eyes darkened and a small smile played at his beautiful, beautiful mouth. "Well, when you figure it out, *ma cocette*, you know where to find me."

Chapter Three

"So, are you seeing anyone?" Jake whispered, closely watching Shell's face as the shadows of dusk settled over the courtyard.

She was quietly rocking her sleeping son and singing along to Rock's rendition of some old Kenny Rogers song. And though Jake reviled all things country with the same passion as a kid reviles peas, he had to admit, he'd listen to Willie, Waylon, and the boys until the cows came home if it meant he could continue to hear her soft voice gently linger in the evening air.

Man, he'd *missed* her. Especially when she slid him a withering look.

She was the nicest, warmest woman on the entire planet. To his knowledge, she'd never missed one of the SEALs' birthdays. She'd always been the first to send flowers to the hospital when they were injured. She'd schlepped through the crowds at the mall to buy extra civvies in order to save them from having to spend their blessedly few personal hours shopping. She'd memorized the names of siblings and parents and family pets and was the first to ask how Uncle Rupert's gallbladder surgery went, or if Grandma Ivy enjoyed her Alaskan cruise.

There'd always been a hot meal waiting at Shell's tiny, one-bedroom apartment for some hungry commando just back from a mission, or a pull-out sofa for some sloppy operator who'd had one too many to make it back to base under his own steam.

In short, she'd been home away from home. A safe harbor for the fighting men to return to after coming back from some of the hairiest missions of their lives.

But she could shrivel most men's berries with that particular look of hers.

Luckily, he wasn't most men.

"My love life is none of your business," she muttered, pursing her lips until he got a very clear mental image of how she'd look with her mouth wrapped around—

Damn. It was way past time he took the advice of the venerable Young MC and *checked his libido*.

"So that's a no," he said, smiling and feeling some of his tension dissolve.

His mission to win her over was going to be a whole hell of a lot easier to accomplish without another man involved. And he was glad for that one small miracle because convincing her he'd changed and that she should take a chance on him would be hard enough all on its own, especially considering the last conversation they'd ever had, the one outside the base's gates.

The memory stabbed into his brain like a hot knife…

It was raining. When she jumped from her car, yelling his name, she was instantly soaked. He felt such desire and rage in that instant. Because he still loved her despite the fact that she no longer loved him. And he knew exactly why she'd come…

"Jake, please!" she yelled, running up and grabbing his arm. "Can we talk?"

"I don't have time," he growled, shaking off her hand and ignoring her hurt expression. "This weather makes

*the brass absolutely giddy, and those sadistic bastards
are sending us out on a training exercise in fifteen. You
can call me tomorrow."*

*"And will you answer?" she asked, her eyes wide and
uncertain. "You haven't the last fifty times I've tried."*

*Yeah, well... "You know what they say, the fifty-first
time's a charm," he mocked.*

*"Jake, please, I—I need to tell you something," she
said, pushing her wet hair back from her face. Her mascara ran down her cheeks in twin rivers, and he assured
himself it was due to the rain and not tears even though
her eyes were red and swollen.*

*Because what the hell did she have to cry about? Her
life was turning out just perfect.*

*"I know what you're gonna say," he ground out. A
crack of thunder split the already charged atmosphere,
fraying his raw nerves.*

"You do?"

"Yeah." He nodded. "And I don't wanna hear it."

*"But I—I thought that—" She shook her head, her
wet hair sticking to her cheeks. "Did Steven tell you?"*

*He laughed, but it had nothing to do with humor.
"Preacher didn't have to say a damn thing. It's plain
as day."*

"It is?"

*"Of course it is." He scowled as he swiped the rain
from his face. "You're trading up. The enlisted man for
the officer. Hey," he shrugged when she opened her
mouth to try to defend herself, "it's no big deal. You
wanted to bag yourself an operator, and Preacher's
a much better bet than me. Not only is he in that
advanced pay grade, but he'll make an honest woman*

*of you. And you know all I ever wanted was a piece of
that grade-A ass."*

She gaped at him in disbelief.

*"Right on!" he told her, not trying to hide his con-
tempt. "You keep that sinfully luscious mouth of yours
wide like that, babe, and you'll have Preacher down on
one knee pledging his everlasting love within a week."*

"Y-you don't mean that!" she cried.

*"Don't I?" He twisted his lips into an ugly sneer, and
all the pain and rejection burning inside him came out in
a flurry of terrible words. "Don't you go thinking you're
any different from the scores of other girls I bagged at
the Clover. The only thing that sets you apart from them
is the fact that you never got me off."*

*She stumbled back like he'd hit her, grabbing her
throat. "I was right about you," she choked, her strangled voice barely discernible above the pounding clatter
of the rain. "You are heartless, and I don't ever want to
see you again…!"*

Yeah, he thought, glancing at her now, the guilt over
how he treated her that day still as fresh as it'd been four
years ago, *convincing her I've changed and that she should
take another chance on me is going to be* far *from easy.*

In fact, considering everything, it was a damned
miracle she deigned to speak to him at all.

But that was Shell for you. Sweet, forgiving Shell…

"You're more beautiful than ever," he told her.

"You've mentioned that already." She rolled her eyes.

He couldn't help but smile, because every time she
did that, every time she rolled her eyes at him, he had to
fight like crazy not to reach over and drag her out of that
lawn chair and onto his lap.

Shit.

And there went his mind again. It didn't help that he'd spent the last four years yearning for her until he actually physically hurt. And now that he was here? Sitting beside her? Dude, he considered it a wonder he wasn't foaming at the mouth like a rabid dog.

And in the spirit of not foaming at the mouth like a rabid dog, he searched for a way to keep the conversation going, because just sitting here looking at her, he could definitely feel the old salivary glands gearing up to work overtime.

He seized on the one thing he figured she'd be only too happy to discuss. "Your brother seems happy."

"Mmm," she agreed, not picking up his tossed conversational ball, the wonderfully obstinate woman.

He tried again. "Never thought there'd be a woman with the intestinal fortitude to handle Boss, but Becky must shit bricks."

"Crude," Shell mused, sliding him a disparaging look, "but accurate. You did always have such a way with words, Jake."

He winked, and she rolled her eyes again.

Rock finished with Kenny and started in on Fleetwood Mac—*at least it's not another country song*—and Jake took the opportunity to rake in a deep breath as he wondered how to broach this next subject.

"Shell," he finally whispered. She turned to him, her eyes particularly stormy-looking in the firelight. Stormy-looking and sad. He hoped to help with that second part starting right now. "I want you to know how—"

He was interrupted by a series of rings and beeps and tinny-sounding rock music that split the easy air in the

courtyard as each of the Knights' cell phones sprang
to life.

Boss dug his phone out of his hip pocket and held it
to his ear, barking only one word, "Go."

The rest of the Black Knights deactivated their
devices and waited for instructions. They weren't long
in coming, but Jake was surprised his name was the first
one Boss called. "Are you carrying, Snake?"

No sooner had the words left Boss's lips than the hard
punch of adrenaline surged through his system. "No.
That big redheaded behemoth at the front gate frisked
me before letting me in."

"Follow me," Boss said with a jerk of his chin.

"Roger that," he came just short of snapping a salute.
Yo, old habits die hard.

He pushed up from his chair and trailed Boss to one
of the little outbuildings surrounding the courtyard
where the big guy pulled out a strange-looking key from
the lanyard around his neck. Inserting it in a complicated
lock, the door sprang open with a hiss.

Okay, so…it was clearly an air-locked environment,
which for a small, private defense firm seemed a bit over
the top.

What the hell are they hiding in there?

Proof of extraterrestrial life? Documents exposing
the truth behind President Kennedy's assassination? A
living, breathing, peanut-butter-and-banana-sandwich-
eating Elvis Presley?

Boss motioned him forward, and he hesitated a
split second—just a split second, mind you, to prepare
himself to be greeted by a colony of little green men—
before peeking in the door.

Um, okay, so no fat Elvis or bug-eyed aliens, but he totally grasped the need for air-tight security. There were enough munitions stored in the building to give all of Bravo Platoon boners.

"Take your pick," Boss said casually, as if it were no big deal to be in possession of enough weapons to outfit an entire division.

"Should I be worried?" he asked, easily recognizing the hard look on Boss's face. He'd seen it often enough during their years together.

"Nah," Boss shook his head, then seemed to rethink his answer. "Look, man, we just caught an assassin trying to set explosives near the western wall—"

"*Assassin?*" Jake interrupted. "Good God, Boss, who'd you piss off this time?"

His former CO shrugged, shaking his head. "It's a long story, and I haven't got time to tell it. All you need to know right now is that there are an unknown number of guys gunning for us and though I'm confident of the security I have in place, I'd still feel better if you kept your eyes and ears open for the next few minutes while you look after Shell and Franklin for me."

"That's a given."

Boss clapped a heavy hand on his shoulder. "Thanks, man. And, believe me when I say it's not going to be an easy task, especially since I need you to convince Shell to stay out here while the rest of us go inside to try and find out what we can from this sonofabitch."

Jake glanced around the courtyard. "You sure it's safe out here?"

Boss nodded. "Right now it's the safest place on the compound."

Jake took Boss at his word, trusting him to know his own security.

"So, assassins, huh?" He shook his head and pointed a thumb overhead at the red-and-white-striped awning covering the courtyard. It hadn't been there last night when he'd arrived from the West Coast. "I guess that's why you guys unrolled the canopy."

"Yeah. A little insurance against prying eyes. That's also why I've been running around all day like a chicken with my head cut off and didn't get the chance to welcome you back properly, man. For that, I'm sorry. So, I'll say it now, I'm glad you're back."

"I'm glad to *be* back." And that was truer than Boss would likely ever know.

Boss nodded and began to turn away. Then he hesitated. "And Snake? Just because I don't *think* there's any cause for alarm, that doesn't mean—"

"Enough said," Jake raised a hand. "I'll be totally frosty."

Boss nodded and took a deep breath. Then his face fell into a series of harsh lines. "You love her, right?"

There was no need to ask who they were talking about.

"I've always loved her. I'll love her until I'm dead and buried."

"So what happened back in Coronado?"

And though he'd known the question was coming, it still caught him by surprise. Especially given the timing. But *okay*…whatever. It seemed they were going to get into this. *Now*.

And damn the assassins trying to blow a hole into the compound…

Boss had always been a multitasker. No reason to assume things had changed.

"I was so screwed up back then," he admitted. "You *know* some of the stuff I was dealing with, what I almost did during that patrol after the barracks bombing. And it all came down to the fact that I didn't feel like I could trust myself anymore. And that scared me shitless." He shook his head, running a hand through his hair. "I thought I'd push her away for a while. Give myself time to figure out just what the hell was going on with me. But I wound up pushing her right into Preacher's arms."

Boss searched his face for a long moment. "And Preacher didn't hesitate to accept that gift, I'm sure."

Yeah, not even for a split second...

"Preacher always was the smart one." He shrugged. "And afterward, I was so jealous I could barely stand myself. Part of that was because I knew Preacher was the better man. He and Shell were both so goddamned *nice*, it was like watching the real-life version of Ozzie and Harriet. It made me crazy."

"Sometimes it's opposites that make a relationship work," Boss mused.

"Yeah," Jake shook his head, "and what? Suddenly you're all Jedi Relationship Master now that you've got yourself a brand-spanking-new fiancée?"

Instead of taking offense, Boss wore the smug expression of a man secure in his woman. "And now? You've conquered your inner demon, and you're ready to do right by her?"

"I wouldn't say *conquered*, precisely," he admitted. "He's still there, still inside me, but he doesn't scare me anymore. And as for Shell, all I'll do is right by her... if she'll let me."

"It won't be easy."

"Nothing worth having ever is."

"Right answer, my man." Boss nodded his approval, and Jake felt for sure the next words out of the dude's mouth were going to be *and may the force be with you*. Instead, he motioned through the door to the munitions shed. "Help yourself to whatever you need."

Amazed at how easily that conversation had gone, Jake went to step into the building, but Boss stopped him again with, "Hey, Snake?"

"Yeah?"

"I'll do what I can to help you with Shell."

He swallowed and nodded his thanks, realizing how much he'd missed the big, mean bastard and how much it meant to be so easily accepted back into the fold.

There was a lightness to his step as he turned and pushed through the door to Arsenal Alley, and then all he was thinking was…*ahhh, yeah*.

Because, as he stood there looking around, he was like a kid in a candy store. A very *deadly* candy store. His eyes pinged from one set of stocked shelves to the next, gleefully noting that each held more impressive weapons than the one before. But his first priority was Shell and Franklin.

So he quickly strode to a nearby shelf and palmed a simple Glock 19. When he slid out the magazine, he found the clip fully loaded. *Nice*. Slamming it back into the grip, he shoved the weapon into the waistband at the back of his jeans, carefully concealing it with the tail of his loose shirt.

Next, he chose a Smith and Wesson five-inch, double-edged boot knife. Once he satisfied himself with its sharpness by checking the tip with his thumb, he slipped it into its custom sheath and clipped it to his front jeans pocket. Again, he was careful to hide it under his shirt. And though he wasn't wearing boots, that didn't mean he couldn't utilize an ankle holster…

Strolling over to the next set of shelves, he let his eyes roam over the array of polished weaponry and chose a Kel-Tec .380 Auto. Sometimes they had the tendency to jam if you soft-wristed them, but he never soft-wristed a pistol. And though its six-round capacity wasn't much, it was the only thing small enough to fit inside the calf of his jeans.

After securing it to his ankle, he grabbed an extra clip for both the Glock and the Kel-Tec and pocketed them before beating feet out of the building.

Securing the door behind him, he turned and glanced around the courtyard at the other outbuildings, wondering what surprises they held.

Goddamn, they really did it, he thought, taking a moment to feel pride in what Boss and Rock had built here in big, bad Chi-Town.

Then his eyes landed on Shell, and any warm fuzzies melted away like sunscreen on a hot day.

Damn.

Ice-cold fear shot through his veins, because even though he'd faced some of the most evil motherfuckers ever to be born and hadn't batted a lash, the thought of something happening to Shell, especially on his watch, was enough to have sweat slicking his palms and sliding coldly between his shoulder blades.

"So?" she asked once he retook his seat, carefully arranging himself so his position didn't impede his ability to quickly grab his weapons. In her chair, she unconsciously swayed side-to-side to soothe the sleeping boy, though the look on her face was anything but calm. "What's going on?"

"Your big brother has made some enemies," he admitted and watched her slim throat work over a hard swallow.

"Wh-what kind of enemies?"

For a moment, he thought of giving her the standard, *don't worry, doll, we got it all under control*. But he knew that wouldn't fly. So instead, he gave her the unvarnished truth. "The kind that want to kill him."

"What?" she squawked. Franklin stirred against her chest, making a disgruntled noise followed by a little snort before she managed to shush him back to sleep. She lowered her voice and asked, "*Who* wants to kill him?"

"Dunno." He shrugged, hoping to fool her with his feigned unconcern. Then he noticed her pulse hammering away at the base of her throat and realized he hadn't quite managed it.

Obviously, you need to brush up on your acting skills, Sommers.

Okay, so he'd try a different tack. "There's really no reason to worry, you know."

"No?" She raised a disbelieving brow.

"Nah," he scoffed, though the hairs on the back of his neck had twanged upright the minute all those cell phones started ringing, and they were still waving around like little danger-barometers even now. "We're secure as long as we stay inside these walls. They're thick enough to protect us from pretty much anything.

Not to mention the security cameras keeping watch around the entire perimeter."

"Yeah," she huffed, hugging Franklin to her chest and burying her nose in the boy's hair. "It's not the security I'm worried about. It's the *reason* for the security that's the problem. I shouldn't have come here. I shouldn't have brought Franklin—"

"Look at me, Shell," he commanded softly, his heart double-timing it when she turned those soulful, gray eyes on him. "I'll never let anything bad happen to you, you hear me? Never."

I'll die first.

And that was the *one* true thing he knew in this world…

Don't say things like that to me! she wanted to scream.

Mostly because they were precisely the kinds of words—sweet ones, not cruel—she'd longed to hear on that rainy day four years ago. And hearing them now only served as a bitter reminder that it was too late.

Too late for anything, for…*everything*.

To her utter chagrin, hot tears hovered behind her eyes, and she'd be damned if she'd let him see. Quickly turning away, she placed another comforting kiss on top of Franklin's head. "Please don't cry, Shell," he whispered and, *crap*, so much for trying to play it cool. "I know you're scared, but I *will* protect you."

He thought she was on the verge of tears because she was afraid?

Well, who wouldn't, you daft woman? There are people trying to get in here to kill your brother!

Okay, and truthfully, she *was* scared. Petrified, in

fact. But that wasn't the reason for her tears. The sweat slicking the back of her neck and dampening her hair? Yep, *that* was from the fear. But not the tears. Oh, no. They were all about him…

Of course, it was best to let him think what he wanted, play to his assumption. At least then she could use the excuse of her fear to keep the conversation on some sort of stable footing because, for the first time, they were alone.

Uh-huh, that had *not* escaped her attention. Especially since she suspected Jake had been waiting all evening for this very thing. It was obvious he had something he wanted to tell her. It was there in his pretty green eyes every time he looked at her.

And she didn't want to hear it. Because no matter what he said, it wouldn't change what had happened. The only thing his words could possibly accomplish was to make her feel more pain and regret, and Lord knew she'd already experienced enough of that to last a lifetime.

"I can't help but be afraid." She turned back to him when she was sure she had herself and her stupid tear ducts under control. "You don't know what it's like to be a mother, Jake. Fear, even under normal circumstances, comes with the territory. When you have a child to keep safe you—"

"I'll protect him, too." Jake vowed.

And there it was again. That look of utter sincerity. *How does he do that?*

"I know you will, Jake." He lifted a brow, and she managed a weak smile. "Even after everything that happened between us, I never doubted your courage."

"Yeah, about that…"

No, no, *no!*

"Can we just be quiet for a while?" She pleaded, this time not hiding the desperation in her eyes. "I just need some peace and quiet to calm my nerves."

His jaw clenched, and she could tell he was biting back his next words but, finally, he nodded. And in the stillness of the courtyard, the only thing she could hear was the pounding of her weak and foolish heart.

Rock stood with Vanessa and Boss at the second floor window of the shop, watching as Wild Bill—their resident explosives expert and Becky's older brother—and Angel—the spooky ex-Mossad agent who'd joined their ranks under mysterious circumstances—made their way through the compound's hand-rolled iron gates, frog-marching their captive across the open expanse.

And even as he observed their would-be assassin struggle in the Knights' grips, his mind drifted out to the courtyard.

I wonder how Snake is farin' now that he has Shell all to himself?

Not too good, he suspected.

One didn't need his particular skills for reading people, or his aptitude for picking up on subtle cues, to see that Shell's feelings toward Snake fell far short of friendly. It was clear as day for anyone with two eyes, because whenever she looked at the guy, she appeared ready to either break down sobbing or turn tail and run. He couldn't help but wonder exactly what had happened between—

"Is Eve on her way?" Boss asked Becky as she strolled up to the group, interrupting Rock's thoughts.

Oui, and there was *another* mystery. Because though it was obvious Eve Edens was a timid woman by nature, that didn't account for the look of stark horror that contorted her pretty face the moment she heard Wild Bill was going to show up. She hadn't been able to vamoose herself from the compound fast enough.

"Yep, she's headed home with her tail between her legs," Becky said, snaking an arm around Boss's waist before turning to watch the trio of men approaching from down below. When they walked beneath the yellow wash of a street lamp, she chuckled before adding wryly, "Well, holy flaming ninjas, Batman."

Rock grinned. The hit man, whoever he was, was dressed all in black. And he'd actually had the *couilles* to deck himself out in one of those tight, eye-slit hooded thingamabobs complete with a pair of weird double-toed, soft-soled boots.

"He looks more like Crouching Tiger, Hidden Dumbass," Vanessa mused.

A snort of laughter erupted from between Rock's lips before he could call it back.

Well, well, well. Aren't you just full of surprises tonight, Miss Cordero?

When she'd flirted with him earlier, he'd been so blindsided by the whole thing that, for a minute there, he'd gone dumb and mute as a bag of hammers. But he was proud to say he'd recovered in enough time to slide her some pretty good one-liners.

Unfortunately, despite their titillating little tête-à-tête, it was obvious she was barking up the wrong damn tree where he was concerned. Because, *merde*, there was more than just lust in her eyes when she looked at him. Lust he could've dealt with quicker than a knife fight in a phone booth. But the visions of white weddings and matching rings he could see dancing around inside her pretty head stopped him cold. Happily ever after wasn't an option for him...

"Hey," Bill yelled from the front door, dragging him away from his thoughts, "what do you guys want us to do with Shogun here?"

"Put him in the interrogation room!" Boss ordered before turning to Rock and asking, "You ready for this?"

"*Oui*, I'm ready." He nodded, taking a deep breath and turning toward the stairs.

As he made his way down to the first floor, he ground his back molars so hard it was a miracle he wasn't shooting little shards of enamel and the occasional filling from his ass. He stalked into the claustrophobic supply closet they'd retrofitted into an interrogation room upon first learning of Johnny Vitiglioni's paid assassins, tossed off his ball cap and tilted his head from side to side, cracking the vertebrae in his neck.

Zut. He hated this next part. Digging around inside a person's psyche always left him feeling dirty...

Chapter Four

GODDAMN, WHAT'S TAKING SO LONG?

Jake wasn't accustomed to being outside the action. In fact, he was accustomed to being smack-dab in the middle of it. So this hanging out in the backyard with his thumb up his ass sucked. Hard.

He felt like a sitting duck, like he'd cut his leg on a piece of coral and was chumming the water in great white shark territory.

Oh, he knew Boss would never have left them if he truly thought there was any immediate danger, and he'd been telling Shell the truth about the level of security around the place, but that didn't stop the hard burn of adrenaline from sizzling through his system, making his knees bounce until the beer in his hand threatened to shoot like a geyser.

With an effort, and so he wouldn't make Shell any more nervous than she already was, he resisted the urge to recheck the clip in the Glock. Then he managed, just barely, to corral his jumpy legs and lean back in his chair.

Unfortunately, none of the physical calm he forced on himself stopped the dark thoughts from endlessly spinning inside his head.

Who would want to kill Boss?

Would this dick-wad try to go after Shell and Franklin?

Did this dick-wad know *about Shell and Franklin?*

Okay, and back to the original question, which was, *Why the hell is it taking so long?*

He covertly glanced around the courtyard, deciding on entry points and escape routes, figuring out where he'd place himself to best protect them on the off chance an assassin came crawling over the wall.

Christ, just the thought...

Well, I can easily hustle them inside the safety of the shop, he assured himself. Then he frowned when he realized that would be the case if the perpetrator tried to come at them from any direction save the northwest corner.

Yeah, that northwest corner was a weakness. It effectively placed an intruder only three feet from Black Knights Inc.'s back door, cutting off their only secure avenue of escape.

So, the far southeast corner it is.

That's where he'd make his stand. From the southeast, he could hoist Shell and Franklin over the wall and into the Chicago River on the other side. They'd both be safe in the water while he dispatched the person or persons stupid enough to screw with those he loved.

And if he couldn't dispatch them? If the number was overwhelming? Well, then, he'd give Shell time to swim to safety with Franklin while he stayed and fought to his last breath and—

Whoa. He'd just unconsciously included little Franklin in with those he loved.

So that meant...what? He loved the kid?

It made sense—he certainly loved Shell, and Franklin was part of the package and, okay, now his pulse was *really* hopping. He'd never been tasked with protecting a child before...

When Shell started gnawing on her lower lip, he decided the silence she'd requested wasn't really doing anything to ease her tension. So, to try to take her mind off the situation, and *his* mind off the memory of what it was like to suck that full lip between his teeth—*come on*, even pinned down by mortar fire he'd still have wild fantasies about that bottom lip—he determined it was finally time to offer up the apology that'd been sitting on his tongue since…well…since forever.

The expression on Jake's face had Michelle's heart flipping over in her chest.

"Shell?"

And when he said her name like that, even after all these years and even though her nerves were stretched piano-wire tight, her stomach took flight. "What?"

"There's, uh, there's something I've been needing to say to you for a long time."

For the first time since her brother had disappeared inside the shop, Jake wasn't craning his neck around every which way. Instead, he kept his eyes glued to the label he was nervously peeling from his beer.

Nervous? Jake?

Flip. Uh-huh, and that would be her heart turning over. *Again*.

Stupid. Stupid. *Stupid*.

Don't fall for it, Shell. Just keep it together for a little while longer.

"Jake," she said, "whatever it is, let's just forget about it, okay? Let's just—"

"I'm so sorry," he blurted before she could finish.

Okay, so…they were doing this.

Taking a deep breath, doing her best to shore up all her emotional walls, she asked, "You're sorry? For what?" She had a whole list.

"For getting Preacher killed," he whispered.

Um, okay, so *that* wasn't what she expected. If he'd suddenly grown whiskers and claimed to be the Easter Bunny, she didn't think she'd be any more shocked. "Jake, that wasn't your fault. You did what you thought—"

"It *was* my fault," he insisted, running a hand over his face and shaking his head.

"No," she assured him. "That's ridiculous." She knew a little of what'd transpired on that wind-swept mountain. Her brother had given her the basics after Steven's funeral. And as much as she'd prayed for the day when she'd see Jake the Snake brought low, she never wanted it to happen this way, with guilt and blame tearing him apart. "It was a vote. Fair and square. Steven made his own decisions that day," she insisted, hoping her tone convinced him, because she was having a really tough time resisting the urge to reach across the small distance separating their lawn chairs to lay a hand of comfort on his muscular shoulder. She knew from experience, once she started touching Jake, it was almost impossible to stop. "Steven was a grown man who—"

He lifted his eyes to her face then. And they were so green, so tormented. "Did Boss ever tell you about the Marine barracks bombing?"

"Uh…no," she shook her head, surprised and disoriented by the lightning-fast change of topic. "He…he never said anything about it."

He nodded and went back to folding and refolding the beer label he'd finally managed to pull from the sweating bottle. Then he glanced up and made yet another visual pass around the courtyard. Yes, he may claim there was no cause for worry, but that didn't mean he wasn't still on high alert.

She supposed there was some comfort in that. Of course, the small relief she garnered from knowing he would hop-to at a moment's notice quickly dissolved when the silence between them stretched until it was a sharp, tangible thing.

When she couldn't stand it a second longer, she cleared her throat and quietly asked, "Were you guys... um, were you stationed there when it happened?"

She remembered watching the footage of the horrendous event on the news. The scenes of carnage and destruction had been enough to have even the most stalwart constitutions running for the nearest toilet. At the time, she'd been beside herself with worry, wondering if her brother and all the men she'd come to think of as family were lying somewhere in that smoldering rubble.

Then Frank had called, joking around like usual, never breathing a word about the bombing, and she'd assumed Bravo Platoon was stationed elsewhere in Afghanistan.

"Do you, um, do you mind if we turn our chairs around?" Jake suddenly blurted, catching her off-guard yet again.

What the heck? This conversation felt more like a verbal scavenger hunt, one where she was missing the clues.

"Uh, sure, I guess" she said, pushing up from her

Adirondack chair and watching in confusion as he hastily turned it, along with his own, away from the fire.

"I want my eyes to adjust to the dark, and I also want to keep watch on that corner," he explained with a jerk of his chin toward the corner in question.

O-*kay*. Her pulse, which hadn't been steady all night, tripped over itself.

"What's over there?" she breathed, trying to see something in all that pervasive blackness.

"Nothing that I can see, and that's the whole problem." Huh?

"Okay," he said, retaking his seat and grabbing his beer, "where was I?"

She wasn't sure anymore. Her head was spinning.

"Oh, you asked if we were stationed there when the barrack's bombing occurred, and the quick and simple answer is yes."

She dropped down into her seat as a wave of dizziness and nausea overcame her. The realization of how close she'd come to losing them all trumped every other thought.

So close. Too close…

"We were housed down the block from the marines. You see, SEALs and jarheads tend not to mix effectively when it comes to housing situations considering we're an unruly, rough-and-ready bunch by nature, and Marine's are a spit-and-shine, follow-the-rules group by training. You've sorta got yourself an oil and water situation there." He grinned then and, even scared out of her mind, sick over the thought of nearly losing her brother and all the boys of Bravo Platoon, she had to mentally scold herself to keep from falling prey to his particular brand of allure as she watched his dimples deepen.

And, yes, considering the danger of her situation and the dreadfulness of their current topic of conversation, she fully grasped how ludicrous that was.

Of course, Jake always had the ability to muddle her thoughts, charming cad that he was.

"But that's not to say we didn't eat in the same mess hall with those dudes or have some brews around the same campfires," he continued, his smile disappearing as his eyes grew shadowed, the memories obviously painful. "During that month, all us frogmen in Bravo Platoon got to know those leathernecks pretty good."

"I've heard it said soldiers in war make friends really quickly," she remarked quietly. "The shared experience and all that."

"Yeah." He nodded and turned away, his expression filled with anguish.

Her heart, the one she had to keep reminding herself to harden against him, proved true to character and softened around the edges.

He was quiet then, and only the gentle hiss and crackle of the fire at their backs broached the stillness of the courtyard. After she'd allowed him some time to gather his thoughts and herself and her idiotic bleeding heart some time to beat back the urge to reach out and touch him, she ventured, "So were you guys…were you on base that day?"

"Yeah." He nodded. "We were."

She knew what was coming next, and she steeled herself to hear it. As much as she'd love to plug her fingers in her ears and sing *ob-la-di, ob-la-da*, she squashed the urge to get up and pretend their conversation never happened. Instead, she pulled Franklin closer to her chest, taking comfort in his presence and his soft, little boy snores as she waited for the horror she sensed was about to fall from Jake's lips.

One thing she'd learned being the sister of soldier: when a fighting man wanted to talk, you let him. No questions. No interruptions. No matter what was going on around you.

And even after everything that'd happened between them, after all the terrible things he'd said and done, she couldn't force herself to turn away from him now, in his moment of need, though she sensed whatever he was about to say might ultimately cause her defenses to crack.

"We were still jocked-up, loaded down with sixty pounds of gear from the mission we'd just come back from when the blast hit us," he said, glancing over his shoulder to throw the mutilated beer label into the flames. It caught fire instantly and burned bright blue, casting strange, dancing shadows around the courtyard. The effect was particularly eerie given the atmosphere, and her breath hitched in her throat. "It sounded like the world was ending, and everyone on base, including us, immediately beat feet. But we weren't running away. Hell no. We were all soldiers, so we started running *toward* the explosion and the fireball billowing into the sky.

"It looked like hell had burst through the Earth's crust," he recounted quietly as he settled back into the Adirondack chair, adjusting himself slightly to accommodate the gun in his waistband—oh yeah, she knew her brother had loaded him for bear even though he'd been trying to act all inconspicuous about it.

And great. Now she was chilled to the bone and sweating through her bra all at the same time. *What in the world were you thinking coming here? Bringing Franklin?* It'd been one thing to pal around with covert operatives and the danger that surrounded them when it was only her. It was another thing entirely to do so now, when she had a child to consider.

She should've never doubted her brother's original decision to keep them far away from the BKI compound...

"I remember the heat," he continued softly. "It was like nothing I'd ever felt, and it was the first thing to hit us as we rounded the corner and got our first glimpse of what was left of the barracks. That and the smell. The smell was indescribable, like death raised to the power of a thousand."

Her nostrils flared in sympathy. Thankfully, the only scents captured by her quickly indrawn breath were that of smoking pine logs and warm boy.

"There was nothing but a crater where the barracks had been. A giant, burning, blackened hole that was at least fifteen feet deep. And all around us, we could see the remains of those two hundred hardcore Marines. There were arms and legs and torsos hanging in burning trees, combat boots and cammies blazing and smoking and raining down like ticker tape at a Macy's Day Parade."

He paused for a beat, raking in a slow, shaky breath, and she blinked back the tears she hadn't realized were hovering behind her eyes. Just when she was about to throw caution to the wind and reach out to comfort him, a small sound, a tiny crackle of movement, like a footfall in a bed of dry leaves, sounded in that corner he'd been so concerned about.

She stared into it as Jake silently drew a huge, black pistol from the waistband of his jeans. His demeanor went from simply alert to that of a jungle cat ready to pounce, and her heart hammered in her throat until it was impossible to breathe. But no matter how hard she struggled to adjust her eyes to the stygian darkness, the only thing she could see was...

Nothing. Not one stinking thing. Just inky blackness. Just like he'd said...

She waited, afraid to blink, afraid to move, even though she unconsciously covered Franklin's head with her hand. Straining her ears, she listened for a repeat of that tiny kernel of noise, that miniscule rustle of sound, but...

Silence.

Except for the chatter of the fire, except for the little snores emanating from between her son's sweet lips, not a whisper broached the stillness of the courtyard and then...there it was again!

"Get behind me!" Jake hissed as he bolted from his chair, automatically placing himself between her and Franklin and the threat.

Shell, wonderful woman that she was, didn't hesitate to scramble from her chair and grab the waistband at the back of his jeans with one hand while she held her still-sleeping son with the other.

"We're going to back up, *slowly*, into that southeast

corner," he whispered from the side of his mouth, steadily aiming his Glock into the darkened northwest corner of the courtyard.

That damned nook was like a black hole, absorbing all light.

Of course, Jake didn't need his eyes to tell him something was moving there. His ears caught it all. Each rustle sounded like soft-soled footsteps on hard, slate stones. His heart—usually so steady when coming face-to-face with armed militants or standing beneath a sky raining mortars—was threatening to beat right out of his chest. Because the thought of someone he couldn't see aiming a gun at Shell's head...dude, that scared the ever-lovin' shit out of him.

Scared him like he hadn't been scared in a long, long time...

And why did it have to be *that* particular spot?

Um, probably because whatever ass-hat was standing there, hidden in those deep shadows, had studied the layout of the place and knew about this one weakness.

At least that's what *he'd* have done and, sonofabitch!, *that* thought certainly didn't ease any of his tension.

"Come out," he commanded in a clear, ringing tone as he continued to inch backward, herding Shell and Franklin toward the only place that offered the possibility of escape.

When no one emerged from the blackness, he added, "I'm gonna start filling that corner with hot lead in about half a second if you don't show yourself!"

And just as his finger began to squeeze the trigger, just as his arm muscles tightened in readiness to both steady the weapon and absorb the kick, a form began to take shape at the exact spot where the north wall merged with factory building.

Slowly at first, and low to the ground, a dark shadow disengaged from the blackness of the corner and slipped inch by inch into the golden circle of light cast by the crackling fire.

"Holy *shit*," he hissed at the same time Shell blew out a shaky breath that ruffled the hair on the back of his neck and sent chills down his spine. Then she burst into the kind of laughter brought on by equal parts relief and hysteria.

He swung around to look at her, his stupid heart hammering like he'd been shacked in a closed-out wave. "It's not funny," he managed to growl as he shoved the gun back into his waistband, though, in all honesty, it kinda was.

"I know it's not," she chuckled, swaying from side-to-side with Franklin, who, somehow, despite everything that'd happened in the last two minutes, was still dead to the world. Jake figured the damn kid might've slept through a nuclear blast. "But can you imagine the look on Frank's face if he came out here to discover we'd mistaken his cat for a killer and filled the poor thing full of holes?"

He glanced down at the cat in question. The thing was butt ugly and, completely oblivious to the chaos it'd created and the closeness with which it'd come to losing one of its nine lives, was winding its rather rotund form around and between Shell's legs while simultaneously staring up at her with adoring yellow eyes.

He opened his mouth to tell her the stupid cat *and*

Boss would've deserved it when, inexplicably and seemingly from nowhere, an entirely different urge overcame him.

He grabbed her, sleeping boy and all, and pulled her to him, sealing their lips in one fell swoop.

———————

Vanessa fidgeted, glancing around at the hard faces of the Knights. They were gathered at the conference table on the second floor of the shop, waiting to see what information Rock could get out of the guy who'd been hired to kill them.

Guy who'd been hired to kill them…

Okay, and the whole situation suddenly felt all too real. No longer could she pretend the price on her head was nothing more than an amorphous threat, because the proof that someone was willing to pay good money to see her dead was sitting down in the interrogation room being questioned by Rock.

A sick feeling bubbled in the bottom of her stomach, and the bratwurst she had for dinner was suddenly threatening to give a return performance.

Just when she opened her mouth to break the strained silence, a sharp slap, like someone slamming their hand down on a table, echoed from below.

Wild Bill winced. "So he's moved on to step two."

"Huh?" she asked, swallowing the acid that inched up the back of her throat.

Someone's willing to pay good money to see me dead…

The thought kept spinning through her head until she thought she'd go completely insane and her baked potato decided to jump in line behind the bratwurst.

"The first step in any interrogation is to try to win over the suspect with friendliness," Angel, the ex-Mossad agent who'd come to work for BKI around the same time she had, said in his raspy voice. "When that doesn't work, you move on to threats of physical pain and the fear that evokes."

She turned to Boss. "Will Rock really beat the information out of him?"

"Hell, no," Boss grumbled, his fingers tightening around the steaming cup of coffee in his hands. "We don't stoop to the level of our enemies."

"Oh, for Pete's sake!" Becky threw her hands in the air. "Would everybody stop pulling the whole oogedy-boogedy say-nothing but mean-everything black-ops bullshit here and just tell the poor woman the truth. She's a Knight now, and she's gonna find out eventually anyway."

"What? What am I going to find out?" She nervously glanced around at the group.

Becky made no attempt to hide her exasperation at Boss before turning to enlighten her. "Rock is an expert interrogator. He can get anything out of anyone because he has this crazy ability to get inside of your head."

What the huh?

"Ozzie says Rock is like Spock," Becky went on and, oh great, a *Star Trek* analogy from Ozzie, the king of all things sci-fi. How appropriate. "He can totally rock that whole Vulcan mind meld thing." Vulcan mind meld. Uh-huh. She said that as if it were a real thing.

The sound of Rock's cowboy boots clomping up the metal risers stopped all conversation around the conference table cold.

"So?" Boss asked when Rock topped the last riser.

"So." He whipped a chair around backward, straddling the seat. When he draped his tattooed forearms
over the back, she noticed the hard muscles in his biceps,
exposed by the short sleeves of his Green Day T-shirt,
twitching fitfully.

He doesn't like doing it, she realized.

Whatever freaky skill he'd been taught, doing so got
him all jammed-up, and not in a good way. Of course,
she could totally understand how unsettling it must be
to go snooping around in someone's head looking for
weaknesses only to turn around and use those weaknesses against them.

"Shogun," Rock said as he shook his head and blew out
a tired breath, "whose real name is Larry Marrow, doesn't
have enough sense to pour piss out of a boot. The stupid
fils de pute thought if he said anythin' about Johnny and
the price on our heads, I'd kill him. No matter how often
I told him I wasn't gonna kill him, that I just wanted him
to answer my questions, he didn't believe me."

As soon as the name slid from Rock's lips, Becky
whipped out a laptop and started digging up everything
on Larry Marrow from his blood type to his favorite
baseball team. She'd been taught her computer skills by
the best. Namely, Ethan "Ozzie" Sykes, because as well
as being the king of all things sci-fi, he was also the
Knights resident computer whiz-kid.

"What else?" Boss asked, ignoring the chatter of
Becky's fingers on the keyboard.

Rock sighed and ran a hand over his goatee. She
noticed it tremor ever so slightly.

God, and now, like an idiot, she was even more

tempted to go all Disney on him. She obviously had a weakness for the whole wounded warrior thing.

"Accordin' to ol' Larry," Rock continued, "all communications between him and Vitiglioni were done through a series of private post office boxes, and Johnny supposedly used an alias. He hadn't the first clue where to find Johnny. Apparently," he grimaced, shaking his head, "and you're gonna love this, but apparently Larry answered one of those crazy cryptic ads in *Soldier of Fortune* magazine."

"You've got to be fucking kidding me," Boss growled. "So now every lowlife, wannabe hit man from here to Timbuktu is going to be gunning for us? Is that what you're saying?"

Rock nodded. "Larry *also* informed me there's a 50k price tag on each and every one of our heads."

Bill whistled, and Becky let loose a string of curses to do Boss proud.

Oh boy, Vanessa thought as she reached for the bottle of beer sitting in front of Becky. "May I?"

"Help yourself." Becky nodded distractedly.

She tipped her head back and gulped down the frothy brew, trying to wash away the bile that'd steadily gathered in the back of her throat for the last half hour.

So, to recap her life in the past few months…

First, she joins a clandestine defense firm. Then, she develops a rather tragic case of *do-me-big-boy* for one of her coworkers. And finally, she finds herself slam-bam in the middle of an unknown number of crosshairs.

Are we having fun now?

Um, hell no. The answer to that question was a resounding *hell no*.

Although, there was some comfort in knowing the other Knights were in those same crosshairs with her, because if anyone could come out of this situation unscathed, it was the hardcore warriors of BKI.

"Do you know how Larry was supposed to contact Johnny for payment once he made a kill?" Boss asked.

Rock reached into the pocket of his frayed Levi's and pulled out a piece of paper. "Supposedly, this address is a meeting place. If Larry had proof of a kill, he would hook-up with Johnny there at nineteen hundred on Friday to collect his reward. If he didn't show up Friday, then he was to meet Johnny on Tuesday at the same time. I guess after that Johnny figured we'd all be dead because Larry-Larry-Bo-Berry didn't have any more dates."

"Hand it over," Becky motioned with two fingers, and Rock passed her the yellow sticky note. "Hey, this is local," she exclaimed excitedly.

"*Oui*." Rock nodded.

"So that means Johnny's here in Chicago?" Becky lifted a brow.

"*Mais oui*. Or at least he will be this Friday and next Tuesday."

Vanessa's temples started pounding in rhythm to her heart at the news. She'd never had a price on her head before, and knowing the guy who'd made a mark of her was going to be so close? Well, it took was what an untenable situation and shot it straight into the atmosphere of planet Oh*Hell*No.

She was sensing a theme here…

"I think we should station guys at the drop point *now*," Bill said, running a hand through his thick brown hair, "so we can watch the comings and goings and maybe do some nosing around. See if anyone in the area has seen him. The sooner we catch him and put an end to this, the better."

"Agreed," Boss said. "But let's think about the logistics here. Everyone is pulling four-on/four-off rotations keeping eyes on the perimeter. And since Ghost decided *this* would be the perfect opportunity to take his new wifey on an ill-timed honeymoon, that only leaves—*Ow!* Why are you smacking me, woman?"

Becky's palm was still connected to the meaty part of Boss's big shoulder when she said, her voice tight with indignation, "First, Ghost took off with Ali because he figured it was the only way to keep her safe from Johnny's vengeance. You know that as well as I do. And second, it's a *honeymoon*. It's never ill-timed." She pointed a finger at his nose. "You remember that."

A muscle in Boss's jaw twitched, and just when Vanessa thought he might put Becky in her place, his scarred face split wide in a blinding grin. He grabbed Becky's hand and kissed the tip of her still-pointing finger.

"Message received." His voice was infused with a hot emotion that certainly wasn't anger.

The two exchanged a look so pointed Vanessa's own cheeks began to heat just as Bill piped up with, "God. I'm more than happy to be pulling surveillance duty in the condo across the river if it means I don't have to watch you two constantly making googly eyes at each other. I think I might puke."

It was true. There was a lot of sexual tension in the air tonight. What with Boss and Becky barely able to keep their hands off one another, and *her* inability to stop staring at Rock and drooling.

Oh yeah, and then there were Snake and Michelle...

The chemistry simmering between those two was enough to make a smart girl reach for a hazmat suit because, *wow*, an explosion of epic proportions was imminent.

"I think you'll survive," Boss grumbled, reluctantly dropping Becky's hand and turning back to the group. "But that brings me back to my point, which is that since Becky has to stay here and coordinate movements and communication between all parties, there's only me and Rock left to recon and surveil the drop point."

"Not to throw a fly in the ointment, Boss," Rock interjected. "But you're not exactly inconspicuous on a good day. With that bright blue cast, you stand out like a back pocket on a shirt."

"Shit!" Boss cursed, glaring at the offending cast like it was a demon sprung from hell.

"I'll go," Vanessa blurted before she could think better of it.

Brilliant, Van. Simply brilliant.

"Have you ever done surveillance before?" Boss asked, eyeing her curiously.

"Of course." What the hell was she doing? He'd given her the perfect out.

"Okay then," Boss slapped his big palm down on the table, the equivalent of a judge's gavel, effectively alerting everyone the decision had been made. "You and Rock go get eyes on the drop point and see if you can't locate Johnny."

Her heart started hammering against her ribs as Rock

sent her a considering look out from under the dense shadow created by his lashes.

Oh man, this is a mistake…

But she didn't have too much time to contemplate the ramifications because Boss continued, "You know what having Johnny out hiring any Joe-Shmoe with an empty wallet and full clip means, don't you?"

"*Oui*," Rock dipped his chin. "It means the only way to get these flies off our shit is to kill or otherwise vamoose dear Johnny."

"Exactly," Boss said, wincing and threading one big finger under his cast to scratch an itch. "We get rid of Johnny, and we take away the money. We take away the money, and we take away the threat."

"And once we do that, how will we disseminate the information so Johnny's *Soldier of Fortune*-reading goons call off the hunt?" Angel asked.

Vanessa looked over to see Bill grinning broadly. "Hey, Becky?" he sing-songed, his tone teasing. Becky gave him a wary glance. "How do you feel about another press conference? The media has loved you ever since you were a pirate's hostage."

"Ugh," Becky groaned. "I thought I was finished with reporters after that whole debacle."

One thing Vanessa could say about working for BKI: it was never boring. Case in point: Becky Reichert had been captured by pirates. Yes, that's right. Pirates. As in *arg*.

If she wasn't mistaken, there was even an eye-patch involved…

"All right, then," Boss pushed away from the conference table and turned to Becky. The look of mortal dread on her face caused him to shake his head and pat her shoulder conciliatorily. "You'll be great, just like you were before. For now, I'll call our friends at the CPD so we can turn Mr. Marrow over into their loving hands. And Bill, you and Angel get back in position. We need to be ready for the next strike."

The next strike…

Like it was a foregone conclusion there'd be one.

Oh, God.

Chapter Five

JAKE'S BROAD PALMS WERE WARM AGAINST MICHELLE'S upper arms, his thighs hard against her own as he curled himself around her and her softly snoring son, kissing her with all the skill and dedication she remembered from four years ago.

Sweet Lord! Help me!

Because right now she was incapable of helping herself.

He tasted the same and smelled the same and, worse, *felt* the same. All corded muscle and smooth skin, prickly whiskers making her lips tingle.

In a word: male.

All the things a man should be.

Making her feel all the things a woman should feel when she was held in strong arms. Cherished, desired, protected…

Oh, how she wanted to go on letting him kiss her to within an inch of her life, kiss her until all thoughts of consequences flew right out of her head. But she'd been on this ride with him before, had witnessed her own father play on this same terrible roller coaster of physical thrill-seeking, and she knew, like always, her heart would be the one to pay the piper in the end.

No matter how much it might feel otherwise right now, she knew the excitement and pleasure of the moment wasn't worth the pain of the crash.

The effort it took to step from his embrace was excruciating, but she managed it. Though it felt like she was leaving her heart behind. And then he went and made everything so much worse when he blurted, "I love you, Shell."

"Wh-what?" she sputtered.

"I love you," he said again. Just like that. So easy. So carefree with those words.

When he took a step toward her, she mirrored his movement, retreating, nearly tripping over the dang cat that was rubbing itself against her calves. He reached out to steady her, and she jerked aside. His fingers were a brand, burning her on the outside as his words scorched through her insides.

"I loved you then, I love you now, and I've loved you all the days in between," he went on, even as his expression fell when she scrambled to avoid his touch.

He tucked his hands into the front pockets of his tattered jeans, and she closed her eyes as her heart, the one she'd sworn she'd hardened against him, shattered anew, along the same fault lines he'd made so long ago...

It wasn't true. He might think it was because they'd never gotten the chance to finish what they'd started and he'd confused unrequited lust with love, but it *wasn't* true. He didn't love her. Men like him didn't know the meaning of the word, yet they were oh so quick to whip it out when it suited them.

Hugging her son to her chest, she fought the urge to burst into tears, just dissolve into a puddle. This was why she hadn't wanted to see him, why the mysterious "they" were obvious imbeciles. This moment right now. Because she wasn't strong enough to resist him. She never had been.

But you have to be, Michelle. For Franklin's sake…

"No, Jake," she whispered, squeezing her eyes shut as she tried to breathe past the iron vice of anguish crushing her chest, "you don't—"

"Tell me there's a chance," he begged. She opened her eyes to search his face, her throat burning like the glowing embers of the fire at his back. "Tell me you still feel something for me."

She swallowed and managed to choke, "You had your chance. You had *many* chances, but you blew them all. Now, it's too late." *Too, too late…*

"No," he shook his head. "I refuse to believe it."

"It's true." She beat back the ocean of tears gathering in her eyes and firmed her resolve, though everything inside her screamed at her to go into his arms, to believe him even though she'd heard all these same lies before. And then she told a lie of her own, "I don't love you anymore."

When he got very still, she figured she'd better deliver the coup de grace before she lost her nerve. "I'm not sure I ever loved you," she whispered hoarsely.

Did he…? Were those tears in his eyes?

Dear God, they were. And just when she thought those tears might actually fall—and heaven help her if they did; she'd never survive it—everything hardened in his face.

The wetness in his eyes vanished so quickly it startled her, forcing her to retreat another step.

"I can change your mind," he declared, lowering his chin so that he was glaring at her from under his furrowed brow.

And *that* was the arrogant man she knew so well, the mercenary man she knew so well. It gave her the courage to shake her head. "No. You won't get the chance to—"

Her brother picked that moment to burst through the shop's back door.

Jake spun, his hand automatically going to the weapon he'd returned to the small of his back, reminding her that, despite the ridiculousness of the debacle with Peanut, they'd been having this entire conversation, engaging in this foolhardy behavior, in the middle of a situation that was downright dangerous.

Her big brother had someone trying to kill him, and she and Jake were standing there kissing? Arguing about their feelings?

They should both have their heads examined.

"Snake," her brother said, "I need you to go to Shell's place and pack a couple of bags for her and Franklin. They're staying here for the next few days."

"*What?*" she yelped, Jake's heart-wrenching words momentarily forgotten as she gaped at her brother. Her outburst caused Franklin to grumble sleepily and root around for his thumb. After shoving the chubby digit between his lips, he once more quieted. Only then did she hiss, "You're insane. We're not staying here!"

In response, Frank leveled her a glare so severe everything inside her shriveled to the size of a pea.

"Yes," he insisted, "you are."

~~~

If Boss hadn't been so butt-ugly and likely to punch him smack in the face for the effort, Jake would've run over and kissed the guy.

He'd been losing the battle with Shell and had been clueless as to what to do to turn the tide in his favor. Enter Boss...

"B-but you can't be serious!" Shell sputtered, absently patting Franklin's bottom when he grunted quietly.

"Oh, I'm serious as a heart attack." Boss ran a big square hand through his hair and settled into a lounge chair. "See, we've got ourselves a little situation here, and I'm afraid it might spill over onto you and Franklin. It's not likely, but I wanna make sure to cover all my bases."

"Little situation? Is that what you call having some-one paint a giant bull's eye on your back?" When Boss glanced over at Jake, she added, "Oh, yeah. He told me someone wants you dead."

Boss lifted a shoulder, and Shell's face filled with incredulity.

"Okay, so when did you know about this *little situation*?" she demanded.

"Yesterday evening was the first time we got credible evidence of the threat. I thought perhaps that might be the end of it, but apparently not. And then tonight the seriousness of the situation became clear."

"*Yesterday* evening?" Jake watched her eyes narrow. He was glad he wasn't the one on the other end of that death-ray stare—for once. "And when did you think you were going to tell *me* about all this?"

"I just did."

"Yes," she grumbled. "Which leads to the next important question, which is why in the world would you bring me and Franklin here when you know you've got guys gunning for you? Why would you bring us to the center of all the trouble?"

"Believe me, you're safer here at the compound than any place else."

"What the heck is going on, Frank?"

"Some guy out of Las Vegas named Johnny Vitiglioni has hired a bunch of backwoods goons to take us out," Boss explained, and Jake resisted the urge to reach out and grab Shell's hand when she gasped quietly. If the last few minutes were any indication, she wouldn't welcome his touch—and he was going to try very hard not to let that hurt him.

Of course, even if it did hurt him—okay, so let's be honest here; it most certainly did—he was determined to take it.

He deserved it, after all…

But if there was one thing he knew about Shell, it was that she couldn't hold a grudge for long. She was too softhearted, the wonderful woman. She'd eventually forgive him for his past mistakes, no matter how egregious they were. That's what he loved best about her, her big, wide-open heart. All he had to do was stick with it, stick with *her* and—

"There's fifty grand on each and every one of our heads," Boss finished.

Oh, hell. His mind was wrenched away from his relationship, or non-relationship as the case may be, with Shell. *So, whoever wants them all adiosed means business.*

Because fifty thousand dollars was a lot of money, even for a professional hit, and when you multiplied that by the number of Black Knights, it became a small fortune.

He listened intently as Boss recounted a story of a

corrupt senator, illegal weapons deals, missing files, and a cross-country chase that ended in two hired thugs being sent to their maker by one of the Black Knights.

"It seems Vitiglioni has sworn a vendetta against us." Boss shrugged like having a price on his head was nothing more than a minor inconvenience, a pesky gnat buzzing around his picnic lunch. "And until we can get rid of him and cut off the money he's willing to supply for our deaths, we have to be extremely vigilant. Hence the need for the guys we've got on the rooftops surrounding the compound and the whole Barnum and Bailey theme going on back here." He pointed to the overhead canopy.

"What's to stop this Vitiglioni character from using an RPG or hand-held missile to try to take out the entire compound in one fell swoop?" Jake asked, his mind spinning with logistics.

"Nothing," Boss admitted. "Except the fact that he's a small-time crook, and it'd be extremely difficult for him to get his hands on anything like that. And given the guys he's hired to do his dirty work answered an ad in *Soldier of Fortune* magazine, I'd bet the farm they don't have anything more than handguns, rifles and maybe a little C4. And just so you know, it'd take a lot more than an RPG to take down the shop." He smiled and winked proudly. "The walls on the factory building are three feet thick and reinforced with the same alloy steel they use on aircraft landing gear. It'd take a two-ton bomb to level Black Knights Inc."

"That's very reassuring, Frank," Shell cut in. "Truly it is. But I really don't understand what any of this has to do with me. I don't understand why *I'd* need to stay here."

"Because when Vitiglioni realizes he can't get to us, he might start going after targets he *can* get to."

Jake nearly tossed his dinner at the mere thought…

"S-so you're telling me you intend to bring in everybody's families?" Shell demanded, her expression filled with disbelief. "Mac's and Ozzie's and—"

"Come on, Shell," Boss cut in. "Everybody else's families don't live here in Chicago, where the hit men just happen to be hanging out. Your situation is different, and you know it. I might've been less worried a week ago. But after that stunt you pulled in the hospital, I have to make sure I take the proper precautions."

Rock had filled Jake in on the situation with Shell and Boss. The fact that Boss had kept her hidden from the employees of BKI and the fact that Shell had recently blown right through that rule.

A little part of him thought, *Go, Shell*. Because he couldn't imagine how difficult it must have been for her to remain separate from that part of her brother's life when she'd grown so accustomed to sharing it. Of course, after everything that'd happened back in California, he could certainly understand why Boss had chosen to do what he'd done, and knowing she'd inadvertently entered the crosshairs by appearing with BKI personnel had him wishing she'd stayed hidden away—permanently.

"You planned this all along, didn't you?" Her eyes flashed, and Jake was pretty sure that had Boss been the least bit flammable, the dude would've burst into a giant fireball then and there.

"What? Planned to have some jack-off Las Vegas mobster put a price on our heads?"

"No. You planned to back me into this corner even before you came to my house this evening. That's why you were trying to convince me to pack a bag so Franklin and I could spend the night."

Boss shrugged. "Yeah? So what? If you'd cooperated, you've have what you need now instead of me having to send Snake after it."

"You deliberately manipulated me!"

"Nope. I just chose not to fight about it at the time. I know how overprotective you are and how you get when something threatens Franklin's schedule."

"You *know* why I'm such a stickler about that," she snarled.

"Just because we had a deadbeat father who dicked up our childhood doesn't mean you have to micromanage every waking minute of Franklin's."

"We. Are. Not. Staying. Here." She enunciated slowly, meticulously.

"Fine," Boss said, and Jake's heart hammered at his easy capitulation. Damnit! He needed Boss's help in this, and if the big guy was going to give up so—

"If you don't want to stay here," Boss continued. "You can take Snake home with you to act as your bullet-catcher."

Oh, you giant, ugly, wonderful sonofabitch!

"No way." Shell was already shaking her head before he finished the sentence. "Send another of the Black Knights home with me but—"

"As it happens," Boss interrupted her, "we're already stretched thin. He's the only man available for the job."

The knife that'd cut straight into Jake's heart when Shell said she didn't love him, the one that'd twisted when she claimed she may never have loved him, stopped turning and began to retreat. Because he hadn't been kidding when he told her he could change her mind. Given the right set of circumstances and enough time, he *knew* he could win her over.

And it seemed Boss was determined to silver-platter the right set of circumstances for him. If the look of horror on Shell's face was anything to go by, she knew it as well.

A small smile tugged at his mouth.

"B-but I d-don't want him to—"

Boss talked right over whatever objection she began to make. "I also think you should tell Miss Lisa to take the rest of the week off. You don't want to have to explain to her why Snake is glued to your side. It'll cause too many questions. Just tell her a friend has come into town who's willing to look after Franklin and that she should use this time to take a much deserved paid vacation. In fact," Boss whipped out his cell phone and handed it to her, "why don't you give her a call right now?"

Jake knew by the obstinate expression Shell wore that she was very tempted to throw that cell phone straight back into Boss's face. Instead, she took a deep breath and grumbled, "There has to be another way."

"Nope." Boss shook his head. "It's either take Snake home with you, or you and Franklin stay here where *I* can keep you safe."

"But I have clients and meetings," she ground out, careful to keep her voice pitched low so as not to wake the sleeping boy. "I can't just hang around here for however long this will take and—"

"Which is why it's best all the way around if you let

Snake act as your bodyguard for the next few days. He'll watch your back and take care of Franklin, and you can go about your business as usual. You okay with that, Snake?" Boss turned to him, and if Shell hadn't been watching, he felt sure the big guy would've winked.

"It's fine by me," he said, still fighting the urge to run over there and plant a big sloppy one on his former CO's face.

"Good," Boss slapped his knee and stood. "Now, there are a few specifics Snake and I need to discuss. Shell, while we're doing that, why don't you make that call to Miss Lisa, then get your stuff and meet us by the Hummer."

"Snake," Boss turned to him, "you should probably perform a few escape and evasion techniques on the way to her house just to be safe. Oh," he snapped his fingers, "and on that note, you'll be taking the river tunnel out of here."

River tunnel? They had a river tunnel?

Too cool.

Once more he felt a jolt of pride at what Boss and Rock had built for themselves here in Chicago. And once more that jolt of pride was quickly followed by a trickle of regret that he hadn't been here to build it all with them…

"We'll have one of the guys ride your bike over tomorrow morning and exchange it for the Hummer." Boss continued.

"Sounds good." Sounded better than good. Sounded *great*, because it meant he'd get to have Shell all to himself.

"Excellent." Boss nodded, then frowned. "Wait a second. I didn't ask if you're okay to drive. How much beer have you had?"

*Not enough to keep me from wanting to toss your
sister over my shoulder, cart her upstairs to one of
those bedrooms, and make love to her until the sun
comes up.*

Of course, there wasn't enough booze on the planet
to keep him from wanting to do that…

"Only two over the last three hours. I'm good to go."

"But I don't *want* him to—" Shell tried again.

"You know what your options are." Boss glared
down at her, one hand raised in mid-salute by that bright
blue cast and the other firmly planted on his hip. Though
the stance was highly ridiculous, Boss still managed to
make it look menacing. "Which is it going to be?"

Shell turned to Jake then, glaring like this was all his
fault. In response, he flashed his dimples and a wink.

"Ugh," she carefully plopped down in a lawn chair,
angrily punching in some numbers on Boss's cell phone
with one hand while she cradled Franklin's back with the
other. "I knew it was a mistake to come here tonight,"
she muttered as Boss once more pointed Jake toward the
munitions building.

After they'd gone some distance, he ventured, "Just
what are the chances this Johnny character will come
after Shell and Franklin?"

"Very remote," Boss assured him, using the key to
open the thick metal door to the armory. "Johnny wants
us dead. We're the ones who killed his cousin and
brother-in-law. But I'd already decided to bring her here
or send one of the boys back home with her even before
you showed up, so I'm glad you arrived when you did.
And now, you've got the chance to convince her you're
not our father."

"Yeah, uh," Jake scratched his ear. "I gather there's a story there, you know, given you called the guy a deadbeat."

His former CO sighed, sliding a surreptitious glance over at Shell who was nodding and speaking quietly into the phone although the expression on her face was anything but conciliatory. "I never spoke much about dear ol' Dad, did I?"

"Much? Try never. I always assumed the dude was dead."

Boss motioned him through the door to the armory and, as Jake stepped inside, he breathed in the metallic scent of the weapons, the slightly tangy aroma of gun oil, and the more acrid smell of cordite. Why he found that combination particularly appealing spoke loudly of the life he'd chosen to live.

"I don't know if our father is dead or not," Boss admitted. "I haven't seen or spoken to the man in almost twenty-eight years."

Jake raised a brow.

"My dad had a thing for younger women and used to pretty blatantly cheat on our mom. When I was twelve and Shell was six, he finally quit trying to play the father and husband and split. Our mother fell apart after that and Shell…well, I guess Dad's leaving probably affected her the most. It made her wary, mistrusting…"

Jake's heart broke for the scared, hurt little girl Shell had once been, and he realized how much courage it must've taken for her to swallow her fear four years ago and give him, a self-described ladies' man, a chance. The same chance he'd immediately proceeded to screw over and toss out the window.

Jesus, you're an ass, Sommers…

"I guess that's why I was so surprised back in California when it looked like you two were starting to hit it off," Boss mused. "Considering your similarities to our father."

"I would never screw around on my wife," he insisted, pissed beyond measure to find himself lumped into a group of cheaters.

"Hell, I know that," Boss scoffed. "But Shell doesn't, and she didn't back then either. I suppose that's why she was so quick to settle on Preacher after things with you two hit the skids."

She'd settled on Preacher because he'd literally thrown her at the guy, and Shell was smart enough to recognize an honorable man when she saw one.

"Why are you telling me this?" he asked, narrowing his eyes as he tried to read Boss's mind.

"Because, like I said earlier, this isn't going to be easy. And I figure you'll stand a better chance if you realize exactly what you're up against."

Yo, as if all the shit that went down between me and Shell wasn't bad enough...

"But she's worth it." Boss watched his face intently.

"Damn, dude, I know that," he huffed. "I just wish I could find your father and gut him like a fish for making my job that much more difficult."

"Ha!" Boss clapped him on the shoulder and spun him toward the shelves lined with every weapon an operator could ever desire. "You'll have to get in line for that. Now, even though I don't think Vitiglioni or his goons are really going to go after Shell, I figure we're better off safe than sorry. Pick out whatever you need."

He started toward the shelves then hesitated, turning

back. "Why are you willing to help me with her?" he asked, gauging the big man's reaction with a practiced eye.

"Because she's a good woman, and she needs a good man. I always thought you were a good man, Snake."

As warmth unfurled in his chest—because, yo, for more than a few years he'd doubted that very thing—he feigned wiping away a tear as he kicked an imaginary rock, "Aw, shucks, Boss. You'll make me blush."

"A pain in the ass," Boss added, "but a good man. Of course, that doesn't mean I won't sneak into your room while you sleep and slit your throat should you hurt her."

Chapter Six

LISTENING TO THE COUPLE GOING AT IT NEXT DOOR, Johnny contemplated shoving his hand down his pants to join in the festivities—sad, but self-service was the only kind of service he'd been getting since he'd gone into hiding—when his prepaid cellular phone buzzed on the nightstand. Startled, he nearly tumbled off the lumpy piece of cardboard that passed as a mattress in this filthy hotel.

"Damnit, what now?" he growled, refusing to answer the vibrating phone. The only person who had access to this number was his sister, and she was only supposed to call him in case of emergency.

Emergency? *Yeah, right.*

So far today, Mary had had three "emergencies."

The first crisis involved her calling to ask for the keys to his Lamborghini. Because she wasn't going to be seen driving to Tahoe in her lowly Mercedes Benz— *the spoiled bitch.*

Next, she'd wanted to know if he could deposit 20K in her checking account. It didn't matter to her that ever since the debacle with the senator, the one that'd gotten both her husband and their cousin killed and caused the FBI to start nosing around his holdings, he'd been forced to transfer all his funds to an overseas account, go underground, and stop making purchases in order to stay under the government's radar. No, none of that mattered to her, because she had her twisted, frigid little heart set on this canary-yellow diamond at Tiffany's, and she was accustomed to getting exactly what she wanted and damn the consequences to anybody else.

Which brought him full-circle to emergency *numero tres*, which, like the other two, hadn't really been an emergency at all. She'd simply called because she was bored and wanted to know if any of the Black Knights or their family members were dead, yet.

Um, *no*. If they were, he'd have called. Just. Like. He. Told. Her. A. Million. Times.

The insistent buzzing of his phone had him cursing and throwing one of the stale-smelling pillows across the room—imagining it was his sister's frail body— before he pushed into a sitting position and pressed the "talk" button with enough force to bend the nail on his finger.

"What the hell do you want now, Mary?" he barked, trying to drown out the sound of the couple in the next room.

"Where are you?" she screeched. He held the phone away from his head and briefly considered flinging it across the room to join the smelly pillow.

"First of all, what phone are you using?" He couldn't take any chances with the Feds on his tail.

She sighed heavily. "The prepaid one. Gimme some credit."

Uh-huh. Credit. Right.

"And where are you calling from?"

"From inside the safe room like you taught me. *Come on*, Johnny. No one's eavesdropping, so cut the crap and tell me where you are."

"I'm at the hotel," he said, grinding his teeth.

"Why aren't you doing something for Chrissakes? Isn't that what you're there for?"

He lifted a hand to his brow and prayed for patience. "I told you I've hired an investigator to dig up dirt on the Knights and their relatives. That takes time, Mary."

"Yeah, and in the meantime, what are *you* doing to avenge the brutal murder of my dear, sweet husband?" she demanded.

Oh, give me a friggin' break.

For one thing, *sweet* was not a word that had applied to Mary's husband in any way, shape, or form. And for another, it was true the guy was murdered, but Johnny could think of a lot more brutal ways to go than a single shot straight to the ol' gray matter that instantly put your lights out.

"If you must know, I followed the Knights to a local hospital yesterday, and while I was there I found out—"

"Well, why didn't you just kill them all while you had the chance?" she interrupted, her voice petulant.

Jesus, Mary, and Joseph, she was clueless. What? Did she expect him to pull his pistol in the middle of the hospital, where there were hundreds of cameras ready to catch his every move and a whole gang of security guards geared up to take him down the minute he opened fire?

Stupid gash. That was just one of the *many* nasty names hovering on the tip of his tongue, but he bit it back along with all the rest. "Killing the Knights doesn't make sense. Killing their *families* does. It's poetic justice. An eye for an eye."

And he couldn't wait to see the looks on their faces when their relatives starting dropping like flies. They deserved all the hell he was about to rain down on them for offing his brother-in-law and cousin. Of course, if he was really honest, he had to admit the great majority of his thirst for vengeance came from the financial hit he'd taken and the business losses he'd suffered when he'd been forced to go off the grid.

He'd succeeded in remaining under the government's radar for fifteen long years, and it severely pissed him off that it was a bunch of leather-wearing bikers who'd managed to burn him.

"Well, if you aren't going to kill them, then why did you take out that ad in *Soldier of Fortune*?" Mary asked.

Her tone infuriated him, and he screwed his eyes closed, rubbing at his aching temples. Just how dense could one woman be? "Because those bumbling, white-trash wankers who answered my ad will hopefully keep the Knights distracted long enough for me to exact revenge on their families."

"And if they actually manage to *kill* one of the Black Knights?"

"Well, that's a bonus, now isn't it? But I seriously doubt any of them will even get close. Last night, I waited at the bar across the street for over an hour for one of those hit-man wannabes to come claim their reward money. Not a single one showed."

Of course, he wasn't going to complain about that. He didn't really relish the thought of handing over fifty Gs even if the cash was going to a good cause.

"So, what did you find out at the hospital last night?" she asked.

"That one of the Knights has a sister and a nephew who live here in Chicago. I tried using the whole flower delivery trick on her this evening, but she's warier than most broads. She wouldn't open the door. It doesn't matter, though. I'm going back tonight, and I *will* kill both her and her son."

"Oh, good," Mary gushed. "Well, keep me informed then."

She clicked off without saying good-bye, but Johnny didn't give a rat's ass how rude his sister was, because the couple next door was ramping it up for the big finish, and despite the crudeness of the show, or maybe because of it, his cock began to throb with interest.

Tonight, he'd visit Michelle Knight, and before ending her life, he planned to put a period on his sexual slump.

A niggle of anticipation trilled up the length of his spine.

―⁂―

If someone had told Michelle when she woke up this morning that she'd be driving through the Black Knights' secret underground tunnel about to take Jake home with her, she'd have said, *Yeah, when hell freezes over*.

Well, the devil and his demons must be sledding and making snow angels, because that's exactly what she was doing.

This can't be happening.

That thought kept circling around in her head, but

all she had to do to convince herself that she wasn't dreaming—or having a nightmare—was look over at Jake's hard profile cast into shadow by the dimly glowing lights on the Hummer's dashboard. If she wasn't mistaken, there was a tiny smirk tilting up one corner of his mouth.

This was exactly what he wanted, no doubt about it.

"I can change your mind." He'd said it with such absolute certainly that just thinking of it now caused a cold shiver to race down her spine. Because there was small part of her, a very small part—okay, maybe not so small—that feared he might be right.

Of course, when he pulled the Hummer out of the dark, dank tunnel and into the parking garage on the opposite side of the river from the Black Knights' compound and she watched in the rearview mirror as the concrete wall silently slid back into place behind them, completely camouflaging their route, she was reminded that Jake was the very *least* of her worries right now.

There were much bigger fish to fry. Fish that came in the form of hired gunmen.

Sweet Jesus. She rubbed her sweaty palms on her jeans and tried to rake in a calming breath. It didn't work. Especially when she realized Jake was obviously thinking about those same fish, because he exited the parking garage like his tires were on fire, careening around the corner and onto the street.

"Sorry," he muttered, glancing into the back of the Hummer where Franklin was strapped into his car seat, still sleeping the sleep of the dead—or the sleep of tired three-year-old boys. "I've got to make sure we don't have a tail."

"Don't worry," she assured him, grabbing the handle above the door, the one Frank always referred to as the *oh shit bar*, when Jake took the next corner like he was manning the wheel of a sports car instead of a big, cumbersome Hummer. She closed her eyes and winced when they missed the back bumper on a parked Mercedes by no more than a hair. "He's like his Uncle Frank in that he can sleep through anything."

"Yeah," Jake said, checking the mirrors, "I've noticed that."

When they'd gone a few blocks, made a few more erratic turns, he blew out a breath and settled more comfortably into the driver's seat.

"We're good?" she asked him.

"We're good." He nodded.

"Oh, good." *Okay*, she rolled her eyes, *and just crown me Queen Lame-Ass. Geez.*

He grinned over at her, his dimples dark shadows in his stubbled cheeks as he reached over and clicked on the radio.

The sound of KT Tunstall's smooth voice drifted softly through the vehicle.

She quickly glanced out the window and for the thousandth time that night found herself on the verge of tears.

It would have to be this song, wouldn't it?

Jake looked over at Shell, wondering if she was thinking the same thing he was thinking.

"Remember this song?" he asked. "It was playing that night me and all the boys of Bravo Platoon built that mammoth bonfire on the beach in Coronado to celebrate our last day of freedom before being required to embrace the suck and head back to Afghanistan. I finally got up the balls to tell you how I really felt that night, soldiered up enough to finally kiss you. Do you remember?"

Her whole body froze. Yeah, she remembered…

He took a chance. "The guys were playing football, we strolled down the beach and you…you told me you'd wait for me."

"And I did," she whispered, her voice strangled.

"Yes, you did. I came home four months later to find you the same wonderful, wholesome, beautiful Shell. But I came back different, didn't I?" He'd been hurt and angry and, worst of all, broken. He'd taken that hurt and anger out on her. He'd said and done things that couldn't be taken back, but they could certainly be explained and apologized for.

He opened his mouth to start in on all those apologies and explanations when Franklin piped up from the backseat. "Mama, I needa go potty."

"Can you wait a little bit until we get home, sweetpea?" Shell asked, twisting around in the front seat, and Jake noticed, even in the darkness of the vehicle, the wetness in her eyes.

As much as he hated to see Shell sad, those tears gave him cause for hope. Because they meant that, despite everything, despite her claims to the contrary, she still cared.

He suddenly felt so light he was sure, had the roof of the Hummer not stopped him, he would've floated right up into the night sky.

"No, Mama." He caught Franklin's vigorous head-shake in the rearview mirror. "I gotta *go wight now.*"

"Jake," she turned to him, "could you—"

"Already on it," he said, hooking a fast right into the parking lot of a gas station, ridiculously happy at doing this, this ordinary, mundane thing of getting the kid to a restroom, this…being a family.

Yo, I could definitely get used to this…

"Oh, this is gonna be fun," Rock murmured as he glanced around the reception area at the pay-by-the-hour roach motel. The one that promised to be his home for the next few days.

There was a sad, lopsided plastic plant in one corner, a couple of painted-up ladies of the evening lounging on a ratty, red velvet settee, and a cigarillo-smoking, stained-wife-beater-wearing guy working behind a set of steel bars that separated the reception desk from the rest of the entryway.

To add to the air of seediness, the smell of sex mixed with the more pungent aromas of bottom shelf booze and stale cigarette smoke.

"I've seen worse," Vanessa murmured as she slipped an arm around his waist and swayed drunkenly.

The drunkenness was all part of the act. It, along with her platinum blond wig, sky-high red patent-leather pumps, nearly nonexistent mini-skirt, slick ruby lips, and enough kohl eyeliner to give a randy raccoon a heart attack, was supposed to fool everyone into thinking she was just another working girl who'd scored herself a high-class john.

Enter him: the high-class john.

The Armani suit he was wearing was stolen from Christian's closet along with the Gucci loafers that were half a size too big and slipping against his heels.

Oui, he was gonna have one hell of a set of blisters by the time this was over. No doubt about it.

He slung an arm around her shoulders and leaned down to whisper in her ear. "Now *that* sounds like a story I'd like to hear sometime, *chère.*"

"I'd tell you," she whispered back, "but then I'd have to kill you."

It was the standard spec-ops comeback, but he threw his head back and laughed like she'd just said the wittiest thing he'd ever heard, because, *mon dieu,* the feel of her pressed against his side seared him like a brand.

The next four days were going to be hell. And he was contemplating this very salient fact when he caught a look at himself in the smoky, gilt mirror clinging to the peeling wallpaper.

He barely recognized his own reflection.

With the neon-blue colored contact lenses he'd popped in his eyes, his hairless chin, and the jet-black dye he'd washed through his hair—not to mention the gold watch and four-carat diamond sparkling in his ear—he looked like a quintessential Chicago mobster.

Shades of Al Capone.

One of the good things about having a non-descript face was that a few small changes completely altered his looks.

"Hi, sugar," Vanessa slurred to the guy working behind the bars, her voice a rough parody of itself, like she'd spent the last fifteen years smoking two packs a day. Rock considered himself a pretty good actor, but Vanessa Cordero, *oui*, she was world class. "We're gonna need a room for—" she glanced up at him, pursing her glistening lips. And though this was all a giant ruse, for a moment he wished he really *was* taking her upstairs to peel away that ridiculously small halter-top and that barely there miniskirt in order to sink into the warm, wet welcome of her body. "How long you want, big daddy? An hour? Two?"

"Let's make it a full night and go from there," he winked, donning his best Chicago-accent while reaching into his jacket pocket to pull out a platinum Bulgari money clip—also on loan from The Christian Watson collection. Rock would never understand the guy's obsession with designer labels. Right now, he missed his jeans like crazy and, oh lordy, what he wouldn't give to have his boots back. "Mr. and Mrs. Smith checking in," he told the guy who cast a jaded eye over his suit.

"That'll be two hundred dollars, Mr...*Smith*," the guy rasped as he chewed on the end of his cigarillo and ran a hand through the ten hairs still left atop his greasy head.

Two hundred dollars?

Uh-huh. Rock highly suspected the rates at the Stardust Hotel worked on a sliding scale. The more money you could afford to pay, the more money your stay was gonna run you.

"We'd like a room facing west," he told the guy as he thumbed off two Benjamins and slid them between the bars. "You know, so the sun doesn't wake us up in the morning." And so they'd be perfectly situated to watch the hotel's front door and the comings and goings at the bar across the street.

The guy threw the crisp bills into an old-fashioned cash register that *dinged* in happiness of yet another deposit before he slid Rock a key with a plastic, diamond-shaped attachment. On the attachment, in chipped white font, was the number 402.

"We've got a delivery coming," he told Mr. Cigarillo, winking and running his tongue over his lips in a lewd gesture. "A few…*provisions* to get us through the night, if ya know what I mean."

The guy stared at him with dead, bloodshot eyes and continued to chew on the soggy end of his cigarillo.

"Anyway," he continued, undeterred by Sir Wife-Beater's bored gaze, "when they get here, just send 'em on up."

Sir Wife-Beater transferred his smoke to the other side of his mouth, flashing one severely crooked front tooth, and Rock figured that was as close as he was going to get to an acknowledgment of his request.

Pocketing the key, he once more slid his arm around Vanessa's shoulders and steered her toward the lone elevator as she pretended to teeter precariously in her high heels. The women lounging lazily on the settee evaluated his suit and shoes and primped by fluffing their hair and their boobs while simultaneously batting their fake lashes.

"You get tired of her, honey," one of them called, "you just come back down here. Candy'll show you a real good time."

"Back off, bitch," Vanessa snarled. Rock bit his lip to keep from grinning. "This one's mine. Go find your own."

"Who you callin' a bitch, bitch?" Candy demanded, showing a set of teeth brown and worn down from too many years smoking unfiltered cigarettes.

"I'm callin' *you* a bitch, *bitch!*" Vanessa retorted hotly, making like she was heading toward Candy.

Rock dragged her back and shoved her in the elevator before Candy could push up from the settee. When the creaky silver doors closed them inside and the elevator began its jerky journey upward, he turned to ask if that was really necessary, even as entertaining as it'd been, but she grabbed his face.

"Let's make it look good for our audience," she whispered, hooking an ankle behind his knee as she pulled him down for a kiss.

He caught the blinking red eye of the security camera mounted in the corner a second before her lips landed on his and then...*rien*—absolutely nothing.

His mind came to a full stop, because her breath was sweet, her lips were sweeter, and her tongue was the sweetest of all.

And suddenly he wasn't playing a part anymore. He grabbed her ass with both hands and spun, pinning her against the elevator wall as he made like Alexander the Great and conquered.

As in, take no prisoners. Full-on tongue action. A real grab and suck.

And just when he was about to remove a hand from her ass in order to palm one of those firm breasts pushed up like an offering in that teensy halter top, the doors opened with a slightly discordant *ding-dong*, like maybe the elevator was suffering from a cold, and sanity suddenly returned.

Holy shit!

He stepped back, his heart racing like a runaway freight train. When he looked down, her sultry eyes, made more so by all that black eyeliner, blinked up at him with equal measures of shock and awe.

"Sorry," he whispered, swallowing and trying to still his racing pulse. "Got a bit carried away there, *mon petite*."

"It's, uh…" she raised a shaky hand to wipe a thumb across his lips. No doubt a good amount of her lipstick had made the transfer. "It's fine. All part of the act."

Uh-huh. Sure.

Well, if she wanted to paddle down that sad little river otherwise known as *denial*, who was he to dissuade her?

Together, they swayed down the hall with its stained red carpet and chipped gray paint before stopping outside room 402. Inserting the key, he pushed open the flimsy metal door and was immediately hit by the overwhelming aroma of Pine-sol, pot, and piss.

Oh, goody. The three Ps. What fleabag, pay-by-the-hour rat-trap would be complete without them?

"It's not so bad," Vanessa murmured, pushing past him into the room.

"And you're a terrible liar," he told her as he took a moment to rearrange the erection he'd sprung in the elevator. Following her across the dingy carpet, he refused to look at the bed. The really big, really *obvious* bed taking center stage.

He pushed back the curtains on the dirty window and glanced out at the bar across the street. The neon sign for In The Mood Lounge blinked bright blue, and he couldn't help but think the only people who frequented the bar were either "in the mood" to contract a lethal case of ptomaine from the food served there, or "in the mood" to come down with a chronic case of herpes from the ladies working the joint.

Johnny sure knows how to pick 'em.

He'd seen some shady places in his life, and In The Mood Lounge rated right up there with the best of them. Especially when you combined it with the rare treasure across the street that was The Stardust Hotel.

"How does it look?" Vanessa asked, pulling on the hem of her mini-skirt. Rock felt that grab and tug as if it'd happened to his dick.

Merde. Get it together, Babineaux.

"It's perfect for surveillance," he told her, refusing to turn in her direction lest she notice the tire iron he was concealing inside his suit pants—Correction: *Christian's* suit pants. Oh, and wouldn't Christian absolutely love that? "Not only can we see the entrances to the hotel and lounge, but also anyone enterin' or exitin' the alley behind the bar. Now all we need is our surveillance gear and—"

A hard knock sounded on the door.

"Ask and ye shall receive," Vanessa drawled as she strolled across the room, now remarkably steady on those towering heels.

When she opened the door, Rock barely refrained from bursting into laughter because Becky stood in the hallway, dressed in a 24-hour delivery service uniform with a short brown wig covering her blond hair. A patchy beard concealed her pretty face, and a pair of Coke-bottle glasses made her soft brown eyes look huge and dull and lazy. She also wore a pair of fake yellow teeth and a monster, hairy mole on her upper lip.

No doubt about it, Rock wasn't the only one who was good with a disguise.

Moley, moley, moley.

"Delivery for Mr. and Mrs. Smith," she said in a deep voice, holding up two giant bags from The Pleasure Chest. A pair of pink, furry handcuffs dangled from one bag while the top of a giant green dildo protruded from the other.

"Well, come in, sugar," Vanessa rasped in her fake smoker's voice for the benefit of anyone out in the hall. Only after she'd closed the door behind them, did Becky drop the act and break out in a huge smile that made the hairs in her mole flicker like a cat's whiskers.

"Oh my God, this is so much fun. Aren't you guys having fun?" she asked gleefully.

Rock could think of a lot of other things he'd rather be doing.

"Now, look," she said, obviously considering her question rhetorical, "I brought a couple pairs of clean undies and a change of clothes for each of you." She set the bags on the sagging mattress and starting digging inside, tossing the handcuffs and the Jolly Green Giant's dick aside like they were nothing. "There's toothpaste, two toothbrushes, some soap, shampoo and, Ta-da!" She waved the collapsible disk on a parabolic listening device. "The surveillance equipment you requested, Rock."

Vanessa held up the green dildo and tilted her head, her eyebrows pulled together in a deep V. The thing was as big around and as long as her forearm, and the sight of her with a dick in her hand, even if it was green and ridiculously oversized, had him fighting to contain the erection that had begun to soften upon Becky and her mole's appearance. "Who in the world can actually use something like this?" she asked absently.

"A professional," Becky replied, still unpacking the

bags. "Or at least that's what I figured when I was picking it out."

"Did Boss let you make this trip on your own?" Rock couldn't imagine. The big guy was like a mama bear with a cub when it came to Becky. And who could blame him really? Especially given the woman's astounding ability to find trouble in the most innocuous of situations.

"Are you kidding me?" Becky made a face that looked wholly absurd given her get-up. "He's hiding in the stairwell with enough weapons to start World War III. But, whatever," she waved a dismissive hand through the air. "I wanna know if there was any sign of Johnny on the way in?"

"He'd be a fool to stay here," Vanessa murmured, looking around for somewhere to store the mammoth rubber cock and coming up empty. She satisfied herself with tucking it under the bed.

Rock wasn't going to complain.

"It's actually not such a bad idea," he muttered, and both women swung around to face him. "If he wanted to keep an eye on the meeting place, there's no better vantage point than this hotel."

"So are you going to go looking for him? Asking around?" Becky asked.

"*Oui*. We'll take turns watching the bar and nosing around the neighborhood. Vanessa," he pointed at the woman as one corner of his mouth twitched, "will go downstairs and have a little tête à tête with Candy— she's one of the lovely ladies you passed on the way in—and casually mention a client who fits Johnny's description. See if it rings any of Candy's bells." He turned to Vanessa. "That is if you two can manage a civil conversation?"

Vanessa groaned. "I make no promises."

Becky crossed her arms and pouted. With the mole and the beard and the teeth, the gesture looked ridiculous. "Man," she grumped, "you guys get to have all the fun."

He waved an incredulous hand around to indicate their less-than-stellar accommodations. "Ya think this is fun?"

"Well, it's better than being stuck at the shop and—" she cut herself off as she narrowed her eyes and took a step toward him. A grin split her bewhiskered face, once more causing the hairs growing out of her fake mole to twang like mini antennae. "Yeah," she said, nodding and looking back and forth between him and Vanessa. She reached up to wipe at his lips. Obviously, Vanessa hadn't completely rid him of the evidence of their little elevator encounter. *Zut!* "I think you guys are going to have lots and *lots* of fun."

He and Vanessa simultaneously opened their mouths to explain, but she waved them off and started for the door. "If you two need anything else, give ol' Duncan here," she tapped the name embroidered over the right breast pocket of her uniform, "a call. Until then," she opened the door and immediately dropped her voice so it resembled a man's, "thanks for the tip."

After she'd gone, Vanessa plopped down on the bed and the mattress springs squeaked as if in agony. "Maybe we should talk about—"

"Help me get this equipment set up," he interrupted her, because, really, what was there to say?

They were professionals on a stake-out.

People were depending on them keeping their eyes

and ears open. They couldn't let the chemistry bubbling between them distract them from the mission.

And since he couldn't *do* anything about the boner in his pants, he sure as hell didn't want to *talk* about it.

Chapter Seven

MICHELLE STARED DOWN AT HER SLEEPING SON, snuggly warm in his little bed with his stuffed Elmo doll tucked up under his dimpled chin, and cursed her brother for putting her in this god-awful position.

It was his fault she was here now, scared for her life and that of her son…scared of how she'd continue to evade Jake's advances.

Crap.

She knew what she needed to do. She needed to go downstairs, walk into her bright, welcoming kitchen, and play the part of the good hostess. Give her guest the lowdown on the accommodations. All those little things, like where to find fresh towels and soap…

But her kitchen didn't seem very bright and welcoming right now, because it currently housed the one man on the entire planet she'd sworn to avoid like last week's fish tacos. The one man who could—no, *would* break her heart again if she gave him the chance. The one man capable of crushing her hard-won resolve with only a kiss.

Oh, that kiss…

It made her remember too much and not enough all at the same time. It was terrible. And wonderful. And so, so dangerous…

With dread weighing down her heart, she softly closed the door to her son's room and made her way downstairs, through the living room, and into the kitchen.

And then she momentarily forgot about everything, because there he was.

The man who inspired all her hottest fantasies. The same one who embodied all her worst fears…

"I checked the perimeter," he said, not bothering to turn toward her as he worked at something on the far counter. "Everything looks good. That security system Boss installed for you is top notch. You don't have anything to worry about. You're completely safe here."

Yeah, right. Physically she might be safe, but emotionally? Now that was another matter entirely.

"I hope you don't mind," he finally turned away from the counter only to find her frowning at his back. His very broad, very strong, very drool-worthy back. *Dangit, Michelle! You have too much sense for this!* "I helped myself to some tea." He held up two mugs, steaming and filling the air with rich aroma.

"You'll have to finish both," she told him, refusing the mouthwatering temptation of a warm nightcap combined with a sexy man. Because, you know, there was an empty sofa in the next room…

"Oh, come on, Shell," he winked and lifted one of the mugs. "It's your favorite. Chamomile."

She wished the fact that he remembered that didn't affect her so.

"I can't," she said. "I'm about two minutes away from needing a pair of toothpicks to prop open my eyelids."

Not really. She'd be hard-pressed to get any sleep tonight given everything that'd happened. Oh yeah, and then there was the fact that Jake was going to be sleeping three doors down from her. A measly twenty feet away. Sprawled all over her guest bed. Naked…

At least that's how she imagined it would be.

God, help me!

"Extra towels are in the hall closet along with extra soap. I put clean sheets on the guest bed." *The one you'll be sprawled in. Naked. Frickin' frackin' fudge!* "Feel free to scrounge anything from the fridge or pantry you want. Although, I see you've already done that, so just," she made a rolling motion with her hand, "carry on."

There. Hostess duties complete. *Now turn around, get your butt upstairs, and forget he's in your house.*

Uh-huh. Right. Like that was possible. Still, the first step was to take the first step. Literally.

"Goodnight, Jake," she said, swinging back into the living room.

"You head upstairs right now, and all you'll do is toss and turn." He set the mugs of tea on the kitchen table.

Busted.

Warily, she turned and watched as he lifted a brow at the roses. "Pretty flowers. Weird color though."

"Did you pick it?" she asked, trying and failing not to drool over the bunch and twist of his tanned muscles as he leaned over to smell the roses.

"What?" He straightened.

"The color of the roses?"

"What are you talking about?" His brow furrowed.

"Oh, uh, nothing. I just…I thought maybe they were from you."

He smiled, and the flash of his dimples had her heart pounding. "When I send you roses, doll, you'll know they're from me. They'll be blood red, none of this blue shit, and they'll come complete with a card that declares my undying love."

"Stop." She raised a hand.

"Shell—"

"I'm tired, and I'm going to bed." End of discussion.

"There are still things we still need to talk about."

Oh Lord.

He could *not* keep telling her he loved her.

Not when she kept fanaticizing about him naked, not when his kiss had caused all those delicious, awful memories to rise too close to the surface, making her feel vulnerable and lost. And certainly not when the fear of what her brother had inadvertently involved her in made her long to seek the comfort of a strong set of arms.

Because she just might convince herself to believe him. And if she convinced herself to believe him then—

No. He doesn't love me. It's lust. It's just unsatiated lust…

"We said everything that needed to be said," she hastily informed him, taking a loose-kneed step back toward the living room, which was made all the more difficult considering each of her feet weighed about two-hundred pounds.

And then his next words stopped her in her tracks.

"I haven't slept with another woman in over two years," he said.

Don't do this to me…

She hesitated, taking a deep breath before swinging around to face him. She shouldn't ask, but she just couldn't help herself, "Why is that?"

"Because I got your letter." Her heart began beating so fast she felt dizzy. "And it changed everything for me."

She resisted the urge to lift a hand to her spinning head. "Wh-what do you mean?"

"I mean, I always figured you hated me. I figured you'd never be able to forgive me after the way I treated you, after the things I said, after what happened to Preacher. But then I got that letter from you, asking me to come here, telling me you, Boss, and Rock were waiting for me, worried for me, and for the first time I began to have hope."

"And your response to that hope was to completely *ignore* me?"

"I wasn't ready yet," he admitted. "I needed to wait until I was sure of myself."

"What are you *talking* about?" she demanded, planting her hands on her hips.

He smiled and took a step toward her, but at her hard look, he halted and tucked his hands in his pockets. "I'll explain everything to you. I promise, I will. But right now, the thing that's most important, the thing I want you to realize, to understand, is that I haven't slept with anyone in two years."

Suddenly, she was unaccountably tired, and the toothpick comment didn't seem all that farfetched. "So what do you want from me, Jake?" she sighed, shaking her head. "A medal?"

"No. No medals. I just told you so you'd know I'm nothing like your father."

Her cheeks stung with swift heat. "Now what is *that* supposed to mean?"

"Boss explained what happened with your dad. He told me what a bastard the guy was and that you think I'm just like him. But I'm *not*, Shell. You can trust me. If you give me your heart, I promise I won't shit all over it like your father did."

"Yeah," she scoffed, amazed at both his audacity and his ability to not only lie to her, but also to himself. He was exactly like her father. He'd proven it time and again. "Because you were sooo careful with my heart the first time."

"So, you admit to giving me your heart? Earlier tonight you said you'd never loved me."

Crap, crap, *crap!*

"Whatever," she waved a hand through the air. Hoping, in the process, to wave away the point he'd made. "The fact of the matter is: Fool me once, shame on you. Fool me twice, shame on me."

"But I didn't fool you. There were circumstances you don't—"

"It doesn't matter," she quickly interrupted, so tired of listening to lies, and worse, actually finding herself wanting to believe them.

He opened his mouth to say something else when Franklin's sleepy voice drifted down from the second floor, "Mama! I'm thirsty!"

"I'll be right up, sweetpea!" she called, beyond grateful for the excuse to quit the field as once again she turned toward the living room.

"We're not finished talking about this," Jake grumbled at her back.

"*Yes*, we are."

From the corner of her eye, she saw him take a determined step in her direction, and she swung around, startled.

He moved with the easy beauty of the supremely fit. Not one ounce of wasted movement. And no matter how hard she tried to tell him she was serious, that she didn't have anything else to say, she could only stare in horrified awe at the resolved glint in his eye.

She finally managed to work her tongue loose. "Wh-what in the world are you—"

He didn't hesitate, didn't telegraph his intentions. One second he was stalking toward her, the next second he had her face cupped between his strong hands and his warm lips settled over hers. The kiss was so tender, so deep, that it forced all the breath from her lungs.

This is a mistake.

He knew it like he knew his name was Jacob Michael Sommers. But he couldn't help himself. She refused to listen to what he had to say, and the only other way he could think to convince her that she was wrong, that there *was* still something between them, something that could grow if only she'd let it, was to prove it to her physically.

"I want you so much," he breathed against her lips, reveling in their lushness, in the sweet taste of the wine that still lingered on her tongue from dinner. "And I know you want me, too."

He could feel it in the way she fought with herself, fought to keep from stepping toward him, fought to keep from fully tasting his tongue.

She failed on all counts.

"No," she shook her head. But when he bent to kiss the side of her exposed neck, she melted instantly, her body language completely at odds with her next words. "I don't want you."

He glanced at her face, gratified to discover she was

lying through her teeth. Because there was no mistaking the hot desire shining in her gorgeous, *gorgeous* eyes.

She licked her lips, her tongue a flash of delicious pink, and he could barely breathe, barely think. His brain cells were no longer receiving enough blood to fire his synapses. So he kissed her again, walking her backward until he pinned her against the wall.

And he remembered this was how it'd been that night at the Clover. The two of them, against the wall of the men's restroom, caught in a burning embrace that threatened to ignite into an inferno at any second.

She'd been telling the truth about one thing tonight...

Some things never changed. Because the passion that flowed between them was as volatile and explosive as ever.

And though he knew he needed to talk to her before he took things any further, though he knew he should slow things down and make her listen to what he had to say, what he *knew* hadn't quite caught up with what he wanted.

Because what he wanted was her. All of her. All naked skin and slumberous eyes. Her body moving beneath him in that sliding, sensual way inherent in the female of the species. And he wanted it now. Right here in the middle of her kitchen.

When she tentatively snaked an arm around his neck, pressing her luscious breasts against his chest, what few thoughts he'd been able to hold onto immediately flew from his head. All he could think was, *Yo, this is* Shell. *Back in my arms. Finally.*

He wanted to yell with the joy of it...or cry. He wasn't sure which. Maybe both.

Michelle was having an out-of-body experience.

That's the only thing that could account for why her arms were around Jake's neck, seemingly of their own accord, and why her tongue was eagerly tangling with his.

But she'd always figured an out-of-body experience left you feeling numb and disconnected, which most certainly was not the case here. *Huh-uh.* In fact, she felt *very* connected.

Every inch of her skin was on fire, her belly roiling, her scalp tingling.

It was exactly as she remembered it. Everything about him, about the two of them together, was exactly as she remembered it, and her heart absolutely ached at the reminder of how it'd once been, how it might've still been if only—

He shifted forward until they were groin to groin and—*oh, mercy, mercy me*. He was hot and hard and throbbing steadily, and she remembered that, too. She wanted nothing more than to—

But she couldn't. She could *not* allow herself to fall for him again. The consequences of that action had been heartbreaking the first time. She couldn't bear to think what they'd be now. Of course, when he slid a hand up her side to gently brush the underside of her breast, her libido screamed at her to throw caution to the wind and just give in. Give in to the lust in his eyes and the pleasure in his touch…

And it was tempting. Oh lordy, it was tempting. But she had other things to consider now besides her own desires.

The little boy sleeping upstairs, for one.

And right on cue Franklin called, "Mama! Where are you?"

Pushing Jake away was one of the hardest things she'd ever done, even harder when she glanced up to see him raking in breaths like he'd just completed a hundred yard dash. Oh, man, his eyes…They were so green, so fierce and bright, and when he looked at her like that—

"Shell, I—"

"It's over," she interrupted and took another step away, scrubbing a shaky fist over her kiss-moistened lips. Her heart felt like she'd popped it in her pressure-cooker and set the temperature to high. "It's been over for a very long time."

"It's not," he insisted, crossing his arms and grinding his jaw until his cheeks muscles twitched. "You kissed me back just now."

He wasn't as big a man as her brother, not as thick or muscle-bound. He was elegantly built, with a quintessential surfer's body. Still, at 6'4" he managed to stand nearly a head above her. The disparity in their heights, particularly when she wasn't accustomed to having to look up at many men, drove home the main reason she couldn't just save herself the headache and heartache and immediately insist he leave.

Because there he stood. Tall, strong, steady. Ready and willing to lay his life on the line. And, *dangit!*, she needed the protection he offered. Her *son* needed his protection.

"Mama!"

"I'll be right up!" she shouted, before turning back to Jake. "If it weren't for my son, I'd throw you straight out the door for that stunt you just pulled."

"You *did* kiss me back. Try to deny it."

She couldn't. "I kissed you back. And it was as big a mistake now as it was four years ago. I'm going to bed. I suggest you do the same. We have an early morning tomorrow."

"Shell, I—"

She turned then, waving off whatever else he might think to say as she calmly strode across the living room, careful not to trip over the toy car lying on its side on the rug. She forced herself not to take the stairs two at a time—though every instinct she had screamed at her to *run*, because she could feel his eyes burning into her, trying to see into her soul. But she carefully climbed each and every step, refusing to give him the satisfaction of watching her flee the scene.

When she reached the landing, she slowly turned toward the bathroom and filled a glass from the pitcher of filtered water she kept on hand for just such occasions. Sedately crossing the hall to her son's room, she watched him gulp it sleepily before once more grabbing his Elmo and settling into slumber. After softly closing his door, she managed to calmly stroll into her own room.

And it was there she let go.

Sinking down on her bed, she dropped her head into her hands, her pulse pounding in her temples as a little *eep* that was one part terror and two parts heartache escaped through her trembling lips.

What am I going to do?

Because Jake was right. No matter what she said, no matter the impossibility of it all, no matter how hard she tried to convince herself otherwise, it wasn't over.

It'd never *truly* be over. At least not for her.

But it had to be. Because there was just no other option.

And then, inexplicably, an image of those blue roses popped into her head. Blue…blue meant mystery, didn't it? So, what? She had a secret admirer? And just like that, the solution to her little problem with Jake presented itself.

Jumping from the bed, she grabbed her purse and fished inside for her wallet. Once she located it—way at the bottom beneath a granola bar, the extra pair of Underoos she kept in case Franklin had an accident, and her travel sewing kit—she flipped through old receipts until she found the business card she was searching for.

Lifting the phone from her nightstand, she punched in the number printed in a firm hand on the plain white cardstock and waited as one ring turned to two, and then three.

"Come on. Be home."

"Hello?" The voice on the other end of the line sounded groggy, and she glanced at the digital clock on her nightstand. 11:30.

Dang.

"I'm sorry to be calling so late, Dr. Drummond," she winced, "er, Chris. But I was wondering what you were doing for dinner tomorrow night…"

"Okay." Vanessa pulled off her wig and flung it on the hotel bed, stepping out of the sky-scraper heels that were absolutely killing her back, not to mention her calves. "The next time you want to pump the lovely Candy for information, you're going to do it yourself."

Rock sat on the chair they'd parked in front of the

window, a pair of optics held to his eyes. "Well, you've still got your eyes, *chère*," he observed in that slow-moving molasses drawl of his as he turned away from the window. "So it couldn't have been *that* bad."

"What's that supposed to mean?"

"I thought she might want to scratch your eyes out after that first scene. 'Who you callin' bitch, bitch?'" he mimicked in a terrible falsetto, grinning and batting his almost girlishly thick lashes. "Remember that?"

"For gals like us," she told him, "*bitch* is a compliment. When I said you'd have to take the next shift with Candy, I wasn't referring to any possibility of a cat fight breaking out. Yeah," she shook her head at the look on his face, "I'm sorry to disappoint you, but we professionals stick together. Anyway, I'm saying you're up next because it's gonna take weeks, and the repeated bleaching of my ears, to recover from the conversation I just had."

He lifted a brow, clearly intrigued.

"Candy saw the, uh…we'll call them *props* that our little delivery boy brought in, and she spent ten minutes regaling me with stories about a guy who used to like to use the same kind of equipment on her as she plucked his chest hair while simultaneously singing 'The Star-Spangled Banner.'"

Rock snorted with laughter. "At least the guy was patriotic. God bless America!"

She sent him a disparaging look. "And that's a clean version of the conversation, I assure you. Of course, given her experience with the equipment, it made it easy for her to believe I'd completely worn you out and left you up here sleeping while I ran downstairs to take a break."

"But given the size of our equipment, shouldn't *you* have been the one worn out?"

She smiled innocently and batted her lashes. "Who says we used the props on me?"

Rock shuddered. "Okay, you may need ear bleach, but now I need brain bleach."

"My work here is done," she chuckled.

"Not so fast," he swallowed and made a distasteful face like he was having trouble scrubbing away the images circling around in his head. "What's the 411 on Johnny?"

"I told Candy I'd *done*," she made the quote marks with her fingers, "a client here once before who paid really well. Gave her Johnny's description. Asked if she'd seen him around lately. She says she thinks maybe she saw him yesterday evening out in front of In the Mood Lounge. She couldn't be sure since she was soliciting another john at the time, but the physical characteristics she described sound an awful lot like Vitiglioni."

"Does she know if he's staying here?"

"Nope." She moved toward the bed, flexing her poor aching toes after flinging herself back on the squeaky mattress they'd stripped of bedclothes and covered with what they hoped were at least semi-clean towels. "She said she hasn't seen anyone who fits his description go in or out of the hotel today, but at least we have a solid lead on the bar. And speaking of, is there anything new over at In the Mood?"

"*Non.*" She stared at the water-stained popcorn ceiling and let his smooth baritone wash over her. "Just sad patrons, tired prostitutes, and lazy pimps."

"Not exactly the glamorous life we're living, huh?"

"It could be worse," he mused. "It could be *much* worse."

She lifted her chin and stared at him, curiosity over-coming her. "Like your other job?"

He spun away from the window where he'd once more resumed his surveillance duty. "What d'ya know about that?"

"Nothing." She pushed to a sitting position. "As far as I can tell, *nobody* knows anything about that."

"And that's the way it'll stay."

Uh-huh. She shouldn't have expected anything more.

"You all have a lot of secrets, don't you? Even from one another."

"What do you mean?" His brows lowered over his perfect nose.

"I mean, there's you and this other job. Boss kept his sister hidden for years. Then there's Snake and this thing with Michelle and Franklin and the—"

"What about this thing with Shell and Franklin?" he demanded, and she realized it might be smart to close her mouth right now.

Like, right now.

Sometimes she just wasn't very smart.

"I, uh, I thought it was obvious."

"What's obvious? What are you talkin' about?"

"Nothing," she shook her head. Far be it for her to be the one to enlighten him.

He narrowed his eyes before pushing up from the chair. Stalking across the room, he grabbed his designer jacket and slung it over his shoulder before dropping the optics on the mattress beside her. "I'm goin' to go make some inquiries at the bar. You stay here and keep an eye on things."

The set of his jaw was hard and unforgiving as he turned and marched toward the door.

"Be careful," she called to his back. "We don't know how many guys Johnny has out looking for us, and that disguise is good but it's not infallible."

He lifted a hand in answer, refusing to turn back to her as he disappeared through the door.

O-*kay*, she thought, *so talk of his second job is* clearly *a big no-no*.

Good to know…

Chapter Eight

BANG!

The sound jerked Michelle from a fitful sleep, and she was out of bed, throwing on her robe, and wrenching open her bedroom door before she was fully awake. Which might account for her momentarily forgetting the fact that she had a very big, very *menacing* houseguest. Because when a large shadow loomed in front of her, she opened her mouth to scream.

And she would have, too. Just let 'er rip with everything she had, if a hard hand hadn't clamped over her mouth.

"Geez, Shell, it's me!" Jake whispered, and she nearly collapsed with relief onto the hallway rug.

Then she remembered what had jolted her awake.

"I heard a noise," she said after batting his hand away, blinking owlishly in the dim glow given off by the nightlight she kept plugged into one of the hallway's outlets.

"Yeah, me too." He pushed the cold handle of her Beretta Tomcat into her shaking hand. The little .32 pistol had been a gift from Steven. He'd given it to her right before he'd left for his final mission, and the feel of it against her skin brought on a deep, aching sadness that took the edge off her momentary panic. She couldn't help but think that none of this would be happening if Steven was still alive…

"I recognized Preacher's lockbox above your refrigerator," Jake said. "And, FYI, you really shouldn't tape the key to the lock onto the actual box, but that's neither here nor there. Right now I just need to be sure you know how to use this thing."

"I know how to use it," she assured him. "Frank made sure of that."

"Good. Now I'm going to check out that noise." He handed her his cell phone. "If I'm not back in five minutes, you lock yourself in Franklin's room, hit one on the speed dial—that'll be your brother—and shoot at anything or anyone that tries to come through that door. You got me?"

"Yes." She nodded again, swallowing jerkily, her heartbeat pounding in her ears, as she followed him the short distance down the hall to plant herself in front of her sleeping son's door.

As Jake silently descended the stairs, she noticed he was naked save for a big, black Glock and pair of boxers covered with...

Were those hearts?

A laugh that was one part incredulity and two parts hysteria bubbled up the back of her throat, but she managed to bite it off.

Now was not the time to lose her mind.

Jake's blood pumped through his system at a rate of about a hundred miles a minute, because someone or something was right outside Shell's back door.

He carefully turned the knob and slowly pushed open the door, stepping barefoot onto the cold concrete of her back steps. With his Glock held ready, he flipped the switch to the outdoor fixture. A sudden wash of golden light bathed the back of the brownstone and part of the driveway in a twelve-foot radius—which meant there was still a whole helluva lot of area left in darkness.

Goddamn shadowy corners. They're the bane of my existence tonight.

Goose bumps pebbled his flesh, but they had nothing to do with the harsh bite in the night air and everything to do with the fact that even though he couldn't *see* anything, his senses—heightened by years of training and living on the edge—told him he wasn't alone.

Come out, come out wherever you are, he silently challenged as he descended the steps, quartering the area with his weapon, ears cocked to the slightest sound. He could smell the sweet, earthy aroma of the purple flowers blooming in the flowerbed beside Shell's driveway and the more pungent smell of newly turned mulch.

Gauging the short distance to the neighbor's house, the street in front and the alleyway behind, he chambered a round and methodically scouted the area.

When he'd decided to come to Chicago to finally lay claim to Shell, he certainly hadn't imagined himself stalking around her backyard in his damned skivvies, acting as her bodyguard and bullet-catcher. Hell, no. He'd imagined himself upstairs, in her bed, sunk deep into her warm, soft body.

Ah, the ever optimistic turn of the male mind…

But given that Shell was about as close to inviting him to bed as she was to starting a career in poledancing, he figured this was as good as it was going to get. And honestly, it did appear that perhaps Fate, the unbelievably fickle bitch, had finally seen fit to throw him a bone.

Because *this* was what he was built for. Fighting. Protecting. Defending. And maybe if Shell began to see him as less like the man he used to be—the one who'd treated her so terribly—and more like the man he was now—the one who'd lay down his life for her and her son—he'd be able to charm his way into that invitation for a sleepover. If the heat of those kisses was anything to go by, *yo, mama*, she was closer to inviting him upstairs than she knew.

Of course, first he had to deal with whoever the hell was lurking around out here. And there *was* someone lurking. He could feel eyes on the back of his head as surely as he felt the cold, damp ground beneath his feet.

Just like back in BKI's courtyard, a tidal wave of anger washed through him at the thought of someone hurting Shell or Franklin. But now, the sensation was much more acute. Because back there, Shell would've simply been collateral damage for whoever was gunning for Boss. But here? Whoever had come *here*, to the sanctity of her home, was aiming specifically for her.

For the first time in a long time, the monster inside him reared its head and blinked red eyes, stretching its claws.

Who are you, you bastard. Where *are you?*

There. By the trash cans. Movement.

Heart pounding in hungry anticipation, monster inside him growling and scratching to be free, he slowly stalked in the direction of his prey.

What the hell?

Johnny had ducked back into the prickly hedgerow when a large man with an even larger gun stealthily emerged from the back door of Michelle's brownstone.

This wasn't what he'd planned for…

Last night, when he scouted out the place, he was gratified to learn that Michelle and her son lived alone. And though she was more suspicious than most women and had a security system to match the Pentagon's, he knew just how get around that. All he had to do was cause a little racket. And when Michelle came to investigate, and she *would* come to investigate—humans were intrinsically curious which, in his experience, also made them intrinsically stupid—he'd simply grab her and drag her back inside before forcing her to rearm her system.

Yeah, that was the idea. But this dickhead, the one wearing the ridiculous boxer shorts, screwed everything up. Johnny wasn't prepared to take on a full-grown man, especially one handling a very deadly weapon. He hadn't brought the correct tools with him.

Shit!

Fury mixed with disappointment to sit like a bitter pill, burning his gut.

He'd *so* been looking forward to this. Dreaming about it all day, in fact. Especially after he'd heard the sound of her smooth, sexy voice when she told him to leave the roses.

But he hadn't gotten to where he was in life by being careless.

So…he'd wait. Again. Go back to the hotel and regroup. Again.

And tomorrow night when he visited them? Well, he'd be ready for *all* possible scenarios, now wouldn't he?

Silently he slid back through the bushes and disappeared into the neighbor's yard. He hadn't gone more than twenty feet when he heard a clearly disgruntled meow followed by a string of curses.

Ah, perfect…

Michelle blew out a relieved breath when she heard Jake close the kitchen door and reset the alarm. Tucking the pistol in the pocket of her robe, she waited for him to mount the steps.

Oh, why did her heart jump into her throat at the mere thought of seeing him in nothing but a pair of boxer shorts?

Because it's a silly organ, that's why. A silly, forgetful, forgiving organ. And, let's be fair, Jake can fill out a pair of underwear like nobody's business…

"What was it?" she asked once he climbed to the landing, fighting not to let her gaze drift down the delicious tan expanse of his naked chest.

"That's the second time today I nearly shot a cat," he mused, shaking his head in disbelief.

"Black with white paws?"

"Yep, and chowing down on your garbage like it was chock-full of tuna fish. He must've knocked the lid off the can, and that's what caused the racket."

"That would be Seymour, the neighbor's cat, and he's obviously getting a lot more resourceful. I thought I'd finally bested him with these new garbage cans. Apparently they only foiled him for a little while."

Jake nodded, rubbing the back of his neck as if trying

to massage away the tension, and she took the opportunity to sneak the *teeniest* little peek at his chest.

Unfortunately, even in the dim hall, she must not have been all that stealthy, because no sooner had she allowed her eyes to drift down to the corrugated muscles of his stomach than she felt it happen.

A subtle shift in the atmosphere…

When he lowered his arm, his gaze zeroed in on her cleavage, revealed by the deep V of her nightgown and her hastily donned robe. She grabbed the robe's satin lapels and jerked the two halves tightly together.

Okay, and turn about was fair play, but it could also get a woman in a crap-ton of trouble.

One corner of his too-sexy mouth hitched at the sight of her nervousness before he cleared his throat and took a step toward her, pinning her with his too-green gaze. "I, uh, I want to apologize for the way I acted earlier. I shouldn't have—"

"No," she interrupted, taking two hasty steps back toward the safety of her bedroom. "You shouldn't have. But it's fine. Just as long as it doesn't happen again."

He tilted his head and smiled as he advanced on her retreat. Those blasted dimples taunted her. "That's one of the main reasons I fell in love with you, you know."

Why did he insist on using that word when he didn't truly understand its meaning?

She knew she shouldn't, but she couldn't help herself. "What are you talking about?" she asked from the relative safety of her bedroom's doorway.

"Your sweet, forgiving nature. I've never met anyone as thoughtful and caring and quick to give everyone the benefit of the doubt as you."

Oh, God. And any sexual heat she'd been feeling was instantly doused.

"I'm not as sweet and thoughtful as you think," she admitted, suddenly fighting the nearly overwhelming urge to cry.

Okay, and maybe she should seek some pharmacological intervention. Because it wasn't normal to feel randy as a teenage boy one second and sad as a circus clown the next, was it?

Of course, she figured she could blame some of her hot/cold emotional seesawing on the fact that about a hundred tons of fear and worry and adrenaline had poured through her system at some point that night. Then again, she knew that was only part of it. Because even under the best of circumstances, she wouldn't have been able to listen to Jake make a list of all her redeeming qualities without suffering a sharp, dizzying stab of guilt.

"Yeah, right," he scoffed, and she could only shake her head helplessly. "Anyway," he went on, "I wanted to call a truce, okay? I'm supposed to be here as your bullet-catcher, and that's all I'll be until this thing with Boss is over. There won't be any more shenanigans. You have my word on that."

She couldn't help but notice he made no promises about how he'd behave when it *was* over. Of course, by then she hoped to have convinced him that he didn't really want her, didn't *really* love her.

"Thank you," she whispered and took the hand he offered.

A jolt of awareness passed from his large palm into hers, but she chose to ignore it as she quickly withdrew her fingers. Ignoring the hard glint of desire in his eyes was impossible, however, as she quickly and quietly shut the door on his damnably handsome face.

—⁓—

The next day…

Jake watched Franklin working with the industry of a three-year-old, tongue held between his teeth, little brow beetled in concentration as he rolled a huge wad of mismatched Play-Doh into a giant, multicolored snake on the coffee table in Shell's cozy living room.

He'd never before thought of himself as the kind of guy who'd enjoy having kids around. But after spending the day with Franklin, following Shell from one appointment to the next, he had to admit, he could get used to the idea.

He actually liked reading those silly Dr. Seuss books over and over again. Playing Transformers was surprisingly fun, especially since Franklin seemed to get such a kick out of his Optimus Prime impression—not to mention all those questions he'd forgotten to contemplate as an adult, but that occurred with regularity in mind of a child.

Why is the sky blue?

Why does the sun follow us when we're driving?

Why do the birds sing?

He'd marveled at Shell's ability to answer each question patiently and honestly and with just the right amount of complexity for a three-year-old to grasp. If he planned to stick around, which he most certainly did—despite the anxious, uncertain looks Shell had sent him all day long, *God love her*—he'd have to learn her technique.

The only time Franklin turned to him with a question, *Why does the Tooth Fairy want so many teeth?*, he'd sputtered and looked around the doctor's office they'd been waiting in, and was saved from having to come up with an answer—thank the Big Kahuna—when another little boy came over to play.

"Yo, little dude," he said now, ruffling Franklin's soft hair, "where'd your mama run off to?"

"She's putting on whipstick," Franklin replied, concentrating on getting the snake's tail just right.

Whipstick? What the hell is whipstick?

"But you can't have any," Franklin continued, turning to him seriously. "It's not s'posed to be used to color, and it's only for girls anyway. And even though it smells good, you're not s'posed to eat it either."

"Do you mean lipstick?" He gestured to his lips, smiling when he realized how Franklin must have reached the conclusion about the non-edibility of lipstick.

The kid was a handful, no doubt.

Franklin ignored him as he grinned, flashing those sweet little boy dimples, and pointed at the clay snake. "Look. It's like your tattoos."

"Just exactly like," he said, pushing up his sleeves to once more show Franklin the twin vipers curled around each of his biceps. The boy had been fascinated by them all day long, constantly shoving up his sleeves and tracing them with a pudgy finger—that is when he wasn't coloring, jabbering, or crashing toy cars into one another.

"When can I get tattoos?" Franklin asked, his big gray eyes, so much like his mother's, staring up at Jake hopefully.

"When you're eighteen," Jake replied, hoping that was the right answer.

Where's Shell when I need her?

Franklin sighed heavily and made a face that said Jake might as well have told him he'd have to wait until he was 150. Then he turned back, frustration worrying his little brow, as he attempted to refine the colorful Play-Doh serpent.

So…why was Shell upstairs putting on lipstick? Was she primping for him?

The idea had warmth settling in his belly along with a heavy dose of satisfaction.

She might claim to have no feelings left for him, she might say things were finished between them. But they weren't. Not by a long shot.

And she knew it, too. Why else would she be upstairs putting on makeup? A woman didn't apply lipstick unless she was trying to impress a man, right?

Right.

Okay, so this is good. This is very, very good.

And why should he be surprised, especially after last night?

Yo, mama! He should've been surprised if she *wasn't* primping. Because, it was obvious the fire that'd raged between them four years ago had turned into a freakin' inferno. And no human on the face of the planet, not even Miss Self-Possessed Michelle Carter, could resist the allure of that kind of heat. Like moths to the flame, humans were irresistibly drawn. It was biological. Some sort of throwback. A compulsion wired into everyone's lizard brains to ensure survival of the species or something.

And you better believe he was grateful for it.

"I'm gonna go check on her," he told Franklin, pushing up from the sofa just as the boy grabbed his round little belly, his nose wrinkling. "What's up, buddy?" he asked, instantly concerned.

"I think I ate too much pssscetti for lunch," Franklin said and, *dude*, Jake could believe it. The rug rat had Hoovered two plates of spaghetti and two adult-sized breadsticks. He highly suspected the kid was in possession of a hollow leg.

"Do you need to take a growler, little man?"

Franklin glanced up at him in confusion, his brow wrinkling. "What's a growler?"

"It's a..." he hesitated and rethought his response. "Taking a growler is another way of saying you're going to the restroom."

Franklin giggled. "No." He shook his head. "I don't need to take a growler."

Oh hell. Way to go Sommers. Shell's gonna kill you.

"Are you sure?" he pressed.

"Yes." Franklin nodded earnestly. "It's gone now."

"Okay, then I'm gonna go see what your mom's up to."

"Okay." The kid said, then set about beating the hell out of the snake he'd just finished perfecting.

Little boys. Ya just gotta love 'em...

Jake quietly climbed the stairs and followed the sound of soft music to Shell's open bedroom door. Leaning against the jamb, he tilted his head and watched as she sat at her vanity in the same pink robe she'd been wearing last night, brushing her long, lustrous hair.

He remembered what it was like to run his fingers through all that living silk, what it was like to pull the fastener from her ponytail and let it spill into his hands. He had a very vivid fantasy about holding on to all that luscious, dark hair with both fists while she was on her knees in front of him, her gorgeous mouth—

Fuck a duck! Get your head in the game, Sommers! And remember the promise you made just last night.

"You don't have to go to all this trouble for me and Franklin," he finally managed, not surprised when his voice sounded like he'd been swallowing glass, all rough and breathless.

She leaned in to swipe mascara over her long, curled lashes, doing that whole open-mouth thing that women do. The one guaranteed to drive every hetero man in the world absolutely batty. The one that once more had him envisioning her down on her knees…

Dude, and *now* he had to adjust his stance or do himself harm.

"I'm not doing this for you and Franklin," she told him. "I'm doing this for Chris."

Everything inside him stilled, the warm glow he'd been feeling chilled in an instant and the wood he'd been sporting shriveled like a popped birthday balloon.

"Who the fu—" he caught himself before he let loose with the granddaddy of curse words. Franklin had ears like a cat. Taking a breath, he tried again, "Who the heck is Chris?"

"Dr. Christopher Drummond. He's my date tonight."

Okay, and the fucker, yes *fucker—fuck, fuck, fuck!*— obviously had a death wish.

"You said you weren't seeing anyone," he growled.

"No." She spun on her stool and stood, hands on hips, three-inch pumps making her look like a Amazonian goddess in a thin satin robe. All that was missing was a strand of pearls around her neck, a metal breast plate, and a spear for each hand. And when she loosened the belt and started walking toward him? *Good grief*, he nearly swallowed his tongue. "That's what *you* said. I just said it was none of your business."

Fortunately, she was dressed under that robe. He might've had a coronary on the spot if she wasn't. Quite a few of his favorite daydreams involved her in a pair of heels…and nothing else.

Unfortunately, what she had on didn't leave much to the imagination. The gathered silk of the little black dress clung to her like a second skin, and the sight of her rated a perfect 10 on his curve-o-meter.

The woman was straight-up slammin'! Jessica Rabbit in the flesh.

"Since you're here, can you help me with my zipper?" She presented him with her smooth back as she let the robe droop around her elbows. He could see her bra strap between the halves of her dress.

It was black.

And lacy.

And now he was determined to kill whoever this Doctor Chris was before the asshole got the chance to see her in it.

Yup. Death. That's what awaited the good doctor, the poor, clueless sonofabitch.

"I can't believe you're going on a date after what happened between us last night," he said, clenching his hands at his sides lest he be tempted to use them, not to zip her up, but to reach inside her dress to run them over all that pale, warm skin.

"Nothing happened between us last night but a couple of kisses, Jake."

"It wasn't nothing, and you know it," he grumbled, trying and failing to rein in his temper. A red haze edged his vision. "I may have called a truce for the time being on any sort of physical contact between us, but that doesn't mean the heat isn't there. Try to deny it."

"Deny it?" She glanced over her shoulder, her profile a work of art, as beautiful as a perfect breaking wave. "Why would I deny it?"

He lifted his chin and some of his tension slid away at her easy acknowledgment. Okay, so at least they could agree on one thing. It was a start.

"But it's just chemistry," she continued, "a biological compatibility." Yeah, okay, that's what he'd been thinking not ten minutes ago. "But if *chemistry* was the only thing needed to make a relationship work, everyone would be in a relationship, and the divorce rate would be a tenth of what it is."

"What about love?"

"You don't love me. Not really."

Damnit. That was it!

He grabbed her shoulders and spun her, causing her hair to whip across his face and the smell of vanilla to tunnel up his nose until he had to grind his jaw to remember his promise and to keep from shoving her back against the wall, engage in a little repeat of that scene in the Clover Bar and Grill.

Only this time, he wouldn't stop…

"Don't you tell me how I feel," he hissed, his nose barely an inch from hers. Her dove-gray eyes were wide and unblinking, and her plump lips, which she'd slathered in berry-red lipstick, parted in a little gasp.

His gaze slid down to her mouth and the flash of tongue inside.

Sonofabitch! He almost lost it. Almost threw his promise right out the window and pressed his lips to hers.

"I'm sorry," she said, pulling out of his grasp. It took everything he had to release her. "I'm not trying to upset you. I swear I'm not. It's just that I don't believe you, Jake. I think you've confused lust with love."

Um…*ouch!* And that hurt worse than her assertion that she didn't love him, that maybe she'd never loved him. Because he'd known when she said those things she was lying. Shell wasn't a very good actress. She couldn't hide her feelings the way most women could. They were always right there, sitting on her sleeve and waving around at everyone passing by.

She *had* loved him once upon a time. So even though it'd stung—oh, buddy, how it'd stung—when she tried to contend otherwise, it hadn't hurt nearly as badly as having her throw his profession of love back in his face.

Because he could tell by looking at her now, she wholeheartedly believed what she was saying.

She *didn't* believe he loved her.

God*damn*it!

"And this Dr. Chris?" He ground his jaws together so hard it was a wonder he didn't break a tooth. "Do you love him?"

If she said yes, he didn't know what he'd do. No matter how satisfying the series of pictures that flashed through his brain, no matter how much he might like to, killing the good doctor was out of the question.

Although, in theory—

"Not yet," she said, and his heart was able to beat again. "But given time, I could I suppose. But what does that matter? I don't need to love a guy to go on a date with him."

Uh-huh. And now for the next important question. There was that whole lizard brain thing to contend with after all. "So, do you lust for him?"

"No! I just—"

"Then what's the goddamned point?" he demanded, wincing and stepping farther into the room when the curse reverberated around the hallway. "You don't love him and you don't lust for him, so there's nothing to build on."

"Would you listen to yourself? To what you're actually saying?" she demanded, her eyes hot though her expression was still sad. Sad and a little desperate. "Of *course* there's something to build on. There's stability and consistency and reliability and—"

"You've got to kidding me!" He threw his hands in the air. "Those are the reasons you choose a car, not a husband!"

"Oh, for goodness sakes! We're not animals! We crawled out of the jungle a long time ago, and no longer choose mates based solely by their muscle mass or how well they fight. Now, we have the ability to use that big round thing that sits on our shoulders and make an intellectual decision about who we want to spend the rest of our lives with."

"*That's* why you want to go out with this doctor guy? Because he stimulates you *intellectually*?"

"Yes!" she nodded, her pulse hammering at the

base of her throat. "I'm not like you." *Or my father*. She didn't have to say the words; they were written all over her face, and he felt ready to pop an aneurism. "I don't base my relationships on the thrill of the moment, because it doesn't last. It burns bright for a while, then it fizzles out. I want something more than that, Jake."

He opened his mouth to tell her, yet again, that *he* wanted more than that too, but she cut him off.

"We're done talking about this." She sliced a hand through the air—at some point she'd painted her nails bright red—and now he was growling in earnest, so much like the jungle animal he was supposed to have evolved past. Because he knew what that particular color meant. Boss always referred to it as screw-me-cross-eyed red.

"You're not going," he said, crossing his arms over his chest, surprised there wasn't steam pouring from his nostrils.

"You can't stop me," she insisted, an angry flush climbing up her throat into her cheeks, making her all the more beautiful.

Fierce and beautiful.

And no way was he letting her go out with some ass-hat of a doctor looking like that.

"Wanna bet?" he smirked, reaching for his phone. "How 'bout I make a little call to your brother. Tell him your plans. See what he has to say about you toddling off, unprotected, with this stable, reliable, consistent doctor while I stay here keeping an eye on Franklin. Have you forgotten that there may be some really nasty characters out there ready and willing to put a bullet in your brain? Because I bet Boss hasn't."

"You yourself said the risks to me and my son are

small. But even so, I *don't* intend for you to stay here watching Franklin while I," she rolled her eyes and made the quote marks with her fingers, "*toddle* off alone with Chris."

"Huh?"

"Well, what I mean is you can if you want. It's your choice."

"What the hell are you talking about, woman?" His head threatened to explode right off his shoulders, but only after his scorching ears exploded right off the sides of his head.

"Frank should be here soon, and it's up to you whether you want to stay here babysitting Franklin, or whether you want to follow me on my date. He'll fill in whichever position you don't."

"Boss *knows* about this harebrained scheme?" he asked in disbelief.

What the hell happened to, *I'll do what I can to help you with Shell?*

Because if Boss's idea of *helping* him with Shell was endorsing her idea to go out with some fancy-schmancy doctor, Jake sure as shit didn't want see what the guy's version of *hindering* him would be.

"It's not a scheme. It's a date. And, yes, he knows. And he's…" The doorbell sounded, a trilling call of three separate notes that reverberated around Jake's head like a funeral dirge. "…right on time," she finished.

He stalked to the top of the stairs as Boss pushed through the front door, easily catching Franklin who jumped off the back of the sofa straight into his good arm.

When Boss glanced up, Jake sent him a look that succinctly conveyed, *Yo! What the hell, dude?*

Boss shook his head, wincing.

Jake jogged down the stairs and pinned his former CO with a hard stare.

"I swear I tried to talk her out of it, man," Boss said. "But she's my sister, not a prisoner. I can't force her to do anything. But that doesn't mean I'm not still on your side. This is just a little hiccup."

Great. Frickin' great. Obviously, there'll be no help from that quarter.

Growling, Jake stomped back up the stairs and straight into Shell's bedroom. Her expression was tight, but she took a deep breath and once more presented him with her bare back.

"Now, would you please zip me up?" she asked, her voice strained.

He considered doing the opposite of what she suggested and pulling that damned dress off her shoulders and down over her hips. He'd show her just exactly what *lust* could bring to the table.

Of course, he couldn't be that crude. He couldn't act like the animal she'd basically already accused him of being. And there was that promise he'd made to her last night…

Still, that didn't mean he couldn't exact a little revenge. Because he was done being Mr. Nice Guy. He'd tried apologizing, and she'd brushed him off. He'd told her he loved her, and she'd thrown his declaration back in his face.

Now the gloves were coming off.

She wanted war?

Oh, he could give her war…

Slowly, ever so slowly, he pulled the tab on the

zipper up, dragging the rough edges of his fingers along her smooth skin all along the way.

He was rewarded with the feel of goose bumps pebbling beneath his fingers.

"What are you doing?" she gasped.

"Just what you asked me to do," he rumbled lowly, stepping close so that she could feel the heat from his body. When he reached the top of the zipper, he brushed her hair over her shoulder, softly skimming the callused pad of his thumb along her neck as he fastened the little eyehook. "There," he leaned in until his breath feathered her cheek. "All zipped up."

Her shiver had a smile pulling at the corners of his mouth.

Uh-huh. He'd definitely tapped into her lizard brain. There was no mistaking that telltale flush on her cheeks or the way her breath hitched.

He knew he was pushing the bounds of his promise. And he planned to push it just a little further...

"And, Shell?" He pressed up against her, butt to nuts in military speak. Only it was a shame to refer to a thing of beauty such as Shell's ass so irreverently.

"H-huh?"

"I *do* love you whether you believe me or not. And not only that," he put a hand on her hip and tucked her more tightly against the erection that inexplicably sprung up anytime he got within three feet of her. "I *lust* for you, as well. And those are the two things *I* think it takes to make a relationship work. You remember that while you're out with this stable, reliable, consistent doctor tonight."

Chapter Nine

THE COUPLE WHO WAS CHECKED IN NEXT DOOR WASN'T screwing like the previous pair; they were fighting.

Johnny preferred the screwing.

At least then he wouldn't have to listen to the woman harp on the guy.

He was two seconds from banging on the wall above his headboard and screaming, *Yes, he screwed Dolores! And he probably did it to get away from your shrew-y, more-annoying-than-Fran Drescher voice!*

And just as he pushed up to his knees and raised a fist, a knock at his door had his head whipping around.

What the hell?

No one knew he was here, save Mary. And she wouldn't step one dainty, pampered foot in this shit-hole hotel, much less deign to ride the creaky elevator up six floors.

"Who is it?" he barked, quietly reaching for the gun he kept on the nightstand.

"You got a delivery," a nasally, disembodied voice drifted through the flimsy metal door.

"You must have the wrong room, man. I ain't expecting no deliveries."

"Are you Mr. Vitiglioni?"

Sonofabitch!

He'd checked in under an alias so…yeah, he slid the safety off on his Ruger.

"Who's it from?" he demanded, carefully climbing off the bed, wincing when the lumpy mattress squeaked out a protest.

"Hey, man," the guy complained through the door, "I ain't your secretary. I just do deliveries."

"Leave it," he commanded, inching his way across the room, his pistol held out in front of him.

"Are you Mr. Vitiglioni?"

He wrenched open the door and pointed the scary end of his Ruger at a bulbous nose situated prominently on a round, acne-scarred face. The delivery man was short, pudgy, and more than a bit careless about personal hygiene if his greasy skin and greasier hair were anything to go by.

"Whoa!" the guy's chubby hands flew in the air, and the overnight package dropped to the hallway floor with a muted thud. "Jesus, man! Chill!"

"Who told you I was here?" he snarled, shoving the Ruger's barrel closer to the man's ugly face.

"No one!" the dude swore as his wide, bloodshot eyes slowly filled with tears. "It's right there on the shipping label."

Johnny glanced down and…sure enough. There was his name in big, bold letters along with the address of the Stardust Hotel and his room number.

What the hell, what the hell*?*

He glanced down the hall in each direction before leaning in close to the delivery man, ignoring the smell of mustard and onions on the guy's breath. "You tell anybody about this," he looked at the nametag sewn into the brown uniform, "*Rudy*, and I'll find you and slit your throat. Then I'll pull your bloated, purple tongue down through the cut I made and watch you bleed out. You got that? Nod once if you got that?"

Rudy nodded once, a lone tear spilling down his shiny, pock-marked cheek.

"Good," Johnny shoved him away and watched him stumble before scrambling toward the elevator. The doors opened with a sickly sounding *ping-pong*, and Rudy jumped inside, cowering in the back corner.

Johnny winked and pointed his gun straight at Rudy's greasy head as the silver doors slid shut. A terrified groan slipped down the hall, and Johnny couldn't help but smile.

He loved that sound. The sound of fear. It was a thing of joy to hear, and he supposed it affected him much the same way a church choir affected others.

He peered down at the package, and once more scanned the hall in each direction before bending to retrieve it. Quickly backing into his room, he locked the door and strode toward the bed. After depositing the package on the faded comforter, he stared at it for long moments.

From Mary?

That's the only thing that made any sense, but would she be stupid enough to send him a package with his *real* name on it considering she knew what he was in Chicago to do?

If so, he was tempted to kill *her* instead of the Black Knights' families. The stupid bitch...

For a moment he considered not opening it. What could she have possibly sent that he'd want to see anyway?

Nothing, that's what. Absolutely nothing.

Then again...

"Oh, what the hell," he grumbled, reaching down to rip it open. He frowned when a thick, brown, accordion-style file folder appeared. With a hesitant hand, he untied the string holding it secure and carefully peeked inside.

"Huh?" His frown deepened as he pulled out a glossy photo. It showed Michelle Carter and her son laughing together at a playground. He dug deeper into the file. More photos. More papers listing names and addresses. More newspaper clippings showing—

Wait.

Names and addresses?

He thumbed back to a previous page and squinted at the typed list. Some of those names sounded familiar. Sykes, McMillan, Weller...

And then it hit him. Those were the last names of the Black Knights. But these photos weren't of the Knights. These were women and children. Young men. Elderly couples and—

Relatives.

This package was from the PI he'd hired, the same PI who wasn't supposed to know where he was.

"You're even better than you led me to believe," he murmured into the silence of the room, impressed by the private investigator's resourcefulness while at the same time a little peeved to have his hiding place discovered.

The PI was obviously letting Johnny know that he wasn't without a certain set of skills. Not so subtly informing Johnny that should Johnny attempt to come after him, you know, just to tie up that last string—which *had* been Johnny's plan from the beginning—he knew exactly where Johnny was and would see him coming from a mile away.

Okay, Johnny could respect that.

The PI would live. For now.

Shoving everything but the picture of Michelle back into the file, he ran a finger over her photographed face.

He'd begin dealing with the Knights *other* relatives tomorrow, because tonight he had big plans for Michelle...

~~~

"Hey! What are you doing?" Michelle demanded when a strong arm wound around her waist, dragging her back from the taxi she was about to step into.

"My job." Jake's voice sounded close to her ear. "Acting as your bullet catcher. So, you're coming with me."

"You can act as my bullet catcher by following at a safe distance. Just like you've been doing all night." And, boy, hadn't that been fun? Glancing in the rearview mirror of Chris Drummond's BMW and seeing Jake behind them, looking mean and menacing sitting on the back of his motorcycle, and too, *too* sexy for words in that thick leather jacket? Not to mention the grumbling roar of his monster bike had made it impossible for her to concentrate on anything Chris said...

Now, she slapped at Jake's arm until he released her, spinning to face him. The chill wind whipping in off Lake Michigan grabbed the flimsy shawl she'd draped over her shoulders and whipped it away. He snatched it before it could fly up into the vortex of air created by the towering skyscrapers and wrapped it tightly around her back, pulling her close to his chest in the process.

"Where'd the good doctor go?" he asked quietly, intimately. His breath smelled crisp, like the lime-flavored seltzer water he'd been drinking at the bar in the upscale

Spanish restaurant while keeping an ever-watchful eye on her and her date.

Her date.

What a joke.

It'd been the evening from hell, and she couldn't say she was sorry it was ending so soon.

Oh, not that Chris Drummond was a jerk or anything. If fact, he was a very nice guy. An exceedingly boring, eye-crossingly somber, nice guy. As he spoke quite elegantly over dinner about his family, his charity work, and his patients, she couldn't help but let her eyes wander over to the bar where Jake sat.

All vigilant and threatening and in no way boring.

And all she'd been able to think was, *I'm doomed.*

Here I am. Out with a handsome, stable, well-to-do man, and I can barely keep from falling face first into my Paella or else running over and jumping on the lap of the cad sitting at the bar.

There was obviously something really wrong with her.

Because even though she *knew* that a smart woman would look at Dr. Drummond and start salivating over what a fantastic catch he was, even though she *knew* he was exactly the type of man she should want, the exact opposite of her father and Jake, she couldn't help but glance across the table at his handsome face, perfect teeth, polite conversation and think…

Borrrring.

Where was the drama? The passion? The fire? The romance?

It was at that point in her spinning thoughts when she'd inevitably glance over at Jake and come back to the whole *I'm doomed* thread. Because *there* was the drama and passion and fire and romance. Right there. Sitting at the bar in biker boots, another stupid Hawaiian shirt, and a pair of jeans that made the temperature in the restaurant jump ten degrees.

Every other man in the place was dressed in designer suits that probably cost more than one of her mortgage payments, and *still* Jake managed to outshine them.

How was that possible?

Or maybe it was just her. Maybe she had some sort of strange weakness when it came to the allure of a rough-and-ready alpha male, otherwise known primarily as Mr. Jerkwad. Maybe it was some deep-seated psychosis brought on by her father's abandonment. Some sort of twisted, perverse Electra complex.

Yep. It's official folks. I'm a total head case.

Because her big plan to prove to Jake that things were really, *truly* over between them by holding up another man as comparison—a smart, handsome, professional man whom he couldn't hope to compete with—had blown up in her face like an overcooked microwave dinner.

Bam!

Doomed. That's all there was to it.

She was *such* a fool…

"The hospital called Chris in," she told Jake now, squirming against his embrace, but that only made him hold her tighter and her pulse, never steady around him, slammed into overdrive when her hardened nipples brushed his chest.

"Quite a guy you got there," he said, a sardonic grin tipping his lips, his eyes flashing in the lights of the passing cars. The city was a cacophony of noises around them, but all she heard was his low, sexy voice. "Leaving you to finish dessert by yourself."

"He had an emergency surgery, you big dolt!" she hissed, then realized she still might be able to salvage this evening and its initial intent. Ignoring the feel of him against her, so large and strong, she smiled and fluttered her lashes. "Oh, did I fail to mention Chris is a surgeon?"

A terribly boring surgeon who any sane girl with half a brain would kill to have. *Ugh!*

"Yo, I don't give a flying fuck if he's the goddamned president of the United States," he growled, pulling her closer until the heat from his big body surrounded her, inexplicably causing goose bumps to burst over her skin. "That doesn't change the fact that you were bored to death."

Had it been that obvious?

Yep, clearly it had been. *Dangit!*

"Fine," she conceded since there was no use in denying it. He'd see her lie for what it was. "I'll give you that but—"

"So, if you did this just to make me jealous, sweetheart," he leaned in close, his nose nearly touching hers, "it worked."

"I didn't do it make you jealous!" She jerked out of his embrace and immediately lamented the move when the cool wind whipped around her. "I did it to prove to you, once and for all, that what we had is over."

"Yeah?" he asked, one brow raised sardonically. She was overcome with the urge to wipe the smirk from his face by smacking him upside the head with her handbag. "And how'd that work out?"

"Oh, what does it matter?" She wrapped her shawl tightly around her shoulders and took a step toward the curb and the waiting taxi. This night couldn't end soon enough. "The date is over. I'm going home."

"Not yet." He grabbed her arm and started herding her down the sidewalk. Pedestrians instinctively gave way to him and female heads turned to watch him walk by. *Ugh!*

"What do you mean?" she demanded, yanking on her arm, but he refused to release her.

"I mean, right now you're coming with me."

When they stopped beside his motorcycle, parked at an angle on the side of the street, she was finally able to wrench her arm from his grasp.

"I'm not riding that," she declared, her tone leaving no room for argument. "For one thing, it's forty-five degrees out here. And for another, I'm wearing a dress."

By way of answer, he shrugged out of his thick motorcycle jacket and slung it around her shoulders. The heat from his body was caught in the leather along with his warm, clean, beachy smell.

God, help me. Her entire body tightened in response.

"The skirt you can hike up until we get there," he said, handing her the helmet he'd draped over a set of sparkling, chrome handlebars.

"I will not!" she huffed. "Even if it wouldn't be nearly indecent, I can't travel twenty blocks up to Lincoln Park. I'll freeze to death before we get there."

"We're not going to Lincoln Park. We're only going as far as Michigan Avenue."

"Michigan Avenue? What's on Michigan Avenue?" she asked, eyeing the smooth way he swung a leg over the menacing-looking bike. With its reptilian paint job, studded black leather detailing, chrome exhaust, and vicious, serpent-inspired rims, the motorcycle looked like something you'd see in a fantasy magazine, not something you'd actually *ride*.

"You'll see," he told her, scooting up on the seat to give her room.

As if she was really going to mount up behind him. The guy had a wild imagination; she'd give him that.

"I told you I'm not going."

"You'll go even if I have to pick you up and set you on the back of Viper myself."

Viper? It had a name?

Of course it did. Men named *everything*.

"I'd like to see you try," she crossed her arms. The move was a bit awkward given she was still holding his helmet. "I'm nearly six feet tall. I weigh a lot more than you think."

A sudden gleam entered his eyes that had her catching her breath. "I didn't seem to have any problem holding you up against that wall inside the Clover." Oh my God! Why did he have to bring that up? Now, she fought the urge to cry. "I figure I'll manage just fine now." He turned his head to the side and lifted a brow. "Or do you need me to prove it?"

"This is ridiculous." She shoved the helmet at him, blinking back sudden tears. "I'm hailing a cab and going home."

"Get. On. The. Bike. Shell," he grumbled, dipping his chin, glaring at her out from under his sandy brows.

"Get bent, Jake," she choked, hoping he mistook her anguish for anger.

"Okay," he sighed, swinging from the back of the bike. "You asked for it."

He lifted her into his arms as if she weighed nothing.

"Hey!" she squawked, her tears vanishing as she smacked him repeatedly with her beaded clutch. "Put me down, you big jerk!"

Unfortunately, he did as she requested. Only when she landed, inexplicably she was astride the big motorcycle. Before she could hop off, he plopped the helmet on her head, swung onto the bike in front of her, and started it.

Viper came to life with a guttural roar and a chest-shaking vibration. And before she could squeak another word of protest, he gunned it.

―――――

They were being followed.

Sitting at a stoplight, Jake glanced into Viper's rear-view mirror at the leather-clad man on the motorcycle who was idling two measly cars behind them. The dude had shadowed their every move for the last two blocks, and Jake was going to make for damned sure that behavior ended.

Now.

A burst of welcome adrenaline burned through his veins as he glanced right and left, gauging the cross traffic.

"Hang on," he gruffly commanded over his shoulder. As soon as he felt Shell's arms tighten around his waist, he punched it.

Viper roared through the intersection, the cycle's fat rear tire leaving acrid-smelling rubber in its wake along with the sounds of angry honking and Shell's shrill squawk of surprise. Blazing down the street like a bat out of hell, he spied a dark alley and quickly hooked a right, darting inside.

"What in the world?" Shell demanded when he toed out Viper's kickstand and swung off the bike. His boots were barely on the ground before he was bodily lifting her from motorcycle and carting her toward a rusted-out blue and white dumpster.

"We've got company," he explained, dropping her to her feet on the dirty concrete behind the dumpster as he bent and retrieved the Kel-Tec from his ankle holster. Pressing it into her hand, he tried not to die a little bit at the spark of fear that instantly lighted her eyes when she pushed up the visor on his helmet.

God, I hate this…

This fucker, whoever he was, was a dead man. Because no one was allowed to scare Shell, threaten Shell, and live to tell about it. The mere thought spiked his adrenaline to the next level.

"Who—"

"Dunno. I can't see anything under his helmet and visor. Do you know how to use this one? It's a little different from the one you have at home," he said, drawing her attention to the silver pistol in her hand.

"Y-yes," she breathed, her chest rapidly rising and falling. "Frank makes sure I get to the gun range twice a month, and he's tested me on multiple sidearms. This is a Kel-Tec, right?"

"Yeah," he confirmed, checking his clip. "So if this asshole somehow gets the best of me—" Her eyes flew wide. "He won't," he assured her. "Remember how I

told you I'd never let anything bad happen to you?" She
nodded. "Well, I meant it. But if hell suddenly freezes
over and the sky falls down and this guy somehow *does*
happen to best me, you plug him with this. And don't
shoot him just once. I want you to unload the clip into
him, you got that?"

She swallowed jerkily but nodded all the same.

And he couldn't help himself.

He leaned in and smacked a quick, hard kiss on her
fabulous lips before turning and hustling back to the
alley's entrance. Pressing his back against the brick
building, he pulled the Glock from his waistband, chambered a round, and waited.

He didn't have long to wait. The vibrating growl of a
V-twin engine sounded out in the street, and a second later
the front tire of a custom Harley rolled into the alley. Jake
held his breath, focused everything on his next move, and
felt his muscles bunch in hungry anticipation of action.

And then, like always, everything slowed.

A motorcycle boot appeared, followed by a jean-clad
leg that led up to a thick, black motorcycle jacket. The
sight of the black helmet was all Jake had been waiting
on. It was his green light to *go!*

He hooked an arm around the dude's neck, instantly
clothes-lining him and dragging him from the bike. The
motorcycle, now absent a driver, rolled a few feet before
teetering precariously and crashing to the alley floor
with a loud *bang!*

Smashing the cyclist's back against the building, Jake
shoved his forearm up under their would-be assailant's
chin and used his other hand to shove the barrel of his
Glock straight into the guy's gut.

"Who are you?" he demanded in a low roar, feeling for the second time in as many days the sharp teeth of the monster inside him. The thing was gnawing on his backbone, begging to be free.

The dude lifted his hands, and Jake told himself that if the asshole reached for anything other than his helmet, he was going to light him up with lead. As it was, his finger twitched on the trigger.

"Goddamn, man!" the guy said as he pushed off his helmet and let it fall to the ground with an echoing crack. "I…I just wanted to get a look at that paint job. It…it's totally cherry and—"

"Sonofabitch!" Jake cursed. The kid, yes *kid*—if the fool was over twenty, Jake would eat his shorts—was nothing more than a motorcycle enthusiast. But just to make sure, Jake patted him down. Once he'd assure himself the guy wasn't packing, he straightened and shoved his Glock back into his waistband.

"Sorry," he told the kid as he turned to right the motorcycle. "I thought you were someone else."

"Damn, man. Damn!" The kid panted over and over again.

Jake pushed the guy's bike up beside him and bent to hand him his helmet. The poor bastard's hands were shaking so bad he could barely take it.

"Look," Jake told him. "This was a mistake." He opened his wallet and withdrew a handful of benjamins. "Here's some green to take care of any damage to your bike's paint."

The kid looked at the money like it might be poison. Jake rolled his eyes and shoved it into the front pocket of the young man's motorcycle jacket. "Now, get outta here," he commanded.

And, yo, the dude didn't need to be told twice. He immediately pushed the start button on his handlebars and whimpered when the Harley only coughed. Jake rolled in his lips and prayed for patience. The kid tried again, and this time the bike came to life.

Jake watched him peel out of the alley and turned back toward the dumpster, shaking his head.

What a goatscrew…

—∙∙∙—

Okay, and now it's official. I'm doomed…

Because watching Jake get physical and rough up that guy should've turned Michelle's stomach. And it did, just not in the way it was supposed to…

Because instead of feeling sick at the near violence, her belly felt like it'd been on a roller coaster of delight, and she couldn't help but think how unbelievably sexy he was.

Crap, crap, crap!

"What was that all about?" she asked as she emerged from behind the dumpster, thumbing the safety back on the little pistol.

"Two cats and now a motorcycle fanatic," Jake muttered, shaking his head. "But I guess it's better to have false alarms than actual threats."

"A motorcycle enthusiast?" she asked, incredulous. *"That's* who was following us?"

"Yeah." Jake ran a hand through his hair as he took the pistol from her and returned it to his ankle holster. Straightening, he swung onto Viper and motioned with his chin that she should mount up behind him.

"I think I've had about all the excitement I can stand

for one night," she told him, crossing her arms inside his thick motorcycle jacket, trying to ignore the smell lingering in the leather. "I'm going to hail a cab."

"Really?" The look he gave her would've curdled milk. "We're going to go through this again?"

"Jake—"

"Just get on the damned bike, Shell. I'm not in the mood to argue."

He wasn't in the mood to argue? *He* wasn't in the mood to—

"Fine," she spat. Because, truth be known, she wasn't in the mood to argue either, especially knowing it'd only end with him forcefully lifting her and setting her on the bike again.

And when her thighs tightened around his hips and her arms slid around his waist, she tried very hard to remember all the reasons why she couldn't just allow herself to love him. Then he glanced over her shoulder, grinning an *I won* grin that deepened his dimples, and all she could think was...*I'm doomed...*

Chapter Ten

"OH NO. NO WAY."

Jake smiled at the touch of hysteria in Shell's voice when he cut the engine, pulled off his helmet, and toed out Viper's kickstand.

"I'm n-not going inside with you," she sputtered. "Not inside a *hotel*. You must think I'm crazy!"

"What?" He grinned at her over his shoulder, loving the way the too-large helmet pressed her hair down over her eyes and the way she kept blowing at it. "You know I'm a man of my word. I promised you no shenanigans, so there'll be no shenanigans. Unless you're worried *you* won't be able to keep your hands off *me* once you have me all alone in a room?"

"In your dreams."

"You have no idea," he grumbled, swinging from the bike.

"Huh?"

"Nothing." He extended a hand. "Come on. Up you go."

"I said no." She crossed her arms mutinously, and the sight of her, swathed in his thick jacket, hair all in her eyes, bare, mile-long legs straddling Viper's seat, was almost enough to have him rethinking this entire idea.

He hadn't brought her here to seduce her. He'd brought her here so they could talk. Just talk. Without the ever-hovering specter of interruption by a three-year-old boy.

And yeah, he supposed he could've taken her to a quiet spot for a drink, but then he'd be watching the door and the other patrons, constantly surveying his surroundings, scanning for threats. And he didn't want to do that. Nope. He wanted to give Shell 100 percent of his attention. Because there were so many things he needed to say. Things he needed her to understand.

"*What* are you staring at?" she demanded, reaching up to remove the helmet and shake her hair loose. The move was unconsciously sexy and despite his intentions to the contrary, his dick perked up at the sight—the thing never did pay any attention to his intentions.

"I'm staring at the most beautiful woman in the world," he said, letting his eyes wander down the incredible length of her legs again.

She rolled her lovely eyes, pursing her lips until he wanted nothing more than to nibble on them right before he reached under that tiny skirt and—

Christ, Sommers, you better check that right here, right now. That's not why you brought her here.

"Come on, let's get inside where it's warm."

"No!"

"Shell, I just want to talk to you. Scout's honor."

"You weren't a Boy Scout," she scoffed.

"Of course I was."

"Oh come on, Jake! I wasn't born yesterday. A man doesn't rent a hotel room just to *talk* to a woman."

"I rented this hotel room as soon as I got into town two days ago, before I knew I'd be staying at your house. If you don't believe me, you can check at the reception desk. But first, you'll have to get off the bike."

"I said no!"

He got the distinct impression she would've stomped her foot if she'd been standing. Funny, he'd actually like to see that.

"Uh-huh," he took a page from her book and rolled his eyes. "And remember what happened the last time you said *no*? Do you need me to throw you over my shoulder again and haul your sweet ass inside?"

The look she shot him should've dropped him like a dumping wave. Instead, he crossed his arms, raised a brow, and waited.

Shell was a smart girl. She knew when she was beaten.

"Fine," she spat for the second time in fifteen minutes, swinging one bare leg over Viper's seat and— *sonofabitch!*—the woman had the best damned gams on the planet.

But that isn't why you brought her here!

Uh-huh. Tell that to Mr. Chubby in my pants…

"I'm giving you fifteen minutes." She wiggled her short skirt down her magnificent thighs, and he nearly went cross-eyed. She had the ability to rev him up like no other. "After that, I'm calling a cab and going home to relieve Frank from babysitting duty."

He followed her to the elevators, only letting his eyes drop down to watch the swing of her ass once.

Okay, twice.

So sue him. Along with a killer pair of legs, the woman had a great ass. He was entitled to give it its due.

He expected her to continue to put up some sort of token resistance. But on the ride to the lobby, they were silent. On the walk through the lobby to the main set of elevators, they were silent. Up to the seventh floor, they were silent. Down the long hall leading to his room…

Yup. Silent.

It wasn't until he inserted his keycard that she spoke up. "Nope. I'm not going inside with you. We can talk right here in the hall. It's private enough."

And there it was. He knew she'd been making it too easy on him.

Wrapping an arm around her shoulders to keep her from bolting, he dragged her into his hotel room.

"Hey! Hands off!" she grouched as he marched her toward the bed. When she saw the direction he was heading, she started backpedaling like he was threatening to throw her headfirst into a volcano.

"Oh, for crying out loud, Shell!" He gently but forcefully pushed her down on the mattress before angrily stalking to the chair shoved beneath the writing desk in the corner. " Just sit there, and let me say what I have to say."

Dragging the chair toward the bed, he swung it around backward and straddled the seat. For a long time, he let his eyes wander over her flushed face, cataloging the features he'd fallen in love with the first time he laid eyes on her.

"Well?" she finally asked, squirming uncomfortably beneath his careful regard. "You got me up here to talk. So talk."

—✺—

"I want to finish telling you about the barracks bombing."

Oh, crap.

And that was the *one* thing guaranteed to have Michelle folding her hands in her lap and squashing the urge to run.

Because what had she said she was supposed to do when a fighting man wanted to talk?

Oh, yeah. She was supposed to listen.

Heaven help me…

When he spoke of such things, she had to fight to remember that he was a womanizer like her father, to remember his callous rejection, his abandonment, the years he'd ignored her plea to return to them, to *her*. When he talked about such things, she had fight to remember he wasn't just a wounded soldier, a warrior who'd experienced enough horror and pain to last a lifetime. She had to fight to remember that he was *Jake*, and that the last thing she should do is trust him…

"Where did I stop last night before we were interrupted?" he asked.

Body parts. He'd talked about body parts.

"The crater left behind and the…uh," she swallowed, "the…bodies of the Marines h-hanging from the trees."

"Yeah." He nodded, and she watched the thick column of his throat work over a hard swallow. "We dug in the rubble for two days. But there were no survivors. Not one. And it was at that moment, after forty-eight hours of sorting body parts and tearing my hands to shreds sifting through broken concrete blocks, that I started to hate them. And when I say *them*, I mean *all* of them. All those backward, medieval-thinking motherfuckers and their misplaced fervor and furor. I hated the way they talked, the way they walked and looked and smelled. I wanted to wipe every last one of them from the face of the planet once and for all."

She nodded in sympathy, trying to imagine anyone witnessing the level of carnage created by that barracks bombing not coming away from it with a heart full of bitterness and rage. One hot, mutinous tear slid down her cheek as the sangria she'd had with dinner turned to vinegar in her stomach.

"Before the bombing, I'd been philosophical about killing the enemy," he explained, briefly scanning her face before once more focusing on his hands, clenched into fists on the back of the chair. "I cut them down, because I was ordered to cut them down and because to allow them to remain alive posed a threat to everything and everyone I loved. But after the bombing," he shook his head, his sun-bleached hair falling over his forehead reminding her of those times she'd run her fingers through it, "something evil and insidious sank its poisoned fingers into my soul, and I started to hate. I hated until I couldn't think of anything else. A few weeks later, four of us were on patrol in the hills, and that hate found an opportunity to manifest itself. You see, we were tasked with questioning the locals about their knowledge of the events surrounding the blast."

She swallowed, lifting a brow.

"I don't know how many people we questioned. Hundreds probably. And, of course, everyone claimed to have zero knowledge of what happened. It was so fucking frustrating. Then one day we came upon a group of men. They were sitting next to this little mud brick house having some kind of meeting. They, too, swore they didn't know anything about the bombing, but their eyes told a different story. Then, when we searched their house, we found news articles about the bombings, framed like goddamned trophies. And I knew then and there that even if they weren't part of the actual bombing—which, as it turns out, they weren't—they were the kind of men who wouldn't hesitate to pick up an AK-47 or RPG and use it against coalition forces. Over there, you get where you can spot a fanatic from a mile away. And these guys…" he shook his head, "…these guys were fanatics with a capital F."

He paused for a beat, seeming to gather his thoughts before continuing. "They weren't armed. They made no moves of aggression toward us, but I took one look at them, at the malice in their faces, and remembered sorting through all those bodies and I…I was absolutely livid. My skin actually itched, like my hate was alive and burrowing just beneath my flesh. I pointed my weapon directly at the leader's skull. I was *this* close to killing him." He held this thumb and forefinger an inch apart. "Just putting a bullet in his brain. It shames me to admit how close I came to becoming a cold-blooded murderer that day."

She nodded and, for the umpteenth time since he'd suddenly *poofed* back into her life, resisted the urge to reach out and comfort him.

"You can't beat yourself up over something you *almost* did."

"Can't I?" His green gaze lasered in on her face, for the first time since this entire conversation began he was really looking at her. The effect was mesmerizing. Her stomach started spinning in circles like she'd tossed it in the dryer. "That incident scared me to death." At her surprised expression, bitterness contorted his face. "Yes, despite what you've been led to believe, SEALs get scared. Honest-to-goodness, pee-your-pants scared.

And that's what that day did for me. It scared me something wicked."

Once again, she beat back the urge to reach for him, curling her fingers into the bed's comforter as she nodded for him to continue.

"I can't describe what it's like to hold the power of death over a person," he admitted quietly, flexing his fingers and staring at his palms as if they belonged to someone else. "It's a heady thing that makes a man feel more godlike than he has any right to. What that day showed me was that the hate had grown in me and made me not only accustomed to that power, but *hungry* for it. I was turning into the kind of man I'd been sent there to exterminate—an indiscriminant killer."

"I don't think you'd have be—" she began to defend him, but he interrupted her.

"And it was that fear, that fear of becoming like the very men I'd come to hate, that played no small part in my decision on the side of the mountain the day Preacher died. I let that fear overrule my own good judgment, my judgment as a soldier, as a SEAL, as a part of a team. I didn't want to give in to the monster and, consequently, I made the wrong call."

"Frank told me about that day. Your orders were to—"

"Fuck my orders!" he growled. "It was *fear* that guided my decision that day. Then when we actually *needed* al-Masri, I let my anger overcome reason, and I shot him in the head. And you know what makes it all so much worse? The fact that I convinced Preacher to go along with me. From the beginning, his vote was to kill the guy and run like hell, but I talked him out of it because I'd lost my edge and was too damn scared of myself. And you know what that got him? It got him fucking killed!" His voice cracked, and he pressed his thumb and forefinger against the inside corners of his eyes.

Another hot tear escaped and coursed down her cheek. Followed by another. And another.

"That's the biggest thing I'm sorry for, Shell," he said hoarsely, refusing to look at her. "For being a coward who was more concerned with harnessing the monster growing inside him than in making the strategically sound decision. The decision that would've kept us all alive, kept *Preacher* alive. Because even though it killed me when you chose him over me, I'd still rather see you two happy, *together*, than know I'm the reason he's cold in the ground."

Oh, Steven. My sweet, sweet Steven.

And my poor, poor Jake…

"Jake," she reached out and touched his wrist. *Oh, you've gone and done it now.* Because the skin there was warm and vibrantly alive, prickly with man hair. It reminded her of what it was like to be crushed up against the length of him, to be held so tightly she couldn't tell which heartbeat was his and which heartbeat was hers. "I don't blame you for what happened to Steven. And you shouldn't blame yourself. No matter what you say, he made his own decision that day."

"But he'd still be alive if we'd killed al-Masri like he wanted to. You'd still have a husband, Franklin would still have his father, and I can't tell you how—"

"Jake," she squeezed his wrist, stopping him midsentence. "Maybe you'd *all* be dead if things had worked differently. Ever think of that? Maybe you'd have gotten pinned on the plateau and picked off one by one. The fact of the matter is, there's no way for you to know how things might have turned out. What you can be sure of is that you didn't do anything wrong."

No matter how much he'd hurt her, no matter how much his continued presence in her life threatened to hurt her still, she couldn't bear to see him wrestling with that kind of guilt.

He searched her eyes, his Adam's apple bobbing in his throat. Warmth spread from his wrist to her palm, up her arm, and across her chest before she hastily withdrew her hand.

"But if you don't blame me for Preacher's death," he regarded her with such intensity she was forced to look away, to busy herself by plucking at a loose bead on her clutch, "then why did you look at me like that last night when I introduced myself to Franklin?"

She briefly closed her eyes and tried without much success to steady her nerves. "Because of all the disappointment and hurt, all the pain and memories, it just seemed so…" She shook her head helplessly. "I don't know, unfair, I guess is the right word to use. That you were able to act like nothing happened. It…it just…it got to me."

He dragged in a deep breath, and she glanced over. He'd rolled in his lips, and his eyes were unusually bright in the dim lights cast by the lamps beside the bed. "From the moment you stepped into the courtyard, I wanted to fall to my knees and beg your forgiveness. If I hadn't thought you'd scoff at my apology, I'd have done just that."

Her heart cracked along another old fissure.

"Well, now you've apologized, and I—"

"No," he shook his head, sliding from the chair to kneel before her, causing her swirling stomach to drop down to her toes. Taking both of her hands, he gazed into her eyes. "I haven't apologized for everything. I haven't apologized for the way I treated you that night at the Clover or the things I said to you outside the base's gates. I haven't apologized for—"

"It's okay." Even more than his declaration of love, his remorse over the way things had happened all those years ago beat against her hard-won resolve, making her regret, making her want to believe that she was wrong about him. Making her start to wonder if she'd made a mistake. And on the heels of that wonder rode a tsunami's worth of guilt. She swallowed and whispered through the constriction in her chest, "Really, Jake. I don't want to hear any more. Let's just leave it."

Stay strong, Michelle. He might be sorry for what he did just like Dad always claimed to be sorry, but that doesn't change who he is…

"You may not want to hear it," he said, "but that's not gonna stop me from saying it."

Please let it stop you from saying it. "Jake," she begged. "It's really not—"

"I'm so sorry, Shell," he blurted. "So sorry for the way I treated you when I got back from that four-month tour. My only excuse is that, even though the teams separate us from society, I'd never really felt like an outsider, like something *other*, until after the barracks bombing. Until after nearly killing that guy in cold blood. I thought if you ever found out what I'd become, you wouldn't want me. And then I treated you like shit when you went and did the smart thing, kicking me to the curb and falling for Preacher, but that was just a broken heart and wounded pride doing the talking. I swear to God, I didn't mean any of it."

Splat!

Uh-huh, and that would be the sound of her resolve getting bashed flat with a sledgehammer.

He smiled sadly and shook his head, reaching to thumb away the tear slowly sliding down her cheek.

Oh, why couldn't you have told me all of this back then? Things could've been so different…

"People talk a good game about what it's like. They toss around words like PTSD and battle fatigue," he went on, squeezing her cold, numb fingers. If only her heart could remain as cold and numb. "But they're only words. No one really knows what it's like until they've lived it and experienced it. *I* lived it and experienced it so much that I became totally detached from myself. Some days I felt like the walking dead, completely numb, and other days my senses were heightened to such a degree that the smallest things would set me off. I should've handled it better. I know that. But I did what I thought was right. I pushed you away to save you from the monster I'd become. From the *killer* I'd become."

"Jake—"

"It took me a long time to get to the point where I could trust myself again, before I felt like I had a handle on all the anger and hatred. Even after I got your letter, there were still times I struggled. But I made a promise to myself then and there. I promised myself that I would come back for you just as soon as I felt strong enough, just as soon as I felt like a reasoning, rational man instead of one motivated by rage and a need for retribution. Shell, I—"

"Oh, please stop," she pleaded, trying to dislodge her hands, but he held tight. "I don't want to hear any more."

"I know you don't, but I have to make you understand—"

And then she did the only thing she could think to shut him up.

She kissed him.

Yo.

The touch of Shell's soft lips was the dead last thing Jake expected to feel. And even when she put her hands on his shoulders and scooted forward until he was between her thighs, he still knelt there like a complete jackass, afraid to move, eyes wide and blinking in astonishment.

She was…kissing him?

Oh, mama, was she ever…

And just like that, the promise he'd made to her the night before was forgotten as old instincts kicked in. He grabbed her face, sucking on the sweet tongue she'd inserted into his mouth as his heart filled with hope. Was that birdsong he heard? Were church bells ringing somewhere?

It was like being in the middle of a Broadway musical. That is until he realized what this kiss *really* meant.

It wasn't about passion or love. Hell, it wasn't even about comfort.

She was just trying to keep her walls from crumbling. To distract him from saying the things that might make her reconsider her opinion of him, the things that might make her start to believe him when he said he loved her.

Well, that was just bullshit.

He pulled back. And the look on her face was desperation tinged with fear.

And just as quickly as they'd begun, the song birds and church bells fell silent. All he heard was his harsh burst of breath as he exhaled, and the heavy thud of his heart pounding in his ears.

"This isn't why I brought you here," he told her. "I just want to talk."

"We're done talking," she said, reaching for him again. Her sweet breath feathered across his lips as the expression on her face turned provocative and slumberous. That look was enough to reduce any man to nothing more than a hard-on with a body attached.

And, yo, you better believe he wasn't immune. Not by a long shot. But that wasn't how he wanted it to be. When they finally made love, he wanted it to be because they'd come to an understanding, an agreement about their future together. He wanted it to be because—

"Aw, hell," he grumbled, completely disgusted by his lack of self-control when she kissed him again.

Chapter Eleven

THIS IS SO WRONG.

Michelle knew it in her heart.

She'd kissed him to shut him up. But she should've known better. Because it was impossible to stop at only one kiss when it came to Jake unless, like last night, she could latch onto some distraction.

Of course, there'd be no distractions here. Not in this hotel room.

It was just the two of them. Alone. So entirely alone…

And Jake was so heartbreakingly familiar. The way he touched her, skimming his hands up her sides until he gently cupped her breasts, his thumbs feathering over the tips.

Oh wow. She'd forgotten how toe-curlingly good that could feel.

The way he kissed her, nibbling on her neck before softly biting the tender skin there, making her arch beneath him. The way they fit together, breast to chest, hip to hip. The way his eyes burned when he looked at her.

Stop this!, her mind screamed, but she refused to listen. She wanted more. Just a little bit more heat, a little bit more pleasure. And then she'd stop…

Shoving her hands under the tail of his silly Hawaiian shirt, she was rewarded with the feel of smooth, hot skin rippling over wonderful muscle. She couldn't see it, but she had a very clear memory of the tattoo covering his back. It was a bold, colorful reproduction of the SEAL Budweiser, the pin all Navy SEALs attached with pride to their uniforms—on those rare occasions they actually *wore* uniforms—an eagle perched atop an anchor and trident. She remembered thinking the tattoo was tough-looking and fierce, like the man who wore it.

Like the man she'd secretly dreamed of for years.

Just a little bit more…

She kicked free of her pumps, and he groaned when the movement pressed her more tightly against his throbbing erection.

Kneeling on the mattress, he pulled her into a sitting position, ravaging her mouth as he unzipped her dress. What'd seemed to take an eternity to do in her bedroom earlier this evening was undone in an instant with no more than a harsh *zziiiipp* of metal teeth pulling free from one another.

And this was it. Here and now. If she let this go any further, there'd be no turning back.

Stop this!, her mind screamed at her again. But that voice was growing fainter and fainter as Jake continued to love her, as her body started a steady chant of *oh wow…oh wow…oh wow!*

And hadn't she already suffered the consequences of loving him? Hadn't she already suffered the heartbreak? So what would be the harm in giving herself this one night to finally *make* love to him?

Sure, that was nothing but a rationalization for what was undoubtedly one of the stupidest things she'd ever contemplated doing, but did she even care?

She'd spent the last few years suppressing her own

needs for those of another. Pretending she didn't miss the feel of a man moving against her, moving inside her. Acting like she didn't burn with a need she refused to fulfill. And tomorrow she'd go back to all that. Tomorrow she'd resume her role, adjust her mask, step back into her mommy uniform.

But tonight?

For the first time in a very long time, she decided to be selfish, to take what she wanted and not worry about the consequences.

Tonight was going to be for her. For the woman she'd been before all the pain and anger and deception. For this one night, she wasn't going to worry what the future might hold, what terrible hurts and revelations it might reveal. For this one night, she was going to forget it all and just…feel.

Having made her decision, however idiotic it may have been—okay, it was undoubtedly idiotic, but she was done caring—she shrugged out of her dress, letting it pool at her waist. Jake pulled back, his eyes hungry as they stared down at her lacy bra and all it supported.

"My God, you're beautiful," he murmured, using one finger to trace the silky, black strap. Following the material to the top edge of one cup, he gently dipped that long finger inside.

Goose bumps tripped up her spine.

She reached for him, and it was then he did something totally unexpected. He jumped up from the bed, turning his back on her and lacing his fingers together on top of his head. "I didn't bring you here for this. I swear I didn't. I *meant* it when I gave you that promise last night."

"I know," she breathed, shimmying out of her dress and panties, unhooking her bra and flinging it to the floor. Since she made her decision, she wasn't going to let him back out.

She deserved this, dangit! She deserved the wantonness and fire and hedonistic thrill. After everything she'd been through, after everything he'd put her through, she deserved it…

He dropped his arms, turning to her, his hot eyes traveling over her naked body before he groaned. "You…" he swallowed, his Adam's apple bobbing in his throat. "You took off your clothes."

"Yes, I did," she whispered. "Now the only problem is that *you* haven't taken off *yours*."

She scooted to the edge of the mattress, kneeling in front of him as she reached for the buttons on his shirt. He didn't stop her, just stood stock-still and watched as her fingers worked the buttons free. She reveled in the thin smattering of hair she revealed, darker than that on his head, although the tips were still golden and sun-bleached. His nipples were little brown disks and when the backs of her fingers grazed his stomach, the muscles beneath quivered in a series of accordion-like contractions. He shrugged his shoulders so she could pull the shirt away, then groaned again when she dropped her fingers to the buttons of his fly.

"Why are you doing this?" He grabbed her hands, stopping her. "Does this mean that you…? That we…?" He shook his head helplessly, the hope in his eyes enough to have a dead weight settling in the center of her chest.

For a moment, she wanted to forget everything that'd

happened, everything he'd ever done, take him at his word when he said he loved her and he'd changed.

But men like him never changed, no matter how much they might believe they had. Eventually, when things got boring, when things got routine, he'd prove himself true to form and go in search of the next thrill.

It was as certain as tomorrow's sunrise…

"Nothing's changed," she told him, reaching up to drag him down for a kiss. "We've always been good at this, or…" She chuckled, and she hoped he didn't notice that the sound was a little desperate, "…at least I *think* we'd have been good at it if we'd ever been allowed to finish."

His eyes were so green, staring at her searchingly, but he didn't offer up further objections as she undid the last button at his fly and yanked his jeans and his boxers over his hips. His erection sprang free and—

Oh…wow…

He was long and pink and…absolutely perfect…

When she reached for him, he stopped her, manacling her wrist. She glanced into his face and saw the struggle in his eyes, in the hard tick of the muscles in his jaw. "This is what you really want, Jake. You know it's only ever really been about this."

Softly she pulled his hand away from her wrist and placed it on her breast. His eyes followed the move and the minute she skimmed his fingers across her hardened nipple, his nostrils flared, and his gaze narrowed.

"Shell," he groaned, his eyes avidly watching the movement of his fingers as he circled and gently pinched at the aching bud. "It *isn't* just about this." But even as he said it, he moved closer, his knees bumping up against the mattress.

She reached for him again, and this time he made no move to stop her.

"Ah, God," he whispered when she stroked her hand up his length.

"Let's finally finish this," she murmured, leaning forward to press her lips to the tip of him, reveling in the smell of aroused man, in the feel of silky hot skin sliding over a column of flesh-and-blood steel.

He made a desperate, hungry sound in the back of his throat before pushing her away so he could hop out of his boots, shedding his jeans and ankle holster in the process.

And then he was there, pressing her back into the mattress, covering her with his long, hard body, kissing her as feverishly as she kissed him, stroking her as hungrily as she stroked him, raking his teeth and tongue across her body when she wasn't doing the same thing to him.

And just when she was about to throw a leg over his hips, when she was about to impale herself on all that hot, vibrant flesh she held in her hands, a seed of sanity bloomed inside her head.

She almost kept her mouth shut. After all, the question she needed to ask was the same question that'd made him come to his senses four years ago. The same question that had had everything coming to a screeching halt in the bathroom of the Clover Bar and Grill.

Still, the good Lord knew she couldn't take any chances...

"You have a condom, right?" she panted, still stroking him. Running her thumb over his soft tip and spreading the silkiness she found there around his plump, smooth head.

He exhaled hard. "Damn, I don't know. They may be in the bag I left at your house."

For a brief instant, she considered throwing caution to the wind, especially when he did something crazy with his tongue.

"I guess," she gasped and licked her lips, her body on fire, "I guess we'll have to improvise."

"Hold that thought," he said, pushing from the bed only to retrieve his jeans from the floor and scrounge through the pockets. His sudden absence, and the cool rush of hotel room air that blew over her skin, was almost shocking.

She had to stifle the urge to launch herself off the bed, tackle him to the floor, and ride him until her eyes crossed.

Instead, she pressed up on her elbows. "What are you doing?" she asked, letting her avid gaze roam over his splendid male body, her eyes alighting on his tattoo, so vibrant and powerful-looking, spread across his beautifully broad back…

"Ah, ha!" He shouted triumphantly as he held up the two foil packages he'd pulled from his wallet. "Always be prepared. I *told* you I was a Boy Scout."

~~~

Shell crooked a finger at him, a living, breathing goddess, beckoning him back to bed.

"Come here," she said and, word up, he didn't need to be told twice.

Okay, and it was official. He was the weakest-willed man on the entire planet, because he knew, without a shadow of a doubt, that he shouldn't be doing this.

But she was naked.

In his bed.

And he loved her…

So despite the myriad reasons why he should put the brakes on this little endeavor, he found himself stalking toward the bed, intent on making love to her.

And it was going to be love. He'd make damn sure of that.

She didn't believe the words when he gave them to her, so he'd show her with his hands and tongue and body just how much he cherished her, worshipped her.

How much he *loved* her.

He crawled up the bed, up her body, letting his eyes drift from sweetly painted toes to softly turned calves. Farther to silky thighs and amazingly curvaceous hips.

She had the cutest belly button. So little and perfectly round. It looked like it hadn't decided whether it wanted to be an outie or an innie, so it'd become both. He couldn't resist it. When he kissed it delicately, she giggled softly, spearing her fingers into his hair. He took that as his cue to continue his journey northward.

Of course when his gaze landed on her breasts, he had to stop again because…*yo*…they were perfect. Large and round, with dark, half-dollar-sized nipples. Nipples begging for his kiss.

He didn't disappoint.

And when he lapped one with his tongue, she sighed. The sound went all through him, turning him on and revving him up.

He sucked her breast gently, loving the way she moaned and arched into him, loving the way his hands were filled to overflowing with her.

Shell wasn't one of those delicate women who'd snap in two if he held her too tightly. She was an armful. A warm, soft, wonderful armful that he wasn't afraid to love.

In a word: perfection.

He figured he could continue to make love to her breasts until eternity, knead their delicate lushness and kiss their hard tips until he went toes up from pleasure, but he remembered how much she loved to have her throat kissed. How it made her tilt her head just so…

He made his way up her soft neck, back to her sweet ear, letting his teeth and tongue graze against soft, fragrant skin and reveling in the way she lifted her chin, giving him all the access he could ever desire, giving in to him in a way he'd only dreamed possible.

He wanted to see her face. That beautiful face, those gorgeous eyes, and those amazing lips…

When he pulled back to look down at her, his heart stopped.

Holy, holy hell. She was something all right. Eyes, heavy with passion. Cheeks, bright with a warm blush. Lips, slick and pink and swollen…just like the flesh between her legs would be.

He couldn't stand it a second longer. He reached down and palmed her gently before inserting one and then a second finger inside her.

She was hot. Wet. A woman ripe with desire. Every dream he'd ever dared to dream. Every hot fantasy he'd conjured up in the middle of the night.

"Make love to me," she whispered, reaching up to nibble at his jaw, and his dick pulsed so hard he had to grit his teeth or come on the spot.

Two years without a woman was wreaking havoc on his control, which had never proved to be very good with Shell anyway.

"Say it again," he commanded, his breath sawing from his lungs, his voice harsh as he watched her face, watched her realize exactly what it was that he wanted.

Love. Even in the context of making it. To hear it on her lips in regards to him.

It wasn't *everything* he wanted. But it was something. Something he could hold onto. Something he could build on...

A flicker of uncertainty passed over her face, and he held his breath, afraid he might have ruined it. Then she reached for him, grabbing his ears and pulling him down to her, murmuring against his lips, "Jake, please make love to me."

—✺—

"Shell," Jake breathed in her ear as he spread her thighs and settled between them.

He peppered her face and neck with kisses, and she heard the crinkle of the foil wrapper. She glanced down, watching his large, tan hands expertly slide the condom on his long, pink erection, and the sight was almost as titillating as the sensation of him when he pressed against her entrance.

He was hot, hard, and throbbing. A second heartbeat to drown out the feel of her own.

"*Yes*," she whispered as he slid the barest fraction of an inch inside.

"Oh, Shell...My sweet, sweet, Shell..." His voice was hoarse, the veins in his neck standing out in sharp relief as he tightened his jaw and slung his chin down to watch the impalement of her body with his own.

It was excruciatingly slow, and wonderfully delicious. Ecstasy and agony all rolled into one giant ball of sensation.

Gradually, and oh so gently, he joined them together, seating himself to the hilt with one final jab that rocked her softly against the mattress. And then he stopped, panting, gazing into her eyes.

"You feel so damned good," he gasped, swinging his hips back only to drive home just as slowly, just as gently. "So damned good."

Good didn't begin to describe it.

Snow at Christmas was good. Homemade lasagna was good. This? This was transcendent.

It'd been years since her body was forced to yield to the intrusion of hard, male flesh. Too long obviously, because suddenly she was shattering.

All around him.

One moment she was exalting in the novel feeling of sex, the sensation of aching delight she'd denied herself for too long, and the next she was flung from pleasure's highest cliff.

It was all so unexpected, she shouted his name, digging her nails into his shoulders as her orgasm burst through her again and again, undulating rivers of ecstasy that had a rainbow of colors flashing behind her lids.

"Oh God," he breathed in her ear, riding the waves with her as he continued to love her so slowly. So expertly.

And when the last remnants of pleasure shivered through her, he lifted himself up on his elbows, gazing down at her with such awe, such desire.

"Jake," she leaned up to kiss his mouth, saying the only thing she could, "again."

He smiled then. That sweet, sexy, dimpled smile that'd captured her heart the first time she'd seen it.

"My pleasure," he rumbled as he began to move.

His body was a machine beneath her fingertips. All oiled muscles and perfectly orchestrated strokes.

He knew exactly how to love her, exactly how to touch her. Oh, the things he did with his mouth and tongue, with the rhythmic, piston swing of his hips...

It was *sooo* unbelievably delicious. It'd never been this delicious with anybody, and she knew it'd never be this delicious again.

Because this was Jake. The love of her life.

It was scary to finally admit that, especially knowing they could never be. Knowing this would be the one and only time she allowed herself to make love to him.

And she wanted it to last forever. She wanted the world to stop, time to stop, so she could live in this moment. Right here, right now.

"Shell, tell me everything you want."

What she wanted? She wanted the impossible.

"Please," she begged, "please don't stop."

"Never," he growled, his hips picking up the rhythm, swinging hard and fast.

And that was just right. Just what she needed to have her teetering on the precipice again. Oh wow. Oh *wow*. *Oh...*

"Shell..."

She heard the tremor in his voice, felt the tension in the muscles of his back where her fingers curled into the deep divot of his flexing spine. He pushed back to look at her, and she could see the desperation in his eyes as he struggled against his release.

She struggled against hers, too. Because if she went, she knew she'd take him with her, and then it'd be over. This wonderful, beautiful moment would all be over, and she wasn't ready yet.

Her inner muscles tightened around him, and she ground her jaw, fighting the pleasure.

"Please," he begged, sweat beading on his forehead, darkening the tips of his blond hair. "Please come with me, Shell."

And that was it.

She exploded.

There was no other word for it.

Her whole world blew apart, her body throbbing and clinging to his as he continued to thrust into her so deeply. She dissolved into a million fragments of pleasure, and he followed her immediately, shouting, "I love you!" over and over.

Then, as quickly as she'd blown apart, all the little pieces of herself began to reform. Those were her arms, clutching him so tightly. Those were her heels, tucked up under his delicious butt. Those were her lips, pressing hot kisses to the side of his neck.

When he gazed down at her, it took everything she had to resist the warmth in his eyes.

"I love you," he said again.

And instead of answering, she choked back her tears.

Give her time, Jake told himself as he watched Shell

close her ears to his proclamation of love once again. *Just give her time to see that you're not going to reject and abandon her like you did four years ago. Then she'll come around. Then she'll see...*

At least, he hoped she'd see. In truth, he was beginning to have his doubts, and that had everything inside him threatening to shatter. Frustrated tears burned up the back of his throat and, okay, he *so* wasn't prepared to be that guy. The one who broke down after orgasm.

"I need to—" he began.

"—take care of the condom," she finished for him, and when he pulled from her body, it felt like he was leaving his soul behind.

After disposing of the condom in the bathroom trash, he glanced at his reflection in the mirror.

She will *come around,* he assured himself. *After all, she just made love to you.*

And he knew she wouldn't have done that if she didn't still feel *something* for him. Shell wasn't one for casual sex.

Feeling a good measure of his old self-assurance return, he walked out of the bathroom only to find Shell kneeling in the center of the bed, the second foil-wrapped condom held between her fingers, a sultry half-smile playing at her delicious lips.

Yo, she'll most definitely *come around.*

In fact, she already was. Though he suspected she hadn't realized it, yet.

His heart began a happy, steady thrum.

"You ready for round two?" she asked with a little smile that caused two small divots to form beside her fabulous lips. For some reason, the sight of those divots drove him absolutely wild. "Or does a man of your advanced years need a few more minutes?"

And this was the Shell he remembered. Warm, teasing…

He wanted to shoot a victorious fist in the air.

Instead, he satisfied himself with raising a brow. "A man of my advanced years?" he chuckled as he glanced down at his dick.

Upon exiting the bathroom and seeing her there, naked in the middle the bed, the thing had started a steady climb to vertical.

Her eyes followed the direction of his gaze. "Well, well, Mr. Sommers," she breathed, licking her lips. "I now see why you were such a hit with all the ladies."

"You ain't seen nothing yet, doll," he assured her as he stalked toward the bed.

She fell back against the mattress, laughing.

But he didn't jump on top of her like he knew she was expecting. Instead, he knelt at the edge of the bed and lowered his face between her thighs, sucking in the wonderfully decadent scent of her musky arousal.

He couldn't resist her. He opened his mouth and kissed her. Her thighs tightened around his ears, but she didn't jerk away. And that was all the invitation he needed.

Sliding his tongue into the hot heaven of her sex, he reveled in the noises she made. They were cries of joy mixed with pure pleasure. She loved what he was doing to her, and she let him know it, especially when she reached down to grab his hair and pull him more tightly against her.

Then her breathing ratcheted up, and the sounds she was making became desperate. "Jake, please," she panted. "I want you inside me."

And, yo, that was another invitation he couldn't resist.

When he moved from his position between her soft, wonderful thighs, he was gratified to see an unwrapped condom in her hand. She smiled seductively as she slowly rolled it down his length.

She was so beautiful. *And tight*, he thought as he slowly pushed his length into the moist welcome of her body. That was all the evidence he needed to know she hadn't been with a man in years. And he was caveman enough to admit that the fact made him ridiculously happy.

"What are you grinning about?" she asked, gasping when he pulled back only to stroke home.

"Just happy," he said as he moved again, careful to caress every last inch of her.

She grabbed his shoulders then, lifting up to kiss him, her nipples hard against his chest, and he quickened his strokes. And then, for a few glorious minutes, there was no need for words.

Because every second was filled with pure, triumphant pleasure.

But suddenly, "Shell," he whispered against her lips. "Oh God. I'm really close."

"Me too," she moaned, moving with him, her beautiful, pale skin glistening with sweat. "But I'm always so close when I'm with you."

And that did it.

Jake's release blasted through him like a cannon shot. "Shell!" He cried her name and felt a flash of relief when her inner muscles contracted around him as she followed him over the edge.

He held her tightly for long moments after the last shivers of ecstasy washed through their joined bodies.

Refusing to break the connection, he rolled them onto their sides, staring into her eyes as he ran a reverent finger over her shoulder, down her arm, across her hip and the faint white scars she'd sustained from her pregnancy.

"Ugh," she wrinkled her nose. "Don't look at those. They're ugly."

"No they're not," he assured her, his heart warm inside his chest. "They're beautiful."

A sheen of tears pooled in her eyes. "That might be the sweetest thing I've ever heard. Delusional. But sweet all the same." She leaned in to kiss him, then pulled back before their lips could touch. Her eyes were huge and wary. "Jake? Is the...uh...are you still wearing a condom?"

Huh?

He reached down between them but was relieved to discover the little plastic ring fully intact and right where it should be.

"Yep," he pulled out of her, then stared in horror at the remnants of the condom. Which wasn't really a condom anymore, just a ragged piece of latex dangling around his junk. "Ah, shit," he said at the same time Shell squealed and vaulted off the mattress.

She pointed at the broken condom like it might grow teeth and bite her. "Wh-what the *hell*, Jake?"

"Hey," he reached for her. "It's okay. These things happen."

"Not to me," she swatted at his hands. "These things don't happen to *me*." Then she turned away and bolted into the bathroom, muttering something under her breath he didn't quite catch.

He sighed when he heard the lid to the toilet slam up followed by the sound of her relieving herself. He wanted to tell her urinating after sex as a way to fight off pregnancy was just an old wives' tale, but she worked in the medical field, so he figured she knew a lot more than he did about such things. Besides, if the last look on her face was anything to go by, she wasn't in any mood to hear his helpful observations.

The sound of the toilet flushing was immediately followed by the hiss of the shower turning on.

Now he figured it was safe to venture forth.

Strolling into the bathroom, he found her bent over the tub, adjusting the temperature. The sight of her bare ass, all beautiful and heart-shaped, had his cock twitching.

Of course, the thing always had been stupidly optimistic.

He was fairly confident there'd be no more playtime tonight. And when she spun to glare at him, hands on hips, accusatory fire shooting from her eyes, he went from fairly confident to 100 percent certain.

"How old were those condoms?" she demanded, her full breasts jiggling slightly when she stuck out her chin.

"Um," he scratched his head. "Two or three years, I think."

"T-two or three *years!*" she sputtered. "And you thought it was okay to *use* them?"

"I wasn't thinking at all at the time," he admitted, taking a step toward her, but she only waved him off. "I guess I just assumed they were like Twinkies. Had a shelf life of, like, a thousand years or something."

It was at that moment that her eyes zeroed in on the offending prophylactic still decorating his happily erect cock—Come on, she was standing there naked. There was nothing he could do about it. It was evolution. Woman plus naked equals erection—and now *she* was the one reaching for *him*.

"Why are you still wearing that useless thing? Just to tick me off? Get rid of it!"

"Okay, I—Hey! Ouch! I'll do it!" He turned away from her very *un*-gentle hands and peeled away what was left of the condom.

When he turned back, she snatched it out of his hand and glared at it. He was surprised the thing didn't burst into flames. Then she tossed it toward the trash like most guys toss a hand grenade before jumping into the shower and slamming the door closed behind her.

"Look," he stood outside the semi-transparent glass. "What are the chances you're pregnant? Where are you in your cycle?"

The door slid open with a snap. "I'm a week past my period, and I—"

"Okay. Okay, that's good, right? You shouldn't be ovulating, yet."

"What the *hell* would you know about it!" she said, her face contorted with fear and something that looked very much like rage.

Was he missing something here? She *was* overreacting a bit, wasn't she?

"Look, if you *are* pregnant, we'll deal with it."

She blinked and opened her mouth, then seemed to think better of whatever it was she about to say, because she slid the door shut in his face, mumbling something he couldn't hear above the hiss of the shower.

He reached up to open the door when a snippet of

music had him rethinking his move. "Uh, Shell? I think your phone is ringing."

"It's in my clutch," she said in a tight voice.

"Clutch?"

"My purse, you big Neanderthal."

Okay. Obviously he *was* missing something here. Because in the space of about five minutes, he'd gone from *Jake, again* and *Jake, don't stop* to *Jake, you big Neanderthal.* "Does that mean you want me to answer it?"

Once again the door snapped open, and she glared at him. "What do you think it means?"

He sighed and shook his head, completely flummoxed as to why this was all *his* fault, before he turned and strolled, er, *limped* back to the bedroom.

Ouch.

He cupped his abused dick in one hand while digging through her little purse with the other. When he located her iPhone, he saw Boss's name on the screen and decided to answer it himself. "Yo," he said, "what's up?"

"Snake?" Boss's voice was tight, and Jake's instincts kicked into overdrive. He bent to grab his jeans.

"Yeah. What's the problem?"

The next words out of Boss's mouth had him cursing and scrambling into his jeans as he yelled for Shell to get her sweet ass out of the shower, double-time.

Chapter Twelve

"THAT WAS BECKY," FRANK SAID, POCKETING HIS CELL phone as he turned away from the gurgling water cooler plunked in the corner of the tidy waiting room at Northwestern Memorial Hospital. "She says she's sorry she's not here now, but Steady and Zoelner caught one of Johnny's goons climbing to the roof of the bagel shop, and Ozzie had to maintain his post until after Rock arrived to question the guy. But Ozzie has finally schlepped his sorry ass—her words, not mine—back to the shop in order to act as her escort, and they should be arriving within the next half hour. In the meantime, she wants me to tell you she's thinking of you and saying a prayer for Franklin."

Michelle was glad the waiting room was empty save for her, Frank, and Jake, or else the occupants would've gotten an earful. Of course, they wouldn't have understood the half of it.

"I know how much danger you guys are in," she said, trying to hold back the tears burning behind her eyes. She didn't want to add a hysterically sobbing woman to the list of things her brother was dealing with right now. "None of you should be here. You should be back at the shop taking care of business. Back at the shop where it's safe."

And they would be if she hadn't taken it into her head to go on that stupid date. Which had led to Jake's hotel room. Which had led to them making love. Which had led to her not being home when her son—

"A hospital is one of the safest places around, Shell," her brother told her. "And the only *business* I want to be taking care of right now is my *family's* business."

Okay, and that did it.

"I'm never going to forgive myself," she sobbed, shoving her fingers back through her hair before she remembered she hadn't washed out the shampoo she'd applied right before Jake dragged her from the shower. Her head was beginning to dry into a crunchy, pasty mess.

Of course, that was the least of her worries.

Because her son, her life, her whole reason for living, was having emergency surgery.

Emergency surgery!

And she hadn't been there to say good-bye before he was rushed in. She hadn't been there to hold his little hand, or kiss his sweet face, or tell him everything would be okay because mommy was here. She hadn't been there to comfort and console him when he was terrified and in pain.

And *why* hadn't she been?

Oh, right, because she'd been screwing Jake Sommers blind, that's why.

She'd been blissfully and willfully forgetting about everything except her need to finally assuage her own desire. In fact, she'd probably been in the middle of orgasm number two or three while Frank was rushing her boy to the hospital.

Selfish, selfish, *selfish!*

What had she been thinking?

Or maybe, the better question would be, what had she been thinking with?

Certainly not her head.

"I shouldn't have gone out on that date. I should've been there when he—" she hiccupped, a wash of fresh tears running into her hands when she pressed them over her eyes. It turned the pasty shampoo on her fingers into a sudsy mess which she wiped off on the hem of her skirt.

"Shell," Frank whispered, coming to sit beside her on the stiff, blue sofa, squeezing her knee. "It's not your fault. You haven't been on a date in years. You were due. No one could've guessed Franklin would suddenly be struck with appendicitis."

Appendicitis. The word sent horror streaking through her heart.

"Yeah, Shell," Jake said from her other side, mirroring her brother's movement and patting her opposite knee. "You couldn't have foreseen this. These things happen and—"

She turned on him then. Grabbing his hand and nearly crushing his fingers. "These things happen?" she screeched. "Is that your answer for everything tonight!"

"I don't..." he shook his head. "I mean—"

"Forget it," she howled, once more burying her face in her hands.

And yes, she knew she was being unfair, taking out her rage and guilt and frustration on him when the blame rested solely on her shoulders. But she couldn't help herself. If it weren't for him, she'd have never gone out on that date in the first place. She'd have been home with her son. Where she belonged...

"Hey, Shell, it's not Snake's fault any more than it is yours." Frank ran a hand over her head and grimaced, glancing at her more closely. "What have you got in your hair?"

She turned to ask what the heck that had to do with anything when a red-haired nurse in baby blue scrubs came to the door. "Michelle Carter?"

"That's me," she jumped up, her stomach sitting in her throat, disgorging all its acid until she couldn't help but wonder if she'd ever be able to swallow correctly again.

"My name is Susan. I'm a nurse on Franklin's surgical team and—"

"Well, then what are you doing out *here*?" she demanded, completely mortified, envisioning Franklin's surgeon going, *scalpel...scalpel...scalpel?* And then looking around and finding Nurse Susan missing.

"Oh, I'm just observing," Susan said, walking toward her. The nurse's hot pink Crocs squeaked against the tile floor.

"Oh, good. So, how's it going?" she asked anxiously. "Is it over so soon?"

"No," Nurse Susan shook her head, pasting on that look all medical professionals perfected over time. The one that gave absolutely nothing away. "There's been a slight complication." At the expression of abject horror that passed over Michelle's features, Susan of the pink Crocs quickly pressed on. "It's nothing major. He just has a few adhesions. Those are connections to abdominal organs by thin fibrous tissue. It's not totally uncommon, but it does complicate the surgery a bit. And in the off chance we're going to need to transfuse, we were wondering if there was anyone in your family with Franklin's blood type who'd like to donate. He's AB negative. And as I'm sure you were told at his birth, that blood type is extremely rare. He could be transfused with A neg, B neg, or O, but an AB donor would be better. Again," she said, "let me stress that the chances of us needing to do a transfusion are *incredibly* small."

The more the nurse spoke, the dizzier Michelle became. But she grabbed on to the back of a chair, steadied herself, and concentrated on the question. "My blood type is A," she said, raising a hand to one pounding temple. The air in her lungs burned like she was breathing kerosene. "What are you, Frank?" She turned toward her brother.

"I'm A, too." He shook his head, his heavy brow furrowed with worry, which made her start to panic. Frank was a rock; he wasn't supposed to get scared.

Don't pass out. Don't pass out.

Although that was a lot easier said than done. Her lungs were working overtime, but she couldn't get enough oxygen.

"It's not a problem," the nurse assured them. "I just thought I'd check and—"

"I'm AB negative," Jake piped up.

"Well," the nurse craned her head around Michelle's shoulder to see who'd spoken. "That's fantastic! Are you the father?"

A fierce, shocking pain slammed through Michelle's chest, and she plopped down on the chair she'd been using as a support. Bright lights flashed before her eyes.

"No," Jake shook his head, pushing up from the waiting room sofa. "I'm just a friend."

"Well, isn't it lucky you were here then?" the nurse chirped, obviously pleased. "Are you willing to donate?"

"Of course," Jake said, frowning when he passed her. "Hey, Shell, are you okay?"

She waved him on as Nurse Susan said, "Please come this way then Mr…"

"I'm Jake," he said, casting Michelle one last worried glance before following the nurse toward the door. "Jake Sommers."

"Well, Mr. Jake Sommers," Nurse Susan crooned, obviously having already fallen victim to his dimples, "let's go relieve you of some of that high octane liquid gold you've got running through your veins."

"Damn," Frank murmured after they'd gone. "It *is* lucky Snake was here."

Yeah. Lucky…

That was the last thought she had before her world went black.

The nurse pointed Jake into a little room where a middle-aged guy in green scrubs and bright orange Nikes was busy washing his hands in a miniature stainless steel sink.

"Jake," she said, "meet Carl. He's the world's greatest phlebotomist. He'll have you a pint low in no time."

"Have a seat." Carl the Great Phlebotomist motioned to a chair with padded arms while snapping on a pair of blue latex gloves. The nurse gave him a wink before turning and squeaking down the hall in her ridiculous hot pink rubber shoes.

"Gotta love Susan," Carl said, watching the sway of

the nurse's rather plump butt with a little smirk before turning back to Jake. "So you're the elusive AB neg, huh?" He handed Jake a squeeze ball, telling him to give it a couple of good pumps while tapping at his inner elbow with a chubby finger.

"So I've been told," Jake muttered, a vague sense of unease settling over him.

It's just worry over Franklin, he told himself, though somehow that didn't seem right.

"Ever given blood before?"

"Plenty of times." Once during a battlefield transfusion that'd saved the life of a fellow operator but nearly killed *him* in the process. Of course, Carl didn't need to know about that.

"Cool, dude. So this is gonna be a piece of cake, especially with killer veins like yours. I always like taking blood from guys who work out. That low body fat really makes the hoses pop, if you know what I mean."

Yeah, Jake knew what he meant. Especially when he glanced down at his inner arm and saw a vein the size of garden snake winding down to his wrist.

"A little pinch now," Carl said as he inserted the large 17-gauge needle. Jake had been shot at, dodged mortar rounds, rolled a jeep during a getaway, and been stepped on by hadjis while having to lay prone in a hide-site, but nothing gave him the heebie jeebies like a good, thick needle.

"Oh, you're a quick one," Carl remarked when his blood raced through the plastic tube and down into the clear collection bag, a red, life-giving river he was happy to know might help save the life of Shell's son. In terms of shedding blood for a cause, he figured it didn't get much better than this. "We'll be finished in a sec."

He continued to squeeze the ball, watching absently while the bag filled, his mind turning over the events in the waiting room. That's what was niggling at him. Something wasn't right. Something didn't make sense. But when he tried to get on top of whatever it was, it flew out from under him like an un-waxed surfboard.

"You're not from around here, are you?" Carl broke into his spinning thoughts.

"What makes you say that?"

"The accent, dude. It's totally So Cal. And I should know. I'm So Cal myself."

"Oh yeah? Where are you from?"

And for the next few minutes, the two exchanged surfing stories, which Jake was pretty sure were mostly bravado on Carl's part, especially when the guy claimed to have done an aerial from an A-frame off Australia's Gold Coast.

But he didn't call bullshit. Surfing was like fishing. Exaggerations were a prerogative.

After the bag was full, Carl stuck a wad of cotton to Jake's inner arm and secured it with a two Band-Aids. Then the surfing phlebotomist handed him a cookie and a glass of orange juice, and it suddenly occurred to him what it was that'd been bugging the hell out of him.

That whole *take your mind off it and it will come to you* thing wasn't just an old wives' tale.

"Hey, Carl," he said with his chocolate chip cookie halfway to his mouth. "You know a lot about blood, don't you?"

"Dude, I'm the Stephen Hawking of blood."

Jake figured ol' Stephen might shudder at that particularly gruesome and, no doubt inaccurate, comparison.

"Why do you ask?" Carl inquired, digging around in the bag of cookies.

"Is it possible for a mother who has blood type A and a father who's O to have a child who's AB?"

Carl shook his head, taking a bite of the perfect cookie he'd finally managed to locate. It was obvious from the paunch around Carl's belly, he didn't do much surfing anymore, and he partook of his cookie stash far more than he should. "Not unless the rules for genetics have suddenly changed."

"Huh, that's what I thought."

Carl looked at him askance. "Uh, oh. I know that look. That question wasn't rhetorical, was it?"

"No, Carl," he muttered, standing and heading for the hall, taking his cookie and juice with him. "It wasn't."

"Ah, hell," he heard Carl grumble as he stomped toward the waiting room.

"Okay, okay," Michelle slapped at her brother's hand, the one that was clamped on to the back of her neck, keeping her head shoved between her knees. "I'm fine now. You can stop with the manhandling."

"Give it a few more minutes," Frank muttered.

"I'm not going to hyperventilate again, I promise. But I might pass out from all the blood rushing to my head if you don't get off!" She swatted at his hand a second time.

When he released her, she sat up and squeezed her eyes closed as stars happily circled her vision. Then the scuffling sound of footsteps had them snapping open again.

Oh, great. The cavalry has arrived.

Becky and Ozzie—Frank's resident computer genius and all-around techy wizard—pushed through the waiting room door in front of Jake, who tossed an empty plastic cup into the trash and—

Oh, dear God, no…

She knew that look on his face. It caused her throat to burn and her stomach to ache and she couldn't avoid it even as Becky rushed over to her.

"It's going to be fine," her future sister-in-law assured her, solicitously patting her arm. "Franklin's going to be just fine. You wait and see. Billy, that's my brother…" she explained for Jake's benefit, though the guy wasn't paying her a lick of attention. He was too busy staring holes through Michelle's soul. "…had his appendix removed when he was twelve, and he was back to wrestling with me within two weeks and—what the hell have you got in your hair?"

"It's, uh…it's…" She didn't finish. Mostly because she'd already forgotten the question. Oh, the look on Jake's face…

"Shell," he said, his jaw working like a rock grinder. "I need to talk to you out in the hall."

"What's up?" Frank asked.

Jake jerked his chin to the side. "I just need to talk to Shell." His voice sounded like it'd been scoured with 24-grit sandpaper.

It was time, as they say, to face the music. She'd hoped and prayed this day would never come, but a large part of her had always feared it would.

Her brother glanced at her concernedly, and she tried to smile and reassure him. But it must've looked a bit sickly, because he only scowled harder.

"Shell? What—" She shook her head, waving away whatever question he might've asked as she stood to follow Jake into the wide, tiled hall.

Oh, sweet Lord. Her worst nightmares revolved around what was about to happen right this very minute, right this very *second*.

With her stomach hanging down to her knees, her heart perched dead center in the middle of her throat, and her head floating up around the ceiling somewhere, it was a wonder she could function at all. But somehow she managed to take a deep breath and face him.

"Th-thank you for donating blood," she whispered, hoping to put off the inevitable for a few seconds longer.

"Who is Franklin's father?" he demanded, his eyes searing into her.

Her heart moved from her throat to her skull, pounding in her temples like the entire percussion section of the Chicago Symphony Orchestra.

"W-who do you think?" she stammered through a throat which, now empty of her heart, was swelling with unshed tears.

"I have no idea!" he hissed. "It sure as hell isn't Preacher. He was a universal donor. Blood type O negative. I know because he was supposed to be our go-to guy for battlefield transfusions. And since you're type A, there's no way the two of you could've produced an AB son."

"You're right," she told him as the hall started closing in around her.

He blinked. "That's it? That's all you've got to say?"

"I—" she began and then had to swallow. Her entire world, the world she'd finally managed to build for herself, the world she'd finally managed to build for her son, was crashing down around her ears. "I made the best decision I could at the time, Jake. I made the decision I thought was right for my child. What more do you want me to say?"

"I want you to tell me who the hell Franklin's father is!" he demanded, nostrils flaring like an angry bull's. The nurse manning the station at the far end of the hall glanced up, her brow furrowed. "Because before you hooked up with Preacher," he lowered his voice, "I thought *I* was the only man in your life. I guess I was wrong, huh?" His expression turned ugly. "And then you married Preacher under the pretense of carrying his child and—"

"Steven knew the baby wasn't his," she interrupted sadly, even as she tried to grasp the fact that he really hadn't put two and two together. It seemed impossible...

"And he agreed to marry you anyway?" he asked incredulously.

"Steven was a sweet, loyal, honorable man. If there was someone in need or in trouble, he was the first to lend a hand. I was both. In need and in trouble." And she desperately missed her husband, her friend, during times like this when she needed a strong shoulder to lean on.

Steven had been her rock, her savior, and he'd deserved so much more than she'd been able to give him. Oh, she'd loved him, there was no doubt about that. But it was the kind of love she'd felt for many of the boys in Bravo Platoon. And then he'd died before she got the chance to give him her whole heart…

God, he was worthy of so much more…

And that was one of her biggest regrets in what was turning out to be a very long list of regrets.

"Yeah, yeah," Jake scoffed. "We all know Preacher was a saint. But that doesn't answer the question of who Franklin's father really is."

She lifted her eyes to his angry face, sadness and regret and…yes, *guilt* threatening to crush everything inside her. "You really can't guess?"

"Well, it wasn't Preacher, and it certainly wasn't me so—"

"Of course it's you, Jake. Who else would it be?"

His chin jerked back like she'd slugged him. "But… but…" He shook his head. "That's impossible! We never—"

"Didn't we?" she asked. "Think back to that night at the Clover. I know you were pretty drunk, but surely you remember at least *some* of what happened."

─────

Remember *some* of what happened?

For fuck's sake, Jake remembered it like it was yesterday…

She was a bright, burning flame in his arms when he pulled her into the restroom. Scorching him down to his soul. Climbing all over him. Her hands, everywhere. Her mouth, hot and hungry.

His body was absolutely rigid with pleasure as he shoved her back against the wall. And she laughed, low and sexy in that way she had, wrapping her beautiful, mile-long legs around his hips.

When her skirt slid up around her waist, he felt the sultry heat of her sex through the thin, lace panties she wore. He felt it all the way through the tough denim of his jeans as his pounding erection settled into place.

"Shell, Shell," he chanted her name over and over again, plying her mouth with his tongue, everything inside him warring with itself. He wanted this so much but...

"Jake," she breathed in his ear. "Take me. Right here. Right now."

And that was it. All thoughts, save her, her soft cries and hot tongue and grasping hands, flew from his head.

He groaned when she eagerly bit the side of his neck. Managing to snake an arm down between their bodies, he pushed aside the elastic of her panties, slipped his thumb between her plump female lips and...

Hot.

She was so damned hot, burning his skin.

And wet.

She was so wet, slick and ready.

He plunged one finger inside her tight sheath and pulled back to watch her gorgeous eyes drift shut. A deep blush stole up her neck and burned in her cheeks as he pressed his thumb against the hard knot of nerves at the top of her sex and circled slowly.

"Oh, wow," she whispered and he thought, Oh, wow is right.

Because she was everything a woman was supposed to be. Lush and lusty. Sweet and sensuous. And she was his. His for the taking. His for the fucking. His. His. His. The monster that'd grown inside him over the last few months roared with pleasure.

And he knew this was the last thing he should be doing. Because as soon as she saw what he'd become she'd—

"I'm going to come," *she announced throatily and, once again, all thought fled as he added a second finger to the first and stroked her deeply even as he increased the rhythm of his thumb against that sweet little knot of nerves.*

Oh, come for me. *He wanted it so bad, more than his next breath.*

It was a primal desire. A primitive need to possess, mark, mate, claim.

He'd never experienced anything like it. That animal-istic drive. And he feared it was the beast slipping loose of its chains making him feel this way.

He felt her inner muscles squeeze his fingers, a hard pulse that nearly had him coming in his jeans. But he gritted his teeth and worked her, endlessly sucking her tongue as his fingers pumped, as his thumb circled and pressed, circled and pressed, until her soft gasps turned to muted cries, until she keened his name and unraveled in his arms.

"Oh, Jake," *she breathed in his ear, and then all he could think was that he wanted inside her.*

Now.

He fumbled with his fly and, when his erection sprang free, it pulsed so hard he saw stars.

Damn, this is getting ridiculous! *He needed to get inside her, and fast, because he was about to embarrass himself like a randy sixteen-year-old getting his first hand-job.*

Tugging the leg of her panties aside, he pushed into her...

And it was like coming home, but to no home he'd

ever known. Because it was right in a way he'd never thought possible. So fucking right. He'd been searching for this, just this, his entire life, and now he'd finally found it. This woman. This moment…

When he pulled back to plunge into her again, to seal them indelibly, she groaned and whispered, "Do you have a condom?"

It was then that reality came tumbling down around him…

He glanced at her now, at the tight expression on her face made harsh by the bright overhead lights in the hospital hallway. "I didn't come," he blurted.

He remembered that very clearly. She'd asked if he had a condom, and he'd come to his senses. He'd pulled out of her, shoved his raging cock back in his jeans, wrangled the demon inside him who'd howled with fury, and marched her straight out of the bathroom and into Preacher's arms.

"Yeah." Her expression was stricken. "I guess you didn't have to."

"But—" he shook his head.

"You know all those warnings about applying the condom *before* making any type of sexual contact?" she asked, swallowing convulsively, her eyes bright with unshed tears. "Well, I'm the walking, talking, cautionary tale as to why that's so important."

He couldn't comprehend. Was she saying Franklin was his son?

No.

No, it wasn't possible.

She couldn't have done this to him. Boss couldn't have done this to him.

"Are you telling me…" he shook his head again, his chest caught in a vice as tight as the one squeezing his brain. "What are you telling me?"

He had to be confused. He had to have misunderstood.

"I'm telling you Franklin is your son, Jake. He's yours."

And with those words, the puzzle pieces clicked into place.

"And you're just now telling me?" he demanded, clenching his fists as his throat filled with unspoken screams of *no, no, no. This can't be real!*

He still didn't want to believe…

"I *tried* to—"

He stopped listening as a deep red haze fell over his vision. He turned and marched into the waiting room, no longer thinking, just acting. Total tunnel vision.

He'd been deceived. By the woman he loved and the best friend he trusted.

And since he couldn't take his fury out on Shell…

He stalked right up to Boss, who was sitting on the sofa. After catching the look on his face, Boss's brow creased in a series of deep furrows, the scar slicing up from the corner of his mouth going stark white.

"Snake?" he asked. "What's up, man?"

"How *could* you?" Jake roared, choking as stupid, stupid tears filled his eyes. "How could you do that to me?"

"Jake." Shell grabbed his arm, but he yanked free of her grasp and went toe-to-toe with Boss, who'd quickly pushed up from the sofa.

"How could you keep something like that from me all these years?" His head was packed with C4, ready to explode at any second. And then a thought occurred to him… "That's why you were so quick to try to help me with Shell, wasn't it?" he snarled. "Not because I'm a good man, like you claimed, but because it'd wrap everything up so nice and neat. One sweet, fucking family unit!"

"What the hell are you talking about?" Boss yelled right back.

"Hey guys," Becky tried to interrupt, but Jake plowed right over her.

"I'm talking about the fact that Franklin is my son. He's mine, and you didn't have the decency to tell me!"

"Franklin isn't yours," Boss scoffed, and Jake's fingers clenched into fists. "He's Preacher's."

"The goddamned cat is out of the bag!" he screamed, angrily dashing away the tear that had the audacity to slip down his cheek. "The blood types don't match. I know I don't have a PhD in biology, but I'm not a *moron* either. Did you expect that fact to just slip by me?"

"Franklin is…" Boss shook his head and glanced over at Shell who was biting her lush bottom lip and wringing her hands as tears coursed, unchecked, down her cheeks.

"Frank didn't know any—" she began as realization dawned on Boss's face, realization quickly followed by rage.

Well, good. Now we're both on the same goddamned page!

One minute he was glaring at his former CO, the next instant his head snapped back on his neck as pain exploded like a frag grenade in his jaw.

Boss might be big and clumsy-looking, but the sonofabitch had reflexes like a cat. Evidenced by the fact that Jake hadn't seen the left hook coming.

"You swore you wouldn't touch her unless you planned to make it legit!" Boss thundered, taking advantage of Jake's momentary astonishment to plant a hard palm in the center of his chest and shove him across the room. It was like being hit with a two-ton wrecking ball, and he tripped over a chair, sprawling on his ass.

Glancing up in time to see Boss steaming toward him like a freight train, the hand raised in the air by that bright blue cast clenched in a big, meaty fist, he scrambled to his feet and assumed the standard bent-knee stance, ready to absorb the kinetic energy of one very pissed off, 245-pound man. Then Becky suddenly launched herself onto Boss's back, clinging to him like a feisty blond monkey. She screamed something in Boss's ear that Jake couldn't understand, but whatever it was, Boss stopped dead in his tracks.

His face was a thundercloud, his chest working like bellows, but he no longer looked ready and willing to kill Jake on the spot.

It was at that point that Shell stepped into the breach. "Frank didn't know anything about it," she said, wiping at her tears with a trembling hand. And yeah, now that the killing rage was waning and cognition returning, Jake was beginning to clue in to that salient little fact. "No one knew but Steven. And he took my secret to his grave."

She hiccupped, glancing around the room at the shocked faces before shakily lowering herself into a chair. She covered her eyes with her hands as her shoulders heaved, but no sound escaped her lips. Which was more awful than if she'd been blubbering.

But no matter how hard he looked inside himself, Jake couldn't seem to find any sympathy for her. His heart, once so full of love, felt like a giant void.

Several seconds passed where no one moved or dared to breathe. It was a real pin-drop atmosphere. And now that his adrenaline was wearing off, his jaw felt like it was sitting on the side of his head.

Word up, Boss packed one helluva punch. He wouldn't be chewing right for the next month.

Lifting a hand, he checked to make sure that, yes, his lower mandible was still located on the *front* of his head.

"Why, Shell?" Boss finally asked, taking a step toward her.

Yeah, Jake wanted to know the answer to that question himself. Not that it really mattered, since there was no explanation she could give that could possibly justify her actions…

Shell just shook her head, stopping Boss from taking another step. The big guy frowned, his face so full of pain and shock and betrayal that Jake couldn't imagine what *he* must look like.

"Okay," Boss said, nodding jerkily. "Okay. We'll talk about this later."

What the fuck ever! Jake wanted an explanation now. Like, right now!

And he opened his mouth to demand just that at the same time Boss glanced over his shoulder at Becky, who was still attached to his back. "You gonna stay back there all night?"

"You gonna do another Mike Tyson impression?" she countered.

"I've got it under control," he told her. But before she

could climb down and Jake could demand his explanation, Nurse Susan reappeared in the open doorway.

"Well, it seems we didn't need your blood after all, Jake," she said, her face wreathed in smiles before she caught a glimpse of Becky and Boss and raised a brow, frowning. She shook her head and turned to Shell. "You'll be happy to know that your son's appendix didn't rupture. The surgeon was able to cut away the adhesions and remove it cleanly, so we don't foresee any future problems. Franklin is in recovery. You should be able to go see him in about fifteen minutes. And if all goes well, you can take him home tomorrow evening."

"T-tomorrow evening?" Shell sputtered, wiping at the tears on her cheeks. "So soon?"

"Laparoscopic surgery doesn't require a long hospital stay. And Franklin will heal faster at home, provided you keep him from getting too boisterous."

"I'll tie him to the bed if I have to," she promised, her voice thick with emotion. "And thank you." She smiled shakily at the nurse before turning to stare at Jake beseechingly.

What did she want from him?

Forgiveness?

No way. He'd always considered himself an easygoing guy. He wasn't one to hold a grudge. But if she thought he would just say, *That's okay, Shell. It's no problem that you hid my kid from me,* she had another thing coming.

Three years.

He'd had a son for three years. And because of her duplicity, her selfishness, he'd missed that first step, that first word, that first...*everything*.

And in that moment, he understood why people said love and hate were two sides of the same coin, because the void that'd become his heart filled up once more.

And this new emotion certainly wasn't love. Although it burned just as brightly...

Chapter Thirteen

JOHNNY STOMPED DOWN THE STAIRS OF THE TOWN HOUSE, the very *empty* town house, with a frown on his face.

All the lights were on, a fire crackled in the fireplace, the TV was blaring a rerun of *It's Always Sunny in Philadelphia*, the refrigerator door stood wide open, and the security system hadn't been armed—which accounted for his easy entrance into the place.

What the hell happened here?

It was almost like they knew he was coming and bolted. But that didn't make any sense.

Ducking back into the cozy living room, he surveyed the ordered chaos of toys, books, and family photos and wracked his brain over what to do next. Mary would be sorely disappointed if he made it to tomorrow without delivering at least *some* form of payback—and he *so* didn't want to have to listen to her bitchy voice howl at him over the phone line.

And then there was the not-so-small fact that he'd already been denied the pleasure of Michelle's company twice. Being robbed of her again was damned near untenable.

She was one hot piece of ass.

For the last hour, he'd fantasized about shooting the blond guy in the head before grabbing Michelle and fucking her bloody. Then would come the intense satisfaction of slitting her pretty throat. He was not a man who liked to be thwarted. Especially not three times in a row.

Unfortunately, he had no idea where to find her.

Except…wait a second…

Hadn't he read something about a nanny in Michelle's bio?

Rubbing his hands together in anticipation, he strolled through the kitchen, stopping to snag a bottle of beer from the open refrigerator and slipped out the back door.

———

"No, no," Michelle whispered into her phone as she lovingly gazed at her son's pale face. She sent another little prayer of thanks skyward—her thousandth since Franklin had come out of surgery. "Don't worry about coming here tonight, Lisa. Just enjoy your time off."

"He complained of a bellyache three days ago," her nanny said, anguish in her voice. "I just thought he'd eaten too much."

"Which would've been my first thought, as well," Michelle reassured her, laughing gently. "Don't go blaming yourself. These things happen."

And as soon as she uttered that last phrase, she thought of Jake and glanced anxiously at the bathroom door. The minute Franklin was transferred to a private room, Jake and her brother locked themselves inside the attached bathroom and proceeded to lay into one another.

Even now, she had a hard time blocking out their heated exchange in order to concentrate on the conversation with the nanny.

"I'll come by the hospital tomorrow evening when

he's released," Lisa said. "We'll get him home and in bed together."

"Franklin will like that," she whispered, wincing when a particularly vile curse issued from inside the bathroom.

She hoped it wouldn't come to blows again. Seeing her brother waylay Jake was almost too much to bear.

Oh, there'd been times she wouldn't have batted a lash to watch Frank put Jake in his place. Times she might've actually *enjoyed* seeing Jake get his ass kicked. That day outside the gates at the Naval Amphibious Base for one. But today it just felt...*wrong*.

Just terribly, terribly wrong.

Because he was absolutely annihilated by the bomb she'd dropped on him. There was no denying that. Not after seeing the stark, unbridled anguish in his face, the disbelief and pain and heartbreak.

It was almost enough to make her think that maybe she'd made a mistake all those years ago. That maybe, even after the way he'd treated her and the things he'd said, even after he ignored her letter begging him to return—especially now that she understood why he'd done all those things—that she should've just told him the truth.

But no, she assured herself, *you did what was right for your child*.

She was sure of that...wasn't she?

She hadn't wanted her son growing up with a reluctant and neglectful father. She knew what that was like, the excruciating, nearly debilitating pain of it. And Jake *would* have been reluctant and neglectful... wouldn't he?

Oh Jesus, it was all so complicated and terrible. She wasn't sure *what* was right anymore...

Fighting back tears of sorrow and regret, she signed off with Lisa, pocketed her cell phone, and rested her head on the rung of the hospital bed. Squeezing her eyes closed, the conversation taking place inside the bathroom filled her ears.

"How can you stand there and tell me you've forgiven her after she's been lying to you all these years?" Jake demanded.

"Because she's my sister," Frank snarled. "And I know two things beyond a shadow of doubt. One, she must've had a damn good reason for doing what she did. And two, she can't lie for shit. And since she was able to pull it off, it means she must have wholeheartedly believed she was doing the right thing."

"I don't care what she *believed*," Jake roared, then lowered his voice when Frank shushed him. "There's absolutely no excuse."

No excuse? Had he forgotten everything?

She reached through the rungs to squeeze Franklin's little knee under the light blue hospital blanket, more to reassure herself than to reassure him, because he hadn't yet woken from the anesthesia. But he would soon, and the thought had dread settling in her stomach like a five-pound pot roast.

What would Jake do when he had the opportunity to speak to his son for the first time? Would he tell Franklin the truth? And how would Franklin react if he did?

Her sweet boy had no experience with a father. The concept, in its solid form, was foreign to him. As far as he was concerned, a *daddy* was nothing but an abstraction. A story like all the stories she read to him before bedtime. How would he handle the appearance of a living, breathing, all-too-real father?

"Snake," she heard her brother say, "I understand how you feel. Really I do. But you need to give her a chance to—"

"She's had all the chances she deserves," Jake snarled. "Three long years of them. When do I get *my* chance? I want my son, Boss."

The room tilted and began to close in on her, and she realized she wasn't breathing. The thought of losing Franklin…

"I know you're hurting right now, man. I know you're pissed beyond measure. And you've got every right to feel that way. But there's no way in hell I'm letting you take that boy away from his mother."

A solid *thump* sounded against the wall, and she was pretty sure Jake had attempted to put his fist through it. That supposition was confirmed when a long silence ensued, which was eventually broken by her brother asking, "Feel better now?"

"Not really," Jake mumbled.

"We're going to find a way to work this out, man."

Really? Did her brother have a time machine? Because, as far as she could tell, the ability to change history was the only way she could fathom them being able to work out anything.

"I want my son, Boss." Jake repeated. "I deserve the opportunity to be a father to him."

-----∿-----

"Hey, honey, you lookin' for date?" The red-haired whore with the gargantuan fake tits grabbed one of her nipples through her bustier and gave it a squeeze as Johnny breezed by her on his way to the elevator at The Stardust Hotel.

"Maybe later," he muttered, too preoccupied with the task at hand to give her much more than a passing thought.

Of course, if he couldn't find Michelle Carter tonight, he might be in need of some relief from the fire in his veins, and the whore, though certainly not his first choice, would do in a pinch.

"Well, I'm here when you need me," she purred.

He winked at her and waggled his tongue as the silver doors closed behind him. Snapping his fingers impatiently, he groaned as the elevator made its noisy, slow journey to the sixth floor. He should've snuck in the rear entrance and climbed the back steps, just like he'd been doing since he'd checked in to The Stardust Hotel. But he'd been too anxious to get his hands on the information and had falsely thought the front door and elevator would be faster.

It wasn't.

But finally, *finally* the elevator door slid open. Hurrying down the smoky hall, he fished in his pocket for his room key. Pushing inside room 602, he rushed to the bed and thumbed through the folder the PI had sent him until he found what he was looking for.

Lisa Brown.

The file said she was a part-time graduate student at Northwestern University in Liberal Studies—whatever the hell that was—and a full-time nanny for Michelle

Carter. Scanning the sheet for the information he sought, he smiled when his eyes landed on an address.

Folding the piece of paper, he tried shoving it in his jacket pocket only to stop when his fingers brushed against something glossy and flat.

He pulled out the photo of Michelle with her son and unfolded it, running a thumb over the full line of her lush breasts. What the red-headed whore in the lobby had paid a plastic surgeon a pretty penny to construct, God had given naturally to Michelle.

His blood began to pound in his cock, and he reached down to adjust himself.

Oh, we're going to have some fun, you and I. A whole lot of fun…

Tossing the photo on the bed—he didn't need it, he'd know her face anywhere—he shoved Lisa Brown's information into his pocket and strolled from his room, whistling happily.

"Snake, can I talk to you out in the hall," Boss asked, causing Jake to glance away from the sweet, innocent face of his sleeping son.

His son…

Yo, it's going to take some time to get used to that.

He was a *father*. He had a *son*. Maybe if he said it over and over again, he'd finally be able to believe it.

"I guess," he said, pushing up from the stiff chair he'd pulled beside Franklin's hospital bed. The boy looked like a little doll among the covers, so small, so pale. He tried to see some of himself in him…

And it rankled more than he'd ever admit to find none

of his physical characteristics in that cherubic little face. It was insult added to injury. After all, he'd already been denied his rights as a father, was it fair the universe had decided to deny his genetics, as well?

Franklin stirred, a small frown wrinkling his brow, and Shell reached up to brush the boy's hair back from his face, whispering words of comfort.

"You comin' or what?" Boss asked.

"Yeah, yeah," he mumbled, striding toward the door, refusing to glance at Shell as he passed her.

Pushing into the hall, he closed the door behind him and crossed his arms as he leaned against the jamb, glaring at Boss. Oh, he knew his former CO was innocent in all this, but it didn't help that the guy was determined to take Shell's side in everything.

He felt like he was fighting a war on two fronts.

"What's up?" he asked when Boss eyed him concernedly.

Screw that. He didn't want concern. He didn't know what he wanted exactly; he was still too shaken up and confused, but he did know it wasn't concern.

"Becky and I have to get back to the shop," Boss said, the scars on his tight face standing out in rigid, white relief. "Rock has finished questioning this latest hit man, and he's on his way back to resume his surveillance and reconnaissance duty at the hotel. Steady's having to wait back at BKI in order to give me the sit-rep on what Rock discovered before he can resume his duties, but before I can take care of that I need to swing by Shell's place and close up. I left in such a hurry, I didn't lock the door or set her security system, and it'll be a miracle if she hasn't already been robbed blind. I'm leaving Ozzie here to look after Shell and Franklin. But what I need from you is some assurances you won't—"

"You don't need to have the kid stay," he interrupted. "I can look after Shell and Franklin until it's time to take them home."

Boss's expression belied his hesitation, and that pissed Jake off all the more. "Look, dude," he ground out, "just because she broke my heart and hid my kid away from me doesn't mean I'll let anything happen to her. She *is* the mother of my child, after all."

The mother of his child. And that was another concept it was going to take some getting used to…

He suddenly had the urge to hit something. *Hard*. And, unfortunately, the wall didn't look sturdy enough to be satisfying.

Boss's eyes narrowed, searching Jake's livid expression, and then the big guy did something totally unexpected.

He grabbed Jake by the shoulder and dragged him into a bear hug.

"W-what the fuck?" he sputtered, trying to push away. But it was like trying to move a mountain.

"I'm sorry," Boss whispered close to his ear. "I'm so sorry this happened. If I'd known…" He let the sentence dangle, and all the rage and frustration that'd kept Jake from breaking down into a pitiful heap of tears and snot vanished like smoke on an ocean breeze.

Oh, fuck a duck!

The first hard sob wracked his lungs and had him threatening to squeeze the life from Boss as he wrapped his arms around the man's back.

"How could she do it?" he choked, burning tears

clogging his throat and blinding his eyes. "How could she do this to me?"

"I don't know, man," Boss patted his back with a big, square hand. "That's why you need to ask her. That's *what* you need to ask her."

"I can't even *look* at her," he admitted, pushing back to wipe his nose. "How can I after what she's done?"

"You can because you remember she's Shell. She may've fallen off that super high pedestal you had her on," Boss said, undaunted by the fact there were big, fat tears streaming down Jake's face, "but she's not the heartless witch you're trying to convince yourself she is either."

And that was the whole damn problem now, wasn't it?

Because he knew she wasn't.

He knew Shell. And there wasn't a malicious or vindictive bone in her body.

Which meant she'd made her decision four years ago, because she'd actually thought what she was doing was right, just like Boss had said. And *that* meant she'd believed him either unable or unwilling to uphold his responsibilities toward her and their unborn child. Which, in turn, forced him to admit that maybe she *was* right. Maybe he would've been unable or unwilling to uphold his responsibilities.

He'd been so screwed up...

"You go back to the shop with your people," he finally managed, taking a step back and scrubbing a hand over his face, hating the fact that it came away wet, because that meant he'd been blubbering like a goddamned baby. *Again*.

One more breakdown like that and he'd have his "man card" permanently revoked.

"I'll watch after Shell and Franklin." When Boss turned his head to the side, his expression wary, Jake blew out a breath and nodded. "I won't say one cross word to her."

"I have your word on that?"

He held up three fingers. "Scout's honor."

"You were never a Boy Scout," Boss scoffed.

"Goddamnit! Why does everybody keep *saying* that?"

Johnny waited on the stoop outside the four-flat building in Lincoln Park with a dozen blue roses in hand until a twenty-something kid wearing a Chicago Bulls cap climbed the stairs and opened the door to the apartment building. The dude was talking into his cell phone—in a fight with his girlfriend by the sound of things—so he didn't see Johnny slip in behind him.

He quietly followed the Bulls fan up the stairs, shaking his head when the kid swore to the woman on the other end of the line that he *wasn't* interested in Gabrielle Eyler, and to prove it, he'd never look at another girl again.

You better man-up, my friend, or else that bitch will be wearing your balls as earrings in no time.

He turned his head away when Mr. Pussy-Whipped stopped on the second floor landing to let himself into his apartment, adjusting the Silly Lilly baseball cap he'd stolen from the shop when he went to get his first bouquet, and quietly slid past as if he was in a hurry to get to one of the top floors. The kid barely glanced at him before closing the door of his apartment behind him.

The stairwell leading to the third floor smelled like

cheap air freshener, and the carpet on the stairs was stained, but other than that, the place was clean.

And *quiet*, he noted with some concern.

Which meant he'd have to be quick and smart with his work. He couldn't have the neighbors calling the cops now, could he?

No. Definitely not.

After all he'd done and gotten away with, he certainly didn't want the killing of some no-account grad student/ nanny to be the one thing that finally landed a needle in his vein.

Hoofing it up to the fourth floor, he slipped on a pair of fitted, leather gloves and knocked quietly, then stepped to the side, away from the view of the peephole as he held up the roses.

"Who is it?" a soft, young voice sounded through the door.

"I'm from Silly Lily Flower Shop," he said. "The guy who lives on the second floor let me follow him in. Are you Lisa Brown?"

"Flowers?" she inquired. "So late?"

"I tried to stop by earlier, ma'am," he explained, "but you weren't home. And since I was in the neighborhood anyway, I figured I'd try again."

"On your own time?" Her voice sounded wary, and he didn't want that. He couldn't let another scene like the one with Michelle happen again. He had to think fast.

"Oh hell no," he chuckled, careful to keep his tone friendly. "We're a twenty-four-hour shop. Because, ya know, we've found most guys who stumble home from the bar at 2 a.m. are less likely to receive any guff from the missus if they have flowers in hand."

"Oh, okay," she said. "Hang on just a second."

Christ, he thought, shaking his head, *most women will believe anything if flowers are involved.* According to Lisa's file, she didn't have a boyfriend, so just who did she think was sending her flowers?

Some clichéd secret admirer, no doubt. She obviously needed to take a page from Michelle Carter's book on "don't open the door to strangers." Of course, he wasn't going to complain.

He listened anxiously as the deadbolt clicked and the chain rattled, his palms itching inside his gloves, the sweet scent of the roses burning his lungs. The minute the door inched open, he planted a booted foot in the center of the thing, sending it crashing backward along with the woman behind it.

He was on her before she had time to scramble up, before she had time to scream.

Securing her arms behind her back and smashing her face into the rug so that all she was able to manage were a few muted whimpers, he quickly scanned the little apartment, checking to ensure she had no guests. When he found everything quiet, he bent to breathe in her ear, "Lisa Brown." He loved the feel of her heaving and bucking beneath him. "I need you to tell me where I can find Michelle Carter."

———

"You owe me twenty bucks," Becky said with a wry grin, sauntering up to Jake and opening her purse to show him the huge assortment of colorful plastic acorn containers you find inside vending machines, the ones filled with cheap toys. "Not to mention repayment on the sliver of pride I lost while plugging money into that stupid machine. The guy working in the gift shop thought I'd lost my mind. On the up side," she wiggled her blond brows, "if you ever have a need for acrylic fashion rings, bouncy balls, or flavorless gumdrops I'm your go-to gal."

"But you were able to finally get them?" he asked with concern.

She winked and held up a small sheet of press-on tattoos, grinning.

He made a grab for the sheet, but she whipped it behind her back, shaking her head. "Ah, ah. You slide me a nice, crisp Andrew Jackson, and I slide you the tattoos. I like you and all. But I'm no gift fairy, and my boss is kind of a tightwad." At this last bit, she turned and winked at Boss who was leaning against the hallway wall.

The big guy blew her a kiss.

Jake shook his head at the pair as he quickly dug into his wallet, pulling out a twenty. He and Becky made the exchange like a drug deal; he palmed the tattoos the instant she palmed the twenty. And once the trade was complete, Boss pushed away from the wall to sling a big arm around his future bride. "Now that that's done," he muttered, "let's get going. Rock is itching to get back to the hotel."

"Oh, I just bet he is," Becky chuckled.

"What the hell is that supposed to mean?" Boss demanded as the two turned and headed down the hall.

"I swear, you men are as blind as bats when it comes to things involving human emotion…"

Jake watched them go until they rounded the nurses'

station and their voices faded. Then he turned back into Franklin's room, avoiding Shell's inquisitive, slightly wary stare.

Going into the bathroom, he wetted a washcloth to take back to his son's bedside and—

His son.

Again the notion hit him like a mortar round, blowing apart his tenuous control, causing his heart to pound and his lungs to seize.

He looked at himself in the mirror over the sink. The hurt was there in his bloodshot eyes, in the heavy lines on his brow and the ones bracketing his thinned lips.

Why did she keep him from me?

And yeah, he knew he needed to ask *her* that question, just like Boss said. But not yet. Not here. And definitely not now.

He needed some time to prepare himself for the heartbreak he knew her answer would bring...

Taking a deep breath, he pushed away from the sink and exited the bathroom. Still avoiding Shell's searching gaze, he strode to Franklin's bedside and pushed up the sleeve on the boy's hospital gown.

"What are you doing?" Shell asked, and her sultry voice affected him the same way it always did. Cutting straight to his heart.

"I'm giving him a press-on tattoo," he mumbled as he placed the small sheet of paper on Franklin's bicep, gently wetting the back with the washcloth in order to transfer the ink.

"I can see that," she said, and her sweet tone made him want to glance up at her. But he couldn't. Not yet. "But why?"

"Because he admired mine all day today, and I want him to see that he has his own the minute he wakes up. It's the only thing I could think to do for him." Since he couldn't comfort the boy like Shell could, with only a word or a touch, with only his simple presence. After all, who was he to Franklin? Nothing but a big stranger who'd played games all day and who was good at doing funny voices.

The hurt began to thrum inside him again, close to the surface like a bad tooth, and he struggled to beat it back.

"That's nice of you," she whispered as he softly peeled away the paper backing, smiling at the coiled green and black snake that decorated Franklin's sturdy little arm. "He'll like that."

"Yeah." He threw the wet paper backing from the tattoo into the wastebasket and resumed his seat in the torture device that passed as a chair. "At least now we have *something* in common."

"What do you mean?"

"I mean…" He stared at the boy's face. "At least now we have matching tattoos. One physical characteristic to tie us together."

"What are you talking about?" There was genuine confusion in her voice.

He glanced up into her beautiful face, trying not to let the concern written there affect him. But it did. Because accompanying that concern were the heartfelt emotional twins otherwise known as *sorrow* and *regret*.

Which made his anger toward her begin to mellow. And he certainly wasn't ready for that.

Reminding himself of the years he'd lost, the years she'd *stolen*, he hardened his resolve and blurted, "I'm talking about the fact that the kid has half of my DNA, but you couldn't tell it by looking at him."

Her face instantly softened, and he glanced away.

"You're wrong," she whispered.

"Yeah?" He grimaced when his stupid voice cracked like a pubescent boy's. "How so?"

She was silent for a long time, and he knew she was waiting for him to look over at her, but he couldn't. Finally, she sighed. "You asked me why I had that look on my face in the courtyard yesterday evening when you introduced yourself to Franklin. You said you thought it was because I blamed you for Steven's death?"

Now he couldn't help himself. He glanced across the bed to find tears standing in her eyes.

Her lying eyes, he reminded himself.

"Yeah? And you said it was because you thought it was unfair that I was able to waltz back into your life like nothing ever happened."

She shook her head. "The *real* reason I wore that expression was because with you two standing together, especially with those identical smiles and those identical dimples, I figured everyone would immediately deduce the truth. That you were father and son. In that instant, you looked so much alike it made my heart stop."

He glanced back at Franklin, at the boy's round cheeks that, even relaxed in sleep, still showed faint, shadowed divots—just like he knew his own did.

For the third time that day, tears clogged his throat.

Yep, there goes my "man card."

"Thank you for that," he managed to whisper.

Chapter Fourteen

"YOU TRY TO SCREAM ONE MORE TIME," JOHNNY sneered, smiling evilly at the stark terror contorting Lisa Brown's face as she sat strapped to one of her kitchen chairs, "and I'll cut out your pretty brown eyes."

He'd never cared much for black women. Not that many of them weren't gorgeous in a darkly exotic way that got his blood pumping. But they were generally too mouthy for his tastes. And Lisa was proving to be no exception.

"However, if you answer all my questions," he continued, "I'll walk out that door, and you'll never see me again."

Right. And I'll also give you my ocean-front property in Arizona.

He watched hope spring up in her dark eyes and had trouble maintaining his poker face. Removing her gag, he grabbed her jaw just to make sure she didn't do something stupid like open her mouth to let loose with another one of those banshee wails she'd managed earlier.

The woman had a set of pipes, no doubt. And that could get him in trouble if he wasn't very, very careful.

"Where are Michelle Carter and her son?"

"Wh-why do you wanna—" she started, and that just wouldn't do.

"Bitch," he squeezed her jaw until her eyes rolled

back in her head, and she began to struggle ineffectually against her restraints. "I'm the one asking the questions here. Where…is…Michelle?"

She shook her head, and he slapped her. Hard. Her head snapped to the side on her thin, fragile neck, and her soft, milk-chocolate-colored cheek instantly burned bright red. He grabbed her jaw again, digging his fingers between her top and bottom teeth.

"You wanna try that again?" he asked.

"Th-they're at the hos-hospital," she managed to garble even though he was squeezing her jaw so hard she could barely form the words. A bright drop of blood leaked from one corner of her mouth, and he knew he'd managed to cut her cheek on her teeth when he slapped her.

He loosened his grip. Not to lessen her pain—he liked seeing her in pain—but to hurry up this little interview. "What are they doing there?"

"Franklin h-had an appendicitis. He…he had surgery. Please," she begged, "you're hurting me."

Oh, you haven't begun *to experience pain. But you will. Soon…*

The thought made his erection throb hard against the fly of his jeans, and one corner of his mouth quirked in anticipation.

"And when will they be coming home?"

Lisa's eyes slid to the side, one frantic glance at the purple, sequined purse lying on the bistro-sized kitchen table. He followed the direction of her gaze and wondered what she could possibly think she had hidden in there that might save her.

Cell phone? Mace? Maybe a little handgun?

Of course, all of those required hands to operate…

"It's too late for that." Resting his gloved palms on the high back of her chair, he leaned in close to her face. So close he could smell her fear, all musky and sour.

Some of the sweetest perfume on the planet…

"You're not getting out of here until I let you," he hissed in her ear, loving the feel of her trembling breath against his cheek. "And I won't let you until you answer all my questions. "Now," he pulled back and smiled, "when will Michelle and her son be coming home?"

Lisa swallowed, running her plump pink tongue over her dusky lips. He eyed the movement with some remorse.

The woman had a mouth made for sin. Too bad he wouldn't be able to use it.

"Franklin's being released tomorrow evening," she whispered. "Now, *please*," two fat tears spilled down her cheeks and dripped off her chin, "let me go."

Johnny winked, then reached up with his knife and slit her slim throat.

He delighted in the surprise that flashed through her eyes. People were always shocked to realize they were actually going to die, which never ceased to amaze him. Especially during times like this.

But hope springs eternal, he supposed.

Reaching into her throat, past the sticky blood that pumped steadily from the fatal wound, he grabbed that pretty pink tongue he'd admired earlier and pulled it down through the torn flesh.

You won't be using those pipes now, will ya?

And, yeah, it was sort of a shame to have ruined that lovely face, and it was certainly a travesty to have destroyed her wonderful tongue, but what could he do? Colombian neckties happened to be his specialty, and he wasn't one to screw with a good thing.

Standing back, he tilted his head as he observed the macabre picture little Lisa presented, eyes wide and dull, blood still flowing freely down her chest, mouth open in a silent tongueless scream.

There was always that moment. After the kill. When the adrenaline wore off. A brief second when he tried to feel something. Anything. A small pause when he searched his conscience for a kernel of remorse. But, just like always, his hunt turned up…nothing.

Oh well.

Shaking himself into action, he washed off his gloves in her kitchen sink before carefully opening her front door to peek out into the hall and down the stairwell. When he found everything quiet, he closed the door behind himself and quickly raced down the stairs.

The instant his loafers touched the sidewalk outside, a contented smile curved his lips.

Now on to Michelle…

"How'd it go?" Vanessa asked, lowering a pair of optics and turning away from her perch by the window.

Just the sight of her pretty face and dark, inquisitive eyes was enough to have the fatigue Rock was carrying lift away like dandelion seeds on a stiff breeze. It was also enough to have the brainless wonder in his pants raising its little head expectantly.

Amazing.

When he'd passed Candy of the Ridiculous Red Hair

in the lobby and she dropped her top in order to give him a look at the goods, he hadn't been able to manage even a modicum of enthusiasm—and that was saying something, considering her plastic surgeon had been more artist than doctor. But one look at Vanessa, sitting there in her ridiculous street-walker getup, her hair pulled back in a sleek, prim bun, and her face washed clean of make-up—one part tramp and two parts lady—and suddenly he could barely manage to wrangle the beast caged behind his zipper.

Correction. *Christian's* zipper…

Zut!

He threw his key on the rickety, plywood nightstand and toed out of Christian's too-big, too-fancy, too-expensive shoes. Sinking down on the lumpy mattress, he ran a hand through his hair.

And noticed his fingers were shaking…

Damnit. They always did this after he'd been required to pry open somebody's mind.

"Ya know how they say you should never judge a book by its cover?" he mumbled, fisting his hands before shaking them in order to try to stop their quaking.

It didn't help. It never did…

"Yeah?"

"Well, they were talking about Joe Bob Bartlett."

She raised a brow, and he blew out a hard breath, swallowing convulsively. "*Dieu*, the guy was so skinny he'd hafta stand up twice to cast a shadow, but he was tough as nails. It took me nearly an hour of interrogatin' to get any information outta him at all."

An hour of begging, cajoling, yelling, and threatening before he'd finally been forced to apply a little pressure, inflict a smidgen of pain, and suddenly Joe Bob couldn't tell his story fast enough…

"Sorry," she whispered, and he glanced over at her.

Now that's a mistake, you big couyon.

Because that brief look was enough of an invitation to have her rising from the chair by the window and padding over to him.

Her feet were bare, and her toenails were painted a sweet pink that looked like cotton candy. When she stopped in front of him, he was left with no choice but to look up into her concerned face. There was understanding in the fathomless depths of her dark eyes. Understanding and something he didn't dare name.

Because they were alone.

In a hotel room.

With a bed…

Merde.

She reached for his hand, chaffing the stupid, shaking thing between her soft palms. "I can't imagine what it does to you," she murmured. "Using someone's fear and weakness against them."

She didn't know the half of it. Because it was more than that. A true interrogator could get inside a person's psyche. And sometimes once you got into a person's head, it wasn't always easy to get out. "You get used to it after a while," he managed.

She smelled so good. Like peppermint and sugar, slightly sweet, slightly spicy…

"Bullshit," she said, then smiled at the look of surprise on his face. "Yes, I call bullshit on occasion."

Okay, their conversation had veered off course. And with her standing so close, touching him, his brain was going all fuzzy. Like he'd had one swig too many of the moonshine his Uncle Beauford used to brew. It was time he got them back on track.

Now.

Before he did something they'd both regret.

"It doesn't matter," he said, softly sliding his hand from between her soft palms, disgusted when his fingers continued to tingle with sensation. "It needed to be done. And now we have two more assassins off our tails."

"Two?"

"*Oui*. That's why Joe Bob was so hard to break. He was protectin' his brother, Jimmy Don, who was holed up back at their hotel."

"Joe Bob and Jimmy Don? Let me guess, they hail from Kentucky."

"Nope. Oklahoma. Indian Territory. The Sooner State."

"Yeah, yeah." She waved off any other titles he might have thrown out there in an attempt to keep their discussion on steady ground. "I get it," she said, then hesitated, her brow furrowing. "Or maybe I don't. Why *is* it called the Sooner State?"

Dieu, she was funny. And pretty. And oh, oh, *oh* so sexy.

He needed to get away from her. Now. Five minutes ago...

"I'm not sure," he grumbled, pushing up from the mattress. "I think it has somethin' to do with the land run. But that's not important right now. What *is* important is two more of our would-be assassins are off the street."

There. All done. Debrief complete.

Now if only she'd take a step back, he could make a break for the sanctity of the bathroom where, undoubtedly, he'd have to spend the next five minutes taking care of the problem in his pants.

Unfortunately, she remained rooted to the spot, blocking his escape.

"Rock?"

His heart stopped dead.

"Yeah, *cheri?*" Was that rough-sounding voice really his?

"Why do you do it if it bothers you so much?" Her eyes were so big, looking up at him so innocently.

He couldn't pretend to misunderstand her question. "Because it's what I've been trained to do. And I'm good at it. Really, really good at it."

She nodded, and he could see the storm of questions swirling around in her head. But she must've known by the look on his face that he wasn't going to give her any more answers.

He'd already revealed more than he should have. "*Tete de pissette!*" he growled, pushing past her to stalk toward the bathroom.

"I speak French, you know," she huffed. "And I don't think I said or did anything to warrant being called a dickhead."

"I was talkin' to myself," he said, turning back to her.

She rolled in her lips, fighting a grin, and the look went all through him.

Merde. What a goatscrew.

Johnny reached into Michelle's refrigerator for another beer but stopped with his hand on the bottle when he heard the sound of a car door slam.

He quickly glanced around the cozy kitchen looking for a place to hide when he spied the large, walk-in pantry. He was there in two strides, slipping inside and closing the door behind him. With his back pressed against a shelf of canned goods, he held his breath, his hand sliding down to his waistband and the grip of his Ruger.

Ten seconds later, the front door opened with a squeak and heavy footsteps sounded in the living room, followed by the television falling silent.

"Yeah, I'm here now," a man's deep voice resonated through the louvered slats of the pantry door. "I'm gonna do a quick recon of her place then lock up. I'll meet you back at the shop in thirty."

Footsteps pounded up the stairs and then stomped around overhead. Johnny glanced around the pantry anxiously, looking for some way to conceal himself more thoroughly.

He couldn't let this jackass, whoever he was, muck up his plans yet again.

There. In the back corner.

A large packing box stood open, an odd assortment of baskets tossed inside.

Slowly, quietly, he pulled the baskets out and stacked them beside a shelf. Then, just as stealthily, he climbed into the box. It was a squeeze, but he managed to fold himself into a ball, carefully keeping his Ruger at the ready should he need it, and pulled the flaps closed over his head.

Then he waited.

His breath caught in his lungs when the footfalls sounded on the stairs again. And then he heard the man enter the kitchen a few seconds before the refrigerator door slammed shut. He swallowed, and it sounded like a gun blast inside the stuffy silence of the box. Sweat trickled down his temple when the pantry door opened, and he blew out a silent breath when it closed again.

The man's cell phone came to life with a blast of rock music, and Johnny listened as the guy answered gruffly, giving instructions to somebody on the other end. When the sound of his voice faded, Johnny soundlessly emerged from the box and tiptoed toward the pantry door.

He tipped his chin until he could see through one of the thin, horizontal openings, blinking at the huge man with a bright blue cast standing in the middle of the living room.

His heart began to pound with giddy anticipation when he recognized the giant.

Frank Knight. Owner of Black Knights Incorporated.

What were the odds?

Pretty good actually, since you're hiding in his sister's pantry.

He suppressed a wry chuckle and thumbed off the safely on his pistol.

He knew this wasn't the plan. The plan was to kill Frank's family. An eye for an eye. But Johnny couldn't bring himself to pass up an opportunity like this.

He started to lift the Ruger, to point it at Frank Knight's back, when suddenly the big man swung around, seeming to stare straight at him. It was like being caught in the crosshairs of a rifle, and Johnny's neck prickled like it was crawling with ants; a bead of sweat slid coldly down his spine.

He held his breath, ready to raise his gun those final few inches and fire the instant Frank made a move in his direction. But the big man turned abruptly and stalked across living room. Johnny's heart tripped over itself as he released his pent-up breath.

Holy fuck, that dude is scary looking. Far more intimidating in the flesh than in his photos. Of course, Johnny wasn't scared. Hell no. He was far from scared. He was downright ecstatic. This was the head honcho right here!

His finger curled around the trigger as his palms began to itch. The air inside the pantry grew heavy and damp with his rapid breathing, with the sweat that broke out all over his body.

"No," he heard Frank laugh. "We are not going down in the river tunnel for a quickie. It's wet and creepy down there. Remember what happened this morning when you thought you felt a spider in your hair, and you started running around screaming? It completely ruined my happy ending. I'm coming out now. Warm up the engine for me, will ya? No," the big guy laughed again. "Not *that* engine. The one on the Hummer."

Carefully, Johnny pushed open the pantry door, wincing when it squeaked. But, fortunately, the sound was masked by a series of beeps coming from the security panel on the wall by the front door. Hurriedly, he tiptoed across the kitchen, silently raising his weapon as he went. When he stepped into the living room, a smile on his face, the Ruger hot in his hand, his finger already squeezing the trigger, he was met by the front door swinging closed.

"Fuck me!" he cursed beneath his breath, racing

across the living room, feeling his opportunity to kill Frank Knight slip through his fingers.

His hand was on the knob, preparing to wrench open the front door and take aim, when the sound of a big engine firing up stopped him cold.

He peeked through the leaded glass at the top of the door in time to see a monster black Hummer pull from the curb.

"Goddamnit!"

For a split second, he contemplated taking aim and filling the SUV full of holes. But he managed to restrain himself.

So okay, he forced himself to uncurl his finger from the trigger, *you missed your chance to kill Frank Knight. Maybe it's better this way.*

After all, dying was easy compared to the suffering the dude would face once Johnny was finished with his sister.

Quickly glancing at the alarm system, he noted the motion detectors were programmed to arm in fifteen seconds, which gave him just enough time to hoof it up to the second floor and get himself into position.

With anticipation burning bright in his heart, he turned and raced up the stairs.

Stupid cell phones! They're always out of batteries when you need them!

Michelle tossed her useless phone into her purse and tentatively glanced across the hospital bed at Jake's rigidly controlled face. He'd stayed in Franklin's room with her all night and all day, and he'd yet to ask the one question she knew must be burning a hole in his brain.

Why?

She saw it in his eyes every time he looked at her, caught it on his expression whenever he gazed at Franklin.

But he hadn't asked it.

And why hadn't he asked it? Why hadn't he given her a chance to explain like her brother had begged him to?

Dear Lord, she'd never meant to hurt him. She'd only meant to protect her child, to do the right thing for her child. And she could explain all of that to him; she *wanted* to explain all of that to him…if only he'd ask.

Because she couldn't be the first to broach the subject. If she did, it might appear as if she was offering excuses and she wasn't. She had no excuses, because he'd never given her any cause for excuses. He'd only ever given her reasons!

She beat back a sharp sob and wondered, now that they were about to check out of the hospital and take Franklin home, what he would do?

Tell Franklin the truth?

Demand custody?

What was he thinking in that head of his? *What?*

She couldn't stand this…this…not knowing.

But she couldn't confront him, couldn't demand he tell her his intentions before he was ready to make them known, because that just might push him to the edge, make him act rashly.

No. She had to keep on doing exactly what she'd been doing. Staying calm. Staying patient.

Even if it killed her…

"Jake," she whispered his name, and he glanced up from the out-of-date *Hot Rod* magazine he'd been reading for the last two hours. "Can I—" she had to swallow past the lump in her throat. "Can I borrow your cell phone? Mine is dead, and Lisa was supposed to be here twenty minutes ago. I'm…I'm getting worried."

In answer, he absently dug into the hip pocket of his jeans and tossed her his iPhone before immediately going back to his magazine.

And the silent treatment continues…

She shook her head, resisting the urge to burst into tears as she thumbed on the phone and quickly dialed Lisa's number. She listened to it ring on the other end and gnawed anxiously on a hangnail before she was forced to leave a voice mail.

"No go?" he asked after she clicked off.

They were the first words he'd spoken to her in hours, and the sound of his voice, even brusque and unyielding as it was, made her chest ache.

"No," she pushed up from the little love seat to circle the foot of Franklin's hospital bed and return his phone.

Her fingers brushed his as she handed back the device, and she was forced to subdue the accompanying shiver. Even after everything, after all the disappointment and betrayal, the mere touch of his skin made her long for…things she shouldn't long for. Things that could never be.

"She's not picking up," she continued, ignoring the desire to fall to her knees and beg his forgiveness, beg him to understand that she'd done what was right, beg him to remember how he'd been, beg him to see that it'd killed her to keep Franklin a secret, but he'd given her no choice. But she knew he was in no mood to accept his part in all this. And, for her part, she had just enough pride left to remain on her feet. "And it's not like her to say she'll be somewhere and then not show up. I'll give it a few minutes just in case she's stuck in traffic or something, and then I'll try her again." She was amazed at how steady her voice sounded given her insides were spinning like a ferris wheel. "By the way, your phone only has three percent battery life left."

He shrugged and went back to reading, and she stood there in front of him, heart in her throat, staring down at the crown of his shaggy, sun-kissed head.

"You're going to have to talk to me eventually," she whispered. "It's the only way to sort everything out."

He rolled in his lips, a muscle ticking in his jaw as he shrugged again, still refusing to look at her, continuing to pretend like he was reading that stupid car magazine.

Heat began to burn over her scalp, but she did her best to ignore it, to maintain her composure.

"You know I'm right, don't you?" she asked.

But when he shrugged *again*, that did it.

She jammed a palm down on each of his big shoulders. "Stop shrugging!" she hissed into his surprised face, surprising herself as well. She was obviously losing it, but she was helpless to stop herself. She couldn't stand this vicious silence a moment longer. Not when each second sliced into her heart like broken glass.

"Please, Jake," she beseeched him, taking a deep breath to try to calm herself. It didn't seem to work. "Please say something. Say *anything*."

And then she got her wish, because the question she'd

been waiting to hear for hours, suddenly flew from his lips like he'd spit out bad sushi.

"Why?"

Chapter Fifteen

"WHY DIDN'T YOU TELL ME I HAD A SON!" JAKE
demanded, ignoring the stricken look that contorted
Shell's face right before she slowly turned and made
her way back to the love seat.

When she took a seat, folding her arms around herself
protectively, the move pushed her breasts together until
her cleavage looked like it could adequately conceal a
Colt .45.

He'd been face-first in that cleavage just last night.
And even after all that'd happened, even after all her
lies, he was disgusted to discover he was more than
ready to dive in again.

He still wanted her. Still yearned for her in a way that
made his blood run hot and his heart beat double-time.

It was completely ridiculous, and he was turning into
a totally masochistic moron.

"Answer the question," he demanded, disgusted with
himself. Disgusted with her. Disgusted with life in general at this point.

Her expression softened as she searched his face.

Oh, and great, now his heart wasn't only galloping, it
was breaking just a little bit, too.

Perfect.

"Do you remember that day I came to see you at
the base?"

He swallowed, nodding, the entire sordid scene

flashing in front of his eyes. He'd been so callus. So cruel. And then it suddenly occurred to him...

"Is *that* what you came to tell me that day? That you were pregnant?"

One large tear spilled down her smooth cheek. She didn't reach up to wipe it away, instead allowing it to roll off her chin and land on her collarbone where it caught the overhead lights and sparkled like a sad little diamond.

"Yes," she whispered, her gaze steady on his face despite the fact that he knew the memory had to be as painful for her as it was for him.

"I..." he swallowed, cursing himself for being a blind, jealous idiot. "I thought you'd...I thought you were coming to tell me about you and Preacher."

She laughed, the sound full of bitterness and regret. "At that point there was no me and Preacher."

He looked at her sharply. "But...by that time you two had been connected at the hip for what? A month? Ever since that night at the Clover—"

"Six weeks," she smiled sadly. "For six weeks, Steven held my hand, patted my back, and told me just to give you time. He said you were going through a rough patch, and I needed to give you a chance to work through it."

"Goddamn," he glanced away, shaking his head when he thought of how different it all could've been if only he'd—

"Steven was my only friend," she continued, cutting into his thoughts. "The only one I could talk to. Any of the other guys would've run to Frank and spilled the beans about what was happening between you and me. And then Frank would've killed you. But you remember how Steven was. If you swore him to secrecy, he'd die before breaking his word. Of course, when I found out I was pregnant, that really put his loyalty to the test…"

It was a good thing his "man card" had already been revoked, because tears gathered behind Jake's eyes. "And when you came to tell me you were pregnant, I accused you of being a gold-digging slut. Which, in retrospect was more than ridiculous, huh? Yo, how many rich Naval officers do you know?"

She reached up to thumb away another tear. "I was hurting too badly to recognize what you were going through. I took your vicious words and the fact that you'd ignored my phone calls for a month and half to mean you didn't love me anymore, if you'd ever loved me at all."

He dug his fingers into the arms of the chair. Just as he'd feared, her answer to the question of *why* made him face the fact that she wasn't the only one to blame for how things had turned out.

Oh, she'd made a mistake by not telling him she was pregnant with his child. There was no question of that. But she wouldn't have done it had he not treated her like garbage, like something that belonged on the bottom of his shoe.

Goddamn him. Goddamn them both.

"And so you turned to Preacher…"

"No," she shook her head. "I decided to get rid of the baby."

His chin jerked back, and she turned to gaze at Franklin's sweet face, the love in her own so bright and clear it was almost like the emotion was distilled down to its purest form.

"I knew what it was to grow up in a broken home, to grow up fatherless," she whispered. "I didn't want that for my child."

"But how—"

"Steven went with me to the clinic that day, still holding my hand, still patting my back." She shook her head and wiped away more tears. "I was a mess. I was crying so hard, I couldn't fill out the paperwork. He had to do it for me. And then, when the nurse called my name, he looked at me…" she turned to him then, her smile watery, "… and he grabbed my hand and ran with me out the front door. You see, he knew me better than I knew myself. He knew I'd regret that decision for the rest of my life. And Steven being Steven, he offered me a solution."

"He offered to marry you, to give you the home and family you'd been dreaming of your entire life." *And it should've been me*. His heart ached so badly it was a wonder the thing still managed to pump blood.

She nodded.

"Did you love him?" He didn't know if he hoped her answer was yes or no. The selfish, jealous part of him wanted her to say *he'd* been the only man to touch her heart. But Preacher deserved so much more than that…

"I loved him," she said, shaking her head sadly, "but I wasn't *in* love with him. Steven knew that, I was honest with him about that, but he swore I'd eventually *fall* in love with him."

"Yeah," he nodded his head as a slideshow of memories of Preacher flashed through his brain. "Preacher may've been a saint among sailors, but he was still a SEAL, cocky as hell. He probably figured there was no way in hell you wouldn't eventually fall for him."

She sighed. "I like to think he was right. I like to think that if we'd gotten the chance…" She trailed off, gathered herself, then continued quietly, "I've struggled every day with the guilt of that decision, wondering if I did the right thing. Wishing I could've given him more."

"You gave him enough," Jake told her, sadness and remorse making his heart feel as if it weighed as much as a B-52 bomber.

"I hope so," she whispered. "I hope I was a good wife to him in the time we had together. I've always—" She stopped and hastily wiped away the last of her tears when the doctor strolled into the room with a clipboard under one arm.

—◊—

Vanessa kicked off her ridiculous high-heeled shoes and raced down the smoky hall, digging into the cleavage of her halter top to pull out her room key.

In her excitement, she dropped it on the floor and nearly split the ass of her miniskirt bending to pick it up. Straightening, she fumbled with the lock and finally burst into the hotel room with, "You're never going to believe this!"

"*Oui.*" Rock sat by the window, gazing down at his phone as if he'd never seen it before. And even watching him do something as simple as thumb off the device, the tendons in his forearm shifting under his tattoos, made her need to catch her breath. Or maybe it was just the fact that she'd run up the four flights of stairs instead of taking the ultraslow elevator that had her lungs working overtime. Yeah, that had to be it. "Who told you?" he asked. "Was it Becky?"

"Huh?"

"That Franklin is Snake's son? I just got off the phone with Steady who found out from Ozzie. Apparently there was a big to-do at the hospital last night involvin' blood, brawls, and bombs of the big-honkin' secret variety." He shook his head in disbelief. "So which grape on the Black Knights' gossip vine spilled the beans to you?"

She was totally confused, and it wasn't just the alliteration and mixed metaphors. "Nobody. It was obvious the other night when I saw all three of them together, but that's not what—"

"Is *that* what you meant with that whole cryptic statement about all of us keepin' secrets from each other?"

"*Yes*," she huffed, tossing her platform stripper shoes aside. "But that's beside the point. Listen, I was downstairs getting clean towels when I ran into Candy who said she saw Johnny come in last night!"

Rock had spent quite a bit of time over at In the Mood Lounge after the first night when he'd questioned the bartender and the guy said he remembered seeing someone who matched Johnny's description. But Rock had turned up a big ol' handful of nothing on that front. And you can bet Vanessa was more than a little happy to be the one to net them some actionable intel.

Girl power!

"Come in where?" Rock demanded, jumping from the chair. "Here?"

"Yes!" She excitedly hopped from one foot to the other. "He's staying here. Right here in this hotel!"

"Your phone is out of batteries now too, damnit," Michelle cursed from the passenger seat of her Hyundai Elantra, clicking off Jake's iPhone. She winced and glanced into the back seat to make sure her son hadn't heard that little slip at the end.

The last few days had seen her vocabulary deteriorate considerably.

Thankfully, Franklin had his headphones on, watching the movie playing on his iPad, his soft cheeks absent their usual rosy glow and his little eyes smudged by dark bruises.

We'll be home soon, she silently promised him, reaching back to pat his knee.

He smiled at her so sweetly, lifting the sleeve on his T-shirt to proudly display—for the twentieth time—the press-on tattoo Jake had given him, and her poor, battered heart melted all over the place.

She winked and pointed at the tattoo, giving him a thumbs up like she'd done twenty times before, and he giggled before returning his attention to the movie. His pale face wrinkled when they inched over a speed bump in Northwestern Memorial Hospital's underground parking garage, causing her to glance at her watch.

It was almost time for another dose of pain medication.

"I'm sure there's a good reason why she isn't here," Jake said from the driver's seat, pocketing the change the parking attendant handed him before pulling past the gate and taking the ramp up to street level. There was still a cloud of tension hanging between them, but after their come-to-Jesus talk he was no longer giving her the silent treatment.

Which was a good thing.

She had enough to worry about without his whole cold-shoulder act adding to it. And for the first time in a really long time, she began to believe there might be hope for the two of them.

Oh, not that she thought there was any room for a relationship. Because Jake would never forgive her...

Heck, after seeing the look on his face when she first told him what she'd done, the shock that'd instantly morphed into rage that'd quickly slid into a sickening kind of anguish, she had a hard time forgiving herself for the pain she'd caused him.

But even if there wasn't room for a relationship, maybe there was room for an understanding.

She would continue to hope so. For her son's sake.

Jake flicked on the blinker, and they exited onto the packed city streets. A line of yellow taxis waited by the hospital's main doors, and The Corner Bakery advertised their daily panini special on a chalkboard easel in the middle of the sidewalk—which reminded her that she hadn't eaten. Jake had come back earlier in the afternoon with a bag of hamburgers after dropping off his motorcycle at her house and picking up her car, but she'd been too busy listening to the nurse and jotting down notes about medication schedules, maintaining stitches, and food restrictions to eat anything.

Now she was starving. And worried.

Worried about Franklin. Worried about Lisa and her brother and...Jake...

"She probably just broke her phone or dropped it in the toilet or something," he assured her, still talking about the nanny. "I bet when you get home, charge your phone and check your email, you'll find she sent you something explaining her absence."

That made sense. Lisa did have a bad habit of going through cell phones. She was always leaving them on the El-train or forgetting them in class…

"Maybe you're right," she said, although she couldn't shake the niggle of unease that teased at the back of her brain. Of course, maybe that was just light-headedness brought on by having gone nearly twenty-four hours without food.

Digging in her purse, she pulled out her emergency granola bar and peeled off the wrapper, eating half the thing in one bite.

"Mmm," she murmured. Never had nuts, fruit, and rolled oats tasted so good. "I'd offer you some," she said around the mouthful, "but I'm afraid I might eat your hand should you reach for it."

He smiled, his green eyes flashing, his dimples deepening in his shadowed cheeks. The expression was so shocking and unexpected given the events of the last day, the granola turned to dust when she tried to swallow it.

Finally managing to choke it down, she decided now was her chance to ask him his intentions.

"What are you going to do, Jake?" The words tumbled from her lips.

"About what?" He turned to frown at her.

"About Franklin." She held her breath.

He glanced into the rearview mirror. "He can't hear us?"

"Not with those earphones on. And he won't take them off for an instant while *Tangled* is playing. He loves the horse."

He nodded, remaining quiet for too long, then, "I want joint custody," he blurted.

She nearly threw up.

"But how...but where...I mean..." There were so many questions, and she had so many objections, she didn't know where to begin. So she just stopped and swallowed the last bits of granola in the hopes that it might actually stay down.

Joint custody?

But then she'd only get to see her son three or four days a week! Just think of all the things she'd miss...

Kinda like the things Jake has missed over the past three years? a little voice whispered.

Oh, dear Lord.

"Boss has offered me a job," he said, oblivious to the fact that she might be having a nervous breakdown in the passenger seat. "So I'll be living here in Chicago. And I know how you are about Franklin's schedule not getting interrupted, but kids are more resilient than you think. I don't see why us splitting time with him should be a problem."

And just as quickly as the panic had seized her, it slid away, leaving her with a feeling of numbness. Helpless numbness.

"You know," she murmured after a while, staring out the window even though she was blind to the traffic whizzing by, "my brother thinks I stick to a routine with Franklin because of our father leaving. He thinks it's a control issue brought on by a childlike need to ensure nothing bad ever happens to me again. But that's not true."

"No?" Jake asked as he inched onto the highway running between the city and Lake Michigan.

"No," she shook her head, absently watching a dog owner chunk a stick into the water at the edge of Oak Street Beach. A black Labrador retriever raced into the choppy waves after it, and for a moment she wondered how the world kept on turning, how everything kept on moving, when her entire life was spinning out of control.

Joint custody…

"Dad was a douchebag of epic proportions; there's no question of that," she admitted distractedly, her mind only half on the conversation. The other half was busy silently screaming. "But Mom was just as bad. Maybe worse. Because even though she stuck around, she was no kind of mother. After my dad left, she decided the best way to bury her sorrow was in a daily bottle of Stoli."

"Christ," Jake spat, and she could feel him glance over at her, feel his sympathetic gaze heating her face and somehow that made everything worse. She didn't want his sympathy. She wanted his understanding. She wanted her *son*. She wanted…so many things that could never be…

"I learned to live in fear of the unexpected. Like the day I came home from school to find the man from next door tearing away my mother's clothes as she lay passed-out on the living room sofa. I don't remember much about what happened after I flew at him, mainly because he hit me hard enough to knock me senseless, but sometimes, late at night when I'm just drifting to sleep, I have these brief flashbacks of Frank barreling through the open front door and tackling our neighbor to the ground."

"Good for Boss."

"Yeah," she nodded, remembering very clearly the fury that'd contorted her brother's young face when he flew through the door. Killing rage. That's how most people would describe it. "At fifteen, he was already bigger than most full-grown men, and though my recollection of the exact chain of events is sketchy at best," she absently drew a broken heart in the condensation that'd formed from her breath on the passenger side window, "I *do* remember three things. The neighbor ended up in the hospital. Frank installed triple locks on our front door. And I was never allowed to walk home alone again."

They drove in silence then, both lost in their own thoughts as the white-capped waves of Lake Michigan rolled onto the beach to their right and the twinkling lights of the skyscrapers cut through the coming dusk to their left. Then Franklin giggled in the backseat—undoubtedly it was a scene with the horse—and Michelle was dragged back into the moment.

"I swore that day, I swore then and there," she breathed, reliving the fear and uncertainty of that instant when she walked through the front door to see what was being done to her mother, "that if I ever had kids they'd *never* have to live through the kind of childhood I had to live through, an unstable environment created by a drunken mother and exacerbated by an absent father."

"Shell—"

"Anyway," she cut him off, still staring out the window, "*that's* why I'm such a stickler for Franklin's schedule. Because I never had one as a child. When I walked through my door each day after school, I never knew what I might find."

"I'm so sorry that happened to you," he said, and there was genuine regret in his voice.

"I'm sorry it happened to me, too," she admitted with a shrug. "Maybe if it hadn't, I would've done things differently. Maybe I would have been braver, not so hell bent on trying to create that perfect family…"

He grabbed her hand, his palm warm against her cold fingers. "Why didn't you tell me about Franklin after Preacher died? After there was no hope of creating that perfect family? That's the part I just can't get past, Shell. You had *four* years."

"I *tried*, Jake," she choked on a sob, refusing to look at him when there were tears standing in her eyes. "I was going to tell you after the funeral, out of respect for Steven, but you left early. And then, when I went to find you, I discovered you'd already transferred to Alpha Platoon, caught a transport OCONUS. You were gone for two years, Jake. For two years nobody knew where you were, so how was I supposed to tell you?"

She turned to him then, her eyes beseeching him to understand.

"But I came back—" he began, and she interrupted him.

"And I sent you a letter begging you to come here."

He rolled in his lips, a muscle ticking in his jaw. "The letter said nothing about my having a son, Shell."

"Yeah," she swallowed, once more facing the window. "I suppose that was a test of sorts. If you'd come, if you'd shown a modicum of interest, I'd planned to tell you."

"You know why I stayed away," he growled.

"Yes," she sighed. "I know now why you stayed away."

Again they fell into silence, only this time the strain

of it was a palpable thing. It stretched between them like the string of a kite caught in the wind, threatening to snap at any moment.

Finally, after several excruciating seconds, Jake ventured quietly, "And after I came here, after I'd explained everything, why didn't you tell me then?"

She swung to face him, her jaw slung open.

He really didn't get it, did he?

"Because you'd already proven yourself true to form!" She tossed her hands in the air.

"I'm *nothing* like your father," he snarled. "And I'm getting real sick and tired of the comparison. I. Am. *Nothing*. Like him."

And for the first time since his arrival, seeing the adamancy and sincerity on his face, she began to wonder if maybe he was right. If maybe *she* was the one who'd been wrong all along. If maybe her own childhood had blinded her, making her jump to conclusions about men and—

Oh God. The thought was too horrific to bear. Because that would mean she'd wronged him, robbed him of the child he would have protected and cherished and loved and—

Remorse and regret settled heavily in her stomach, making the granola she'd eaten turn to burning acid that scorched her throat.

"I'm sorry, Jake," she finally whispered. And that didn't even begin to cover her nearly paralyzing sorrow over the way things had happened, over her role in the way things had happened.

She felt him relax next to her then and wished she could do the same. But her nerves were stretched so tight she was afraid to move, even an inch, for fear she'd completely lose what little control over herself.

"We both made a lot of mistakes," he sighed. "Mistakes that are hard to forgive, but we'll manage."

She didn't see how—

"And don't worry," he continued, his next words like arrows to her heart. "We'll find a way to work out Franklin's schedule so that it's not too hard on you. You'll see."

Oh, sure. They'd work it out.

And all it would take was for her to give up her son…

Chapter Sixteen

"LISTEN UP, YOU GREASY PIECE OF SHIT," ROCK growled, and Vanessa raised a brow, doubting name-calling would get them very far with the wife-beater-wearing guy working the reception desk. "We know this sonofabitch is staying here, and we need his room number. Now!"

Rock shoved a photo of Johnny at the receptionist, whose dull eyes barely glanced at the thing before he switched his cigarillo to the opposite side of his mouth, chewing sullenly.

Rock made a move toward the pistol he kept concealed in his suit-jacket, and she grabbed his arm, sidling up beside him. "Look, sugar," she said in her gravely smoker's voice, trying to ignore the sour aroma of body odor that assaulted her nostrils when she leaned in close to the bars protecting the man working the desk. The guy was like the Land that Hygiene Forgot. "We need to find this man. He owes me lots of money. And my new best friend here," she jerked her head toward Rock, "has agreed to help me get it back. Now," she winked and licked her lips, "I can make this worth your while."

The receptionist glanced at her boobs, a spark of interest igniting his vacuous gaze. She didn't have great, huge jugs like good ol' Candy, but hers obviously worked in a pinch. Sir Smokes-A-Lot seemed to enjoy them.

"What didja have in mind?" he asked, pulling the cigarillo from his mouth and sucking on his stained teeth.

She smiled even as her stomach revolted at the sight. Reaching into her top, she pulled out a wad of hundred dollar bills. Peeling off two, she waved them through the bars. "How 'bout we start here. And then, once I get the rest of my money back…" she stuck a finger in her mouth, sucking it slowly before inserting it into her cleavage, "… I can give you a little freebie just to show my appreciation."

The receptionist's Adam's apple bobbed in his dirt-ringed throat as he watched the movement, then he hastily licked his thin lips before turning and plucking a key from a hook on the wall. "Room 602," he said and snatched the key back when she went to swipe it. "Now, I don't want no mess to clean up," he warned.

"Don't you worry, sugar," she purred, leaning in even closer, until her boobs smashed against the bars. "I want my money, not a jail sentence."

He considered this bit of logic for a while before handing her the key. "I'll be expecting my freebie when I get off at 2 a.m.," he called to her when she turned toward the elevator, dragging Rock with her.

"Sure thing, sugar." She blew him a kiss over her shoulder. "I can promise you at 2 a.m. you'll be getting off, and then you'll be *getting off.*"

The sound of his sickening chuckle gave her a good case of the heebie-jeebies, but she managed to control her shiver of abhorrence until the elevator doors closed her and Rock inside.

"I could've just threatened to shoot him," Rock drawled, grinning down at her.

"Yeah," she said, "but then he might've been inclined to make a call to the room and warn dear Johnny. This way, he'll be inclined not to."

Rock's brows climbed up his forehead as his eyes pinged down to her halter top. "Who knew a pair of great funbags could come in so handy outside the boudoir."

"You did not just use the term funbags," she said, shooting him a look of disgust as the elevator doors chimed and opened to sixth floor.

"Get him upstairs and into bed," Michelle said, setting her purse on the kitchen table and rolling her head around her shoulders. She didn't remember ever being this exhausted, this emotionally wrung-out. Not only was her heart bloody and desecrated, but her entire body was one giant throbbing ache. Her bones actually hurt. "I'm going to try to call Lisa one more time."

"You heard your mama," Jake said, Franklin cradled in his strong arms, their matching dimples winking in their cheeks until she was forced to look away. "It's up you go, little dude."

"But I d-don't wanna go to s-sleep," Franklin cried, his bottom lip sticking out so far it was a wonder the thing was still attached to his face. The doctor had warned her that children his age often became emotional after surgery, after coming down off anesthesia. "And my b-belly hurts, Mama," he sniffed and tucked his head up under Jake's stubbled chin.

Her gut twisted into knots until it ached as much as her heart.

She checked her watch. "It's time for another dose of

pain meds," she said, amazed she was still able to function given the nearly overwhelming urge to lay down on the floor and cry. Cry for the physical pain her son was in. Cry for the emotional pain she'd caused Jake. Cry for the spiritual pain she'd suffer only getting to see her son part-time. Just cry, cry, cry.

Of course, that would help no one. And, as a mother, she didn't have that luxury. She dragged in a breath to steady herself before striding back to the table to dig in her purse. When she found the liquid medicine, she handed it to Jake along with the plastic measuring cup that'd come with it.

And this was how it was going to be from now on. This splitting of parenting duties…

Oh, God.

She barely beat back a sob of hysteria before gathering her courage once more and calmly instructing, "He's supposed to get one tablespoon," she instructed before turning to her son. "You want to finish watching *Tangled*, don't you, sweetpea?" she asked.

He shoved his little thumb in his mouth and nodded, his eyes bright with unshed tears. "The horsh ish funny," he said around the chubby digit.

"Yes," she smiled weakly, leaning in to ruffle his hair and kiss his pale cheek. The smell of her little boy combined with Jake's beachy aroma was an aromatic assault, reminding her of all the things she loved and all the things she'd already lost and was poised to lose still.

Joint custody…

The term sounded profane.

"That ol' horse *is* funny," she managed, though her

throat was clogged with tears. "And I'll be up to check on you and bring you some ice cream as soon as I call Miss Lisa."

Franklin's tired face crumbled, and he started crying in earnest. "I m-mish Mish Lisha," he wailed, hiccupping.

Yeah, I know exactly how you feel. She wanted to break down right along with him...

"I think it's time we got this little warrior dosed and into bed," Jake observed, and she took a step back, nodding, watching the two of them cross the kitchen and disappear into the living room.

How was she ever going to survive this?

———

When they exited the elevator on the sixth floor of The Stardust Hotel, Rock's deep, rich chuckle made the butterflies in Vanessa's stomach once more take flight.

That's all it took. One look from him. One word. And she felt like she was plummeting down that first steep hill on a roller coaster.

Gee, Van, you're one sad sack.

Yeah, there was no question of that. Because if any other guy referred to her breasts as funbags, she'd be sorely tempted to land a knee in his family jewels right before she crowned him King Asshole. But Rock said it, and she got all gooey, thinking he was the cutest, funniest thing to ever walk on two legs.

Ugh. The reasons why she obviously needed professional, psychological help just kept piling up.

"You okay to do this?" he asked once they reached Johnny's hotel room.

In answer, she kicked out of her stripper shoes and

reached beneath her skirt for the .38 Special she kept strapped to her thigh.

"*Mon dieu*," he whispered, screwing his eyes closed for a brief second, "that might be the sexiest thing I've ever seen."

She grinned as she quietly inserted the key into the lock. Before she turned it, he grabbed her hand, shaking his head. "I'm goin' in alone first. You follow behind me when I give you the all-clear."

"Oh, don't go getting all testosterone-y on me now," she hissed, frowning up at him. "I can take care of myself. There's no need for this He-Man crap."

"*Non.* This isn't a negotiation. I'm—"

Oh, whatever...

Before he could finish, she turned the lock, threw open the door and barged into the room, her pistol quartering the area.

Rock let loose with a string of French curses, but he was barely a split second behind her, both of his guns up and ready and sighting around the room. Once he realized the place was empty and she wasn't in any immediate danger, he turned and barreled toward the attached restroom. She heard the shower curtain rings squeak against the rod as he yanked the curtain aside. Then he appeared in the bathroom door, his face like a gulf hurricane.

"*Damn*," she cursed. "So no Johnny?"

He didn't waste any time laying into her, breaking out a thesaurus's worth of words for dumbass, but she waved him off as she padded toward the rumpled bed.

Picking up a creased photo, her blood began pounding in her ears.

"Oh, shit," she breathed, turning it around for him to see.

~~~

Jake looked down at the face of his drowsy son, his heart nearly bursting with a love he'd never known.

It was an amazing feeling. An overwhelming feeling. A *scary* feeling.

He was a father. He had a son. A little boy whom he was responsible for shaping into a good, honest, loyal man.

"You getting tired, little bro?" he asked, brushing a lock of soft hair back from Franklin's brow.

"Nuh-uh." Franklin shook his head against the pillow as his big, gray eyes drifted closed, and his plump little thumb found its way between his lips.

Jake smiled and tiptoed from the room, partially closing the door behind him. The pain medication was fast-acting, and he was glad for it. Because every time Franklin's face scrunched up, his little cheeks draining of blood, Jake felt like someone shoved a hot knife in his gut. And considering that was his reaction after only having been a father for one day, he couldn't imagine what Shell must be feeling.

Shell...

Damn, we sure made a mess of things, didn't we?

With a heavy heart, he lumbered to the guest bedroom, unbuttoning his shirt and tiredly dragging it from his shoulders as he pushed through the door.

A sound in the corner had his head whipping around. He had just enough time to register he was wasn't alone and drop his shirt to the floor while simultaneously reaching for the pistol in his waistband...

But he wasn't quick enough.

A muzzle flash blazed through the darkened room a split second before agony exploded in his head, and he knew no more.

---~~~---

"Come on, come on," Rock growled. "Pick up, Snake… *Merde!*" He resisted the urge to throw his phone out the window of Christian's Porsche as he and Vanessa sped north on the highway toward Lincoln Park.

"Michelle isn't answering either," Vanessa said from her position in the passenger seat. "Her phone goes straight to voice mail."

She grabbed on to the dashboard when he swerved around a slow-moving Peapod delivery truck but didn't utter so much as a squeak. The woman might look fragile, what with that small Latina frame of hers, but she was turning out to be incredibly tough.

When she'd stormed into Johnny's hotel room like Captain frickin' America, *¡ut!*, he'd nearly vomited his own heart.

"Try her home phone," he instructed as he shifted into a lower gear, working the pedals.

"I don't have that number. You try her at home. I'll call Boss."

"*Oui,*" he said as he cut across three lanes of traffic, the Porsche's fat tires clinging to the asphalt like they were coated with glue.

Christian might have a terrible eye for sensible clothes, but Rock could totally get behind the Brit's taste in vehicles.

He quickly thumbed through his contacts on his

phone as he flicked on the Porsche's blinker and took the next exit in a squeal of burning rubber. Keeping one eye on the road and one eye on the old lady in the Caddy who could barely see over the steering wheel in the lane beside him, he found Shell's information. Pressing the number for her land-line, he held his cell phone up to his ear.

"Sonofabitch!" he cursed when the old lady changed lanes without looking, effectively cutting him off. He had to work the wheel, gearshift, and pedals as he listened to it ring on the other end. And he prayed to a God he wasn't sure he believed in anymore that she would answer...

Michelle was in the middle of scooping chocolate chip ice cream into Franklin's favorite Mickey Mouse bowl while leaving yet another message for Lisa—she'd already checked her email; there was nothing, and now she was *really* worried—when her land-line call-waiting sounded.

Thank, God, she thought right before she clicked over. "Lisa? Where the heck are you? I've been wor—"

"Listen, Shell—"

"Rock?"

"*Oui, chère,* now listen closely, and don't interrupt." The tone of his voice had the hairs on the back of her neck standing up. "Johnny knows about you. We found your picture and your information in his hotel room and—"

The sound of a gunshot exploded overhead, and her entire world came to a screeching halt.

Franklin…

She dropped the phone and raced into the living room, jumping over the toy fire truck in the middle of the rug and banging her hip against the end table upon landing. It sent the glass lamp sitting on top smashing to floor, but she gave it no mind as she sprinted to the stairs.

*Franklin…*That's all she kept thinking over and over again. *My boy…*

She'd only made it halfway up the staircase when a dark shadow appeared on the landing above. Instinctively, she jerked back, her foot slipping on the tread below causing her to lose her balance and land in a heap on the cold, hard tiles of the foyer.

Scrambling to her feet, she wasted no time trying to determine if she'd broken anything in the fall—with the surge of adrenaline racing through her system, she wasn't feeling anything anyway—as she attempted to make out the man's face in the shadows.

She couldn't. It was too dark with the hall lights off.

Of course, there was one shape she had no trouble discerning, and that was the distinctive outline of the pistol in his hands.

It was pointed straight at her head.

She threw her hands in the air as she glanced past his shoulder and screamed, "Franklin!"

She choked with relief when he called, "*Mama?*" His voice was high and frightened, but that didn't matter because it was his *voice*. His sweet, sweet little voice. "What happened, Mama? What's that noise?"

Her heart tripped over itself even as she sent a prayer of thanks skyward. And then she realized exactly what it meant that her son was still alive and well and asking questions…

Oh God, Jake. Oh, sweet Jesus…

"If you value your son's life," the man—Johnny?—hissed, slowly descending the stairs, "you'll tell him to stay exactly where he is."

She opened her mouth, but she couldn't speak.

Jake's dead. Jake's dead. Jake's—

The thought raced around and around inside her head, endlessly spinning until bile crawled up the back of her throat and the room began closing in on her. Then the sound of Franklin's voice dragged her back from the edge of darkness.

"*Mama!*" he screamed again, and she was reminded her son was still alive. She had to keep it together, stay strong and smart for his sake.

She managed to swallow in order to yell, "S-stay in bed, sweetpea! I dropped a pan, that's all. I'll bring your ice cream to you in a little bit. Just watch your movie!"

"Nicely done, *Mama*," Johnny jeered, his face coming into view when he reached the middle of the staircase and the light from the foyer washed over him.

He looked exactly like she imagined he would. The quintessential Italian mobster complete with slick dark hair, swarthy skin, leather jacket, and an expression that was 100 percent sociopath.

He'd have been handsome if it weren't for the pure, black evil shining in his eyes.

"Back up," he commanded, "into the kitchen."

"My son—" she started, but he cut her off.

"Little Franklin will be just fine as long as his mama plays nice." At the look of horror that washed over her face, he chuckled dryly. The sound was like a snake moving through dead leaves. A shiver raced down her spine in response.

"W-what do you want?" she managed, slowly backing toward the kitchen, wracking her brain for a way to save herself and her son.

Or, perhaps, just her son...

If she screamed at him to use the fire escape ladder stored beside his toy box to climb out his bedroom window, could he do it with his injury? They'd practiced the maneuver a lot, and each time he'd accomplished it with no problem, but he'd been healthy then. Or maybe she should yell for him to get up and run for the front door. But would she be able to wrestle with Johnny long enough to give Franklin a fighting chance? And would he actually leave if he saw her struggling with a strange man, or would her little warrior try to help?

"What do I want?" Johnny grinned, flashing a set of bleached teeth that were startlingly white. "Just to have a little fun." The way he said the word *fun* made it sound filthy. "Don't you want to have some fun?" He crudely waggled his tongue before winking.

Jake had a small armory upstairs. If she could just get past Johnny, she might be able to—

"I can see those wheels turning in that pretty head of yours," he taunted, still herding her toward the kitchen, "but I can assure you there's no escape. You see," he moved his free hand up to his shoulder in order to remove the duffel bag she hadn't realized he was carrying, "I have all the things that go *bang-bang* right here in this little bag. That guy I just popped sure liked his guns, didn't he?"

Oh, Jake. I'm so sorry. So unbelievably sorry you only got to be a father for one day... "What was he expecting? A zombie apocalypse? Or did you guys know I was coming?" Johnny cocked his head and eyed her speculatively before shrugging. "Doesn't matter. Because along with confiscating his little arsenal, I was also careful to remove all the knives in your kitchen."

She glanced over her shoulder to see her empty knife block.

"So, since I'm the only one with a weapon," he waved his pistol from side-to-side when she turned back to him, "I'm calling the shots."

Her hip bumped against the edge of her kitchen table, halting her retreat.

"Now turn that chair around," he ordered, "and have a seat. It's time for the games to begin."

"Mama?" Franklin called, and she was forced to admit she was out of options. Her only hope now was that she could keep Johnny occupied long enough for Rock to get here and save her son from whatever fate Johnny had planned for him.

Oh, she knew that line about Franklin being fine as long as she played nice was nothing but bullcrap. From everything she'd heard about Johnny Vitiglioni, he wasn't in the habit of leaving witnesses behind. Of course, he didn't know the cavalry was on its way.

And she planned to use that to her advantage...

"Mama!"

"Don't you get out of that bed, young man!" she yelled, hoping her tone sounded stern instead of terrified. "The doctor says you're supposed to stay in bed, and I swear if you step one foot out of it, I'm giving you a spanking!"

She'd never given Franklin a spanking before, and she hoped the threat of one would scare him enough to make him mind her.

Please, God, she prayed as Johnny smiled evilly, uncoiling a length of rope in his gloved hands, *please let him mind me. I don't want him to see this...*

The world came back to Jake a little at a time...

First there was pain. Terrible, burning pain in the side of his head.

Then there was light. A weak shaft that fell across his face and hurt his eyes when he opened them to blink in blurry confusion at the fixture burning out in the hallway.

And finally there was realization. He wasn't dead. He'd been shot. In the head. But he wasn't dead.

Huh...

Gritting his teeth against the excruciating agony, he reached up and—

Well, that's good. His muscles actually responded to his command, which meant he wasn't paralyzed. A fine start...

Running his fingers through his hair, he encountered blood. Lots of it. But there didn't appear to be any holes. No wet, soggy void for his finger to dip into. His scalp, on the other hand, was a mess. It was ripped in a deep gash and part of it was hanging away from his skull like some sort of gruesome earflap.

Disgusting, to say the least. But in the grand scheme of things, and considering he'd be a corpse if that bullet had hit him one inch to the right, it wasn't so bad.

He started cataloging the rest of his body parts, testing his limbs, when it suddenly occurred to him just *exactly* what had happened.

Yes, he'd been shot. That he knew. Case in point: the pool of blood and ripped scalp. But what he'd forgotten for a moment was that he'd been shot inside *Shell's* house.

Where she and Franklin…

Sonofabitch!

He pushed up from the hardwood floor and slipped in the puddle of his own blood before managing to gain his footing. Reaching into his waistband, he discovered his pistol was gone and bent to check for his reserve weapon despite the fact that the move sent a thunderbolt of agony blasting through his skull.

Nada. Nothing but an empty leather ankle holster…

Not wasting one moment, he ran toward the closet where he'd stored the rest of the weapons he'd taken from the Black Knights' armory only to discover his duffel bag missing from the top shelf.

"Fuck a duck!" he hissed, flying across the room, feeling the seconds piling up against him. He skidded to a halt when he saw the scarf draped on the edge of the mirror above the dresser. Barely giving his gruesome reflection a glance—yeah, he could be an extra in a slasher film—he pushed the flap of torn scalp firmly against his skull and then quickly wound the scarf around his head to hold it in place when he remembered…

My knife!

He'd stored an extra KA-BAR beneath the mattress. A second later, he had the thing in hand, its deadly, seven-inch blade glinting in the overhead light as he silently stepped into the hall, cocking his head, listening…

The house was quiet. Too quiet.

How long had he been out? Was he too late to…?

He didn't get any further in that line of thinking before he bent at the waist and vomited quietly onto the hallway rug. He'd like to say it was the head injury and the accompanying nausea that had him tossing his cookies—and that was certainly part of it—but the real truth of the matter was that the thought of losing his son and the only woman he'd ever loved had his stomach trying to exit his body through his throat.

Please, God, please, if you let them be alive, he bargained with the Big Kahuna as he heaved again, *I promise I'll love them and protect them until the day I die. No more secrets. No more running. No more blame. I'll make this family work and—*

The sound of the cartoon playing in Franklin's room drifted to his ears and had him stumbling forward. In a split second he was across the hall, pushing into the bedroom, nearly fainting with relief when he saw his son's wide, *alive* eyes staring at him from the middle of the bed.

The boy's bottom lip began to quiver, his face scrunching up—uh-huh, Jake knew he was quite the sight, especially to a three-year-old, but there was nothing to be done for it now. So he simply held his finger to his mouth.

"Shh," he whispered as he rushed across the room to kneel beside Franklin's bed. "I need you to be really quiet for me, buddy. Can you do that?"

"J-Jake?"

"Yeah, little bro, it's me." He patted Franklin's leg beneath the covers then winced when he saw the big, bloody handprint he'd left behind.

"You've g-got bwud," Franklin announced, staring at him in wide-eyed horror.

Nope. The problem wasn't that he *had* blood, but that he'd lost too much of the stuff. It was hard to concentrate beyond the dizziness that had his head spinning on his shoulders.

"It's not as bad as it looks," he assured his son as he grasped the edge of the mattress to steady himself. "Now, I need you to listen to me. There's a bad man in the house, and I need to hide you. Do you know of a good hiding place?"

Franklin shook his head.

Shit.

"Okay," he said, pushing up from his kneeling position to sprint to the window, quietly throwing open the sash.

A two-story drop.

There was no balcony, no patio roof, no lattice work attached to the side of the house. Nothing to help his son reach the ground save for a two-story drop.

He could fashion a sling out of the bedclothes maybe, and lower Franklin that way, but it would take up precious time and he needed to go find Shell.

"Where's Mama?" Franklin whimpered, and Jake spun back into the room.

"She's safe." *Please let that be true*. "And now I need to get you safe, too."

"Mama said she'll spank me if I get outta bed," his bottom lip protruded even farther.

"She did? When did she say that?" Then Jake shook his head when he realized time meant nothing to a three-year-old. "Never mind, buddy. Listen, I promise you your mama won't be mad or spank you. She wants me to help you get out of the house."

"Sh-she does?"

"Yes," he whispered, wracking his brain for another solution. Then, magically, Franklin offered one up.

"You could use the wadder."

"What, buddy?" His control was fraying with every ticking second. Every second he couldn't afford to lose. "What's a wadder?"

"The fire wadder," Franklin pointed toward his closet door with a shaky finger. "Mama keeps it beside the toy box."

A half-breath later, Jake was across the room, sound-lessly throwing open the closet door and nearly weeping with gratitude at the sight that met his eyes.

In a matter of seconds, he'd attached the emergency rope ladder to the windowsill and was lowering his brave son onto the first wrung.

"Now when you get to the bottom," he instructed quietly as he watched the boy scramble down the device—it was obvious by his sure footedness, despite his young age, that Shell had practiced with him many times, the brilliant woman, "you run next door and ring the doorbell. Tell whoever answers that there's a bad man in your house and they need to call the police."

"Okay," Franklin whispered, and Jake took a moment to sigh with relief when his son's foot touched the ground, then he was back through the window and racing downstairs, the monster he'd learned to control over the years was screaming for release.

And he did what he hadn't done in a long time. He turned it loose...

Chapter Seventeen

"Mmm," Johnny sucked his teeth and dropped his hand to rub at the bulge in his crotch as he cut through Michelle's last bra-strap and her breasts spilled free.

She bit into the gag and turned away. She wouldn't give him the satisfaction of watching as he ogled her. Nor would she give him the satisfaction of hearing her whimper, though there was definitely one building at the back of her throat.

"Look what we have here," he taunted, and she squeezed her eyes shut, curling her tied hands into fists when she felt his gloved fingers move over her left breast. He twisted the nipple. Hard. But she still refused to cry out. "I've been waiting to get my hands on these puppies for a couple of days now," he drawled. She could feel his fetid breath on her cheek. "And thanks to the info I got outta Lisa, now I've got my chance."

She jerked her head around, unable now to stop the tears spilling from her eyes or the hard sob that sounded around the gag.

Lisa? No!

Johnny smiled with nauseating delight. "Yeah, I paid a visit to your nanny last night. She was very accommodating."

If she hadn't been wearing the gag, she would've spit right in the middle of his evil, smirking face.

Of course, that would've been a mistake.

Because even though she'd most certainly derive at least a small measure of satisfaction from hocking a giant loogie in his eye, it didn't change the fact that Lisa was dead—oh, sweet Lord, the thought made her ill with grief and bile instantly coated the gag in her mouth. But she couldn't break down. No amount of histrionics would bring poor Lisa back. Plus, spitting in Johnny's eye might piss him off just enough to forgo his so-called "fun" and kill her immediately.

She couldn't have that.

Not if she hoped to give Rock and the rest of the Black Knights time to save Franklin.

"Tell me," Johnny placed his hands on the table behind her back and leaned in close, his lips moving against her ear. He smelled like beer and expensive cologne, and the need to barf down the back of his leather jacket nearly overwhelmed her. "Have you been enjoying the flowers? I was so upset when you didn't want to play that first night."

Oh God. Her instincts had been right. And instead of trusting herself and telling Frank about it, she'd simply dismissed the entire thing.

Stupid, stupid, stupid!

And now she was really battling the urge to throw up, especially when he continued. "Do you like getting titty-fucked? With jugs like these," he reached down and squeezed her breasts; the pain had her wincing and biting into the gag until she tasted blood along with the bile, "I bet you do."

He shoved his tongue in her ear, a brief glimpse of the violation to come, and she started to close her eyes, to ready herself to withstand the rest of it, when a movement at the doorway caught her attention.

For a moment, she couldn't understand what she was seeing.

It was a man. Shirtless. With some sort of turban on his head. Completely covered in blood from head to toe until the whites of his eyes were the only discernible feature on his whole person. They shined like beacons. Fierce and bright.

And then she got it.

Jake!

He was alive!

She nearly choked on the sharp relief that burst through her chest before she caught herself. He lifted a blood-coated finger to his blood-coated lips—wow, there was a lot of blood; she didn't know how he was still standing—and she blinked twice, hoping he understood the move for the affirmative it was.

Johnny pushed to a stand and started working at the buttons of his fly, and it took everything she had to keep her eyes on his sadistic face instead of watching as Jake silently slid up behind him.

She stopped breathing when Jake raised his blood-soaked hands.

A split second later, one of those hands was on Johnny's forehead while the other dragged a knife across Johnny's throat.

It didn't make any noise. Not one sound. And Johnny didn't have time to squeak a protest before dark blood flowed from the wound on his neck in a thick, terrible rush.

It was weird, that macabre silence. That brief moment

when time stood still and nothing moved save for the blood pumping freely from what used to be Johnny's throat. Then he dropped to his knees, his hands scrabbling at his neck, a terrible gurgling sound coming from his gaping mouth until she yearned for the strange quiet of the split-second before.

Watching him struggle, she attempted to summon up some sympathy, especially when she saw the astonishment in his eyes. But no matter how hard she tried, she couldn't seem to find any. Not after what he'd done to Lisa. Not after what he'd nearly done to her. And certainly not after what he'd no-doubt planned to do to her son.

And then something really strange happened. Johnny's hands dropped to his side, and his expression became one of…realization was the only word she had to describe it, right before he fell face forward. His head smacked against the leg of the chair she was tied to with a sickening *thud*, keeping his chin raised and his throat wound gaping open so that an astonishing amount of blood poured onto her kitchen floor in a matter of seconds.

Jesus! She never knew a human body held that much blood…

Jake wasted no time cutting her hands free, and she wrenched the gag from her mouth, bending to scrabble with the ropes around her ankles. She needed to get upstairs. Get to Franklin. The thought of him coming down to see this…

"Franklin—" she began, but Jake was quick to reassure her as he bent to help her with the rest of her restraints.

"I used the fire ladder to lower him out the window," he said, his voice hoarse. "He's with the neighbors."

"Oh, thank *God*," she breathed, lifting her toes from the floor to avoid the expanding pool of Johnny's blood as Jake used his knife to saw at the bindings.

The second she was free, she jumped away from the horror and carnage just as her back door burst open and Rock came barreling into the kitchen, a gun in each hand. He skidded to a halt, taking in the scene, and she raised her hands to cover her naked breasts.

"*Dieu*, Shell, did he…?" Rock couldn't finish the sentence, and she was momentarily confused until the realized what he was thinking.

"No," she assured him. "Johnny didn't get that far. Jake came before…before…"

"Good." Rock swallowed and blew out a hard breath, shoving his weapons into his waistband.

"Yeah, dude." Jake pushed to a wobbly stand and grabbed the table, panting slightly. "We got it all under control here. No problemo."

Then he stumbled once and, much to her horror, fell to the floor in strangely graceful heap.

"How's little Franklin?" Nurse Susan asked from the doorway of Jake's hospital room, dragging Michelle's attention away from the news playing softly on the television.

The top story was what had happened at her house and Becky, looking very official on behalf of Black Knights Inc., was in the middle of spinning a tale for the eager reporters about Johnny Vitiglioni and his warped sense of revenge. According to her, Johnny had somehow come to blame the employees of BKI for the killing of his brother-in-law outside the gates of her custom motorcycle shop—even though everyone knew that Mr. Costa had been gunned down in a terrible drive-by shooting and the hardworking, honest mechanics at BKI had nothing to do with it. But Johnny was a sick individual, obviously mentally unstable, and decided to get even with the employees of BKI by murdering one of their very own, very innocent family members.

A whole strange, biblical, eye-for-an-eye thing.

Luckily, the innocent family member in question had had a houseguest who, in a heroic struggle, was able to kill Johnny before any real harm could be done. And no, neither the family member, nor the courageous house-guest would be available for interviews.

It was quite an amazing story, really. Close enough to the truth to be believable, but in reality a complete and utter load of hogwash. Of course, what it managed to do was keep the true nature of Black Knights Inc. a secret while disseminating the fact that Johnny Vitiglioni was dead, whereby eliminating the price on the Knights' heads.

Genius. Pure and simple genius. But that was the Black Knights for you.

Michelle could only shake her head as she lifted the remote to mute the television, glancing briefly at Jake's sleeping profile before turning to Nurse Susan, who was decked out in purple scrubs tonight. And, joy of joys, she was still wearing those bright pink Crocs.

Michelle was beginning to love those bright pink Crocs...

"Franklin is doing great, all things considered. My brother is keeping an eye on him, and at the last check-in, he'd fallen into a coma brought on by pain medication and chocolate ice cream."

"That's good," Susan smiled, leaning against the jamb. "When it comes to little boys, there's no better cure for physical and emotional trauma than ice cream and sleep. Poor guy's been through the wringer the last few days, huh? First with the appendicitis and now with this," she tilted her head toward the silent television.

Becky was still answering the reporters' questions, and Michelle could only marvel at her future sister-in-law's composure. Becky even managed to get in a plug for the custom motorcycle business. At least, that's what Michelle figured she was doing by holding up a Black Knights Inc. T-shirt while flashing a winning smile into the cameras.

Wow.

Her brother had certainly made the right decision three and a half years ago when he hired her to be the cover for his clandestine defense firm. The woman was a gem, no two ways about it.

"He has been through the wringer," she sighed, wishing she could throw her arms around her son right then, but he was safer and far more comfortable with Frank back at the compound than he'd be with her here. And she couldn't abandon Jake after all he'd done for them. Saving their lives. "Of course you'd never know it by the way he was acting. From the story he gave the police, it was all one great big adventure. In fact, he handled everything far better than I did. I was a nervous wreck giving my statement."

"Kids are resilient," the nurse said.

"And thank God for that," Michelle nodded in agreement.

"Speaking of," Susan shook her head in wonder. "He works in mysterious ways, doesn't He?"

"What do you mean?"

"I mean, Mr. Sommers here donated blood for your son's surgery, and lo and behold, barely a day later, he comes in needing that same blood. I'd say that's a miracle."

"Yeah, miraculous," she murmured, though, for her part, she was just happy and thankful Jake was alive.

All that'd happened out in California, the rejection and abandonment, didn't matter anymore. His ignoring her letter, refusing to come to her even when she begged him, didn't matter anymore. Even his demanding joint custody of Franklin didn't matter anymore.

All that mattered was that he was alive. Because despite everything, maybe *because* of everything, she loved him.

And even if there was no future for them, even if he was never able to forgive her for what she'd done, she'd go on loving him. Because she didn't want to imagine, could not *fathom,* a world without him in it...

"How's our resident man of the hour?" Rock asked, leaning against the door jamb Nurse Susan had vacated not more than ten minutes before.

Michelle glanced at Jake lying in the hospital bed, frowning at his pale cheeks, which came frighteningly close to matching the white gauze wrapped around his head. Without his deep, California tan he looked...not weak, he was still roped with muscle, all big and imposing in that hospital gown...maybe the word to use would be vulnerable. For the first time in their long history together, Jake appeared vulnerable.

"Forty stitches," she murmured, marveling once more at the strength it must have taken for him to function with that type of head wound long enough to get Franklin to safety and to save her as well, "a pint of blood—maybe more to come, the doctor says we'll wait and see—and a moderate concussion. I'd say our man of the hour is in rough shape, but I've been told he'll pull through."

"Never doubted it for an instant, *chère*," Rock winked.

"No?" She slowly pushed up from the lumpy love seat and softly padded across the room, backing Rock out into the hall so their conversation wouldn't disturb the small amount of sleep Jake was able to snatch between doctor's visits. With a concussion, he was prodded awake and bombarded with questions to check his cognition every hour on the hour. "You didn't even doubt it when he did a swan dive into my kitchen floor?"

Lord knows *she'd* suffered a moment of uncertainty. Especially when it seemed to take for-freakin'-*ever* for the ambulance to arrive, and all the while Jake's breathing was rapid and shallow, his pulse thready. Holding his ravaged head in her lap, applying pressure to that gruesome wound, she'd made a deal with God.

Let Jake live, and she wouldn't fight him over the joint custody of Franklin.

It was a deal she planned to keep even though doing so was going to kill a little part of her…

"*Non*, not even then," Rock said, leaning back against the wall and crossing his arms over his chest. They were silent for a while before Rock spoke again. "I'm, uh," he scratched his ear and grimaced. "I'm sorry about your nanny. If Vanessa and I had found out about Johnny earlier, we could've—"

"No," she stopped him, shaking her head as her heart bled with remorse. Lisa Brown had been a sweet, beautiful woman with a bright future, and Michelle didn't think there was a level of hell nasty enough for the likes of Johnny Vitiglioni after what he'd done to her. Every time she thought of it, she wanted to slit Johnny's throat all over again. And she'd learned from the investigating officers that they'd found a dozen blue roses in Lisa's apartment. Those goddamned blue roses. Michelle never wanted to see another one in her entire life. "You can't blame yourself. Johnny was a monster. And we have to take comfort, small as it may be, in the knowledge that he's dead. That he'll never do to another woman what he did to Lisa."

"*Oui*," Rock sighed, and once again they fell into silence, each lost in their own thoughts, their own grief. Then Rock cocked his head, letting his eyes run over her face.

"What's that look for?" she asked. "Do I look as bad as I feel?" When this was all over, when everything was finally said and done, she was going to sleep for a week. Maybe two weeks…

"Ya know you're always beautiful to me, Shell. No matter what."

She snorted and rolled her eyes, not buying Rock's whole charming-southern-gentleman act for an instant. She hadn't looked in a mirror, but she was pretty sure she could pass for an extra in *The Walking Dead*. "*Okay*," she crossed her own arms, mirroring his stance, "so then what's with the look?"

"You've been keeping secrets, *ma petite soeur*."

And yep, the Black Knights grapevine had obviously been hard at work.

She sighed with resignation. "And *you're* one to talk?"

"You've got me there," he slung an arm around her shoulders, pulling her back until she leaned against the wall beside him. "So what are you guys going to do?" he whispered in her ear after a long pause, hugging her close to his side.

And suddenly the need to cry was overwhelming. She'd held everything together all night, but now that the adrenaline had worn off, she was teetering precariously close to the edge of an emotional breakdown.

A *well-deserved* emotional breakdown, as far as she was concerned.

"We're going to split custody." Just saying the words out loud felt like a punch in the gut. "Jake says Frank offered him a job, so he's moving here to Chicago. It'll be a struggle, no doubt, given the nature of the work you guys do and how inconsistent his schedule will be, but we'll figure it out."

Rock turned toward her, his brow furrowed. "You mean ya'll aren't gonna try to make it work?"

A hard stone of remorse settled in the pit of her stomach, making her nauseated on top of her nearly overwhelming grief. "It's impossible," she shook her head. "He'll never forgive me."

"Are ya sure about that?"

She searched Rock's hazel eyes, her own hot with unshed tears. There was so much she could cry about, so much she *should* cry about, but she was afraid to start. Because once she did, she might never stop. "How could he? I kept his son from him and I—"

"You thought you had your reasons," he interrupted.

"I *thought* I did," she hiccuped, unable to stop the tear that spilled onto her cheek. "But I was wrong. So wrong. He's nothing like my father, Rock. Because my father was an incredibly thoughtless man who only ever really cared about one thing, himself. But Jake," she shook her head, "Jake cares so much about all of us that he took himself away from everything and everyone he knew and loved in order to—" She choked on her tears, unable to go on now that she was admitting the truth to herself. The awful, horrible truth...

Rock pulled her into his embrace, and she wished she could find comfort there. Unfortunately, she feared she'd never be comforted again.

"Now don't go making a martyr outta him, *ma belle*," Rock crooned. "He made his share of mistakes, too."

She shook her head against his shoulder. "But they're nothing compared to—"

"*Chère*," he held her at arms' length. "You both share in the guilt on this one. You *both* do. Doncha go shoulderin' it all by yourself."

She nodded, gulping down the sobs that threatened at the back of her throat, wishing she could believe him.

They were silent then. Her wiping away the hot tears on her cheeks as she tried to get herself back under control. Him watching her so intently it wasn't helping matters in the least. Then he went a made things oh so much worse by asking, "Do you love him?"

And yep, so much for getting herself back under control. A new torrent of tears spilled from her eyes. "Of course I love him," she admitted aloud for the first time ever. The words seemed to hang in the air, buoyant in their freedom. "I've always loved him," she finished quietly, her shattered heart cutting at her insides until she thought she might die from the pain of it.

"Well then, there ya go. Love conquers all."

Oh, if only it were that simple…

———ᴡᴡ———

Balancing three cups of coffee in her hands, Vanessa carefully made her way down the hall of Northwestern Memorial Hospital. When she reached Rock—looking far too sexy leaning back against the wall, *grrrr*—and Michelle—looking like she'd been through nuclear winter, poor woman—she handed off two of the cups and then popped the lid off the third, blowing over the top of the steaming, brown, life-saving liquid.

Since joining BKI, she'd learned it was almost possible to live on the stuff.

"So what's up," she asked, taking a sip and glancing back and forth between the two of them. "What are you two chitchatting about?"

"The fact that love conquers all," Rock said, sipping his coffee and eyeing her over the rim.

"Does it?" she asked, quickly glancing over at Michelle.

Michelle opened her mouth to respond but shut it again when Rock's phone made a really weird *pinging* noise.

"*Merde*," he cursed, digging in his hip pocket and pulling out his phone, frowning at the screen. "I've got to go."

Uh-huh. And she knew what that meant. His *other* job was calling.

"When will you be back?" she asked, surprised to discover she was holding her breath, waiting for the answer.

"Dunno," he shook his head, turning away. Then he seemed to hesitate, swinging around to pin her with a hard stare. "I want you to know…" He slid a sidelong glance toward Michelle. "I…I just wanted to say that I enjoyed our time together," he swallowed and scratched his ear. And with that heart-stopping declaration, he turned and strutted down the hall with that loose, hip-shot swagger that drove her insane.

She turned back to Michelle. "And with that," she snapped her fingers, "*poof.* He's gone."

"Welcome to the wonderful world of Black Knights Incorporated," Michelle muttered, her expression filled with understanding. "Of course, if it's any consolation, I've known Rock a long time, and I've never seen him look at another woman the way he looks at you."

She snorted. "Fat lot of good that does me considering he seems determined to keep me at arm's length."

Resignation flickered through Michelle's swollen, bloodshot eyes. "From the little Frank has told me about what Rock's involved in, from the little Frank *knows*, it's probably best that Rock does keep you at arm's length."

"Yeah, well, a girl can always dream, can't she?"

Michelle smiled sadly and patted her on the shoulder before they both turned and headed into Snake's hospital room to sit vigil. Only they hadn't gone more than a few feet when Michelle abruptly stopped in front of her.

"Damn," she cursed, spilling some of her coffee on the floor when she slammed into the woman's back. "What gives?"

Then she glanced around Michelle to see Jake's very pale, very awake face.

"I heard what you and Rock were talking about," he said, and Michelle jerked upright like someone shoved a cattle-prod straight up her ass.

"Which part?" The poor woman's voice was barely a whisper, her eyes wide and unblinking.

"All of it."

Vanessa looked back and forth between the two of them, and her "angst light" clicked on. Big time.

Okay. Time to beat feet, Van.

Glancing at her watch, she announced, "Look at the time. Man, it's getting late. I'm sure I'm late for something. I can't think of what, but I'm sure it's important and—" She stopped, swallowing, smiling weakly before deciding to cut her losses.

Then she did the smart thing and turned to make her escape.

Jake watched BKI's communications specialist turn tail and run before he let his gaze linger on Shell's anxious expression.

There were a dozen stiletto-wearing demons tap-dancing on his brain every time he opened his eyes, but he'd take the pain. Oh mama, would he take the pain, just to see Shell's face when she finally told him she loved him.

"But you're wrong," he murmured, "about one very important thing."

She choked, her shoulders hitching up around her ears, "I am?"

"Yes." He nodded, despite the fact that it caused the demons to start in with their best impression of

River Dance. "Because I can forgive you, Shell. I *have* forgiven you."

――∿――

Michelle couldn't help it.

Blame it on the fear of the last few days. Blame it on the emotional upheaval or the exhaustion or the soul-deep grief over Lisa's death. Heck, blame it on the fact that, besides a granola bar, she hadn't eaten in…well, she didn't even know how long anymore.

Because those words, those beautiful, selfless words had her dropping her face into her hands and bursting into tears.

"Not exactly the response I was hoping for," Jake muttered.

"S-s-sorry," she sobbed, everything inside her, everything she'd tried so hard to keep together, unraveling so quickly it actually physically hurt. And it was either sit down or fall down, so she stumbled to the love seat beside his bed, sinking onto the threadbare cushions. "I-I just――" She couldn't go on; she was crying too hard.

And it appeared the emotional breakdown that'd been threatening for a long time had finally come home to roost.

Perfect. Just…perfect.

"Rock is right," he whispered, surprising her when he reached over to hook the edge of his hand beneath her chin, forcing her to look up at him. "We both made a lot of mistakes. *Both* of us."

Yes. Yes they had. But her deception was so much bigger than any he'd ever――

"Did you mean that other stuff?" he asked, his eyes even more brilliant green against the paleness of his skin.

She sniffled. She wasn't surprised to find her hands shaking when she reached up to wipe her cheeks. "Wh-what other stuff?" She'd said so much. Admitted so much...

He smiled at her then, genuinely smiled. And the sight of those devilish dimples caused a fresh wave of tears to climb up the back of her throat, choking her. She began sobbing uncontrollably all over again.

"Damn," he cursed, leaning over to grab the Kleenex box from the little table beside the bed. "It looks like the main pipe has busted."

"S-sorry," she sputtered, relieved and embarrassed all at the same time. Relieved because, for the first time since her brother told her Jake was back, she thought maybe, just maybe, everything might actually work out, maybe they'd actually be able to reach some sort of amiable understanding. Embarrassed because, come on, she was blubbering like she belonged in a straightjacket. Or sedated. Or maybe she was blubbering like a person in a straightjacket who'd been sedated.

Either way, she was making a total fool of herself but, again, she just couldn't help it. Everything was so overwhelming. Jake was overwhelming. Her feelings for him were overwhelming. The fact that he could actually forgive her for what she'd done was overwhelming...

"I'm talking about the fact that you admitted you don't think I'm anything like your father," he said, solicitously handing her a tissue.

"I *don't*," she assured him, indelicately blowing her

nose. "I know now that you were only doing what you thought was right."

"Yo," he chuckled, and the sound was so welcome a new torrent of tears spilled onto her cheeks. He was right. The main pipe *had* busted. "We both royally fucked up by trying to do what was right. Talk about killing each other with kindness, huh?"

All she could do was nod helplessly as she tried to smile at him.

God, she's beautiful.

Even with mascara running down her splotchy cheeks and her ponytail falling out all over the place, she was still the most beautiful woman he'd ever laid eyes on.

And he was finished waiting to hear her say the words he'd dreamed of every night for four long years.

"Okay, so now tell me," he demanded, his heart pounding with hungry anticipation. "Tell me to my face."

She shook her head, confusion in her eyes—those gorgeous eyes she'd passed down to their son, those gorgeous eyes he hoped she passed down to *all* their sons. "T-tell you what, Jake?"

"What you told Rock."

She swallowed and wiped her nose on the tissue, apprehensively searched his face. "What do you mean?"

The pain in his head made the thread by which he was holding on to his patience stretch paper thin. "Tell you *love* me, woman."

For a long while she said nothing, just stared at him, seemingly paralyzed. Then, when he was about half a second away from jumping out of bed and shaking the truth out of her, she murmured, her fabulous lips trembling delicately, "Of course I do, Jake. You know that. You've always known that."

"Yes," he admitted, his heart shouting with victory, his shoulders drooping in relief. "But you've never said it."

"Never?"

God love the woman.

"*Never*," he breathed, his expression loudly broadcasting the fact that she still hadn't.

Again she just looked at him, dragging out the suspense until he thought he'd scream—and damn the high-heeled demons! Then she sniffed, blew out a shaky breath and said, "I love you, Jake. I love you with all my heart."

And there they were.

The words he'd been waiting to hear since…well, since forever.

He nearly passed out from the hard burst of joy that shot through him. But he didn't want to miss a minute of having Shell beside him, loving him, *admitting* she loved him.

And speaking of…

He scooted over in the bed to make room for her. "Get that fine fanny of yours over here."

Her eyes widened with shock. "Jake, I'm sure I'm not supposed to—"

"Ass. In. Bed." He enunciated slowly, holding up the thin sheet, pasting on a look that brooked no argument.

She bit her bottom lip uncertainly before climbing in next to him, gingerly laying her cheek against his chest as he wrapped his arms around her.

Her.

Michelle. Shelly. Shell.

The woman of his dreams.

"I love you, too, you know," he said, squeezing her tight when she hiccupped on another sob that turned into a dozen more.

Yo, he was surprised she wasn't shriveled up like a raisin from dehydration after all the tears she'd shed. But that was Shell for you. Soft, tender-hearted Shell.

And he wouldn't have her any other way.

For long moments he held her, rocking softly as her tears drenched the thin cotton of his hospital gown. Eventually she quieted, eventually she stopped shaking like a leaf in his arms. And it was then he said, "So let's start talking strategy here."

"Wh-what do you mean?" she asked, tensing in his arms.

"I think we should get married right away. Once I start with the Black Knights, it might be a while before I have enough vacation time socked away for a decent honeymoon."

She pushed up to stare down at him, longing and disbelief in her eyes. "Married? Y-you want to marry me?"

Silly woman. Yo, what did she think? After everything they'd been through he'd just want to be friends?

"Of course I do. I mean, we already have a son together and," he pressed his palm against her belly, "it's likely there will be more."

And then they were both thinking about the hotel room and all the things they'd done to one another that culminated in one sadly broken prophylactic.

A delicate blush stole up her cheeks and, inexplicably, he felt his dick stir with interest.

Just goes to show, the male is programmed to mate at all costs. Because, *damn*, he barely had enough blood left to remain conscious.

"I love you, Shell. You love me. There are no more secrets and—" he hesitated, looking at her from the corner of his eye. "Or are there? You don't have another one of my kids squirreled away somewhere, do you?"

"No," she choked on a laugh, her eyes bright with more tears. "There's just the one."

"Well, we'll have to work on that," he promised, watching as his words caused the tears to spill down her cheeks. This time, though, they were tears of joy.

"Oh, Jake," she breathed against his lips.

Her mouth was soft and warm. *She* was soft and warm. Everything he'd ever wanted. Everything he'd ever dreamed. And despite the little demons and the blood loss, his below the belt region responded with a resounding *yes!*

She gasped when she felt him pulse against her leg. "Jake," she giggled. "We can't do this here. The doctor is going to be coming in ten minutes."

"Okay," he groaned, nibbling on her smooth, fragrant neck, loving the way she tilted her head back just so. "But I promise, as soon as they let me out of this hack shack, I'm taking you to bed and not letting you out for a week."

"I'm holding you to that," she sighed, and the sound was seductive and happy and filled his heart to bursting.

In life there are few perfect moments, but he was having one now. Because he held the woman of his dreams in his arms, and with her came the promise of happiness, of family, and a priceless, second chance at love.

READ ON FOR A SNEAK PEEK
AT JULIE ANN WALKER'S

Hell on Wheels

AVAILABLE NOW
FROM SOURCEBOOKS CASABLANCA

Jacksonville, North Carolina
Outside the Morgan Household

THOSE SCREAMS...

Man, he'd been witness to some bad shit in his life. A great deal of which he'd personally perpetrated but very little of which stuck with him the way those screams were going to stick with him. Those soul-tearing, gut-wrenching bursts of inconsolable grief.

As Nate Weller, known to most in the spec-ops community simply as "Ghost," gingerly lowered himself into the Jeep that General Fuller had arranged for him to pick up upon returning CONUS—continental U.S.—he figured it was somehow appropriate. Each vicious shriek was an exclamation point marking the end of a mission that'd gone from bad to the worst possible scenario imaginable, and a fitting cry of heartbreak to herald the end of his best friend's remarkable life.

Grigg...

Sweet Jesus, had it really been just two weeks since they

were drinking raki in Istanbul? Two weeks since they'd crossed the border into Syria to complete a deletion?

And that was another thing. Deletion. *Christ*, what a word. A ridiculously euphemistic way of saying you put a hot ball of lead that exploded with a muzzle velocity of 2,550 feet per second into the brainpan of some unsuspecting SOB who had the appallingly bad luck of finding himself on ol' Uncle Sam's shit list.

Yep, two lines you never want to cross, horizontal and vertical.

"Get me out of here," Alisa Morgan choked as she wrenched open the passenger door and jumped inside the Jeep, bringing the smell of sunshine and honeysuckle with her.

Ridiculously pleasant scents considering Nate's day had begun in the seventh circle of hell and was quickly getting worse. Shouldn't that be the rotten-egg aroma of sulfur burning his nose?

He glanced over at the petite woman sitting beside him, stick straight and trembling with the effort to contain her grief, and his stupid heart sprouted legs and jumped into his throat. It'd been that way since the first time he'd met Ali, Grigg's baby sister.

Baby, *right*.

She hadn't been a baby even then. At seventeen she'd been a budding young woman. And now? Over twelve years later? Man, now she was *all* woman. All sunny blond hair and fiercely alive, amber-colored eyes in a face guaran-damn-teed to totally destroy him. Oh buddy, that face was a real gut check, one of those sweet Disney princess-type deals. Not to mention her body. Jesus.

He wanted her now just like he'd wanted her then.

Maybe more. Okay, definitely more. And the inner
battle he constantly waged with his unrepentant libido
whenever she got within ten feet of him coupled with
his newly acquired, mountainous pile of regret, guilt,
and anguish to make him so tired. So unbearably tired
of…everything.

"What about your folks?" he murmured, afraid to talk
too loudly lest he shatter the tenuous hold she seemed
to have on herself. "Don't you wanna be with them?"

He glanced past the pristine, green expanse of the
manicured, postage-stamp sized lawn to the little, white,
clapboard house with its cranberry trim and matching
shutters. Geez, the place was homey. So clean, simple,
and welcoming. Who would ever guess those inside
were slowly bleeding out in the emotional aftershock of
the bomb he'd just delivered?

She shook her head, staring straight ahead through
the windshield, her nostrils flaring as she tried to keep
the ocean of tears pooling in her eyes from falling.
"They don't…want or…n-need me right now. I'm a…a
reminder that…that…" she trailed off, and Nate had to
squash the urge to reach over and pull her into his arms.

*Better keep a wrinkle in it, boyo. You touch my baby
sister and you die.* Grigg had whispered that the day
he'd introduced Nate to his family and seen the preda-
tory heat in Nate's eyes when they'd alighted on Ali.

Yeah, well, *keeping a wrinkle in it* was impossible
whenever Ali was in the same room with him, but he
hadn't touched…and he hadn't died. Grigg was the one
who'd done that…

Christ.

"They want you, Ali," he assured her now. "They need you."

"No." She shook her head, still refusing to look at him, as if making eye contact would be the final crushing blow to the crumbling dam behind which she held all her rage and misery. "They've always been a pair, totally attuned to one another, living within their own little two-person sphere. Not that they don't love me and Grigg," she hastened to add as she dashed at her tears with the backs of her hands, still refusing to let them fall. "They're *great* parents; it's just…I don't know what I'm trying to say. But how they are together, always caught up in one another? That's why Grigg and I are so close…" Her left eyelid twitched ever so slightly. "*Were* so close…*God!*" Her voice broke and sympathetic grief pricked behind Nate's eyes and burned up the back of his throat until every breath felt as if it was scoured through a cheese grater.

It was too much. He couldn't stand to watch her fight any longer. The weight of her struggle compounded with the already crushing burden of his own rage and sorrow until all he could do was screw his peepers closed and press his clammy forehead to the backs of his tense hands. He gripped the steering wheel with fingers that were as numb and cold as the block of ice encasing his heart. The one that'd formed nearly a week before when he'd been forced to do the unthinkable.

A barrage of bloody images flashed behind his lids before he could push them away. He couldn't think of that now. He wouldn't think of that now…

"Nate?" He jumped like he'd been shot when the coolness of her fingers on his arm pulled him from his brutal thoughts. "Get me out of here, okay? Dad…he shooed me away. I don't think he wanted me witnessing Mother's breakdown and I think I can still hear her…" She choked.

Uh-huh. And Nate knew right then and there those awful sounds torn from Carla Morgan's throat weren't going to stick with just him. Anyone who'd been within earshot would be haunted forever after.

And, god*damn*it, he liked Paul Morgan, considered him a good and honest man, but *screw* the bastard for not seeing that his only daughter needed comfort, too. Just because Ali put on a brave front, refusing to break down like her mother had, didn't mean she wasn't completely ripped apart on the inside. And damn the man for putting Nate in this untenable situation—to be the only one to offer Ali comfort when he was the dead-last person on Earth who should.

He hesitated only a second before turning the key and pulling from the curb. The Jeep grumbled along, eating up the asphalt, sending jarring pain through his injured leg with each little bump in the road. Military transports weren't built to be smooth rides. Hell no. They were built to keep chugging and plugging along no matter what was sliding under the wheels. Unfortunately, what they gained in automotive meanness, they lost in comfort, but that was the least of his current problems. *His* pain he could deal with—brush it aside like an annoying gnat. He was accustomed to that, after all. Had trained for it and lived it over and over again for almost fifteen years.

Ali's pain was something else entirely.

Chancing a glance in her direction, he felt someone had shoved a hot, iron fist straight into his gut.

She was crying.

Finally.

Now that she didn't have to be strong in front of her parents, she let the tears fall. They coursed, unchecked, down her soft cheeks in silvery streams. Her chest shook with the enormity of her grief, but no sound escaped her peach-colored lips save for a few ragged moans that she quickly cut off, as if she could allow herself to show only so much outward emotion. As if she still had to be careful, be tough, be resilient.

She didn't. Not with him. But he couldn't speak past the hot knot in his own throat to tell her.

He wanted to scream at that uncaring bitch, Fate. Rail and cry and rant. But what possible good would that do them? None. So he gulped down the hard tangle of sorrow and rage and asked, "Anywhere in particular y'wanna go?"

She turned toward him, her big, tawny eyes haunted, lost. "Yeah, okay." He nodded. "I know a place."

After twenty minutes of pure hell, forced to watch her struggle to keep herself together, struggle to keep from bursting into a thousand bloody pieces that would surely cut him as deeply as they cut her, he nosed the Jeep along a narrow coast road, through the waving, brown heads of sea oats, until he stopped at a wooden fence. It was gray and brittle from years spent battling the sun and weathering the salt spray.

He figured he and that fence were kindred spirits. They'd both been worn down by the lives they'd led until they were so battered and scarred they no longer resembled anything like what they'd started out being— and yet they were still standing.

Right. He'd give anything to be the one reduced to

an urn full of fine, gray ash. Between the two of them, Grigg had been the better man. But on top of being uncaring, Fate was a *stupid* bitch. That's the only explanation he could figure for why he'd made it out of that stinking, sandy hut when Grigg hadn't.

A flash of Grigg's eyes in that last moment nearly had him doubling over. Those familiar brown eyes... they'd been hurting, begging, resigned...

No. He shook away the savage image and focused his gaze out the windshield.

Beyond the fence's ragged, ghostly length, gentle dunes rolled and eventually merged with the flat stretch of a shell-covered beach. The gray Atlantic's vast expanse flirted in the distance with the clear blue of the sky, and the boisterous wind whipped up whitecaps that giggled and hissed as they skipped toward shore.

It just didn't seem right. A day like that. So sunny, so bright. Didn't the world know it'd lost one of its greatest men? Didn't its molten heart bleed?

He switched off the Jeep and sucked in the familiar scents of sea air and sun-baked sand. He couldn't find his usual comfort in the smells. Not today. And, maybe, never again. Hesitantly he searched for the right words.

Yeah, right. Like there *were* any right words in this God-awful situation.

"I won't offer y'platitudes, Ali," he finally managed to spit out. "He was the best man I've ever known. I loved 'im like a brother."

Talk about understatement of the century. Losing Grigg was akin to losing an arm. Nate felt all off-balance. Disoriented. More than once during the past week, he'd turned to tell Grigg something only to remember too late his best friend wasn't there.

He figured he wasn't suffering from phantom-limb syndrome, but phantom-*friend* syndrome.

"Then as a brother, tell me what happened…what *really* happened," she implored.

She'd always been too damned smart for her own good.

"He died in an accident. He was cleanin' an old gas tank on one of the bikes; there was a spark; some fuel on his rag ignited; he fell into a tray of oil and burned to death before anyone could get to him." The lie came out succinctly because he'd practiced it so friggin' often, but the last word still stuck in his throat like a burr.

Unfortunately, it was the only explanation he could give her about the last minutes of her brother's life. Because the truth fell directly under the heading *National Security Secret*. He thought it very likely Ali suspected Grigg hadn't spent the last three-plus years partnering with a few ex-military, spec-ops guys, living and working in Chicago as a custom motorcycle builder, but it wasn't *his* place to give her the truth. The truth that Grigg Morgan had still been working for Uncle.

When he and Grigg bid their final farewells to the Marine Corps, it was only in order to join a highly secretive "consulting" group. The kind of group that took on only the most clandestine of operations. The kind of group whose missions never made the news or crossed the desk of some pencil-pushing aide at the DOD in a tidy little dossier. They put the *black* in black ops, their true identities known only to a select few, and those select few were *very* high up in government. *High*. Like, all the way at the friggin' top.

So no. He couldn't tell her what *really* happened to Grigg. And he hoped to God she never found out.

She searched his determinedly blank expression, and he watched helplessly as the impotent rage rose inside her—an emotional volcano threatening to explode. Before he could stop her, she slammed out of the vehicle, hurdled the fence, and raced toward the dunes, long hair flying behind her, slim bare legs churning up great puffs of sand that caught in the briny wind and swirled away.

Shit.

He wrenched open his door and bounded after her, his left leg screaming in agony, not to mention the god-damned broken ribs that threatened to punch a hole right through his lung. *Blam!* Wheeze. That quick and he'd be spending another day or two in the hospital. Fan-friggin'-tastic. Just what he didn't need right now.

"Ali!" he bellowed, grinding his teeth against the pain, running with an uneven, awkward limp made even more so by the shifting sand beneath his boots.

She turned on him then in grief and frustration, slamming a tiny balled-up fist into the center of his chest. *Sweet Christ…*

Agony exploded like a frag grenade. He took a knee. It was either that or just keel over dead.

"Nate?" Her anger turned to shock as she knelt beside him in the sand. "What—" Before he knew what she was about, she lifted the hem of his T-shirt, gaping at the ragged appearance of his torso. His ribs were taped, but the rest of him looked like it'd gone ten rounds with a meat grinder and lost.

"Holy shit, Nate!" He almost smiled despite the

blistering pain that held him in its teeth, savage and unyielding as a junkyard dog. Ali never cursed. Either it was written somewhere in her DNA or in that contract she'd signed after becoming a kindergarten teacher. "What happened to you?"

He shook his head because, honestly, it was all he could manage. If he so much as opened his mouth, he was afraid he'd scream like a girl.

"Nate!" She threw her arms around his neck. God, that felt right...and so, so wrong. "Tell me! Tell me what happened to you. Tell me what really happened to Grigg." The last was breathed in his ear. A request. A heartrending plea.

"Y'know I can't, Ali." He could feel the salty hotness of her tears where she'd tucked her face into his neck. Smell, in the sweet humidity of her breath, the lemon tea she'd been drinking before he knocked on her parents' door and told her the news that instantly blew her safe, sheltered world apart.

This was his greatest fantasy and worst nightmare all rolled into one. Ali, sweet, lovely Ali. She was here. Now. Pressed against his heart.

He reluctantly raised arms gone heavy with fatigue and sorrow. If Grigg could see him now, he'd take his favorite 1911-A1 and drill a .45 straight in his sorry ass. But the whole point of this Charlie Foxtrot was that Grigg wasn't here. No one was here to offer Ali comfort but him. So he gathered her close—geez, her hair smelled good—and soothed her when the grief shuddered through her in violent, endless waves like the tide crashing to shore behind them.

And then she kissed him...

Chapter One

Three months later…

SHE HAD THAT FEELING AGAIN.

That creepy, crawly sensation prickling along the back of her neck. The one that made her shoulder blades instinctively hitch together in defense.

She was being watched.

Ali Morgan hastened her steps. Her black, patent leather, ballet flats slapped against the hot pavement as she darted a quick glance across the street.

Nothing.

Not that that was unusual. She rarely saw him, the man she'd begun to think of as her elusive shadow. But somehow she sensed he was there…somewhere…

Snapping a fast look over her shoulder, she rapidly scanned the faces of the pedestrians behind her. Nope. He wasn't back there, either. Not that she'd ever seen him full-on, but she'd caught enough glimpses of him to know her elusive shadow wasn't the middle-aged man caring the brown-bagged loaf of French bread, nor was he the black-and-yellow-rugby-jersey-wearing guy who—

Yikes, who let him out of the house this morning? He looked like a giant bumblebee, and the fact that he was gazing through the front window of the flower shop momentarily overcame her mounting fear. She snorted a giggle. Then the baby-fine hairs on the back of her neck twanged a loud warning, freezing the laughter in her throat like it'd been hit with a harsh blast of dry ice.

Crapola. Maybe she really was going crazy.

She'd had that thought more than a time or two in the past three months, because it wasn't like Jacksonville was a huge place. It wasn't necessarily abnormal to see the same faces over and over again.

"But that's the whole problem now, isn't it?" she muttered to herself.

She'd never actually *seen* her elusive shadow's face. Maybe if she had, maybe if she'd gotten the chance to look into the guy's eyes, she wouldn't be feeling this alarming sense of…pursuit.

A sudden chill snaked down her rigid spine as her palms began to sweat. Her tight grip on the handles of the plastic grocery bags started slipping, and she adjusted her hold, hoisting her purse higher on her shoulder in process.

Two more blocks…

"Just two more blocks and then I'm home free," she murmured, realizing by the quizzical look of the couple passing on her right that she was talking to herself again. That was another little eccentricity she'd picked up since Grigg's death. The whole going-crazy thing was starting to look more and more likely.

She trained her eyes on the bright pink flowers of the potted begonia bushes positioned in front of her condo building—the ones the amiable Mrs. Alexander from 3C had planted just last week.

Just one more block. Just one more block and then she could throw on her front door's chain lock, twist the dead bolt and finally take a normal breath.

She was so focused on those potted plants and the sanctuary they promised, she didn't see the hulking shadow lunge out at her from the deep, murky alley.

It wasn't until the first brutal, bruising jerk of her purse strap against her shoulder that she realized she might be in serious trouble. The second hard yank had her spinning around like a top, sending her shopping bags flying out of her hands, their contents scattering in the busy street like edible confetti.

A maroon sedan mowed over her sack of pecans, the shells exploding in a series of loud *rat-a-tat-tats* frighteningly similar to the sound of automatic gunfire.

"Hey!" someone yelled. "He's trying to mug her!"

That was enough to snap her out of her momentary shock, and she grabbed hold of her purse's inch-wide leather strap, pulling with everything she had. According to every self-defense guru on the planet, she should just let go. A purse wasn't worth her life. But this particular Coach satchel had been a gift from Grigg…

The guy clutching her purse in his meaty fist was built like a German Panzer, all brutal, bulging muscles and non-existent neck supporting a ski mask-covered face. He easily could've ripped her little Coach from her desperate grasp if he hadn't been simultaneously trying to fend off the strangely heroic man beating him about the head and shoulders with a hard loaf of French bread.

"Call the police!" Mr. French Bread bellowed, landing blow after blow until the loaf began to disintegrate and the smell of fresh-baked bread filled the humid air.

That was just the impetus needed to yank the frozen, slack-jawed onlookers into action. As Ali and Mr. French Bread wrestled with her mugger, people started pulling cell phones from various pockets and running in their direction.

The guy in the rugby jersey was the first on the scene, and he jumped on her assailant's broad back, wrapping an arm around the guy's meaty throat and squeezing until the mugger's eyes—the only things visible inside that frightening mask—bugged out like a Saturday morning cartoon. Ali was suddenly sorry she ever compared Rugby Jersey guy to a giant bumblebee.

"Get his legs!" Rugby Jersey yelled, and Mr. French Bread dove at the mugger's knees, tackling him and sending the three of them sprawling onto the sidewalk in a tangle of thrashing arms and legs.

Somehow her assailant managed to disentangle himself from the pile. He pushed his substantial bulk up off the concrete only to dart across the street, dodging traffic and nearly getting hit by a speeding UPS truck in the process. For such a *large* man, he was surprisingly agile. The UPS driver slammed on his brakes with a squeal of melting rubber and leaned from his doorless truck in order to shake a fist at the fleeing man's back.

Ali dragged in a ragged breath and tried to keep sight of her assailant as he zigzagged around people and parked cars. Then she stopped breathing entirely, more stunned than if she'd been hit by lightning, when her elusive shadow suddenly emerged from Swanson's Deli across the street.

At least she *thought* it was him. She could never tell for sure because he always wore a baseball cap that effectively shielded his face. Still…this man had the same solid build, the same square jaw…

Okay, it was getting too weird.

"Hey!" she yelled at the guy as both Mr. French Bread and Rugby Jersey picked themselves up off the pavement.

The man in the baseball cap gave no indication he heard her.

"Hey, you!" she called again, stepping off the curb. She was gosh-darned sick and tired of every day feeling this sense of…*paranoia*. If she could just get a look at him, she might—

The mysterious man took off like a shot.

What? Was he really running away from her?

When he hopped into a big, tough-looking SUV, quickly gunning the engine, she had her answer.

He *was* running away from her.

What the h-e-double-hockey-sticks?

Just when she would've taken off after him, she was jerked back onto the sidewalk by Mr. French Bread. "Whoa, there," the guy said, still trying to catch his breath. "The dude's long gone. Don't go getting your-self run over trying to catch him."

Mr. French Bread gave up attempting to appear col-lected and bent at the waist to put his hands on his knees and drop his head between his shoulders, panting like a dog in the summer heat.

He thought she was going after her attacker, of course, which yeah, probably made a lot more sense than running after some elusive man whom she was sure had been shadowing her every move for the past three months.

Laying a comforting hand on her savior's sweaty shoulder, she reached into her purse—the mugger had *not* succeeded; score one for Alisa Morgan and her two unlikely heroes—and pulled out her BlackBerry.

Zooming in, she snapped a quick photo of the SUV's license plate right before it careened around the corner. Then she bent to peek into Mr. French Bread's red, perspiring face.

"I don't know how to thank you," she said, glancing up to include Rugby Jersey. The guy was also blowing like a winded racehorse, leaning limply against the front window of the hardware store. Obviously neither of them was accustomed to much physical activity, which only made their actions all the more heroic. "You both risked an awful lot—"

Rugby waved a hand, cutting her off. "Damsel in distress and all that," he chuckled, wincing and grabbing his side.

Great. Just what she'd always dreamed of being. Not.

"Are you hurt?" she asked, dismayed by the thought of him getting injured while trying to save something as insignificant as a purse.

"Nah. I think I just bruised a rib."

She opened her mouth to thank him again when the piercing cry of a siren interrupted her.

"Looks like the cavalry's almost here," Mr. French Bread observed.

Black Knights Inc. Headquarters on Goose Island
Chicago, Illinois
The next day…

"Yeah, right. This is a chopper shop. Just a little ol' custom motorcycle business…and I'm the queen of England," Ali muttered beneath her breath, as she glanced through her front windshield at the expanse of the…*compound* was the only word to describe it.

No wonder Grigg had always insisted she stay at a hotel whenever she managed to make it to Chicago to visit him. He'd claimed the loft he lived in atop the "shop"—which would heretofore be referred to as Fort frickin' Knox—was too small to sleep a guest comfortably, but she'd suspected he was feeding her a line of bull even then. And now?

Now, she *knew* it was bull.

Most folks would look through the huge iron gates at the multitude of small brick structures tucked around an immense factory building and dismiss it for simply what it claimed to be on its website, a top-notch custom motorcycle shop. Most folks would disregard the ten-foot-high brick wall topped by huge rolls of razor wire and the 360-degree pivoting cameras as the necessary precautions taken by savvy businessmen who had a small fortune in tools, bikes, and equipment, and who knew this wasn't Chicago's nicest neighborhood.

Yes, that's what *most* folks would do.

She wasn't most folks.

She'd had a Marine for an older brother who'd taught her a thing or two about security, and Black Knights Incorporated had it out the wazoo.

Unwelcome tears suddenly pooled in her eyes, because here was the proof that Grigg hadn't trusted her. He'd died and she'd never really gotten the chance to—

"You'll have to leave your vehicle at the gate, ma'am," instructed the redheaded giant manning the gatehouse. He had a thick Chicago accent, turning the word *the* into the more percussive sounding *da*. "We don't allow unsecured vehicles on the premises," he went on to explain. "Someone will be down to escort you to the main shop momentarily."

"Uh…oh-*kay*," she said as she pulled her lime-green Prius to the side and parked, shaking her head. She glanced in the rearview mirror and dabbed at the tears still clinging to her lashes before pocketing her keys and slinging her beloved purse over her shoulder. Exiting the vehicle, she strolled back toward the gatehouse and the behemoth inside.

"So," she said as she leaned an elbow on the sill of the window and eyed Big Red, "have you worked for the Black Knights long?"

"Long enough," he grunted, never taking his gaze from the series of TV screens showing different angles of the grounds around the compound.

Ah, a talkative one. Wouldn't it figure?

God, what was she doing here?

Nate Weller certainly wouldn't welcome her. For Pete's sake, he didn't even *like* her. Always eyeing her with such cold calculation. Those fathomless black eyes of his following her like she was some strange bug, and he was the dispassionate scientist charting her activities.

Sheesh.

Okay, so maybe she had the tendency to talk too much. But that was partly his fault because he *never* talked, instead remaining constantly and aggravatingly aloof, which was a state so totally foreign to her that she, in turn, started jabbering like her mouth was attached to a motor.

Which was lovely, just lovely.

So fine. He didn't like her. As far as she was

concerned, he could just take his opinion of her and stuff it where the sun never shined. He didn't have to like her in order to help her.

And why she was even mentally chewing over the state of his rather glaring lack of regard was beyond her. Because to tell the truth, she didn't particularly like *him* either.

He was too solemn, too remote, too…*something*.

She could never determine just exactly what that something was—which was extremely irksome. But she'd have to deal with it, or ignore it, because she'd made her decision. She was here.

And speaking of here, where the heck was her escort? She tapped her fingers and glanced around impatiently. "Do you own one of their custom bikes?" she asked, just to have something to talk about because, yeah, waiting to see Nate was driving her crazy.

Big Red made a noise vaguely reminiscent of the bellow a mildly annoyed grizzly bear might make, and she didn't know whether to take that as a *yes* or a *no*.

Great. Just great. This is turning out even worse than I imagined.

Author's Note

For those of you familiar with the vibrant city of Chicago, Illinois, you'll notice I changed a few places and names, and embellished on the details of others. I did this to suit the story and to better highlight the diversity and challenges of this dynamic city I call home.

Acknowledgments

First and foremost, I must thank my dear husband. You never chastise me when, in the middle of a dinner conversation, my mind wanders off because it's been taken over by the characters in my head. You just order another glass of wine and wait patiently for me to return to Earth. I'm forever grateful for that…

Secondly, as always, I must give major props to my agent, Nicole Resciniti. This book was a labor of love between the two of us—emphasis on the *labor*. I couldn't have done it without you, and that's a fact.

Thirdly, I want to give a shout-out to my editor, Leah Hultenschmidt. You've been ever-patient in molding me as an author, gently and persistently making my writing better. I appreciate your vision and wisdom more than you know.

And, finally, *thank you* to our fighting men and women, those in uniform and those out of uniform. You protect our freedom and way of life so we all have the chance to live the American Dream.

About the Author

Deep in the heart of the Windy City, three things can be found at Julie Ann Walker's fingertips: a keyboard, a carafe of coffee, and a sleepy yellow Labrador retriever. They, along with her ever-patient husband, keep her grounded as her imagination flies high. Visit her at www.julieannwalker.com.